Also by Erin Hart

Haunted Ground
Lake of Sorrows
False Mermaid

THE BOOK OF
KILLOWEN

ERIN HART

SCRIBNER
New York   London   Toronto   Sydney   New Delhi

SCRIBNER
A Division of Simon & Schuster, Inc.
1230 Avenue of the Americas
New York, NY 10020

First Scribner trade paperback edition March 2014

SCRIBNER and design are registered trademarks of The Gale Group, Inc.,
used under license by Simon & Schuster, Inc., the publisher of this work.

For information about special discounts for bulk purchases,
please contact Simon & Schuster Special Sales at 1-866-506-1949
or business@simonandschuster.com.

The Simon & Schuster Speakers Bureau can bring authors to your live event.
For more information or to book an event contact the Simon & Schuster Speakers Bureau at
1-866-248-3049 or visit our website at www.simonspeakers.com.

Designed by Carla Jayne Jones
Cover art © The Stapleton Collection/The Bridgeman Art Library
Cover photograph © Richard Cummins/Corbis

Manufactured in the United States of America

1 3 5 7 9 10 8 6 4 2

The Library of Congress has cataloged the hardcover edition as follows:

Hart, Erin.
The book of Killowen / Erin Hart. —First Scribner hardcover ed.
p.   cm.
1. Women pathologists—Fiction. 2. Archaeologists—Fiction. 3. Ireland—Fiction. I. Title.
PS3608.A785B66 2013
813'.6—dc23   2012028465

ISBN 978-1-4516-3484-6
ISBN 978-1-4516-3485-3 (pbk)
ISBN 978-1-4516-3486-0 (ebook)

To Bonnie, and to Betty and John
and all those who find themselves enfolded
in the mysteries of the vitae aeternum

Ireland

N
W   E
S

Belfast

Irish
Sea

Dublin

Galway

Aran
Islands

County
Tipperary

Cork

Celtic Sea

ATLANTIC OCEAN

| 0 | Miles | 50 |
| 0 | Kms | 80 |

County Tipperary

Area of detail

OFFALY

CLARE

LAOIS

KILKENNY

LIMERICK

CORK

WATERFORD

Birr

Ballyinderry
Ballyingarry
Borrisokane
Cloughiordan

Roscrea

Nenagh

Toomyvara
Silvermines
Ballyinderry
Borrisoleigh

Templemore

Templetouhy

Thurles

Gortnahoe

Ballina

Newport

Upperchurch

Holycross

Cappawhite

Boherlahan

Killenaule

Mullinahone

Dundrum

Ballinure

Golden

Cashel

Tipperary

Rosegreen

Fethard

Emly

Bansha

Cahir

Clonmel

Carrick on Suir

Ardfinan

Clogheen

Ballyporeen

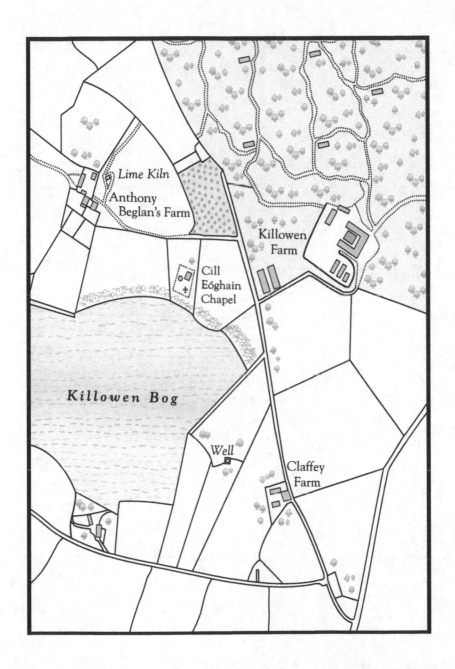

Lime Kiln

Anthony
Beglan's Farm

Killowen
Farm

Cill
Eóghain
Chapel

Killowen Bog

Well

Claffey
Farm

Omnia mutantur, nihil interit.
Everything changes, nothing perishes.
—Ovid, *Metamorphoses*, Book XV

Contents

PROLOGUE

Domfarcai fidbaidæ fál fomchain lóid luin lúad nad cél.
Huas mo lebrán indlínech fomchain trírech innanén . . .
Fommchain cói menn medair mass himbrot lass de dindgnaib doss
debrath nomchoimmdiu cóima cáinscríbaimm foróda ross.

A hedge of trees surrounds me:
a blackbird's lay sings to me
praise which I will not hide . . .
Above my manuscript—the lined one—
the trilling of the birds sings to me.
In a gray mantle the cuckoo sings
a beautiful chant to me from the tops of bushes:
may the Lord protect me from Doom!
I write well under the greenwood.

—Verse written in the margin by an Irish scribe
who copied Priscian's *Institutiones Grammaticae*
(a Latin grammar) in the mid-ninth century

Anno Domini 877
An Feadán Mór, Éile Uí Chearbhaill, Éiru

The oak wood was still. All sound seemed soaked up by the thick car-
pet of moss underfoot. Eóghan stood gazing up into the branches of a
giant oak. He stretched as tall as he could, but the gallnuts hung just out
of arm's reach, dangling from a branch above his head. He knew from
experience that this particular nut contained the worm of a wasp—and
the handiest substance for making good dark ink. Eóghan threw his
arms around a stout low-hanging branch and swung his legs up over it.
He was an agile climber, having spent many hours in the oak grove near
the monastery where he had lived as a child. Soon he was buried in
thick sprays of foliage, straddling the branch and inching out toward his
quarry, the galls that hung like brown fruit from clusters of leaves. From
this perch, he could see his master walking in the morning sun along the
edge of the bog where they had spent the night.

Eóghan felt the tension building inside him, then a sudden rush of
air as a bewildering noise erupted from his throat. "Cuh-cuh-CUH!"

The master was well used to such outbursts. He turned and raised a
hand to his eyes, peering up into the tree. "Ah, you're awake. God be
with you, Eóghan," he said.

"Cuh-cuh-CUH!" Eóghan shouted again, in reply. Out here in the
wood, his voice blended with the sounds of birds and animals, absorbed
by the forest floor. Back in the world of men, his yelps and cries had
rung out against stone, echoing and reverberating, out of place and rude.
Here he was a part of nature, another element in the seamless world of
wonders rather than an aberration.

Eóghan could not help what was happening. He had ever been like
this. *Devil-touched*, his own father had called him, and had beaten him
sorely nearly every day of his life, in a vain attempt to chase away the
demons. When she could bear the beatings no longer, his mother had
carried him to the monastery—he was still a child—and persuaded the
monks to take him in, to train him up in their ways. The brothers had

not been unkind, but in truth they held out little hope for him. They'd thought him simple and put him to work plucking birds for the cook, or gathering nuts and mushrooms in the wood, where his shouting and random gestures could disturb no one but the other wild creatures.

Eóghan inched forward, keeping his oak gall quarry in sight, remembering those early days at the monastery, considering how they had brought him to this place. He had often been set under the kitchen window, where the cook could keep a close eye on him. As he worked, he used to watch the monks strolling from the church to the Scriptorium.

The Scriptorium began to intrigue him. Whenever he was sent to fetch water, he would upend his bucket and stand upon it to peer through the windows, spying on the monks at their writing desks, each with a sheet of calfskin in front him, covered in black marks and designs such as Eóghan had never seen before. At a table in one corner, one brother often worked stitching together calfskin pages, marking them with barely visible lines, or tooling the leather covers that would eventually bind them. Around the walls of the Scriptorium hung leather satchels filled with books, for that was what they were called, these monks' writings. For months, he had lurked outside whenever he could, watching their painstaking work, fascinated by the brother who made the inks, his crocks full of insects and dried berries, his beakers of wine and blocks of crystal gum. Eóghan had longed to be inside, not just to be near the fire but also so that he could see how everything was done. He had to take great care not to be noticed at his hiding place outside the window. When the shouting fits came upon him, he would stifle the sound with his fist, punching the words and noises back down his throat.

Eventually he had begun to steal into the Scriptorium at night, to gaze upon the work on each writing desk, the pots of ink in every hue. He studied the marks the monks had made, recognizing the same shapes repeated over and over, each page recognizable for its subtly different hand. He traced the shapes of elaborate capitals, studying how the scribes had devised their miraculous designs. To him, every codex hanging from the pegs upon the walls was a living thing, a great soul-cry come to life in a myriad of shapes and colors, in the wild eyes, the bared teeth, and talons of the long-necked peacock, the calf, the dog, the eagle. In his dreams, the animals from the manuscripts moved and spoke, fought fierce battles. It seemed that a kind of secret life was hidden everywhere and in everything, and books were no different.

As he worked in the kitchen, he began to mark out the shapes he'd seen in pig's blood, or the juice of a beetroot, tracing over and over, seduced by their sinuous outlines, taking care to destroy any recognizable character whenever the cook passed by.

On one of his nighttime forays into the Scriptorium, he found a wooden cask full of oak galls, more crushed in a mortar on the ink maker's table. He had seen these growing in the grove whenever he was gathering mushrooms or acorns for the cook. So he had begun collecting galls each time he went to the oak wood and secretly adding them to the ink maker's store. Then one night, as he was leaving his gift of gallnuts, the door of the Scriptorium had burst open.

"There he is!" shouted Brother Alphonsus, the ink maker. "I knew someone had been here. Catch him!"

Eóghan smiled, remembering how he had led the monks on a wild chase that night, leaping over writing desks, spilling ink everywhere. He was younger and more agile than any of them, and by the time they finally caught him, the whole monastery was awake. Faces crowded into the doorway, and the Scriptorium was filled with flickering candlelight.

All at once, the crowd at the doorway parted, and a single figure approached. He was short in stature and quite rotund, with a kindly face and a ringing voice. "Unhand the boy," he commanded curtly, and the monks complied, releasing Eóghan's flailing limbs and backing away. The newcomer was a visiting scholar and evidently a man of some importance, to judge from the way the monks bowed to him.

"What are you doing here, boy?" the scholar asked. "What business do you have here in the Scriptorium—in the middle of the night?" His voice, though strong, was also gentle.

Eóghan felt himself color, even now, years later, remembering his response. "Arse-lick," he'd replied. His hands felt blindly for the galls in his bulging pockets, mortified at his own words but unable to stop them. "Cuh-cuh-cocksucker. Arse-lick." He'd heard the sharp intake of breath, watched the faces around him drain of blood waiting for the visitor's response.

"Why don't you show me what's in your pockets?" the scholar had calmly replied.

Eóghan had rubbed his hands together and touched his forehead three times, then reached into his pocket and brought out a handful of galls. A new light of understanding shone from the scholar's eyes.

"He's mad," came the abbot's voice, trying to soften things. "This boy works in the kitchen, Excellency. He's simple in the head, doesn't know what he's doing."

"On the contrary, I think he knows exactly," said the scholar. "You may leave us."

"But Excellency, if this boy was stealing from the Scriptorium, he must be punished."

"You would flog the lad for replenishing your stores? That's what you were doing, wasn't it, boy?"

"Cac-cac-cac," Eóghan had replied, flushing and nodding furiously. "Cac-cac-eater!"

And so it had begun that night twenty-seven years ago, his apprenticeship as a scribe. His protector, the visiting scholar, had eventually left them, but not without exacting a promise from the abbot that he would be brought up in the way of the scribes. At first the monks resented him, a mere boy plucked from the mud at the scullery door, but none would deny his growing skill. At the beginning they allowed him only to gather the gallnuts for their ink. When he'd proved himself adept at that task, they had shown him how to crush the galls with mortar and pestle, then soak them in wine to extract the essence. They'd taught him how to boil that essence down and mix it with gum arabic and vitriol to make a strong black ink. How to mix copper ash for purple, white flake for red, hawthorn berries or eel gall for yellow. In seven years, they had taught him nearly everything contained in their Book of Secrets, and he had learned it well. He had shown himself so diligent in the study of inks and ink making that the monks began to teach him how to cure and stretch the calfskin for vellum, how to measure and mark pages for a gathering. Still not satisfied, he begged to be allowed to take up the pen. To write.

And that was when he had truly surprised them all. For the act of writing stilled his tongue, his hands. He never once shouted or touched his head while copying. At the lettering, no hand was steadier. What magic was there in word making that kept him steady? God was with him then, the monks said. It was sacred, that moment—mind and hand together distilling thoughts into words. How could any human creature know greater joy? It was only when he laid down the quill that the fits came upon him again.

When they taught him to read, how he had pored over the precious gatherings, breaking the rules and burning a lamp into the wee hours to soak up all he could, his soul burning like his illicit flame, with a desire to know. Eóghan had begun to understand that he had suffered all these years from a surfeit of words, too many for his heart and mind to contain, so they kept spilling out of him. *In principio erat verbum*, the Scripture said—In the beginning was the Word, and the Word was with God, and the Word was God. *Verbum, verba, verbi, verborum, verbo, verbis, verbatim, verbalis, verbosus.*

Then his master the scholar had returned and taken him abroad to the Frankish court, where they worked for nearly twenty years, translating and creating new thoughts from old, the master reciting great strings of words, Eóghan diligently writing them down. At the start of all that, he had previously made only faithful copies; this work in which the master was engaged was something new, connecting his own fleeting thoughts to concrete words, and not only that, but also creating in their arrangement an object of profound beauty, like a spider spinning a web.

Three months ago he and his master had set out upon this pilgrimage, from Laon back to Éiru, the place of their birth. Eóghan did not know the master's reason for this journey. When he asked, his master replied only, "Even wild creatures return to the places whence they've come." Two nights ago, they had lodged at the monastery not far from here, where he and the master had met, where he had learned the secrets of the scribes.

Eóghan looked down from his perch in the tree at the master, still sunning himself by the edge of a bog pool. The oak leaves around him stirred in the breeze, and morning sunlight played on the water, making a golden checkerboard that seemed to move and meld together, and Eóghan was filled with such an unaccustomed feeling of well-being, his mind combining the contours of the oak leaf with the glinting ripples—all part of the enfolding mysteries of *vitae aeternum*—and he knew exactly what sorts of embellishments he would try out on the pages his master would dictate today. They would argue, and Eóghan would ask questions. He had become a part of the master's work. He was even allowed to add a gloss from time to time, adding the warmth of his breath to amplify the master's thoughts and words. It was a joyful thing, seeing their two hands on the page side by side.

All at once, Eóghan's thoughts were disturbed by a distant, faint sound of horses approaching. A jagged panic shot through him. From childhood, his first impulse at the prospect of meeting unfriendly stares had always been to hide. And so he climbed higher in the tree, hoping to conceal himself amid its leathery green leaves. As he slipped from sight, a pair of horsemen came charging through the wood, pausing directly below the tree where he was concealed. The forest floor muffled any hoofbeats; all Eóghan could hear was the squeaking of leather saddles, the rasp of labored breathing.

"There he is," the first horseman said to his mate, pointing through the trees at the master. "I confess it's beyond me why anyone should be frightened of such a weak old man." The second rider only grunted. They were so close below Eóghan that he could smell the rank odor of their bodies. There was an edge in the speaker's voice that said these two were fighting men. They seemed to know his master—what were they after?

Eóghan felt a sudden whirlwind of words in his throat, trying to force their way out, and his first instinct, as always, was to keep them from escaping. He stuffed his fist into his mouth and bit down hard, pain erasing for a brief moment the overpowering need to speak.

The first horseman spurred his mount out of the wood and down to the bog's edge, his silent second following. The master turned to them, offering the traditional greeting: "God be with you." In answer, he received a clout across the face that bloodied his lip and robbed him of breath. He staggered slightly but did not cry out.

Hidden in the oak, Eóghan felt the air around him crackle with danger. He must do something, help the master, but how?

"Are you called John?" the first horseman demanded.

"After the Baptist," the master replied mildly. "The very same."

The first horseman gestured to the leather satchel at the master's feet and exchanged a glance with his mate. "Where's your servant?"

"I wish I knew," the master replied. "He disappeared last night. Took our store of food—I'm left here with nothing to eat but my own words." He gestured to the satchel on the ground.

Eóghan nearly cried out. He had taken nothing. Why was the master lying? He felt a slowly rising horror as the horsemen dismounted, and each drew a knife from his belt. The pair of them fell upon the old man, thrusting their blades with an upward motion, again and again and again. Over the assassins' shoulders, the master raised his eyes to the tree where Eóghan crouched, hidden among the leaves. "The beginning and the end," the old man wheezed. "Alpha and omega."

At last the two horsemen stepped back and let the master's lifeless body topple to the ground. Eóghan could hardly breathe, but he felt the uncontrollable sounds begin to rise within him once more. He bit down on his fist again, this time tasting salty blood. *Shield me, cover me*, he prayed to the tall oak, to each of its branches and leaves. *Hide me from the conspiracy of the wicked, from the noisy crowd of evildoers.*

Suddenly a third horseman burst through the woods, pulling his beast up short and dismounting beside his fellows. "So you found him. Good." He spat on the master's body. "How goes it for you, heretic? No king to protect you now!"

The third man snatched up the satchel from the master's feet and looked inside, removing the book he found there and paging through it hungrily before flinging it aside. "Bloody fools!" he shouted. "*Amadáns!* You should have checked the book before you killed him. It's not the one we're after; it's only a bloody Psalter!"

Eóghan felt the last word like another blow. The Psalter was his own, the one he'd copied out for himself. But if the master had his Psalter, what was in his own bag? He suddenly felt the weight of the satchel pulling him down like a stone.

The third horseman wasn't finished. "What about the idiot servant?"

"Gone. We looked everywhere," the first assassin lied.

The third man narrowed his eyes, trying to gauge whether his defiant underling spoke the truth. "Well, see that you find him. It shouldn't be too difficult. They say he howls like a banshee." He swung his leg over his horse again. "Now get rid of the body—see if you can manage to get that right."

Eóghan could only watch as the two men dragged his master out onto the bog. They pushed the body into a dark pool, waiting until it was swallowed up without a sound. Almost as an afterthought, the second horseman reached for the Psalter and satchel and flung them into the pool as well. Still hidden in the tree, Eóghan covered his mouth and wept silently, watching as the open book seemed to float for a few seconds, like a pale pair of wings, and then submerged.

As the assassins remounted their horses and began to ride away, Eóghan felt a noise building up inside him, and this time there was nothing he could do to stop it. "Cuh-cuh-CUH!" he shouted.

The noise being sufficiently inhuman to their ears, the horsemen never even turned around but kept riding eastward, the direction from which they'd come. Perhaps they mistook him for a bird, nothing more than a corncrake clattering for his mate.

Eóghan waited in the oak tree for what seemed like hours, starting at every noise, listening for the sound of horses, but the assassins did not return. Finally he uncoiled himself, stiff from clinging to the sturdy branch, and crept down from the tree.

He knelt at the pool's marshy verge and hung his head in shame. His master was gone, sunk forever into this soft and treacherous bog. Eóghan tried in vain to remember the office for the dead, but each time he tried to sing, he found he could not bring forth any sound but weeping.

At last, he reached for the satchel that hung by his side and opened its flap, drawing out the simple leather-bound volume. The master had surely switched Eóghan's humble Psalter for his own codex, but why? This was the book they were inscribing together, by turns, the continuation of the master's great work. Eóghan remembered the assassin's voice: *No king to protect you now.* Were the words on these pages really worth a man's life?

Alpha and omega, the old man had said. The beginning and the end.

Eóghan's lips began to move as he recited the words that always calmed him. *In principio erat Verbum, et Verbum erat apud Deum, et Deus erat Verbum.* In the beginning was the Word, and the Word was with God, and God was the Word.

He suddenly understood that he could not return to the monastery. Slinging the leather satchel across his body like a sword belt, he set off in the opposite direction. Preserving the precious codex had become his sacred charge. He vowed to protect this book, defend it if necessary, and keep it safe from all harm.

Book One

For chubus caich duini i mbia ar rath in lebrán col-lí
ara tardda bendacht for anmain in truagáin rod scribai.

Be it on the conscience of every person who shall be
graced by possession of this beautiful manuscript,
that he bestow a blessing upon the soul
of the poor wretch who has copied it.

—A colophon from the *Book of Deer*, a ninth-century manuscript

1

Kevin Donegan grasped the twin joysticks and thrust the right one forward, feeling the fierce hydraulic power in the arm of his backhoe. He loved working the controls. Truth to tell, he often dreamed that he was not driving the machine but part of it, wielding not just one but two scoops like gigantic hands. He smiled, reveling in his rusty strength, iron fingers cutting through soft peat, huge arms knocking evildoers on their arses left and right, riding to the rescue of a bewitching blonde who couldn't wait to show her undying gratitude. He was the mighty Diggerman, feared by all who dared oppose him. Invincible.

It was early enough that mist still covered the lowest parts of the bog, an eerie presence that muffled the sharp cries of birds, the unearthly keening of a hare. He'd been on this bloody job for two days, trying to get the drain cut, and it would likely take another three days before he could be on his way. Nobody had said what the peat would go for—not that he gave a rat's. Not his job. Diggerman just dug the holes, cut the drains, and then moved on to the next job: trenching for gas lines, foundation excavation. Whatever. He was in at the start of the job, not to see it finished. Never saw much of anything finished. Better that way.

As he saw it, Diggerman wasn't about putting down roots; his job was turning things up. It was pretty much the same in the romance department. He usually liked being the first to open a trench, and he much preferred girls who were a little nervous and inexperienced. In and out he was, just like Diggerman, and then gone like the wind.

Remembering the ever-so-pleasant bottle blonde and the happy ending of his recurring dream, Kevin thrust the joystick forward again, maneuvering the digger's huge arm into position for another scoop of wet peat. He jammed the left lever forward to let the bucket drop. This time it landed with a loud *clunk*.

That was odd. Apart from the noise of the machine, cutting a drain was usually dead quiet. He lifted the bucket and set it down again.

Clunk. Could be something dangerous—a drainpipe, maybe a gas line nobody had bothered to flag. Holy Jaysus.

Kevin jumped down from his seat and grabbed the spade he kept always at the ready in case of emergency. The teeth of the bucket had struck something hard, punctured it, from the look of things. He began to recognize painted sheet metal, a bit of chrome, and . . . was that a tail-light? It was. What kind of a fuckin' bollocks would go and bury a car in the bog? That's what it was, and no mistake. Not something you'd see every day. He started using the spade to clear away all the peat on top of the boot, which was badly creased by the blow from the heavy bucket. As soon as the weight was lifted, the boot popped open on its own, and Kevin's mind groped to put a name on what lay before him.

He was staring down into the sunken, sightless eyes of a wizened, bluish-brown face. He felt an almost irresistible urge to scramble up the bank, but fought it, fascinated and repelled by the horror before him. At last he managed to assemble a coherent thought. A body. His eyes traveled along the limbs sprawled in the peat—a forefinger and thumb, a shod foot, a knob of bone protruding from a twisted joint. This was a man, all right, but the parts of him were mixed up, a foot where a hand should be. This wasn't just any dead body—it was murder. He remembered grisly accounts he'd heard of people topped over drugs and sacks full of cash. Kevin suddenly felt the blood drain from his head, and he leaned on the spade handle to keep from swaying. But he could not look away.

The possibilities skittered around in his brain: he could run, he could check for a stash of drugs or money in the boot, he could ring the Guards, ring the boss. Which was it going to be? One thought pushed its way to the fore. The job had been very hush-hush from the start. The boss, Claffey, advised him not to mention to anyone where he'd be working the next few days. Had to be off the books, illegal somehow. He usually never gave a fuck about permits or planning permission—not his trouble, and besides, he badly needed the work. Claffey might tell him to get on with it or get out. Although Kevin had realized ages ago that he didn't have many scruples, somehow ignoring a thing like this wouldn't seem right.

He began to recall reports of a bog man uncovered over in Offaly awhile back. That poor bugger turned out to be a couple thousand years old. Who was to say this fella wasn't as old as that?

Suddenly he saw himself on camera, being interviewed about this body. All the television crowd were bound to cover it. He could see the reports on RTÉ, UTV, TG4, maybe even Sky or the BBC—a bog man like this was big news, no matter how old he was. It began to dawn that people would be asking him about this moment for years to come. He'd be something of an instant celebrity, if he played it right. He imagined women gathering around him, female voices breathy with a mixture of curiosity and pity.

Kevin reached for his mobile to ring emergency services, hoping to Christ he'd get a signal way out here in the middle of the bog and relieved when the call finally went through. Conscious of an unwanted edge of excitement in his voice, he started explaining to the operator exactly what he'd been doing when he found the body. He knew emergency calls were recorded—the television people might even play a bit on the news reports. Had to make sure he sounded unflappable, in control.

The operator told him not to touch anything and assured him it would be no longer than twenty minutes before the Guards arrived on the scene.

Nothing for it now but to wait. He climbed back up into the digger to break out his lunch, three cello-wrapped sandwiches and a couple of boiled eggs he'd picked up at a petrol station this morning. Biting into one of the boiled eggs, he caught the empty eye sockets staring up at him from the car boot, the dead man's mouth hanging open like the beak on a hungry fledgling. Suddenly he had no appetite.

As he thrust the half-eaten egg back into the carrier bag, the presence of malice overwhelmed him, a roundly sweeping paranoia, bringing with it all the nights he'd spent as a child listening to his grandparents sitting around the fire with the neighbors, as each in turn described the eerie happenings they'd witnessed or heard tell of.

At that exact moment, a dark cloud passed in front of the sun, casting the whole bog into shadow. Kevin reached down to roll up the cab window. Why take a chance? The scorching weather they'd been having these past couple of weeks was well known to bring on chills. He checked his mobile—only four minutes since he'd rung off with the emergency services. Kevin shoved the phone back in his pocket. And suddenly twenty minutes seemed like an awfully long fuckin' time to wait.

2

Claire Finnerty set down her nearly full egg basket beside the massive oak and checked the path behind her to make sure she hadn't been followed. She crouched beside the tree and, reaching deep into its woody hollow, drew out a battered tea tin. Settling into the natural seat provided by the old tree's twisted roots, she opened the tin, pushing aside the small green booklet with the gold harp stamped on the front, and took out a box of matches, a packet of rolling papers, and small bag of cannabis. She fashioned a thin joint with practiced hand, lighting it with the last of the matches—she must remember to bring a fresh box tomorrow.

Drawing the smoke deep into her lungs, she leaned back and looked out through the trees to her private patch of ripening meadow. Not many people in this upland corner of Tipperary, an untraveled cul-de-sac that pushed its way north into the Offaly boglands. That was one reason she'd finally settled here. This ancient oak had grown up beside a crumbling wall and slab of limestone embedded in the earth, probably the last vestige of some monk's retreat. She understood why he had built his shelter here: the field laid out beyond the trees was covered in blue pincushion plant, dark pink marjoram, sweet clover, and white sprays of cow parsley. Looming low and purple to the southeast lay the Slieve Bloom Mountains.

These few snatched moments in the mornings were her only real opportunity for solitude and privacy. While everyone else at Killowen was busy with chores, she could sit here for a few minutes and indulge in her one remaining vice—and try not to think about the troubles that pressed in upon her, more each day. Christ, how she detested being in charge.

Claire took another long toke and her limbs began to relax. She could actually feel her brain switch into a lower gear as the buzz kicked in. A thick cloud of guilt began to descend upon her, one of the unwelcome side effects of the pot. She ought not to be coming here.

On the other hand, if she were to give it up, she'd have to have a little chat with Enda McKeever. Claire had never thought of the boy as her dealer, though the police certainly would. To her, he was just the polite, enterprising lad who cycled up the lane once every fortnight to swap a small bag of homegrown cannabis for the three dozen eggs she left beside the gatepost. He was responsible for feeding his eight brothers and sisters, she was sure of it. Money was of no use to Enda; his mother was away with the fairies a good portion of the time, and that shiftless, ne'er-do-well father of his was on the way to drinking away every cent they'd ever had, and the farm as well, no doubt. What Enda's brothers and sisters needed most of all was food, and the boy would rather starve than take anything that smacked of charity. So what would the family do for their breakfast if she suddenly decided to turn over a new leaf?

Besides, she needed these few moments of peace to get through the rest of the day. Always so much to be done. The eggs and the milking were just the first chores, then there were the herbs and vegetables to tend, tools to keep in good repair, meals to prepare, not to mention the cleaning and mowing and trimming, and all the paperwork that came with juggling visiting artists and their schedules. Even with a full complement of eight workers, they had a difficult time keeping it all under control.

She still couldn't believe that there were seven other people now living at Killowen. How on earth had that happened? In some ways, she had been better off alone, those first years. There were days she missed it dreadfully, the silence, the weeks and months of soul-scouring solitude. Asking two human beings to live in close quarters without coming to blows was hard enough—but *eight*? And all eccentrics, to boot—everyone at Killowen was an oddball in some way, there was no denying it. She must have been out of her mind. Look at her, retreating to this private bolt-hole every day, thinking she might avoid dealing with the whole situation by coming out here and getting stoned—again. Pathetic, that's what it was, really and truly. If she had any sense, she'd have left long ago, before the place had turned into something . . . unmanageable. But when was that point, exactly?

When she arrived here, the first imperative had been putting distance between herself and what had happened. That was the way she thought about it now. On that fateful day so long ago, she had just started walking away from the blood and the chaos, the sound of the sirens. And she had kept walking, thumbing a lift when she could, until by sheer chance she had arrived here. For the most part, she had succeeded in walling off her past. There was no reason to return. Claire took another drag and held the smoke inside her lungs. That familiar, comforting buzz was becoming a little harder to achieve, a bit more difficult to sustain every day. Claire leaned back, letting the weight of her body slump into the oak tree's gnarled roots, remembering. She watched the smoke curling around her head, suddenly back again in the warmth of a pub's wooden snug, the lofty words and ideas wafting as dense as the curling cigarette smoke in the air. The conversation, fueled by whiskey and porter, was no more than youthful railing against the status quo. Nothing was ever resolved—did anyone really expect resolution? Once in a great while, she allowed herself to miss the innocence and arrogance of those days, when action was still only hypothetical, and idle words had no consequence. Raising one hand in front of her, she studied the worn palm, the stretched skin and enlarged knuckles. Who'd have thought, after everything, that she'd end up as a farmer?

The place had been an absolute tip when she arrived, abandoned for years. The eighteenth-century granary, now the main house, had been a complete ruin, just four walls and gaping windows. The cottage roof was stoved in and the windows were broken, the frames peeling paint; every wall seemed invaded by damp and mold. There was no electricity, no plumbing to speak of. The sad death and even sadder life of the last bachelor-farmer occupant was evident in the mismatched jumble of crockery still on the table, the remains of a final dinner left to molder on the range. She had slept poorly that night, on the old farmer's rough straw mattress. The following morning, she had staked her claim. Picking up a rusty sledge from the shed, she'd gutted the whole cottage in a single day, right down to bare stone. In the days and weeks after, she had cleared away cartloads of mildewed junk and found scraps of sheet metal that would do for temporary roofing. When at last the cottage was marginally livable, she had dug in beds for herbs and vegetables, built a chicken run out of scrap lumber and odd bits of fencing, started trading eggs for paint and lamp oil. It had taken her more than a year to make the place habitable, but after months of hard labor, the cottage walls were finished and fairly glowed with several coats of fresh whitewash. She often thought back to the texture of those early days, the bone-weariness that allowed her nights without dreams. Occasionally her precarious standing as a squatter had triggered a sleepless night, but eventually even that fear had worn away. What might happen was kept at bay by the here and now. And the combination of work and solitude had suited her then. There were times when she'd spoken to no one for weeks on end.

But the need for companionship must have been much more deep-seated than she realized and reared its head quite unexpectedly. She remembered the day in great detail. She'd been taking advantage of rare good weather, staking out beans in the garden, when a middle-aged couple on a walking tour stopped to ask where they might find lodging.

"We've no guesthouse nearby," she'd told them, "but you'd be welcome to stay here. I won't say the accommodation's deluxe, but it is free—that is, if you'd be willing to lend a hand for a day or two."

Her own words had taken her by surprise. But the offer, once made, could not be withdrawn. That couple—Martin and Tessa Gwynne—planned to stay on only a few days at Killowen. Eighteen years later, they were still here. She couldn't imagine how she'd ever got on without them. Martin, tall and slender, with elegant long hands, was an artist with the quill, something she found out only after he'd been at Killowen for more than two years. Tessa was nearly as tall as her husband, with a cascade of dark hair long since turned to white, and hands strong and sinewy from playing the harp. They were both like characters from the ancient sagas, out of place in the present. Martin, in particular, had made himself indispensable, with his esoteric understanding of compost toilets, wattle-and-daub construction, and drystone walls, all subjects about which Claire herself knew next to nothing. Even after all this time, she still knew precious little about Martin and Tessa, except that they were roughly fifteen years older than she was and had lived and traveled the world—London, Switzerland, Paris, North Africa. Claire knew virtually nothing about what had led them to those places, but if she had been forced to speculate, she might have guessed that they were on some sort of spiritual quest. That was quite all right—as long as they didn't try to tell her about it. She had a low tolerance for that sort of thing.

For years, it had been just the three of them. Then, nearly a decade ago, Martin had proposed converting the ruined granary into an art-ists' retreat, and everything else had progressed from there. It had never been Claire's aim to create anything; to her way of thinking, Killowen had just *happened* as she was trying to survive. But they had built something here, bit by bit, as the years piled up, the tilling and planting, the circle of seasons, round and round.

Over time, a whole rootless menagerie of misfits had arrived on her doorstep like strays, all looking for something. Some never found what they were seeking and moved on; some stayed, perhaps content just to work in a garden after being chewed up and spat out by the world. At Killowen, they were fairly well insulated from all that. It wasn't that they were purposely egalitarian, it just worked out that way. They all pitched in with the farmwork, according to their interests and abilities, shared cooking duties in turn, and had time to pursue their own creative inclinations. A French couple had come to stay last year, through a scheme that matched volunteers with small organic farms. Lucien and Sylvie had launched a cheese-making operation and now supplied local co-ops and farmers' markets. Claire didn't really understand what had drawn them to Killowen, but she needed the extra hands—and, she had to admit, the overall quality of the communal meals had vastly improved since the Francophone contingent had arrived.

She had purposely avoided asking questions of the residents, knowing all too well that any idle curiosity might be turned back upon her. No one at Killowen knew of her former life either. It was almost as if the past didn't exist, as if in coming here everyone had acquired a fresh start.

None was more enigmatic than one of their latest arrivals. Eighteen months ago, Martin had discovered a stranger, apparently ill and wandering the bog on foot—with no identification and no sign of where he'd come from. It being the depths of winter, Martin really had no choice but to bring him back to Killowen before he froze to death. Claire closed her eyes, remembering her first glimpse of the man at the door of her cottage—wet and wild-eyed, ill clothed, chilled to the bone.

"Bring him inside, Martin," she'd commanded. "Put him in my bed." While Martin stoked the fire, she had wrapped the shivering stranger in blankets and watched over him for three days and three nights as he sweated and chattered and mumbled about fierce beasts and mysterious visions like Tom O'Bedlam. For three days and nights, she had studied his face against her pillow—dark hair and eyes, flawless pale skin that had somehow retained the high color of youth, though he was probably at least forty. He was in a bad way those first few days, sweating through the bedclothes several times a night. Claire felt her face burn, remembering the illicit ache she had experienced each time she lifted the drenched linens from his nakedness. After living alone for twenty-two years, it was the first time another prospect had entered her mind.

When the fever broke, the stranger in her bed seemed perfectly sane, but he claimed not to know his own name. She had been deeply skeptical at first, but as the days wore on, he seemed utterly sincere in his ignorance. In the end, they had to take him at his word, which also meant they had to christen him. Martin had suggested Diarmuid, after the most famous abbot of the now-ruined monastery near the bog where he was found, and Claire herself had added a surname, Lynch, after her maternal grandmother. And so Diarmuid Lynch he became. As his physical health returned, Diarmuid had moved from her cottage to his own room in the main guesthouse. She had taken to watching him secretly as he went about his work, trying to convince herself that she was concerned only for his well-being but knowing it was just cover for a vaguely unhealthy obsession. For his part, Diarmuid seemed to suffer no anxiety over his lost identity, no hint of curiosity about what he'd been doing on the bog. On the contrary—he'd fallen quite easily into life at the farm, helping Anthony tend the cattle and goats, taking up stone carving and carpentry as if born to that work, even though his soft hands hinted otherwise.

Still an air of mystery remained. She had once caught a glimpse of him lying prostrate in front of the altar stone at the ruined chapel down by the bog. He was speaking in a low voice, but she'd not been close enough to hear. She had not seen him there again.

And Diarmuid wasn't the only mystery. Anonymous notes had begun arriving about four months ago. The first had been left outside her cottage door, a blank envelope with a handwritten message inside, block capitals in blue ink: I KNOW WHO YOU ARE. Cheap writing paper, available from any newsagent. She had studied the handwriting, trying to divine who the anonymous accuser could be. Arriving at the stump the next morning, she'd been seized by paranoia, imagining that her tin was in a slightly different position from where she'd left it the previous day. And yet nothing was missing, the papers hidden there seemed undisturbed. Since there was no name on the envelopes, she even wondered whether the messages had been intended for her or for someone else. What did it really matter, in the end? The person she had been ceased to exist long ago.

A noise sounded on the path behind her. Claire snatched up the egg basket and leapt to her feet as a lanky figure, dark haired and bearded, plunged through the underbrush.

He pulled up short when he caught sight of her.

"What is it, Diarmuid? What's wrong?"

"Claire." He was out of breath from running, and bent forward, hands on knees. "The Guards are down at the bog. Three cars . . . I saw them on my way back from the lower pasture. It looks as though someone's been digging there. I saw an excavator, a small JCB."

Claire's stomach dropped. "That bog is protected."

"The coroner's van is there as well. I think they've found a body."

3

It was just gone half-eight on Thursday morning when Detective Stella Cusack arrived at Killowen Bog. The local coroner had already set up a wall of tarps to shield the body from view. A mechanical digger, arm poised in midair, sat a few yards from the wall, and she spotted a young man, presumably the driver, being interviewed by her partner, Fergal Molloy. The scene-of-crime squad had been waiting for her before they began photographing the body and collecting evidence. She pulled a white Tyvek coverall from the kit bag she kept in the boot of her car, shaking out the flaccid, papery limbs as she prepared to step into it.

When she was suited up, Stella stepped around the tarp wall and slid sideways down the plank into the partially cut drain. The vehicle was a gold Mercedes SL, with a Dublin number plate intact. The first two digits on the plate said the vehicle was two years old; they'd have only to run the number to suss the owner. That alone might tell them whether the dead body in the boot was a kidnapping gone wrong, a gangland murder, or a domestic dispute. Stella couldn't immediately recall any high-profile cases still open, but Molloy would. He was good at that sort of thing, facts and details.

Even after hearing about a car in the bog, the sight of a huge machine submerged in peat was still surreal. As was the body itself. Stella peered down at the leathery face in the boot, letting her eyes and ears absorb details of the scene. This was her first up-close encounter with a bog man—though he looked to be fairly recent, not like one of the ancient corpses you might see in a museum. Perhaps most curious, no cloying smell of death hung in the air. All her nose detected was the usual clean, earthy scent of bog. No doubt it was a man, with all that gingery stubble covering his face. His mouth gaped open; along with the open eyes, the expression made it seem as if he'd been taken by surprise. She was struck by the awkwardness, the indignity of his pose, and for the first time began to notice that the hands and feet were not exactly where they ought to be, as if the body had been rearranged somehow. Stella's rapidly downed breakfast of instant porridge rose in the back of her throat.

Fergal Molloy poked his head around the edge of the tarp. "Dr. Friel is here, Stella."

Catherine Friel was the chief state pathologist. Her job entailed traveling all over the country to crime scenes involving suspicious deaths, conducting autopsies, and testifying about her findings in court. Stella had worked with her only twice before. There had been rumors that Dr. Friel had been seeing Liam Ward, one of Stella's fellow detectives, but they'd somehow managed to keep the relationship pretty well under wraps.

"Thanks for getting here so quickly," Stella said. "I hope the journey wasn't long."

Dr. Friel had lost her Guards driver to austerity cutbacks and now had to make her own way to crime scenes at every hour of the day and night. She offered a tiny smile. "Well, I happened to be stopping near Birr last night, so not the worst. Although some days it definitely feels as though I'm running on caffeine." She had quickly suited up and was now stepping into white Tyvek booties. "What can you tell me?"

"Body was found by an excavator clearing a drain. In the boot of a car, apparently buried in an old cutaway. Looks to be dismembered—but you'll see for yourself."

They rounded the end of the tarp and Dr. Friel sidled down the plank. She got down on her knees, probing at the body with a gloved finger, peering closely at the disarranged limbs through a magnifying glass. After less than a minute, she turned to Stella. "I'm afraid you won't find this man's killer."

Stella felt the first prickle of intrigue. "So he was murdered?"

"Well, I think it's safe to say that he didn't just fall in. I'm seeing what look like several sharp-force wounds to the torso. Of course I won't be able to say for certain until the postmortem."

"Why won't we find his killer?"

"Because the one thing I can tell you with fair certainty is that this man died at least five hundred years ago."

Stella stared at the pliable flesh before her. "But that's not possible. He's so—" She struggled to find the right word. "I don't know how to say it—so *fresh*. How can you tell he's been here for that long?"

"There are several clues, but first off, the color of the skin says he's been in the peat for a good long time. Based on my experience with bog remains, I'd guess at least a few hundred years. And the bones are almost completely decalcified. When a body's been in peat for a long time, everything—even the bones—becomes soft as wet pasteboard. Very easy to pull apart in that state." She pointed to the toe of a shoe sticking up from the peat. "And, unless I'm very much mistaken, his footwear doesn't appear to be the latest style." Dr. Friel reached into her pocket and handed over a business card. "So you see, it's not me you need, it's someone from the National Museum."

Stella glanced at the card: Niall Dawson, Keeper of Conservation, National Museum of Ireland.

"Best to ring straightaway," Dr. Friel said. "They won't want to lose any time. You might want to pack some extra peat around the body until Dawson can get a recovery team here."

Stella thought she'd misheard. "Sorry?"

"It helps to preserve the body." Dr. Friel stooped to collect a large handful of sopping peat from the cutaway floor, applying it gently to the corpse's right arm. "Like this. You'll want to make sure he's completely covered. Niall Dawson will thank you for taking the trouble, believe me." She eyed her watch. "Sorry, I've got to dash. Urgent case up in Westmeath."

"Wait a minute. If this man is five hundred years old, how in God's name did he get into the boot of a car?"

"No idea," Dr. Friel said. "Perhaps that's worth investigating."

Cormac Maguire stood at his bedroom window, looking down into his back garden. Not just his garden or his room anymore. Nora Gavin had shared his bed for the last twelve months. It seemed impossible that so much time had passed.

When they'd returned to Dublin last fall, he had urged her to request a sabbatical, to allow herself a period of recovery after everything that had come to pass on that barren headland in Donegal. The Trinity medical school had granted her request, so she had spent the past year here in his house, reading, walking, digging in the garden. It was a necessary period of decompression, a slow readjustment after being so long submerged in grief. As he had anticipated, the guilt that had anchored her for five years proved difficult to cast off. In the past couple of months, however, he thought the weight seemed to be lifting, little by little—that was all he could say.

Be with me, he'd said to her at Port na Rón. Summoning his own words, and her unspoken response, never failed to fill him with a potent longing. He wanted nothing more than to be with her. But her mere physical presence wasn't what he meant when he'd said those words: Be with me. Some part of her was still holding back, unwilling to allow him entrée to the very deepest, most hidden recesses within herself. Perhaps it was only that she had never dared imagine her life beyond a certain point—the point where she managed to bring her sister's killer to justice.

He'd had his own period of adjustment since moving his father here last summer. The old man had suffered no permanent paralysis or lateral weakness from the stroke he'd suffered a year ago. He could dress and feed himself without difficulty, and for that they had reason to be thankful. But the brainstorm had left a different sort of damage: severe aphasia that showed no signs of abating. It was clear from the old man's demeanor that he could understand them. He could also speak quite fluently, but only in strings of gibberish, as if all the words stored in his brain had suddenly become untethered. He seemed to harbor suspicion that everyone around him was deliberately obstreperous, or perhaps even a bit thick. Attempts at conversation frustrated and exhausted him. He'd recently begun regular twice-weekly sessions with a speech therapist—Cormac had heard the poor young woman from the next room, cheerfully trying to pull his father through the prescribed exercises: she would list the days of the week, the months of the year, try to coax answers to simple yes-or-no questions: *Does glass break? Can fish fly?*

Cormac crossed to his suitcase, lying open on the bed, waiting to accept the last few items he would need on this pilgrimage. For some reason he had fixed upon that designation for the trip he and Nora and his father were about to make. What else would you call a visit to a holy site, for the purpose of collecting relics?

The call about the body had come about forty minutes ago. Niall Dawson from the National Museum had rung to ask whether he and Nora would be part of the recovery team for a set of human remains that had just turned up in a remote Tipperary bog, beside the ruins of a medieval monastery.

Nora had come into the room just as he set down the phone. "Who was that?"

"Niall Dawson. A body's been found in Tipperary, and he wanted to know if we could help with the recovery."

"What did you say?"

"That I'd have to talk to you and ring him back."

"You'd normally jump at a job like this. Why are you hedging? Do you think I'm not able to judge for myself whether I'm ready or not?"

"I didn't say that. It's just that this bog is way off down in Tipp somewhere. Who's going to look after my father?"

"We've got that young woman from the agency coming, haven't we?"

The old man's regular caregiver, Mrs. Hanafin, had just left for two weeks at her son's holiday home on Mallorca. He'd already arranged for a substitute caregiver from a local agency. Nora continued: "I'm not saying we should leave him alone with a new minder, but surely the agency won't mind if we take your father and this new caretaker along with us. It's only going to be a day or two, and it might be a good thing for him, getting out of the city."

She was standing in front of him, her face only a few inches from his own. Her voice softened. "What is it? There's something else, isn't there? Tell me."

"Niall didn't have many details on the body, just that it was old . . . and it turned up in the boot of a car buried in the bog."

He watched her features cloud over as she took in this new information.

She touched his face. "Oh, Cormac, I do love you for wanting to spare me. But you can't do it forever. You have to stop trying."

And so after a few hasty phone calls, it had been arranged: they would take part in the recovery, and Joseph and his temporary caretaker would travel with them to Tipperary. Dawson had arranged a place for them to stay.

In some ways, this trip would be déjà vu all over again. He and Nora had first come together over the corpse of a red-haired stranger, a tragic story sealed for centuries in a bog. They had managed to set her story free, but what would they discover about the current specimen?

The bell sounded in the front hall. Cormac opened the door to a pretty dark-haired woman whom he guessed to be in her midtwenties. She was casually dressed; a small rolling bag stood beside her feet.

"Ah, good, you're all set. Come in, come in. We've been expecting you," he said, extending his hand. "Cormac Maguire."

"Eliana," she said. "Eliana Guzmán. I was looking for Joseph Maguire?"

"Yes, my father," Cormac said. "I'm sorry to spring travel plans on you with such little notice. Did the agency explain? We only just got the call and have to get down the country as soon as possible. You're all right about leaving as soon as we have the car packed?"

He sensed a slight flicker of hesitation in her eyes, then it was gone. "Yes . . . where is it we are going?" she asked.

"I'm sorry. I did explain all this to the woman at the agency but it's all been so rushed. We're headed to Tipperary, it should only be for a day or two. The lodging is all sorted—we're staying at some sort of artists' retreat. You'll have your own room, of course, and access to kitchen facilities, everything you'll need to look after my father—although we won't really have to fend for ourselves; it's the sort of place where the cooking is done for us. Nora and I will be able to help you, when we're not out at the site."

"Tipperary?" she said. "I didn't know there truly was such a place."

"Oh, yes," Cormac said. "And not even such a long way as you've probably supposed." He checked his watch. "In fact, if we can manage to push off soon, we might even arrive in time for lunch."

5

They had just crossed the Tipperary border outside Birr when Nora glanced down at the map. Better start paying attention; she was meant to be navigating this last bit of the journey to their lodgings. The drive had taken them out of Dublin, southwest along the M7, through Kildare and Laois, and now into the area known as Ely O'Carroll. She rode in back with Joseph nodding beside her; Cormac and Eliana sat in front, and she enjoyed listening to the buzz of their conversation without hearing exactly what was said. Now and again a word or phrase would float back to her—Cormac inquiring about Eliana's home in Spain, she asking a few general questions about the daily routine. Nora was grateful to be left alone with her thoughts.

She let her gaze caress the back of Cormac's head, admiring, as she so often did, the curve of his skull, how pleasingly it intersected with the angle of his jaw. Whenever he turned to speak she once again remembered the meandering path those same lips had traced across her bare skin only a few short hours ago.

That intimate portion of her life, in particular, didn't seem quite true. She felt the unreality most acutely each morning when she awakened beside him. Would she ever learn to stop holding her breath, waiting for the next bad thing to happen? Lately she had begun to feel a gradual easing, another few degrees of difference each day, but would it ever be enough? After wandering so long in the underworld after her sister's death, the past year had felt like trying to claw her way back into the realm of the living. She had yet to face the fight for her niece's good opinion, a struggle that hadn't yet begun. Elizabeth refused to see her, wouldn't even speak her name. You couldn't blame the child for clinging to her father's memory, refusing to accept the part he had played in her mother's death. Cormac kept saying that Elizabeth would come around, but it hadn't happened yet. And Nora refused to press. How could you ask a twelve-year-old to see such things?

She glanced over at Joseph, nodding beside her. In some ways, he remained in a shadowy otherworld, bound by a tangled thicket of words without meaning. As she studied the delicate, translucent skin at his temples, the darting movement under his eyelids, she wished for even a fleeting glimpse of the images taking shape inside his head. Were a person's dreams transformed when words slipped their meaning?

They had spent a lot of time together in the back garden these past few months—she on her knees in the dirt, Joseph basking in a chair—on the days when the sun god deigned to show his face. After her own father, she'd taken to cultivating roses and had found restoration in tending to growing things. Cormac's father, too, seemed to find a sense of calm in being surrounded by virescent life. The back garden had become an oasis for the two of them.

In all the days they had spent together, she had yet to discern any sort of pattern in Joseph's speech, or to crack the garbled code of his stroke-damaged brain. He could speak quite easily, and indeed often rambled on and on, but there seemed no logic to it—one day "fork" meant "tree"; the next day it meant another word entirely. That was the trouble—if there was a code, it was corrupt, the circuits faulty. Only his frustration level remained constant.

Once in a great while, he would have a small breakthrough. Two days ago, she'd been standing at the kitchen sink doing the washing up after supper, looking out into the garden and absently singing under her breath the words of an old song that she and Tríona used to sing to pass the time on long car journeys:

> *Up the airy mountain,*
> *down the rushy glen,*
> *We daren't go a-hunting*
> *for fear of little men—*

She heard a noise and turned to find Joseph standing behind her. He'd looked agitated, his collar askew, white hair sticking straight up from the side of his head.

"Can you do her angle?" he said, and opened his mouth. "Bowling over, to-to-to give it up. Get up the barking again."

Did he want her to keep singing or to stop?

"The barking! Um, umma." He took her by the hand and gestured to his mouth, to suggest something pouring out. "Do-do the hemming!"

She began to sing once more, slowly drawing out the words—"Up the airy mountain, down the rushy glen"—and watching as his lips began to move, following along.

He joined in then, each word perfectly formed and clear: "We daren't go a-hunting for fear of little men."

She pressed on: "Wee folk, good folk, trooping all together."

Joseph finished the line once more, on his own, in a scratchy but rather tuneful baritone: "Green jacket, red cap, and white owl's feather!"

He let her hand drop and shook his head. "Ah, God, a shinna what's gone," he said. And then, with sudden vehemence, "Feckin' gyroscope!"

They stared at each other for a long moment.

"You can say that again," she'd offered.

"Feckin' *gyroscope*," he growled.

It had taken her a moment to realize that he had repeated himself—on purpose. He seemed to detect that some shift had occurred as well. His face began to screw up. She had thought at first that he might weep, but the sound that trickled from him was a barely audible chuckle, which grew into a chortle, and then to a full-throated guffaw, which Nora couldn't help joining in—especially when she realized that it was the first time she had ever heard him laugh. When Cormac had entered the kitchen a few minutes later, he'd found them both propped against the cupboards, weak from laughter.

The stroke literature talked about how memorized words and phrases were sometimes unaffected by stroke damage, how they were apparently stored in a separate place in the brain. Joseph had once come out with a few phrases in Spanish, but since neither she nor Cormac spoke Spanish, they couldn't tell whether he was making sense. So many mysteries left inside the human skull. She often imagined how much more difficult the current situation must be for Cormac than it was for her, since she had never met Joseph Maguire before his words had become disconnected. To Cormac, the contrast between this absurd, nattering old man and the larger-than-life figure his father had once been must be more than shocking.

A few words of conversation floated to her ears from the front seat.

"—and is this your first time in Ireland?" Cormac was asking Eliana.

"Yes. I wanted a bit more time speaking English before I begin my studies in September."

Glancing at Joseph, Nora could perceive that his eyes were open, though his drooping posture still feigned sleep. There was probably more understanding than they knew.

"Where will you go to school?" Cormac asked.

"Trinity. I'm excited—such a historic place."

Nora knew from teaching there about Trinity's high admissions standards. This girl must be exceptional. She leaned forward to join the conversation. "What will you study?"

"English literature," Eliana said, turning slightly to include her. The girl had an especially striking profile: delicately arched brows and dramatically sculpted cheekbones, a generous, bow-shaped mouth. Dark chestnut hair and deep brown eyes set off her complexion, which was a pale shade of ivory. Suitable pallor for a bookworm, Nora thought.

"I love the sound of English," Eliana was saying. "I don't know why, it seems sometimes quite . . ." She hesitated, searching for the right word. "Plain? Is that the right way to say it? Unlike Spanish!" She laughed lightly, and the sound seemed to rouse Joseph from his false slumber. His eyes opened wider as he concentrated on the girl's profile and seemed suddenly tuned in to the sound of her voice. All at once his eyes began to brim. His face was immobile as bright, shivering tears traced shining trails down his cheeks.

6

Cormac was looking forward to meeting Niall Dawson and tackling the job at hand. It had been well over a year since he'd been out in the field, the longest he'd ever gone without getting his hands dirty, and he missed it. They were on their way out to the site, after dropping his father and Eliana at the lodging Dawson had set up for them. Killowen was a working farm but also some kind of artists' colony, and while not exactly posh, the place was immaculately clean and quite comfortable. And whatever they were cooking for lunch smelled fantastic. He felt a twinge of guilt, leaving the old man in a strange place with a caretaker he'd only just met, but realistically speaking, what other choice did they have? If they wanted to improve the bog man's chance for survival for a few more centuries, there was little time to waste.

He looked over at Nora and reached for her hand. "Thanks for agreeing to this job. You could have said no."

"Yes, well, in our line of work, it's not like we can just wait around when a bog man turns up. Best to take the opportunity we get, isn't it?"

As the car crested the top of the drive from Killowen, a swath of bogland hove into view just beyond a formidable wall of furze bushes. Cormac turned left out of the drive and then down a narrow, rutted laneway a short distance from the farm. Killowen Bog lay at the bottom of a hollow between rolling hills. Random fir trees and scrubby birches sprouted from its damp center. The blades of a wind farm spun lazily, silently on top of the next ridge. Cormac tried to imagine what the place must have looked like when the bog man sank to his death many centuries ago. This whole area east of the Shannon had once been wall-to-wall monasteries, little islands of learning in the midst of wild bog. As a kid, he'd loved reading about the illicit graffiti scribbled by Irish monks at the edges of their manuscripts. There was one in particular he remembered: "I am Cormach, son of Cosnamach, and there is some devil in this ink." He had felt an immediate kinship with his namesake, imagining him young and perhaps a bit gawky, fed up with errant splodges as he struggled to make it through his copying. Remembering that tiny flare of fellow feeling, Cormac couldn't suppress a smile.

"What is it?" Nora asked.

"Nothing, just imagining what it must have been like here long ago."

Cormac found himself a little unprepared for the carnival-like activity at the site. Upwards of twenty people were standing around, including Guards officers and a few local gawkers. A couple of television vans stood along the road, their camera crews off vying for interviews with the digger operator. There was even a van peddling fish and chips and burgers, no doubt hoping to cash in on feeding the pack of journalists. A small swarm, some journos and some locals, had gathered out at the edge of the drain. They were being kept well away from the body by uniformed Guards officers and crime scene tape, but they still craned to catch a glimpse past the white tarp wall erected by the coroner's crew.

He slowed the car to a crawl, trying to get through the crowds. "Bloody hell. Niall's not going to be happy." At last a space opened at the side of the road and he pulled over and looked at Nora. "This is it. Look, I'd understand if you want to change your mind, especially with all this."

Her eyes held his gaze, steady and calm. "No," she said. "Let's go."

They collected their site kits and started out across the bog. A dark-haired woman stood beside Dawson—she must be the police. Dawson was about to speak when the woman stepped forward and introduced herself: "Detective Stella Cusack. Before you begin, I want to stress that the site is still technically a crime scene—that is, until we can figure out what the body's doing here, or if the vehicle is connected to any crime. At the very least, we could be talking about disturbing human remains, but that's still a chargeable offense."

"We're always careful to document everything as we go along," Cormac said. "And of course we can defer to you or the crime scene investigators whenever you think it necessary."

Stella Cusack seemed satisfied. "At this point we're thinking the car may have been involved in a hit-and-run. Some *amadán* out for a joyride gets into a smashup, thinks he'll just scuttle the evidence. Obviously didn't reckon on a bog body turning up."

"Anything else we ought to know?" Dawson asked.

"Well, Dr. Friel—the state pathologist—said she thought there might be evidence of sharp-force wounds. So it may be murder after all, but I think we're safe filing it as a cold case."

She led them past a group of people standing just beyond the police line near the tent. Dawson followed along and spoke under his breath, "Sorry about the mob scene. I'd love to know who went and blabbed to the press. We've tried a couple of times to get people to leave, but of course when the media got here, the landowner insisted on staying. That's him at the end of the barrier—Vincent Claffey. Been a right bollocks, to be perfectly honest."

"How long is all this going to take?" The shout came from the man Dawson had pointed out as they passed. "This is my property, and you've no right to keep me off it."

Niall Dawson cringed. "You see what I mean."

Cormac glanced over in the direction of the small crowd. The speaker was a wiry specimen, midforties, with shirtsleeves rolled up past the elbow, sideburns trimmed just a little longer than the current fashion, a broad midlands accent. Cormac watched Detective Cusack take a moment to steel herself before turning to face the man. "We're only following the law, Mr. Claffey. As I've explained, we have to give the National Museum charge of the site until they're finished."

Claffey was not satisfied. "Fuckin' government intrusion, that's what it is. This is private property. And am I going to get any compensation for whatever you find here? Not fuckin' likely. Not to mention that I've got to spend all day down here looking after my own interests, because I can be fuckin' sure none of you lot will be doing it for me." He'd gone red in the face and began stabbing a forefinger through the air. "I'm warning you, if there's anything valuable turns up here, it's mine by rights, d'ye hear me? I want it down in writing somewhere."

Niall Dawson spoke, an unfamiliar edge of irritation in his voice: "We haven't found anything of monetary value, Mr. Claffey. You'll be the first to know if and when we do."

Claffey narrowed his eyes at Niall Dawson. "You'd better be telling the truth. What about them two?" Claffey jerked his chin toward Cormac and Nora. "Who are they, more pigs at the public trough? If there's something you're not telling me . . . ."

The teenage girl standing behind Claffey rolled her eyes. "Ah, for God's sake, Da, can we just go?"

Claffey turned on her. "And leave this lot to say what they found or didn't find? I'll not have any of this bunch of cute hoors trying to smuggle away our good fortune, and that's that. What are you doing here, anyway? Who's minding the chipper? Get back there, yeh little slapper!" He pointed the way.

Deflated, the girl turned and trudged toward the van parked at the roadside. Claffey turned back to them, folded his arms across his chest, and planted his feet. "Well, what are ye all lookin' at? Get on with it, why don't ye?"

Detective Cusack pressed her lips together as if to keep from saying something she might regret. She turned her back on Claffey and continued leading them to the white tarps set around the drain.

"Before we begin," Cormac said, "I wonder, could you point out whoever it was found the body? Just in case we have questions for him."

Cusack nodded toward the boilersuited young man being interviewed by a television journalist about fifty yards away. "That's him, the digger operator—Kevin Donegan. Not sure he'll have time for you between media interviews, but you can ask."

"He was cutting a drain here, is that right?" Cormac asked.

Cusack nodded. "I don't know what Claffey's up to, or whether it's even legal, to tell you the truth. Right, I'll leave you to it. I'm still trying to track down the car's registration. You'll keep me posted if anything important turns up?"

7

Nora followed behind Cormac as Niall Dawson led them around the tarp wall, where a partially cut drain ran straight up to the open boot of a car that had been completely submerged in the bog.

"Dr. Friel asked Cusack to pack extra peat around the body after she was here," Dawson said. "Nobody's disturbed anything since then."

Nora knelt beside the drain as Cormac stepped down into it and began removing a few handfuls of peat. As he picked away at the soggy pile, the wrinkled sole of a foot began to materialize from the dark wetness. The skin appeared brown, with a faintly bluish cast. A bone jutted from the peat, and a litany of Latin words began humming through her head: *caput humeri, tuberculum majoris, infraspinatus, teres minor.* All part of the minutiae she had absorbed years ago, names for the various parts and surfaces belonging to the long bone of the upper arm. She recognized the humerus by its distinctive rounded cap, the pair of fan-like tuberosities. And she knew from the exposed surfaces that the bog man's arm had been literally wrenched from the socket.

A faint, electric tracery of adrenaline flushed through her, something she didn't generally experience in the presence of the dead. It was a reminder of the day she'd given up working with live patients, unnerved not only by surgery but even the act of piercing a vein to draw blood, the sight of a wound or scar. But they had been warned about the state of this body. What was it, then? Perhaps the fact that whoever had put the bog man in the boot had been in such a hurry that the remains of a fellow human had been nothing more to him than a nuisance.

"According to Donegan, the fella who found him, the legs and feet are at the left side, the head and torso toward the right side of the boot," Dawson said. "At this point we're not sure if he was dismembered before he went into the bog, or if he was pulled apart by the digger that buried the car. We know a digger was used from the backfill around the car. But whoever dug the hole wouldn't have been best pleased to find a body—must have decided to chuck the bog man into the boot with his spoil."

Nora stared down at the protruding bone, now seeing the folds of flesh and connective tissue that surrounded it. The usual procedure for remains found in situ was to remove the whole block of peat containing the body and return it intact to the lab at Collins Barracks for processing and examination. Since this body had already been disturbed, the usual protocol was out the window. Instead, they would have to extract the body parts right out here on the bog and go through the rest of the spoil in the car boot one handful at a time. They'd already been robbed of a whole range of important clues—the body's position in the bog, composition of the original surrounding material, proximity to any artifacts that might have been nearby.

Niall Dawson said to Cormac, "I've got some boards and a roll of polythene in the back of the Rover. Give us a hand?"

Cormac climbed out of the hole and the two men ducked around the tarp again, leaving Nora alone with the body.

No matter how many times she encountered a human being preserved like this, it was impossible not to feel dumbstruck. She stepped down into the drain and sank slowly until her face was level with the bone, trying to let the minute details sink in. These moments of silent observation were not exactly prayerful in any traditional sense, and yet she felt something sacred in them, something reverential in the acknowledgment of a common thread of humanity. She tried to imagine the quicksilver thoughts, the fears and desires that had once coursed through these limbs, this heart, this brain. How had he ended up here, separated from the rest of his tribe, floating alone in the middle of a bog?

If they were fortunate, all that would come; his story would begin to emerge, little by little, as they dug into the peat. Nora pulled a camera from her bag and zoomed in on the shod foot and its cutwork shoe. Very like one discovered in a Westmeath bog fifty years ago—she'd seen it in reserve collection storage at the National Museum last year. She set the camera down and began removing peat from around the shoe, only to discover a second foot—this one bare—a few inches removed from the first. A few more handfuls and she could see that the ankle was fully flexed; a few inches below the furrowed arch, five toes lined up neatly, one tucked under the next, like peas in a pod.

Was it possible to read a part of this man's life story in a thickening of his rounded heel, the flattening of his metatarsal arch? It was apparent that he had walked—a lot. His feet offered a record of the accumulated miles of a lifetime. Not at all like the sacrificial victims of the Iron Age, who were more often strapping young men who went to their graves untraveled and uncalloused. This man was different. His knobby toes and the sole of his foot bore proof of experience, of a long life, fully lived. She would be wise to linger over details like this now, while she had a chance. Once they'd removed the remainder of the peat, there wouldn't be any time for leisurely study; they'd have to get him into the container and packed off to the fridge at Collins Barracks. In some ways, finding a body like this was like opening the pages of an ancient book, getting a direct glimpse into another time.

Nora climbed out of the trench and started snapping photographs of the drain where it met the buried car. A grave often told more about the person who dug it than the person buried there. She could see the toothmarks of a mechanical digger and places where the spoil had clearly been backfilled around the car. It occurred to her that whoever had buried this car might be here right now, watching the police and archaeologists at work, worrying about what they might find.

She climbed back into the cutaway and moved on to the area beside the bog man's feet, carefully picking away the wet peat with gloved thumb and forefinger, reserving the spoil in case they had to go through it again. Bit by bit, the outline of a head and upper torso began to emerge.

If Killowen Man's bare foot had made an impression, his distorted face, with its gaping mouth and unblinking eye sockets, formed an image that was utterly unforgettable. He had a high forehead; his cheeks had apparently been shaved a few days before he died, and the extra folds of skin about his neck seemed to confirm what she had guessed earlier about his rather advanced age. Tucked around his torso were folds of a thick woolen fabric, perhaps a cloak. There were the slits Dr. Friel had seen as possible stab wounds. Beneath the material she could trace the outline of a shoulder and flexed arm, following the curve of the elbow until she saw, nestled in the folds of the cloak, a curled fist, the right thumb and first two knuckles of the forefingers on his hand clearly visible. Reaching for her camera, Nora focused in on the thumbnail and pressed the shutter release, capturing the image. At least this portion of the body seemed intact. If they could manage to extract the head and torso without doing any further damage . . .

She snapped a few more pictures and glanced at the framed image on the camera's small screen. One more shot. This time, as she zoomed in on the curled fist, something stood out from the glistening peat beside the bog man's elbow. Another half-moon shape, almost like another thumbnail.

She peered into the boot and pushed aside the surrounding peat. This seemed like an awkward spot for his left hand. Then again, she reminded herself, if poor Killowen Man was indeed in pieces, there could be body parts crowded every which way in the boot. She could be looking at a toenail rather than a thumb.

Nora set aside the camera and her pulse quickened as she began scraping away the peat from around the second nail. She hadn't been mistaken. Definitely a thumb, and then a whole hand. Another right hand.

Killowen Man was not alone.

8

Cormac hefted two sheets of plywood near the edge of the cutaway, wondering how much weight each would bear and calculating the full weight of a bog man with his swaddling of soggy peat. Might be better to take him in sections, if he was already divided that way. They had to be able to lift the bloody things. Nora was standing in the trench beside the half-buried car, camera resting in her left hand.

He set down his load a few paces from the cutaway. "How are you getting on?" he asked. When she didn't respond right away, a spark of fear flared inside him. "Nora, is something wrong?"

She stepped aside without a word, and he looked into the boot. The bog man's right fist lay curled against the peat. Beside it was a second hand, this one poking out of a sleeve that sported three knotted leather buttons at the cuff.

"Jesus." He quickly jumped down into the trench to get a closer look. Nora handed him a magnifying glass, which he used to examine the sodden sleeve and the oblong signet ring that seemed to wink at them from the peat. The block capitals of a monogram were upside down but clearly visible: BKA.

When Nora spoke, her voice was calm. "You'd better fetch Cusack."

They could hear Niall rounding the corner of the tarp wall. As soon as he saw their faces, Dawson grasped that something was wrong. "Hey, what's up?"

"Complications," Cormac said.

Dawson came to the lip of the cutaway and looked down into the boot. He swore softly. "We'll have to get Cusack and her crew back in here. Do you want to go, or shall I?"

"I'll go," Cormac said.

So the car was a crime scene after all. They'd been here less than a full hour, and already he was starting to have a very bad feeling about this place. Once again he and Nora were unraveling connections between the living and the dead. Some of those connections were to be expected in their line of work. But some could be dangerous, particularly when people preferred that they remain buried.

He began to make his way across to the road, feeling the eyes of the bystanders upon him—and the landowner, Vincent Claffey, in particular. Why was Claffey giving out like that when they arrived, and what exactly did he imagine they would find here? He was obviously unfamiliar with the law on treasure trove. The government had claim on any artifact found on Irish soil, even on private property.

Cusack was still on her mobile as he approached. He could hear her end of the conversation: "Benedict. And the last name, is that with a C or *K?*" A pause. "Right. Kavanagh with a *K* it is. Thanks." Cusack snapped her phone shut. "Well, we've got a registration on the car's owner, but nobody's seen hide nor hair of him for the last four months."

"I think we found him," Cormac said.

"What do you mean?"

"There's a second body in the boot. Clearly not as old as the—"

Cusack held up one hand. "Wait. Back up just a minute. *Another* body?"

"Looks like he's been pushed into the back of the boot."

Cusack paused for a moment, trying to get her mind around this new information. Her joyriding theory had suddenly vanished, replaced by something much darker. All the tumblers that had begun lining up in her brain would have to be recalibrated.

"We've stopped the recovery work, obviously," Cormac said. "At least for the moment. But we can offer our assistance if you need it—"

Without a word, Cusack began marching over the bog once more. Cormac had to jog along beside her to keep up.

"Did I hear you say the owner of the car was Benedict Kavanagh?"

Cusack gave a sideways glance. "Why? Do you know him?"

"Not personally, but I remember thinking when he went missing that someone must have done him in."

Cusack pulled up short. "Why would you think that?"

"You never watched his television program?"

She kept walking. "No."

Fair enough, Cormac thought. Spending a Friday evening watching tweedy intellectuals lock horns in epistemological debate was not everyone's idea of a good time.

"It was a chat show, but not like the usual—philosophy was Kavanagh's hobbyhorse. He'd spend the first twenty minutes teasing out his guests' ideas, grilling them about their latest book or whatever. You could feel him digging the ground out from under their feet. Then in the last few minutes, he'd prove his guests not just sadly mistaken but wrong on every possible level. He was brilliant. But I couldn't help feeling there was something a little sadistic underneath it all. I'm amazed that anyone ever agreed to be on the program. I mean, surely they knew what was in store for them. Or they imagined themselves somehow able to fend him off, unlike the last poor sod."

"So you think he may have been murdered by a disgruntled guest?"

"Well, perhaps not—that would be too bizarre. But I'll admit it was my first thought when I heard the name."

9

Stella Cusack wished that her instinct about this case had been wrong. But there was no mistaking the age of the second body; she stared at the three buttons on the tweed jacket, the gold signet ring a few inches from them. There was no mistaking the initials on the ring either: BKA. She spoke to Molloy. "Give Dr. Friel a quick ring, Fergal. We'll need her back as soon as she can manage. The crime scene detail as well. And ring up central records in Harcourt Street, tell them we need everything they've got on this man." She reached for her notebook and ripped out the page on which she'd written the name of the car's owner. "Missing person case."

She turned back to the archaeologists, who were standing above her at the edge of the cutaway. "I understood there was some urgency in getting your bog man out of here."

Niall Dawson rubbed his chin. "There is. I was just going to say, we've got to extricate him sooner or later. So I was thinking, it's probably better for all concerned if we just press on."

Stella knew that the decision—and the consequences, should something go wrong—would be on her.

Dawson looked at her hopefully. "Dr. Gavin has been an official consultant to the state pathologist on bog remains, and Dr. Maguire has extensive crime scene experience, documenting mass grave sites in Bosnia. They're both well up on the protocol for clandestine burials."

Stella knew she had to make a decision. "All right, carry on, then. But I want all your photos and drawings. And I want scene-of-crime to go through everything you're planning to take away."

"Done," Dawson said. "And we can see about keeping our bog man on ice at the local mortuary until you're ready to release him."

As she stepped around the edge of the tarp again, Stella found herself scanning the faces in the small crowd that still lined the perimeter of the site, thankful that at least she'd not chased them off. They were bound to guess that something was up when the state pathologist made a return appearance. The new body changed everything. Vincent Claffey claimed to own this parcel of bogland, but what exactly was he up to here? He'd hired Kevin Donegan to cut a drain, but there were no milling machines or baggers lined up to turn this bog into garden-grade peat moss or extruded turf. Whatever he was doing, it had to require planning permission, so had he filed the necessary paperwork, or was he trying to get away with something?

Would Claffey be giving out like this if he'd known about the car and the two bodies—if he'd actually put them there, for instance? Feigning ignorance could just be a way of pointing suspicion away from himself. Stella was familiar with Claffey's form; he'd never been what you might call a hardened criminal, just a small-time schemer who always walked a fine line when it came to the law. Probably due up in court next month for not paying his television license. Claffey and his moneymaking schemes were the stuff of local legend. There was the time he tried offering stump removal with an ancient Massey Ferguson tractor. He ended up rupturing a gas line, barely escaping with his life. The tractor had been blown to smithereens. Or that December night a few years back when the Christmas turkeys he was rearing in a heated shed had all escaped and perished out in the frosty fields. It wasn't just where did he get such hare-brained notions, but where on earth did he get the money? Somehow there was never a shortage for the next big project. Burying a car in the bog was exactly the sort of thing Vincent Claffey might do, but was it in him to cross over the line into something like murder? Still, it was possible to underestimate the man.

Then again, it might also be significant who was *not* standing around at the perimeter of the crime scene. This bog bordered on three farms: Claffey's place, Anthony Beglan's property, and Killowen, and yet neither Anthony nor Claire Finnerty had even ventured over to see what was going on. Might be wise to leg it over there soon.

Stella's phone began to vibrate, then she heard that wretched Lady Gaga song her daughter Liadán had programmed in as her personal ringtone. Bloody teenagers. She fumbled for the phone, trying to shut off the embarrassing noise as quickly as possible.

As usual, Lia didn't bother with a greeting. "I'm going to stay at Da's tonight. He said we could get an early start on the weekend, if it's all right with you. And before you ask, I've collected the mail, folded all the laundry, and finished the washing up."

Jesus, Stella thought, did she really sound like that to Lia? Had the past twelve months of single motherhood turned her into a total nag and a killjoy?

"So, is it?" Lia prompted.

"Is it what?"

"Is it all right with you if I head over to Daddy's tonight instead of waiting until tomorrow?" Lia spoke each word distinctly, as if her mother was suddenly deaf as well as clueless. Stella heard the note of exaspera-tion and could imagine the eye rolling going on at the other end of the phone. She considered the alternatives. Lia would be seventeen next Tuesday week. She had begun to spend every other weekend with her father these past few months, though they hadn't worked out any sort of formal arrangement. In fact, Barry hadn't pressed for specific visita-tion—probably just as glad not to have his daughter around, especially as he was busy bedding women closer to his daughter's age than his own. The very thought made Stella ill. But as it turned out, Barry had very little to say about his part in their daughter's custody; Lia had latched on to the idea of weekends at her father's place when she learned that she could get away with murder. He let her eat what she liked, never made a fuss about her staying up all hours. She understood that if she said yes, she was being overly permissive; if she said no, she was being too hard. Those were the choices; there was no middle ground.

She had dragged out the decision as long as possible. "Well, since you've got everything in hand, I suppose it's all right. But you'll be back by five on Sunday, as usual?" Stella heard the subtle note of pleading in her voice and hated it, hated herself for allowing it to creep in. She had no doubt that Lia heard it, too.

"Yes. See you Sunday. Thanks, Mam."

A loud click told her Lia was already gone.

Stella snapped her phone shut. It wasn't as if she'd be home all week-end anyway, not with another dead man in the boot of that bloody car.

Fergal Molloy approached. "I got on to the revenue crowd about the property records. This bog is split into three turbary allotments, one for each of the adjoining properties, as you might expect. One belongs to Anthony Beglan, one is part of the Killowen parcel, and the other is attached to Vincent Claffey's land."

"So Claffey is the legal owner, as he says?"

"Looks like it. But here's the thing he didn't mention. This bog was designated as Special Area of Conservation two years ago. Claffey and his neighbors are getting compensation for not cutting here—a thousand euros per annum, each. I suppose Claffey wanted to be having his cake and atin' it, too, probably counted on nobody checking." Molloy jerked his head in the direction of the car. "Is it really him in the boot, Benedict Kavanagh?"

"We'll find out soon. What news from Dublin?"

"Harcourt Street are sending the file over. Looks like Kavanagh went missing four months ago. He taped his television program on a Thursday afternoon, as usual—that was April twenty-first. But he wasn't officially reported missing until the first of May."

"Who made the report?"

"His wife, Mairéad Broome. She's a painter—pretty famous in her own right, evidently."

Stella felt a pinprick of irritation and told herself Molloy didn't realize he was being patronizing. It was just what people said.

"What about a photograph?"

"They're sending pictures to both our mobiles. Should have them here in a tick." Molloy looked sideways at her. "You ever watch his program? Kavanagh's, I mean."

Why was everyone asking that? "I suppose you did."

"Once in a while. Bit out of my depth, really. But it was amazing what he got away with. I think half the people who watched didn't give a fiddler's fart about philosophy; they just liked seeing your man have a go. Fuckin' deadly with words, he was."

These minor details were revealing a side of Molloy that Stella had never glimpsed before. All she knew was that he'd been born and reared in this part of the country, and had been seconded to the Antiquities Task Force before landing in Birr last year. What else did he do in his spare time? From the way he dressed, she'd already guessed he wasn't in a darts league with the local Guards contingent. Molloy had been her partner for only a few months, and these things took time. But it had been brought home to her only too recently that you could work with, even live with, someone for years and never get a glimpse into his inner life.

"Any idea who tipped the media?"

Molloy shrugged. "Well, Claffey brought the chipper. Ask him."

"Did you notice there's no one here from Killowen?"

"You sure they've heard about all this?"

"Not much goes on here that Claire Finnerty hasn't got a bead on." Stella had investigated a suspicious fire at Killowen about three years ago. Hooligans, most likely, not enough evidence to pursue anything. But the investigation led to a few interesting chats with Claire Finnerty. There was something that nagged at her about the woman; she couldn't say exactly what it was—a certain guardedness, perhaps, that helped kick her detective's instincts into overdrive. "I'll have a word with Claffey. Why don't you have another little chat with the digger operator, see if he has any more to tell us."

"You mean like why he was digging a drain in a protected bog, for instance?"

People who didn't actually do police work might imagine that detectives were trained to deal only in facts, but the bottom line was that a large part of the work was sorting fact from fiction—also from hearsay, misremembered details, outright lies, ingrained biases, and personal opinion. There was no such thing as "the facts." She tried to keep all that in mind as she rambled over to Vincent Claffey.

She could see him feigning surprise. There was no real place to conduct interviews out here, so she'd have to steer him away from the other gawkers.

"What's happening? What's all this commotion about?" Claffey's grating voice was even louder since he'd spied the archaeologists calling her back to the site.

"The team is just going about their work, Mr. Claffey, and had a question for me. No cause for concern. But I wonder if I could have a word?"

He eyed her suspiciously. "What about?"

They were finally far enough not to be overheard. Stella tried to fix Claffey with a steady gaze, but his shoulders twisted nervously.

"We checked the property records for this bog," she said.

Claffey looked insulted. "Didn't I tell you it's mine? I can show you the papers."

"That's all in order. But Detective Molloy also happened to run a check on Special Areas of Conservation."

Claffey looked sideways, caught. "Ah, well, now, there's a slight difference of opinion on that," he said. "That law is weak."

Stella knew she had him. Cutting turf in a protected bog could bring a stiff fine. "What are you doing with the peat, Mr. Claffey?"

"Sure, what would I be doing with it? Only gettin' me bit of turf mold for sowing potatoes—"

In the course of her work, Stella had driven past the Claffey place on numerous occasions and had never once seen a green leaf of any vegetable growing amid the rubbish and rusted-out machinery that filled his haggard. Vincent Claffey wouldn't know a potato plant if he tripped over it. So what was he really up to, going for his bit of turf mold with a digger?

Her phone vibrated once—the photo of Kavanagh. She held up the screen to show Claffey the image.

"Do you happen to know this man? Ever seen him around here?" The photo triggered a subtle change in Claffey's demeanor. Stella could see his thoughts zigzagging like a hare. He'd been his old cute, cunning self up to that point, and it was definitely the photo of Kavanagh that tipped him over. She said, "We've just found that the car in the bog belongs to him. Benedict Kavanagh. Ring any bells?"

"Kavanagh? No . . . no, can't say that it does."

"So you've never seen him before?" She held up the phone again. "Take another look."

Claffey glanced once more at the image, shifted his weight. "No."

"You're sure?"

Barely a thrust of the chin this time, and he'd managed to suppress the glint of panic in his eyes. "Look, are you finished with me? I'm dyin' for a slash."

He had been dancing a jig along the tape for the past few minutes. "Just one more thing," Stella said. "If you suddenly remember seeing Mr. Kavanagh anywhere, I want you to ring me." She handed him a card. "My mobile's on there."

He took the card and pretended to study it before slipping it into his pocket. "Can I go now? I'm about to burst me fuckin' bladder."

She waved him off, and he legged it over behind the chipper and ducked around back. Stella made a mental note to stay away from the cod and chips—and almost anything else on offer from that van. No matter how hungry she got, she'd wait until Molloy could bring them some grub from the nearest Supra station. The girl in the chipper folded and refolded her gray rag, no doubt wishing she were somewhere else. What must it be like, having a man like Vincent Claffey for a father?

After a moment, Claffey emerged from behind the chipper, zipping his trousers as he returned to his position at the tape. Stella circled around until she stood beside the van, out of his line of vision. More than one way to skin a cat, as her mother used to say. She stepped up to the chipper window. "Hullo, Deirdre, isn't it?"

"Yeh."

Stella's gaze lingered on Deirdre's forearms, which sported a few yellow patches at the wrist, the telltale remains of bruises. Suddenly self-conscious, the girl pulled down the sleeves of her jumper and balled both hands into fists. No good even asking, Stella knew. She would have a ready story about knocking into something. Everybody knew about Claffey's wife scarpering years ago, leaving the child behind. Everyone also knew how Vincent Claffey worked his daughter like a navvy, and even worse suspicions had cropped up when she'd fallen pregnant. But the way the system worked, you couldn't bring a parent up on charges on the basis of whispers and nasty rumors. And to complicate matters, whenever the girl had been questioned, she defended the bugger.

"Your father says you'd been helping him out here on the bog."

Deirdre frowned, unsure whether to believe her. "I only work in the chipper. That's all."

"But he told you what he's doing here?"

"No, he didn't. My da is into all sorts of stuff I know nothin' about."

Thus sparing you from prosecution, Stella thought. *Very decent of him.* She'd have to try a different tack. Glancing over the tired-looking menu board with its hash of mismatched letters, the spattered fryer and the bags of crisps on their clipboard, the cans of Sprite and Diet Coke stacked up against the back wall, she was caught in the undertow of memory. "I worked in a chipper once—I was about your age." All right, so she was fishing, trying to soften the girl up, but it was the truth. "Hated that fryer with a passion—it seemed like I could never get the stink off me—but at least the job got me out of the house at weekends. You do meet all sorts, working in a chipper."

The girl almost smiled. "Yeh, most of them stocious."

Also true, Stella thought. She felt the tug of memory, of the late-night conversations she'd carried on with maggoty young fellas at one o'clock in the morning after the pubs closed. "I used to like market days," she said. "People always seemed in a cheery mood when they were making a few bob." Fishing again, hoping the girl wouldn't notice.

"Yeh—" Deirdre started to say, when the startled noise of an infant came from somewhere near her feet. She stooped to pick up a baby from its carrier and rested him on her hip. She reached for a bottle of formula and slipped it into the baby's mouth; he helped hold it in place. After his nap, the child appeared plump and rosy; he beamed at his mother. Deirdre's eyes, too, lit at the sight of her child.

"I wonder, you wouldn't remember if you ever saw this man anywhere around?"

She held up her phone with the photo of Benedict Kavanagh. Watching Deirdre Claffey's eyes dart away, her expression flattening, Stella picked up another whiff of a scent. *Hold up,* said the voice in her head. *Don't pounce. Just let her talk.*

"Dunno," Deirdre said. She fiddled with the front of the baby's jumper, switched him to her opposite hip. "Like you said, you meet all sorts."

But not many you remember so well, Stella thought. And surely not many who ended up dead at the bottom of a bog hole.

10

It was nearly eleven by the time Nora returned to her room at Killowen. The National Museum team had worked into the night, lights rigged up inside the tent, which glowed out in the darkness of the bog like a giant luminaria. After they'd recovered as much of Killowen Man as they could from the boot, the coroner's team had come in and removed the second body. Both sets of remains were now headed to the morgue at the regional hospital, where they'd each undergo a preliminary postmortem in the morning. Nora had elected not to go along, partly because she wanted to give Cormac a chance to catch up with his old friend Niall Dawson and partly because she was desperate for a bath after the day's grubby work.

They'd not taken much time to get Cormac's father settled in before heading out to the bog, so it was only now that she began paying attention to the surroundings at Killowen. A small sign marked COTTAGES pointed down a path to the right as she pulled Cormac's jeep into the car park alongside the main house.

"House" was probably a misnomer, because the place still resembled the barn or granary it had once been: although two stories, the broad-beamed structure seemed to hug the ground, with vine-covered limestone walls and a slate roof. The entry was a graceful glassed-in room built out from the arch of an old doorway. A few lights glowed in the upper windows now, and Nora realized that she hadn't met any of the residents except for Claire Finnerty, who'd greeted them when they arrived. It turned out that Killowen was no ordinary bed-and-breakfast guesthouse but an artists' retreat. She crunched across pea gravel in the car park, wondering if she'd have to disturb someone to gain entrance this late, but the front door was unlocked. They mustn't be too concerned with security way out here—or maybe it was a philosophical statement about the nature of property. Either way it was curious; the crime rate in the countryside was usually higher than one might want to admit.

The kitchen at the back of the house was dark but for tiny spotlights above the sink and a set of French doors that looked out onto an herb garden. Mealtime had come and gone, and she was positively ravenous. She opened the refrigerator to find a glass-covered cheese plate front and center with a note taped conspicuously to the bell. *Niall, et al., Please help yourselves to anything you may like here. Fix yourselves an omelet if you like, or there's salad on the shelf below. The cheese is our own, and there's wine, bread, and butter on the table.* The note was signed CF.

Nora nibbled some bread and cheese, to take the edge off. She might have something more, perhaps a glass of wine, with Cormac and Niall when they returned.

Making her way silently up the stairs, she knocked softly at Eliana's door.

"Eliana? Are you awake?"

After a few scuffling noises, the door opened.

"Just checking to make sure—" Nora stopped speaking when she saw the girl's face, slightly blotchy, the eyes red rimmed as if she'd been crying. "Is everything all right, Eliana? Are you alone here?" Nora's eyes instinctively checked over the girl's shoulder. There was no one else in the room, only a book overturned on the writing desk, a small volume bound in yellow leather.

"Yes, I'm all right. It's just . . . a sad story." She smiled. "Everything was fine today. We had an excellent dinner."

"And you think Joseph was comfortable about being here—away from home, I mean?"

"Yes. But he seemed rather tired after the meal and went to bed about half past eight," Eliana said, her voice steadier now.

"That's not unusual; he sleeps quite a lot these days. Well, I didn't mean to disturb you," Nora said. "I'll let you get back to your story. See you in the morning."

Inside her own room, Nora gathered up the items she'd need for a bath and left a note for Cormac: *Gone in search of promised thermal suite. Join me if you like.*

She headed down the stairs and turned toward the old stable block adjacent to the granary that had been converted into a kind of spa. The sleeping rooms at Killowen were all en suite, but Claire Finnerty had urged them to take advantage of the new whirlpool and steam room.

Because they'd been expected down at the bog, they hadn't taken the time upon their arrival to have a look.

As Nora turned down the corridor to the spa, an eerie noise came from the far end. It sounded almost like a moan. She stopped to listen. There it was again, a strange wavering contralto. Impossible to tell whether it was a human voice, or just the wind crossing a chimney pot, or a piece of furniture being dragged across a flag floor. Then it was gone.

She kept walking, looking at the frescoes on the walls: long watery ribbons of intertwined pigment, in subtle layered shades of blue green, echoing the variations in the limestone outer walls. The place was a retreat for artists, and someone had put in a lot of time, making Killowen itself into a work of art.

Everything was silent now. And no wonder: the walls upstairs and here in the stable block were at least three feet thick. She hadn't heard anything through the rough-hewn doors upstairs as she passed—no conversation, not even snoring. Quiet as a cloister, this place. She finally came upon a door with a hanging wooden sign: BATH SUITE.

The sight that greeted her as she switched on the light was a spacious room painted a stormy-sea shade of green, the same as the hallway outside. The outside wall was set with frosted-glass windows at regular intervals, the inside wall devoted to four roomy shower stalls. Nora ranged around the room, exploring. She peered through a small window into the steam bath; behind a folding screen at the opposite end, she found a massage table and a large oval tub sunk into the floor, with steps spiraling down along the rim. Nearby shelves held stacks of folded towels, bath salts, and dried seaweed in large apothecary jars. Alongside the jars lay several long clear plastic tubes, cinched at each end with metal clasps. Nora picked one up. "Tir na nOg," read the brand name in large letters on the label, "Authentic Irish Moor Peat." She'd heard of spas where you could steep in a hot peat bath, or detoxify by smearing moor mud on various parts of your anatomy. The scientist in her naturally discounted most of the outrageous health claims, but peat did have some pretty remarkable chemical and biological qualities that weren't completely understood. Maybe she ought to give it a go, although her main concern at this point was getting at the muck lodged under her nails.

She kicked off her shoes and felt a delicious warmth radiating from the stone floor. Turning on the taps, she began to fill the tub, thinking about what she'd seen so far of Killowen. Through the French doors in the kitchen, she had spied a large empty room in the adjoining wing that looked almost like a yoga studio. She'd still not seen any of the residents besides Claire Finnerty, but they must have staff. It would take a lot of effort to keep this place running. Especially if most of the food came from the farm. Claire had explained that residents and guests took meals together in the main kitchen; the rotating cooking detail and menus for the week were sketched out on a chalkboard on the wall. Communal living did seem to have some advantages. Nora supposed her own current arrangement with Cormac and his father had similar perks and pitfalls. But the homemade bread and cheese she'd just consumed let her imagine an idyllic existence here: What could be better than following the creative impulse, living on the bounty of the earth just outside the door? Of course there must be downsides: lack of privacy, for a start, which she understood firsthand. And there were always undercurrents of tension wherever human beings tried to work in concert. No doubt the rifts would become apparent the longer she stayed. But at least for tonight, it seemed easy enough to admire the beautiful façade.

When the bath was full, she stripped off her clothes and lowered herself into the water, snipping the end off one of the tubes of moor peat and squeezing it out onto her knees. This peat was the next thing to mud, but not remotely mineral—its texture was smooth and silky, its color the darkest chocolate. She rubbed the ooze between her palms until it finally dissolved, turning the steaming bathwater a dark brown. This was the same peat that preserved bog butter, wooden roads, all those ritual sacrifices. Ten thousand years, that's how long it had lain in a suspended state in the bottom of a bog, and now it was being disturbed, for what? Beauty treatments whose effects were at best transitory. The impossible quest for youth. She thought of all the endangered bogs and suddenly began to feel guilty for enjoying the fruits of such exploitation.

As she closed her eyes, the vision of the two men in the car boot resurfaced—limbs at all angles, intertwined like two figures in a medieval knotwork design. The first corpse she'd already begun to refer to as Killowen Man, with his delicate hands and cutwork shoe, who, despite being dead, had also become a miraculous survivor in a way. She was eager to begin learning more about him tomorrow. Those cuts in his garments said he hadn't simply fallen into a bog and drowned, but his remains were too recent to have been a ritual sacrifice. So maybe he was the victim of a crime of passion, a domestic dispute, or a robbery gone wrong? One thing was certain: people murdered one another centuries ago for the very same reasons they did today.

It was the other man, the one they believed to be Benedict Kavanagh, who was more unsettling, especially as he might have been pushed into that boot by a killer who was still nearby. Perhaps very near. Nora tried to shove that thought out of her mind, realizing that she hadn't even thought to lock the door behind her.

As if on cue, she heard a small *whoosh* as the door to the thermal suite began to swing open. She sank down, keeping as still as possible and letting the peaty water lap against her chin. She held her breath.

"Nora?" The sound of Cormac's voice loosed a small flood of relief. "Are you there?"

"Back here. And there's definitely room for two, if you—"

"Say no more." In a few seconds, he had peeled off his damp clothing and sunk down into the bath beside her. "Great stuff," he said. "Somehow I had forgotten all about the grinding physical labor involved in fieldwork."

Nora slid closer. "Well, then, a spa treatment is just what the doctor ordered."

He leaned in, brushed his lips against hers. "Thank you, Doctor."

"Did you get something to eat? And did you check on your father?"

Cormac nodded. "Yes and yes. Sleeping peacefully."

"And you got the two gents settled at the mortuary?"

"Ready and waiting for your ministrations in the morning. Anything strange here?"

Nora considered for a moment. "I'm not sure. I looked in on Eliana just before coming down here, and she seemed to be crying. She said it was the sad story she'd been reading, but I don't know."

"It's possible that she's just homesick. I got the feeling that she's led a rather sheltered existence up to this point." Cormac frowned. "And you know yourself what a confounding old goat my father can be, even at the best of times. We'll have to make sure she doesn't feel like we're abandoning her here, expecting her to be alone with him all day long. I know it's only temporary, but—"

The door swung open and they both started in surprise, though not as much as the astonished female who'd just walked in on them.

"Sorry!" she said. "I didn't realize anyone was in here. We usually flip over the sign on the door." A fellow American, Nora noted, thirtyish, with an uncomfortable smile and a pair of bright blue eyes that she was trying studiously to keep averted.

"No, we apologize," Nora said. "We haven't been here long enough to know the house rules. Just arrived today."

The woman's voice brightened. "Oh, you're the archaeologists from the National Museum. Me, too. I mean, I'm an archaeologist—Shawn Kearney." Then, suddenly realizing that she was still the only person in the room wearing a stitch, she put a hand to her eyes and blushed furiously. "Sorry! Not the best time to chat. I'll just—sorry!" She flipped the sign on the door and was gone.

"Not quite how I imagined getting acquainted," Nora said, when she and Cormac were alone again.

"Good to know about the sign, though," he said. "We must employ it in future."

Cormac's forefinger traced an elaborate cipher along her collarbone. "You know, there was something else I noticed out on the bog today. I hate even to bring it up, but—" He seemed to be fighting with himself. "Well, it was strange. When Niall found out the car was registered to Benedict Kavanagh, he never said a word."

"And why is that strange?"

"Because he knew Kavanagh. They were at university together. We were all there at the same time, Niall and Robbie McSweeney and I—and Benedict Kavanagh, though I didn't know Kavanagh personally. He and Niall were best mates in their first year. I know it's a long time ago, but still, you'd think Niall would have mentioned that he and Kavanagh were acquainted."

"You said they were good mates, past tense. Was there some sort of falling-out?"

"You could say that. It only started coming back to me as we worked. The Philosophical Society had this tradition of sponsoring a head-to-head debate between their two most promising undergraduates. Philosophy became a spectator sport eight weeks into the fall term, because you were guaranteed a bloody good argument. I mean, rooting sections and everything. But that year, it was even more interesting, because the two chosen combatants happened to be best mates."

Nora nodded. "Niall and Benedict Kavanagh. So what happened?"

"I can't quite recall the topic of the debate, but it was impossible to forget the outcome. Poor Niall was left sputtering, while Kavanagh ran rings around him. I've never seen anything like it, before or since."

"And you think Niall remembers, too?"

"I don't see how he could forget. The way I heard it, the whole experience made him chuck philosophy. He very nearly dropped out of university altogether. It was only his good friends—Robbie and a few others—who saved him from going down the rabbit hole."

"And you think he may have held a grudge against Kavanagh all these years?"

"That's what's strange. From the little I know, Niall never held Kavanagh responsible for his failure in that debate. He blamed himself for being ill prepared."

Nora was thinking aloud. "So, if he didn't hold anything against Kavanagh, why not mention the old connection to Cusack?"

"Exactly what I was wondering. It's not like he could keep it from surfacing sooner or later. He and I have never spoken about Kavanagh. I don't know if Niall's even aware that I was at that debate. We didn't meet until he switched to archaeology—"

A noise came from the direction of the doorway. Surely not the embarrassed intruder again, Nora thought. Cormac put a finger to his lips, and they both froze in place, waiting. Then the bathroom door closed with a loud click.

11

Stella arrived home well after midnight, greeted by an empty house. A sense of impending doom washed through her, thinking about the mortgage she could barely afford, all the other bills that had to be paid now out of one pay packet. Yet another reason for Lia to prefer her father's place. He wasn't exactly flush, given the current state of the economy, but at least he wasn't trying to scrape by on a Garda detective's salary. There had been a time not so long ago, Stella thought, when she felt strong, decisive, like she was actually capable of making her own choices. Now, more and more, the choices seemed unworkable, and she seemed to be sinking in a swamp of indecision.

She thought of the words Barry and Lia and her colleagues at the station in Birr would use to describe her: reliable, thorough, organized, responsible, competent, sensible, words that enclosed her like the bars of a prison cell. She was all those things, to be sure, but wasn't there even a spark of something more, or had she become just another steady plodder? Whatever happened to that bracingly alive creature she had once been, the one who jumped into everything with both feet?

Looking in the mirror each morning, she could see how her hair, her eyes, had gone dull. Her eyesight was going; she had to squint to read anything. She felt the scratch of the safety pin hitching up her brassiere strap and glanced down at the hem of her sleeve, held together with a staple. Pathetic. She was barely holding it together most days—maybe no one had blamed Barry Cusack for walking out. What happened when you turned out to be a stranger, even to yourself?

Stella ripped off her rumpled suit with its stapled sleeve and flung it on the floor. She stripped off her blouse and bra and knickers, and dumped a whole drawer full of faded, worn-out underclothes onto the pile. Into the feckin' rubbish bin with all of it—she was sick to death looking at it. It was only when she put her hand on the kitchen door handle to peg the pile of clothes outside that Stella realized she was stark naked. Retrieving one pair of knickers, she put on her favorite plush tracksuit and returned to the kitchen, where she poured herself a large glass of wine, and pushed everything from the table.

She pulled out the missing person file on Benedict Kavanagh. The photo inside was the same one she'd received on her phone: a vigorous face, perhaps forty years of age, with intense blue eyes, an aristocratic-looking nose and cheekbones, well-formed lips. He was clean shaven and beginning to gray at the temples. Dynamite on television, one would imagine. Stella tried to visualize this man cocking an eyebrow and delivering a verbal deathblow to his debating opponent.

She started making a list of the interviews they'd have to launch: Kavanagh's wife and all known associates, anyone else who might have benefited from his death. Surely a serious scholar like Kavanagh would have professional rivals. He was also on television, which meant he could have been killed by an obsessed viewer who took exception to something he'd said or, as Maguire had mentioned, perhaps by one of the many guests he'd enjoyed humiliating. Then there were the locals: Vincent Claffey and his daughter, Claire Finnerty and her crowd. A long list.

But the wife was first priority—after all, who had more motive for killing a man than the one person who knew him most intimately? The next thought unsettled her. What if the person who knew a man most intimately wasn't his wife? Happened all the time. And yet another motive for the spouse. Kavanagh's wife had kept her own name— Mairéad Broome. Molloy's "in her own right" comment pricked at her again. According to the file, at the time of her husband's disappearance, Mairéad Broome had recently been elected to the Aosdána, the national artists' association, and had just launched her first solo show. How was Benedict Kavanagh reacting to his wife's increasing success? On that, the file was mum.

Stella reached for a fresh sheet of paper and began listing locations she ought to visit: the crime scene at the bog, Killowen, Claffey's place; an arrow pointing eastward stood in for Kavanagh's home in the city and the Dublin Academy for Advanced Scholarship, where he was a fellow. What did that mean, exactly? Did he teach, or was it mostly research? And what sort of research was involved in a field like philosophy? Stella had little exposure to the world of academia and found herself intrigued by people who could work up a froth splitting hairs over a single word. Then there was the whole political side of things, the usual hurts about who got passed over for chairmanships and committees, the pressures of publication, how the system turned a few academics into stars and the rest into pillocks. All of Stella's firsthand knowledge of workplace politics came from her time in the Guards, but how different could it be, really? Human beings were essentially the same selfish, venal creatures no matter the sphere.

She flipped through the contents of the files: interviews with his wife, the producer of his television program, his colleagues at the academy, the neighbors. Everyone had a slightly different take, it seemed, so the portrait of Kavanagh ended up like one of those dotted paintings she'd seen once in a museum. Stand too close, and you couldn't make out the image. Only by stepping back could you get any perspective. She forced herself to focus on Benedict Kavanagh's habits, his routines. From what she was gathering, he'd had a rather light teaching schedule—one seminar, which met once a week on Monday afternoon. He wrote every morning between eight and eleven, and prepared for his television program after lunch. The show taped from four to six on Thursday afternoon.

Stella had an impression that the interviewees were holding back, not telling all they knew about Benedict Kavanagh. Words like "difficult" and "brilliant" seemed to recur with regularity, almost always in the same breath, as if you couldn't be one without the other. He had gathered a chosen few around him, a coterie that his larger circle— behind his back, of course—had gleefully dubbed "the Children of a Lesser God."

Benedict Kavanagh had grown up in Dalkey, the pampered only son of a prominent heart surgeon and his wife. Had a stellar career as a student, earned multiple degrees at University College Dublin, and slipped naturally into a cushy post at the Dublin Academy for Advanced Scholarship. What he did there apart from the single seminar was anyone's guess, but he was paid a decent salary for it. Nothing out of place in his financial dealings. From the look of things, he traveled and lectured in Europe and America, on his particular area of expertise, listed as "Neoplatonist Philosophers of the Carolingian Court." Someone had included the title of one of Kavanagh's papers: "Eriugena's Commentary on the Dionysian Celestial Hierarchy." Stella stared at the words on the page, struck by the notion that they were legible, neatly typed, and in English. They might as well have been Swahili or Cantonese for all they communicated to her. What prompted people to delve so deeply into a subject that their work was incomprehensible to the vast majority of the planet's population? Perhaps this was a man who'd been raised to believe that he had no equals. That kind of thinking led to all kinds of dangerous situations, in her experience.

The details surrounding Kavanagh's disappearance had been tracked four months ago, as far as possible: he'd taped his program as usual on a Thursday afternoon, and no one reported him missing until his wife phoned the Guards on the first of May. After the taping session, the trail had gone cold. His seminar was not scheduled to meet on the following Monday because it was a bank holiday weekend; there were no cash-point withdrawals, no credit card receipts, nothing to pinpoint where he went or with whom. His car did have an eToll tag, but he'd evidently avoided the M7 motorway on his route to Killowen; there was no record of his tag activating the system. Was he deliberately trying to evade detection for some reason?

Stella found herself resenting the fact that this case would probably be handed over to Serious Crimes in Dublin, as if she and her colleagues weren't capable of investigating a high-profile murder. But that was the way politics was played these days in the Garda Síochána—the big-city task forces wanted any case guaranteed to bring them a dose of media attention, which helped justify their existence in the minds of people in charge of budgets and bottom lines. But even if it came to that, they couldn't stop her from doing her own inquiry. She kicked herself for not going to Dublin herself right away, this evening, to speak with Kavanagh's wife.

Even though Benedict Kavanagh was a minor celebrity, and news of his disappearance had been all over television for a short time, no one had come forward to report seeing him after he'd finished the taping session. His wife had been out of town herself and only reported him missing ten days after he was last seen. News of his body turning up might now bring out someone who remembered clapping eyes on him, and then again, it might not. Serious Crimes would be working that angle anyway; using the media to flush out witnesses was their specialty, not hers. But she had tools of her own. She had seen the body out on the bog—those bulging eyes, the distended cheeks. This crime was not about money or abstract intellectual principle. Benedict Kavanagh's death had been intensely personal for someone. The question for Stella was: For whom?

Book Two

Truagh sin, a leabhair bhig bháin,
tiocfaidh an lá, is budh fíor,
déarfaidh neach os cionn do chláir:
"Ní mhaireann an lámh do sgríobh."

This is sad! O little white book!
A day will come in truth,
when someone over your page will say,
"The hand that wrote it is no more."

—Verse written by an Irish scribe in the margin of a medieval manuscript

1

The kitchen at Killowen was filled with morning light. Cormac found his father sitting at the table, and Eliana nowhere to be seen.

"Have you had your breakfast?" he asked, then noticed a scattering of crumbs on the table before them, an answer to his question. "Where's Eliana?"

Joseph's eyes flickered to the window. "Ticka boffing majuscule." He shielded his face from the figures in the garden, where Cormac could see Eliana talking to Claire Finnerty.

"What is it? Something about Eliana?" Cormac was conscious of the girl's dark head glinting in the bright sunlight outside.

Joseph seized his hand. "She's the porpoise—no, no, these are bad wugs."

"Is something wrong? Are you not happy with Eliana?"

The old man's lips worked, hands fluttering in vague gestures above the table's surface.

He'd been making progress over the past three or four months, even incorporating a bit of sign language into his speech therapy sessions. Most of the signs concerned everyday occupations—eating, getting dressed, all the tasks that came with trying to relearn the words for items a person might use in any ordinary day. They hadn't progressed to the more difficult concepts.

Cormac remembered glancing into his rearview mirror yesterday, seeing his father's eyes locked on Eliana. Was he ill at ease with this new caretaker? Cormac had tried making a study of his father's various facial expressions over the past twelve months, but this latest agitation was something new, like nothing else he'd seen. So many possible shades of meaning in the touch of his hand—fear, urgency, panic.

"I'm sorry. I don't understand." He watched the old man's face crumple in frustration, feeling helpless and dull-witted, bereft of words himself. Words were a false currency in expressive aphasia, a translation machine gone seriously haywire.

Out in the garden, Claire Finnerty turned and led Eliana back into the kitchen. Joseph dropped Cormac's hand and stared at the tabletop, unable—or unwilling—to make eye contact with any of them.

"Look what Claire has brought for our lunch today," Eliana said. "I like the name I read in a book once—'string beans.' That's quite funny, isn't it?" She held up a perfect specimen in front of Joseph's face. "Perhaps you would help me." She gestured, showing how she was going to snap their tender necks.

Joseph didn't look up; he made a noise halfway between grunt and sigh. Eliana looked at Cormac. "Have I said something wrong?"

Cormac shook his head. "No, Eliana, I'm sure he'd be glad to help." Seeing the expression on his father's face, like a man being led to the gallows, Cormac crouched beside him and spoke quietly: "I've got to go now—we'll talk later, all right?" He took his father's hand again, offered a reassuring squeeze. The old man pulled his hand away and stared out the window.

Cormac headed out to wait for Niall Dawson, wondering if he was missing something important because he was distracted by this work out at the bog. How ironic that he should be the one feeling guilty, this late in the game, when it was his father who had been missing for so much of his life.

While he waited, he rang Nora, who was on her way to the hospital in Birr.

"Everything all right?" she asked.

"I'm not sure. My father was trying to tell me something. Something about ticks, or porpoises. He didn't want me to leave." Cormac hesitated. "I suppose whatever it is, we can sort it out this afternoon. Eliana seemed in great spirits, by the way." He remembered the gentle playfulness in the girl's face as she offered his father the beans. "Whatever upset her last night seems to have passed."

"I'll be back from the hospital after the exam, so I'll try talking to Joseph."

He was silent for a brief second. "You're so good with him, Nora—"

She cut him off. "Ah, now, remember our agreement."

Early on in their odd household arrangement, they had agreed that there would be no silliness about things like indebtedness between them. They were all just doing what was necessary, what had to be done. And it was as if she had understood quite clearly from the beginning that she would be a kind of buffer between father and son, taking the role that Cormac's mother had once filled, if only briefly. Whenever he closed his eyes, he saw the three of them—himself, Nora, and his father—holding hands in a line, like a group of children striking out into uncharted territory. The stroke had picked them up and landed them in a place where nothing was familiar, but Cormac knew it was the only place he wanted to live.

2

Stella rose before dawn on Friday and took the M7 into Dublin, enjoying the smooth comfort of the motorway but quite missing the drive
through the winding old coach roads, the sight of the pubs where her
father invariably stopped for refreshment on the way in and out of the
city, following his true religion—sport, and championship hurling in
particular. But time was money these days, and the gleaming white concrete motorways were a sign of the new religion.

She'd decided late last night to make this trip herself and not leave
it to anyone else. This was her investigation, and Serious Crimes could
get seriously stuffed if they hadn't made it over to interview the victim's
spouse by now.

It was just gone half-eight when she pulled up in front of Benedict Kavanagh's house in the city center. The Kavanagh/Broome residence was one of those Georgian monstrosities on North Great George's
Street. Artists and other creative types had snapped up these grand but
crumbling houses for next to nothing back in the eighties, living with
scaffolding for years until development made the street fashionable
again. Stella stood before the door, painted a brilliant aquamarine under
the fanlight, and rapped twice with the huge brass knocker shaped like a
fist. Had to be a story behind that. There was a story behind most things,
if you were paying attention.

When the door swung open, it revealed a barefoot and stylishly
stubbly young gent in black jeans and an expensive cashmere jumper.
"We're not open." He pointed to a brass plaque beside the door: TUES-
DAYS AND THURSDAYS ONLY, BY APPOINTMENT.

"That's all right," Stella said, producing her ID. "I'm not here about art."

The young man's eyes narrowed as he comprehended the nature of
her visit. He ushered her into the foyer, and she saw that the whole
ground floor was done up as a gallery, with large paintings that nearly
covered the walls. The cracked plaster behind them was real, impres-

sions of centuries behind wallpaper, a fresco of evidence to a trained eye. Here and there a chair or a table with a vase of flowers that beautifully set off the paintings. What was it like to have such an eye? Stella wondered, thinking of her own drab sitting room with its insipid wallpaper and matching suite.

The young man left her alone while he went upstairs, giving her a chance to look around. The paintings in the front room were angry seascapes, thick-painted stormy skies and waves and weather, the paint applied with such passion that you could almost hear the surf. Not just grays and blues and greens, but also shades of yellow, brown, and purple. Stella went up close and studied the nearest canvas. How did a person work at close range like this and understand what effect the brushstrokes would have at a distance? There was mystery in it, how the eye perceived the parts and the whole. She glanced up the stairs and saw no sign of the young man returning. So she made a quick round of the ground floor, from the rooms in front, with their large casement windows that looked over the street, to the back rooms—a galley kitchen stocked with wineglasses, coffeemaker and tea urn, industrial dishwasher. The kitchen adjoined a tiny room that functioned as an office, with desk, file cabinets, and a glowing laptop. On the laptop screen was a spreadsheet with recent sales to museums. Stella had to stifle a curse as she glimpsed the number of zeros behind each figure. She slipped from the room and took up her previous position just as the young man appeared again at the top of the stairs.

"Mairéad says she'll talk to you in the studio. I'm sorry I neglected to introduce myself—Graham Healy, I'm her assistant."

Stella followed him up a graceful cascade of pale marble held in place with a wrought-iron railing. Orchestral music poured down from above, louder and louder as they traveled upward, past the living areas on the first floor, all the way up to a garret at the very top of the house, transformed by a bank of windows on the north wall into a painting studio. A whiff of mineral spirits assaulted the nostrils, and music blared loudly from speakers all around the room, filling the airy space with the throb of violins and cellos, the crash of cymbals and booming kettledrums. Mairéad Broome signaled the young man to turn down the music, and as he did so, Stella's gaze traveled through an open doorway to a bedroom where the walls, sheets, and furniture were all stark white. Amid the rumpled luxury of bedclothes, she spied a few discarded garments—his and hers, from every appearance. Stella turned to give Kavanagh's wife her full attention.

Mairéad Broome couldn't have been more than thirty-five, but her hair was prematurely white. It was short and asymmetrical—an artistic statement. She had the fresh and slightly weathered complexion of someone who spent days out of doors—perhaps she painted at the seaside as well. When she turned to set down her paintbrush and rag, the dark brown eyes she fixed on Stella radiated curiosity and intelligence. "You're here about my husband," she said. A statement rather than a question. She'd been expecting a visit like this for some time.

Stella appreciated directness and decided that she ought to respond in kind. "Yes. A body has been found, and we have reason to believe it might be your husband." She watched for an initial reaction. There was none. Mairéad Broome's steady look never wavered, as if something she already knew had been confirmed. The young man began to speak, but she stopped him with a glance. "Where did you find the body?"

"A few kilometers from Birr." Stella felt as if she ought to say more. "You may have heard news of an ancient body that turned up yesterday. Your husband was later found at the same location. His car was submerged in the bog."

At this news, Mairéad Broome stood frozen, staring at Stella as if seeing through her. "I'm sorry, where?"

"Eight kilometers outside Birr, just over the Tipperary border."

"I see. And my husband?"

"I'm afraid he was inside the car."

A short pause, then, "How did he come to be driving in a bog?"

"We're not sure he was driving. It doesn't appear to have been an accident."

"You're saying my husband was murdered?"

"That's what we believe, from the evidence so far."

Mairéad Broome shook her head. "But how do you know it was murder?"

"I'm sorry, I can't really share any details at this point."

"Because I'm a suspect?"

"Until we know more, everyone's a potential suspect."

Mairéad Broome's gaze followed Stella's, through the bedroom door. "It's easy to jump to conclusions, isn't it, Detective? But people's lives are complicated. They don't fit into tidy categories. Surely that's one thing you learn from police work."

Stella moved to her next question. "I have to ask if there was anyone who would profit from your husband's death."

"Apart from myself, you mean? My husband had a pretty sizable family trust. Since there are no children, I suppose it would come to me. But I didn't marry Benedict for his money. I didn't give a damn about his bloody money."

"What did you care about?"

"Difficult as it may be to believe—and not to mention as difficult as he tried to make it sometimes—I did love my husband."

"You were married for how long?"

"Seventeen years." She took in Stella's curious look. "I'll save you the trouble of doing the sums, Detective. I was fifteen when we met and eighteen when we married. Benedict Kavanagh was . . . well, he was unlike anyone else I'd ever known." Her voice fell to a whisper. "Bastard."

"How did you meet?" Stella asked.

"At my parents' house. Benedict was a colleague of my father's, a rising young star at the academy. He used to come to dinner about once a month. My father loved to sit around the table and talk philosophy, and of course Benedict was brilliant at it. No one better. I was young and easily dazzled. There was a minor scandal when we eloped. My parents were furious, but what could they do? Force an annulment? Not quite the thing for a couple of radical advocates of free will. I was so certain about what I wanted then. The path seemed so clear."

"Not as clear since?"

She turned and looked at Stella directly for the first time. "Are you going to tell me you've never had any regrets, Detective? Anyone who makes that claim is a liar in my book."

"Your husband was gone more than a week in April before you reported him missing."

Mairéad Broome's eyes flashed. "I was out of town. I didn't know he'd gone missing until I returned home."

"You still waited three days."

"I explained all this to the police at the time. There had been a couple of . . . previous instances . . . where it turned out that he was simply caught up in his work. I didn't like the idea of wasting police time if

Benedict was just buried in old books—" She stopped short and turned away, apparently remembering where her husband's body had turned up.

"Can you tell me about the last time you spoke to your husband?"

"It was just before I left for Cork. April fourteenth. It was my first solo exhibition."

"So you never phoned him while you were away? And—you'll forgive my curiosity—your husband couldn't find time to attend your first solo exhibition?"

"We had our own work, Detective, our own schedules. Benedict was as busy as I was—busier, even—with his writing, and his work at the academy, and the television program. With my odd hours up here in the studio, there were some weeks we hardly saw one another."

"You wouldn't happen to know what your husband was working on at the time of his disappearance?"

Mairéad Broome sighed. "He often traveled to London, to the British Library, and to the Bibliothèque Nationale in Paris, usually something to do with his old manuscripts. When he got back from his last trip to London, he did mention something about a breakthrough. He didn't say much more, just that he'd found something that would turn the world of philosophy on its ear. I remember his exact words. He said, 'This is going to rattle some bones.' You could see that he relished the prospect—he loved lighting fires under people. It's always been a mystery to me how a few words scribbled down a thousand years ago could be so earth-shattering today. But that was what my husband lived for."

"Did he have any enemies?"

"Well, since you tell me that he's been murdered, obviously at least one. There's a long list of people who disliked him, Detective. It's no secret that my husband was good at stirring things up. One of the things I admired about him, actually. He never shied away from controversy. On the contrary; he refused to let people hide behind comfortable hypocrisies, and if he made enemies, well, he looked upon that as their problem, really, not his."

"I understand he had some rather lively debates with colleagues on his television program."

"Just because he could run rings around those phony, full-of-themselves so-called intellectuals doesn't mean they wanted to see him dead. It was a game to them—all that mock quarrelling and backstabbing. You can't think any of them took it seriously. It's their stock-in-trade, lobbing firebombs, insulting one another's intelligence. They thrive on it."

As she spoke these last words, her voice faded, and it seemed as if the floor had begun to fall away beneath her. Stella realized, almost too late, that Mairéad Broome's legs were about to give way. Healy moved quickly to scoop a chair under her. He knelt on the floor beside her. "Let me bring you a glass of water, Mairéad—"

She snapped at him weakly, "I'm all right, Graham. For God's sake, stop fussing."

Stella waited as the young man ignored the instruction and fetched a glass of water anyway. She was glad she'd made the trip herself and not let Serious Crimes handle the interview. Was this genuine grief she was witnessing, or some version of relief, now that the wait for the missing husband was finally over? Impossible to tell. She said, "I'll need to speak with you at greater length, to go over all the details of your husband's disappearance. But there was another reason for my visit here today. I wonder if you'd be willing to come to the hospital in Birr to identify your husband's body."

Mairéad Broome looked up, as if startled to find Stella still there.

"I can drive you down to Birr, if you like," Stella said.

This consideration of practical details seemed to bring Mairéad Broome back to herself. "No, I'll come on my own. Graham will drive me."

The young man leaned in. "We'll need a few minutes to gather up some things. I'm assuming we'll stay on for a day or two."

"I think that would be wise," Stella said. She turned to Mairéad Broome. "I wonder if I might have a look through your husband's papers. I understand he kept an office here in the house."

"Yes, Graham can show you." Mairéad Broome stood and turned away.

Graham Healy led Stella downstairs to the study on the first floor. He pushed open the door to the book-lined room. "That wasn't like Mairéad, what you saw up there. Must've been the shock."

It was unclear what he meant. Was it the matter-of-fact way the wife discussed her husband's death, or was it her collapse at the end that was so uncharacteristic? Stella studied the young man. Definitely an art student, she decided, unconvinced of his own talent but finding his true calling as the assistant, disciple, and younger lover of a famous artist. The whole situation had a slight whiff of scandal, but of course no one would have blinked if the genders had been reversed.

"What does a painter's assistant do, exactly?" Stella asked.

"A bit of everything, really. I clean brushes, stretch canvases, order supplies, work on the inventory, and keep up all the gallery and collector contacts, the publicity and mailing list, maintain the website."

"And how did you come to be working here?"

"Mairéad came to an exhibition at my school last year," he said. "Favor for a friend, I think. Not that she isn't interested in encouraging young artists—she is, of course—but she was under tremendous pressure, getting ready for her first big solo exhibition. I offered to help out, do whatever I could."

"Because?"

"Because it was a great opportunity, and because Mairéad Broome is a great artist, the sort of artist I'll never be."

"So you left art school and came to work here full-time? Do you also live here?"

The young man's eyes locked on hers, showing a hint of defiance, then flicked away. "That's my room upstairs, next to the studio."

"How well did you know Benedict Kavanagh?"

"Not well. I mostly stayed out of his way, but that wasn't difficult. Like Mairéad told you, they had different schedules."

"Would you say they led separate lives?"

"Listen, when Mairéad realized Benedict was missing, she was beyond distraught."

"Pardon me if this sounds cold, but she does seem to have recovered somewhat. Perhaps with your help?"

"Think what you like, Detective. I've not done anything I'm ashamed of. I doubt whether Benedict Kavanagh could have said the same."

Stella turned back to him. "Enlighten me, please. What do you mean?"

Healy was clearly uncomfortable, but he pressed on. "Well, you hear things—about how the rumors used to fly whenever a new intern turned up to work on his program—it was always the same. After a few months, he'd tire of them, and in would come someone new. Mairéad's not stupid. She knew—everyone knew. The way that bastard treated her." He glanced up at Stella. "As if she didn't exist."

"Do you mind telling me where you were yourself, the last two weeks of April?"

"I was wondering when you'd get around to that," Healy said. "This is all in the file."

"Indulge me," Stella said.

"It was Mairéad's first solo show in Cork. We went down to supervise the installation on the fourteenth. The show opened on the twentieth, and we were back in Dublin on the twenty-eighth."

Stella feigned ignorance. "So you stayed on in Cork for a few days after the opening?"

Healy's eyes flicked away, uneasy. "No, we took a sort of miniholiday after the frenzy of mounting the show."

"Where, exactly?"

"Sorry?"

"Where did you go on this miniholiday?"

"Mairéad's agent has a cottage in the Slieve Bloom Mountains, near Mountrath. We stopped there to decompress."

"And you have someone who can vouch for you, I suppose?"

"We were alone. The owners were away, in Australia. That's why we went."

At least what Graham Healy was saying matched the statements he'd given in April, Stella thought. Still, not exactly what you'd call an airtight alibi. And all far from the motorways with camera systems.

Graham Healy looked at her intently. "I know what you imagine, Detective, but it's not like that."

"What is it like?"

"The marriage was over when I arrived on the scene. There's nothing sordid—"

Stella cut him off. "Thank you, Mr. Healy. I'll be fine here."

He stood at the door for a moment, about to speak, then turned and left her alone in Kavanagh's study.

The crime scene technicians would go over this room again, of course, but Stella always found it revealing to visit the place where the victim had lived or worked. She switched on the desk lamp. Stacks of paper formed lopsided battlements around the edge of the large desk, notes for some dry academic treatise, from the look of it. A pile of dog-eared novels and a nest of scribbled notes and drawings filled the center of the fortress. No sign of a laptop, no phone. A large tea stain showed where a spill had been rather ineffectively mopped up, and biscuit crumbs with attendant blots of grease dotted the papers. Were these Kavanagh's leavings, or had someone else been using his desk in the meantime? The room didn't strike her as a shrine, kept exactly as it had been left by its last occupant. Did the person who had sat here recently have firsthand knowledge that Benedict Kavanagh would never return? Stella studied the crumpled-up sketches on the desk. Perhaps Graham Healy had usurped Kavanagh's place in his study as well as his bed.

3

Standing at the foot of a stainless-steel slab in the morgue, Nora gazed upon the bog man, released from his swaddling and roughly articulated upon the table, following the anatomist's urge to understand everything in its proper place. She tried to take in the whole man, as she had taught her students to do in gross anatomy lab, the whole impression of the person laid out before them on the table. There was a lot more to be gleaned from a cadaver's life and death than a collection of parts, and it was important for future physicians to understand as much about what went right for people as what went wrong. The fact that the patient had died probably ten centuries earlier was neither here nor there. For Nora, every encounter with a cadaver was an occasion, a chance to increase human knowledge and understanding.

The head, upper torso, and arms were still attached, but they had been separated from the legs just above the pelvis. The weakest parts tended to fall asunder first—which usually meant the unsupported spine in the lower back. The man's head was only slightly misshapen from the weight of the peat, the features still readable. Eyes and mouth open, perhaps an expression of surprise at his grisly fate.

Wet bog-brown cloth clung to the torso and limbs, following their contours, apparently torn by the same rough force that had dismembered the fragile body. Because this man had not been found in his original place, a lot of information about how he had ended up there had been lost. Had he gone into the bog standing up, facedown, supine? All these details could speak about the circumstances. Had he gone in whole, or already in pieces? The answer to that was likely the former, judging from how the clothing was torn and the fact that he was obviously much later than naked Iron Age bog men who appeared to have suffered perimortem dismemberment as part of their ritual sacrifice. The other detail that stood out was the stretching and pulling of the muscle fibers, which suggested that the body had been intact until unearthed by someone or something with enough force to pull it apart.

Nora paused to check the spray bottle of deionized water she'd brought with her from Dublin. There could be no dillydallying; she'd have to take her photos and measurements and get Killowen Man's remains back into the container as quickly as possible, to keep him from being exposed to the mold- and bacteria-laden air.

The morgue at the regional hospital was much more used to preparing the remains of elderly patients for removal by undertakers, not so much used to the state pathologist or the National Museum descending upon them en masse. She could see hospital staff occasionally peering through the small window in the autopsy room door.

Nora knew the full team back at the Barracks could probably determine lots of things: when and how his hair had been cut, how much work he'd done with his hands, perhaps even the menu of his last earthly meal, and with it, the time of year in which he'd died. It was a major break that he was wearing clothing; it could be analyzed by experts in fiber analysis, garment and footwear construction, and other arcana of the archaeological profession.

Her job today was to examine the body, take measurements, note her observations while the corpse was still fresh, so to speak. Try to hazard a few conjectures about which types of damage were perimortem and postmortem.

She began to take photographs, starting at the head and working her way down to the corpse's pointed toes. Even after several years in Ireland, working on remains recovered from the peat, she remained in awe of a bog's protective power. This man was clearly at least hundreds of years old, and yet a section of his limbs would show nerves, blood vessels, bone and marrow, the same as a person only recently dead.

Although it was digital, her camera shutter clicked and whirred just like the real thing. The thickened sole of the unshod foot again pulled at her imagination, as it had out on the bog. Part of his story was written there, she was certain. Calluses and fallen metatarsal arches spoke to a lifetime of wandering. The ankle showed signs of gout, suggesting a rich diet, and yet his cheeks were slightly sunken, a sign of deprivation. Was he an outcast or an exile?

She worked her way around to the other side of the body, snapping photographs of the right hand, whose thumb and first two fingers seemed stained darker brown along the distal interphalangeal joints. An anomaly of coloration from the bog, or something else? She circled again to examine the left hand, but it was clenched tight. Setting aside the camera, she began to probe at the clothing that twisted around the man's torso, her eye drawn to the edge of a hole in his cloak. She gently moved aside the wet wool that shrouded his rib cage. There was not just one, as it turned out, but several holes of similar size, and definitely cut rather than torn through the cloth.

The door at the head of the table swung open, and Catherine Friel's face brightened when she saw Nora. "Thought you'd have him back at the Barracks by now. Isn't that the usual protocol?"

"Detective Cusack asked us to hold up here for a while, since evidence from her case could be intermixed with the older remains."

"Wise choice," Dr. Friel agreed. "I'm here for the PM on the other gentleman. Maybe you'd give me a hand? I'd be happy to reciprocate."

After she had Killowen Man safely stowed in the cooler, Nora stood at the other mortuary table, taking in the details on the recent murder victim. In contrast to the ancient bog man, Benedict Kavanagh's corpse was not only intact but surprisingly unmarked. Of course they were still waiting for final confirmation that this really was Kavanagh, but everything pointed that way. Nora couldn't help thinking about what Cormac had said last night, that Benedict Kavanagh and Niall Dawson had been best friends at university. Why would he keep silent?

The mortuary technician had already cut the clothes off and removed the personal effects. Because Benedict Kavanagh's body had just come out of the bog, the limbs were still quite pliable. The corpse now looked like a slightly shrunken effigy laid out on the slab.

A line from a Seamus Heaney poem, the reference to "a saint's kept body," circled through Nora's brain. But by all accounts, this dead man was not a saint, and his face was not the calm visage usually associated with a holy man's death mask; the eyelids were open, and the somewhat shriveled eyeballs still seemed to bulge slightly from the sockets. His jaw gaped open, the muscles of his cheeks stretched tight. As Dr. Friel turned to mark the autopsy diagram, Nora said, "There's something inside his mouth."

"Yes, I saw that," Dr. Friel said, setting down her clipboard. "First priority, I think." She worked two gloved fingers between the dead man's teeth and eventually removed a slightly misshapen black object about the size and shape of a large marble.

"What is it?" Nora asked.

"Not sure, but there's more than one." Catherine Friel's fingers were still wedged between the dead man's teeth. "At least two more." She tightened her grip on the corpse's chin and leaned down to get better leverage.

"Do you think it's possible that he choked on them?" Nora asked.

"Well, they'd be about the right size to block the airway. We can put obstructive asphyxia on the list of possible causes."

Nora pulled the magnifier down to examine each small black orb in turn as Dr. Friel removed it. "Looks like a puncture in this first one," she said, moving on to the others. "A couple of the others, too. No, not a puncture. It's more like a tiny drilled hole." She had a nagging feeling that she'd seen something like this before, but she couldn't say where.

"That's it," Catherine Friel said as she managed to extract the last of the strange objects. "Half a dozen whatever they are."

"Definitely plant material," Nora said. "Possibly a seed pod."

"Take a look at this." Catherine Friel was still holding the dead man's jaw open. She pulled the lighted magnifier closer and suddenly the presence of the pods seemed to fade into the background. Despite the discoloration of the tissue inside the corpse's mouth, Nora could make out a thin layer of epithelial cells, the lamina propria and papillae surrounding thick muscle. Benedict Kavanagh's tongue had been split in half lengthwise, straight down the center.

4

Stella was about twelve miles from the hospital when she rang Molloy. "I've got Kavanagh's wife on her way to identify the body. How's Dr. Friel getting on with the autopsy?"

"Almost finished."

Stella checked her watch. "Can you let her know we'll be there shortly, see how much longer she'll need? I'd rather not have to delay once we get there. Thanks, Fergal."

As Stella drove, she kept glancing at the two figures reflected in her rearview mirror. Mairéad Broome's car, a black BMW, was much more conservative than her husband's gold Mercedes. As she checked the mirror again, she could see Kavanagh's wife in profile, staring out the window and occasionally turning to speak. Stella tried to imagine the conversation going on in the other car.

The regional hospital in Birr was a former tuberculosis sanatorium, a grim complex of single-story pebble-dashed buildings painted pale yellow. As Stella knew from many visits in the course of her work, recent budget cutbacks meant fewer beds, which meant fewer staff, which meant overcrowded casualty departments, and more sick and injured people lying on trolleys in the corridors. You could be bloody sure all the politicians in charge of health services had private insurance and wouldn't be caught dead in one of these places. Entering the hospital car park, she drove around to the back and led Mairéad Broome and Graham Healy through the back door. Whatever their conversation had been on the road, both were silent now.

"We do appreciate your help with identification," Stella said. "If you'll give me just a minute, I'll just see whether they're ready."

Stella pushed through the door to the morgue. It wasn't set up like some of the more modern hospital facilities, with a video camera or separate viewing room. You had to get close to death here. The body lay on a trolley, covered by a sheet. Catherine Friel stood at the sink, preparing to remove her gloves and apron, with Dr. Gavin beside her, still wearing protective gear as well, evidently after assisting with the postmortem. It struck Stella that she was in the presence of a pair of women who had chosen to look at the face of death every day.

Dr. Friel lifted her eyes as Molloy quietly entered the room and joined them at the trolley.

"I've brought Mr. Kavanagh's wife to help with an ID," Stella said. "Any news on the cause of death?"

"The only outward trauma is some swelling in the occipital region at the back of the skull, but I don't believe it was severe enough to be fatal. No fracture, and the swelling would actually suggest that he was alive after it occurred. And we found these in his mouth" Dr. Friel brought out a tray containing what looked like six small black walnuts.

"You think he choked on them?"

"I'm not sure. There's no evidence of petechial hemorrhage, but that's often absent with obstructive asphyxia. There was one of these pretty far down in his throat. Let me show you something else."

Dr. Friel pulled back the sheet and opened the dead man's mouth.

Molloy couldn't manage to stifle a reaction. "Jesus, what happened to his tongue?"

"Split along the median groove, with a fairly sharp blade. But the amount of blood present says it was most likely done postmortem."

Stella was still trying to figure all this out. "So he was hit over the head, possibly asphyxiated with some of those . . . whatever they are . . . and *then* his tongue was cut? I'm not sure I follow."

"Neither do I. I'm just showing you what the evidence so far suggests. I'll have to let you work out the sequence." Dr. Friel gently closed the corpse's mouth and replaced the sheet. "In any case, we're finished here, if you want to proceed with your identification."

"Thanks." Stella was poking at one of the black walnut-like things with a gloved finger. "No idea what these are, you said?"

"Dr. Gavin thought possibly some sort of seed, but we'll let the lab sort it out. You can bring his wife in now, Detective."

Stella stepped into the corridor to speak to Mairéad Broome and her assistant. "We're ready for you now."

Stella knew it was odd, but she always felt strangely energized watching the reaction in situations like this. Most identifications she'd handled were car accidents—there had been a couple of drownings as well—but murder was something entirely different. Mairéad Broome must have realized that she was going to be under scrutiny, which made her first reaction all the more surprising. When Dr. Friel folded back the sheet to reveal her husband's face, Mairéad Broome didn't back away or flinch. On the contrary, she stepped forward. It was as if she wanted to experience her husband's appearance, with every detail burned into memory.

After a long moment, Mairéad Broome spoke: "This man is my husband." She continued to stare at the corpse, and Stella noted with dismay that Kavanagh's mouth was open, the two ends of his split tongue protruding slightly.

Mairéad Broome saw it also and twisted away with an anguished cry, "My God, what's happened to him?" It was only when Graham Healy moved to place a hand on her shoulder that she darted forward to grasp the edge of the sheet, and with one swift motion, she ripped the cover away, exposing the body in all its gruesome nakedness—the shrunken-looking privates nestled in reddish pubic hair, the bare chest bisected by the roughly stitched Y of the autopsy incision. For a moment, Mairéad Broome stood quite still, staring at her dead husband. Dr. Friel and Dr. Gavin stooped in unison to collect the sheet from the floor and pull it back over the corpse.

Healy seized Mairéad Broome by the shoulders and spun her around. Her arms hung limply by her sides; she looked at him blankly, as if she could see his lips move but couldn't hear what he was saying. After a few seconds, she took a deep breath, and her limbs began to flail. Healy tried to hold on, but she was a whirlwind. "Get off me! Get off!" she shouted, slapping at his chest and the hands that held her. Her eyes flashed with dangerous, pent-up fury. "Christ, Graham, can you not just leave me alone?"

Healy backed away, hands in the air. Mairéad Broome's chest heaved, her head drooped forward, and she began to sob.

Graham Healy approached her again and spoke gently. "If we're finished, Mairéad, let's leave here." He carefully slipped one arm about her waist, and this time she didn't resist.

Stella said, "I'd like to speak with you both again before you leave."

Healy's eyes implored. "Give us just a minute?"

Stella nodded and hung back as he led Mairéad Broome into the corridor. She called Molloy over. "Fergal, hang on here and get the autopsy report from Dr. Friel. I'm going with those two."

Stella crossed to the table where the bagged evidence lay. "Just going to borrow these for a bit. I'll bring them right back." She left the room and placed herself where she could see Healy and Broome down the corridor. She feigned making a call on her mobile, so that she could pace up and down while observing the scene. Healy's ministrations were being rebuffed once more. Mairéad Broome broke away, planting herself on one of the hard benches along the wall, bent at the waist, arms wrapped around herself, head bowed. Her young man sat on his hands, his face grim.

How would it feel to have taken the great chance, killed for someone, only to find out that she still loved the bastard? How had Mairéad Broome put it, only a short while ago? *I did love my husband.* Past tense, Stella noted. *As difficult as he tried to make it sometimes.*

What had Benedict Kavanagh done to try his wife's affections? It wasn't hard to imagine. The possibilities were endless, actually. There was the old standby, apparently true in this case, getting off with other women—or even other men. Such things happened, and Healy hadn't mentioned whether the interns on Kavanagh's program were male or female. Not to mention all the countless ways he might have found to humiliate his wife, in public or in private, especially given her reaction to the body just now. What was Mairéad Broome looking for under that sheet?

Or was all her sudden anger directed at Benedict Kavanagh for getting himself killed and leaving her hanging all these months? Just because you didn't love your husband any longer, that didn't mean you stopped worrying about him. If Kavanagh had been getting a leg over, they'd know soon enough. How did these eejits not realize that they couldn't keep their affairs completely secret?

Mairéad Broome had admitted that her marriage was in tatters when she spoke in that careful code about the pair of them being busy with their own work. Bollocks. She probably knew about her husband's bits on the side, and if she did, what would have moved her to do something about it? She'd said she didn't care about money, but as soon as someone made a claim like that, you were almost assured that the opposite was true. Stella made a mental note to check the terms of the family trust, whether it specified what would happen in the event of a divorce or a childless marriage. If leaving Benedict Kavanagh was out of the question, how long before the constant weight of indignity forced his wife's hand? Time to start asking those questions. Stella pretended to ring off the mobile and made her way down to where Mairéad Broome sat.

"I'm all right now, Detective. It was just the shock."

Stella said nothing but reached into her pocket for the bag containing the pods from the dead man's mouth. She held them out to Mairéad Broome, who took the bag and peered at the blackened knobs through the polythene.

"Am I meant to know what these are? Because I don't."

Beside her, Graham Healy shook his head as well, blank. "Not a clue."

"Are they something to do with my husband's death?"

Stella wasn't prepared to part with that information at the moment; instead she tucked the bag back into her pocket and decided on another approach. "When you reported your husband missing, you said you couldn't think of any particular enemies he might have had, but you admitted that he sometimes rubbed people the wrong way—"

Graham Healy exploded: "He was a fucking bollocks!"

"Graham!"

"He ought to have kissed the ground you walked on, Mairéad, with all that you did, all you sacrificed for him and his brilliant fucking career. But no, he was far too busy poncing about on television, stirring the shit and dragging people down. That's all he ever did—"

"Graham, stop it!"

"I'm only speaking the truth, Mairéad, and you know it." He turned to Stella. "She should have walked out years ago. All the international recognition she's been getting, it's only happened since he's been out of her life—"

"Graham, stop it, that's enough!"

He threw up his hands and walked away. They'd clearly had this conversation before.

"I've already told you, Detective, my husband was not an easy man. He was impatient with people who weren't as clever as he was, and that included me. But there were other sides to him, certain aspects that were so . . . well, so simple, in a way. Despite all his intellectual gifts, there were ways he was still a child, emotionally. It turned out that his philosophical high-wire act was just that—an act. All my husband's theories about the nature of the divine, the existence of good and evil, all that bore no connection at all to the way he lived his life."

"Are you trying to say that your husband was a hypocrite?"

"I'm saying that he delighted in the abstract and abhorred the specific, especially when it came to examination of his own behavior. So why don't you just come out and ask me what you want to know, what everyone's dying to know: whether I, or Graham, or Graham and I together killed my husband. The answer is no. And yes, for the record, Graham and I are lovers, and have been ever since the day he came to work for me—"

"Mairéad—"

She silenced him with a look. "Why waste any more of this woman's time, Graham? I'm so tired of pretending. I can't be bothered to keep up appearances. I really can't. If this woman is a proper detective, she'll know everything soon enough. How I was a child when I married Benedict, how he grew bored with me before I'd reached the ripe old age of twenty, and about all the years I've spent since then trying to regain any scrap of dignity and self-respect. And now he's back from his grave, trying to take it all away from me again. Well, he's not going to succeed. This time I'm going to beat Benedict Kavanagh at his own bloody game."

"Why did you stay married, if you don't mind my asking?"

Mairéad Broome looked at the floor. "Cowardice, I suppose. I'm not proud of it. I would have been alone, and my husband had money, he had status and connections. For most of the time we were married, I was just a struggling painter. In some ways, I think he enjoyed having me beside him, all part of the Benedict Kavanagh show. But the threat was always there, under the surface, that he could make my life miserable if I left him, and I had no doubt that he would."

"And yet he tolerated your relationship with Mr. Healy, presuming he knew about it."

"Oh, he knew. But it happened to serve his purposes—let him feel magnanimous, I suppose. And letting me have Graham meant he could do whatever he liked."

"And what was it your husband liked?"

Mairéad Broome raised her weary eyes to Stella. "I'm afraid I can't tell you, Detective. I couldn't bring myself to find out. There are some things even a wife is better off not knowing."

Stella felt the words like a knife. Denial was the default. In a world filled with all manner of bad behavior, why did society insist upon a façade of normality, tidy exteriors that masked the messes inside? How many women knew the truth about their husbands but refused to acknowledge it, because doing so would raise the possibility of more than one reality within themselves?

"Thank you for coming," Stella said. "I'll be in touch if I have any more questions. When will you be heading back to Dublin?"

"We're going to stay on for a day or two," Healy answered. "Mairéad has friends who run an artists' retreat not far from here. A place called Killowen."

5

Cormac rose from his crouch and stood by as Niall Dawson directed the workmen out on the bog. After hours of clearing peat, they'd finally removed enough weight that the buried car could be lifted. A flatbed lorry was in place, waiting to transport the vehicle to the crime lab in Dublin. Cormac watched as the car slowly ascended, pulled upward out of the muck by the arm of the huge digger. The mud-caked vehicle swayed briefly, still dripping, before the machine operator set it down gently on the back of the lorry.

In addition to himself and Niall and the removal workers, the scene-of-crime officers were still on-site, searching for any useful evidence in the apparent murder of Benedict Kavanagh. No one had yet advanced any theories about what Kavanagh was doing out here in the back of beyond, or who might have had reason to wish him dead. Nor had Niall Dawson said a word about his own acquaintance with Kavanagh. Strange.

While his crew covered the car in black polythene for its trip to Dublin, the head of the crime scene detail jumped down onto the boards that rimmed the excavation area, leaning forward to examine the impression of the vehicle's underside, the depressions where the four tires had rested in the peat. "Looks like we're through here, lads," he said. "Let's let the archaeologists have their site back again." He took the hand Niall Dawson offered and heaved himself up out of the pit. "We're heading back. Be sure to let us know if anything else turns up."

Cormac had watched them go over the car, collecting anything that might have a bearing on the case, which meant everything they could find—even the older bog man was forensic evidence in the case they were investigating. The gap where the car had been was roughly four meters by six, a couple of meters deep. The surface was churned up in some places, flat in others where the vehicle's undercarriage had been pulled away.

Cormac eased down one of the stout planks the crime scene crew had placed around the perimeter and his perception began to shift. Since everything in a bog tended to be the same color as peat, you had to keep an eye open for subtle differences in texture. Would they happen upon another item of clothing belonging to Killowen Man, any items he might have been carrying on his person when he went into the bog—his other shoe, or a walking stick, perhaps, or a sack of provisions? Or maybe they'd find evidence of an ancient road, the reason someone would be out here in the middle of a bog. His eye caught upon the fringe of a willow hurdle, a type of woven fencing laid over brushwood centuries ago to make a footpath through soft bog. It was about chest-high in the wall, and ragged, cut through by the digger but amazingly intact, the bark still on the osiers used to weave it. He shifted the planks, stepping from one to the next and pulling the other board to set in front of him. At the far end he found more evidence of a roadway, birch branches thick as a man's arm, eaten up centuries ago by the encroaching moss.

Dawson came back from seeing the scene-of-crime officers on their way with the shrouded vehicle. "Down to us, now," he said. "Let's see what we can find."

Gathering their tools, they began measuring and marking out a grid on the floor of the pit with stakes and string, as they would with any excavation. The surface of the peat was uneven, revealing the impression of a muffler and driveshaft, the axles of the car. Niall was down on his hunkers, taking photos and sketching the features of the surface in his allotted squares from the grid; Cormac did the same in the opposite corner. He leaned in to snap a photo of a shallow pool that had formed under the car's chassis.

The site was deserted now. They worked in silence for twenty minutes, each caught up in his own thoughts. Cormac wondered about Dawson and Kavanagh again. How had Niall Dawson come to know about Killowen? He'd mentioned the farm as a place to kip when they'd discussed coming down to help with the recovery. Before they even knew about Benedict Kavanagh. A small detail, easy to overlook. Cormac knew what it was like to be suspected when you were innocent, but there were so many things about people that were impossible to fathom, even if you'd been friends for years. There was no explaining the way people behaved sometimes. Perhaps he should urge Dawson to come clean, to get the connection with Kavanagh off his chest.

"Look, Niall, I don't know how to say this except straight out. You and Benedict Kavanagh were friends at university. I was there, too, remember? I watched him destroy you in that debate. So why didn't you say anything to the police? When we found the car was his, even when we found the body?"

Dawson's trowel stopped moving. "I haven't seen Benedict Kavanagh for nearly thirty years, Cormac. Surely you don't think—"

"No, of course not. I just can't understand why you kept quiet."

The trowel hung loose in Dawson's hand. "Because it's water under the bridge. I didn't see a need to dredge any of it up again. I'm more than satisfied with my life now, you know that. In a way, I was grateful to Benedict, for opening my eyes." He gestured to the plot they were excavating. "This is my life's work. Getting trounced in that debate made it clear that I wasn't cut out for the philosophical rough-and-tumble. Not in the same way Benedict was, certainly."

"Maybe the rough-and-tumble got a bit too rough. The man was murdered, Niall."

"Well, not by me. Is that what you want to hear?"

"I'm not trying to make a big deal of this. I just thought you might be better off mentioning your old connection to Kavanagh, before someone else does."

"Perhaps you're right," Dawson said. "I'll have a word with Cusack."

As he turned back to his own work, Cormac's eye caught on a shape about an arm's length in front of him. A flat strip, like a belt, with a loop projecting just slightly from the peat's surface. "Niall, take a look at this." Cormac's bare fingers continued scraping at the peat, uncovering more of the leather strap.

"I see it," Dawson said. "Keep going."

The strap was long, and at last Cormac reached the place where it joined another piece of leather. The peat was very wet here, squelching as he worked his hand into the material. He could feel the thickness of the leather, swollen with water, and formed a picture of it in his mind as he worked. Generally rectangular, rounded at the corners, stitching on the inside. He turned to Dawson. "It looks like a satchel—do you see the flap in front? Do you suppose our bog man could have been carrying this?"

"And if there happened to be a book inside—" Dawson sounded short of breath with excitement. "You know, that's been one of our leg-pulls for years. I phoned up Redmond in the conservation lab not three weeks ago and told him some poor sod had stumbled on an illuminated book in a bog. He always knows straightaway I'm taking the piss. What's he going to say now?" Dawson used his fingers to lift the front flap and reached into the satchel's open mouth. Almost immediately, his posture signaled disappointment. "Nothing there. It's empty."

Cormac began to have a strange feeling, the same sort of presentiment he occasionally got while working on a site, as if he could see down through all the layers of history and sense the connections between things that seemed completely unrelated. Perhaps it was only coincidence that Kavanagh's body had come to rest here in the bog in the very spot where some ancient scribe lost his life, or perhaps there was more to it, something they had yet to discover.

Dawson glanced up at the clear sky. "It's warm. Let's get this covered up again, quick-like. Hand us that roll of cling film, will you?" Oxygen was the enemy here. They carefully replaced the wet peat over the satchel, then laid several sheets of film over the sodden mess. After dipping a roll of resin bandage in a nearby water-filled bog hole for a few seconds, Dawson began, with Cormac's help, to stretch lengths of tape across the satchel to preserve its shape, careful to press out any air between the wet peat and the film.

Dawson was thinking aloud as he worked. "If only there had been a book. I mean, Jaysus, think of it. How many early medieval manuscripts have survived in Ireland—a dozen, give or take? If you think about it, there must have been hundreds. Every monk had his Psalter."

Cormac had been pondering the same thing as they worked on the satchel. Now he said,

"Niall, don't you think it strange that Benedict Kavanagh happened to be found here?"

Dawson looked up. "What do you mean?"

"Well, wasn't that his specialty, early medieval philosophy?"

"What difference does that make?"

"I just find it odd that he should be buried here with someone who's probably from the very same era that he studied. A rather amazing coincidence, don't you think?"

6

On the way to Killowen, Stella checked her messages. Nothing from Lia since yesterday morning. Second-guessing was the worst sort of disease, an incurable affliction. Perhaps if she'd been stricter? Or more permissive? Which was it, and where was the magic balance point? Lia's schoolwork was gone to hell last spring, lost in a different, brand-new immediacy—the scent of a boy's neck, the electric torch of a warm hand inside a blouse. What dusty old book could compete with that biological imperative? She felt herself carried back on a memory, locked arm in arm with her classmates, all half pissed on stolen altar wine and possibility as they made their way home on a warm May evening after a snogging session in a nearby orchard with the lads from Saint Anselm's, the boys' college down the road. They'd been falling all over one another, laughing and singing at the top of their lungs:

I am eighteen years old today, Mama, and I'm longing to be wed.
So buy for me a young man, who will comfort me, she said.
You must buy for me a young man, who will be with me all night,
for I'm young and airy, light and crazy, and married I long to be.

She remembered what came after as well—being called on the rug before Sister Geraldine, the mother superior. Breaking the rules didn't bring chastisement from Sister Geraldine but something even worse—a feeling that one had disappointed her. In some ways, that was punishment enough. Stella had often wondered about Sister Geraldine's background, about what had made her choose the veil. What had drawn any of the nuns to that life, away from society, from the world of men? It wasn't as if the choice had lifted them to a higher plane of existence, above the worldly fray; there were obvious frictions among the sisters at the convent—you could see it in the pursed lips, the clipped way they spoke to one another at times. But she had since come to realize that these were intelligent, educated women, scholars who were often deeply immersed in their own subjects—biology, mathematics, literature—and curious about the world. Stella found she had a much greater appreciation for them now that she was trying to raise a daughter with even a fraction of the nuns' self-respect and self-possession. She'd not appreciated them at the time, just as Lia was having a difficult time understanding or appreciating her—that circular curse of youth and age.

Stella pulled into the yard at Killowen and parked opposite the farmhouse, beside Mairéad Broome's black BMW. A few ducks and a gaggle of geese roamed around the driveway. The slate roof on the main building looked new. This was definitely a working farm, and yet there was simplicity and order, as well as a certain creative vibe to the place. As Stella climbed out of the car, the geese began to waddle in her direction. The gander darted forward, hissing a warning, and a voice came from the doorway: "Mind that fella, he's the next thing to a guard dog."

Stella turned to find Claire Finnerty standing in the entry. "I expect you're here about the bog men," Claire said. "Hard to keep a thing like that under wraps. Boot of a car, we heard." Claire herself was dressed for work, in cargo pants, striped jumper, and fleece vest. Her thick dark hair was tied back in a no-nonsense plait, her feet firmly planted in a beat-up pair of wellingtons. "I'm the only one here at the minute, apart from a couple of guests."

"I'm happy to begin with you," Stella said.

"Come in, then." Claire Finnerty led her into the house, through the large open sitting room and kitchen that formed the main portion of the ground floor. Thick oak beams spanned the width of the building, and the far wall was almost all glass—three sets of French doors that looked out over an herb garden in the back courtyard. The table was covered at the moment with small heaps of fresh-cut oregano, thyme, and rosemary that gave the kitchen a pungent aroma. Claire Finnerty returned to her task, bundling the herbs with elastic bands. "Have to keep at this," she said. "We've a market in Banagher first thing tomorrow."

"Her car's outside, so no doubt you already know what I'm going to ask: How long have you known Mairéad Broome?" Stella asked.

"She's been coming here about six or seven years. We offer a place to work with a minimum of interruption. That's why we're here."

"How often does she come?"

"I'd say about twice a year, on average."

"Regularly?"

"Not really; it depends on her exhibition schedule."

"What about last spring?"

"I don't remember the dates on every booking. I'd have to check—"

"Please do."

Claire Finnerty rose deliberately and led Stella to a small cluttered office adjacent to the kitchen. It was a cozy and gloriously eccentric space, walls the color of cinnamon and carved wooden and woven grass masks hanging on nearly every inch of space that wasn't occupied by bookcases. The shelves were packed with books this way and that, not in disorderly fashion but so that every possible inch was filled, no wasted space. Horticulture, spirituality, Irish history, art, architecture, teach-yourself titles on every conceivable topic, including worm propagation, organic farming, *How to Grow Your Own Hemp*. At the center of the desk, a small laptop gave off a cool blue light. "When were you looking for?" Claire Finnerty asked.

"The last two weeks of April, this year."

Finnerty tapped on a few keys to bring up the booking calendar. "Oh, no, I thought we'd taken care of that." She turned to Stella, all concern. "We had a computer virus that wiped out our scheduling program for the first five months of the year. I know that Mairéad was with us sometime in the spring, but I can't remember whether it was February or March—but definitely not April."

"How do you know?"

"We were getting in a new geothermal system, and with all the upheaval of construction, we decided it would be better not to have resident artists during that time."

"Since you're a friend of Mairéad Broome's, you must also know that one of the dead men found in the bog yesterday was her husband." Stella held up the photo on her mobile and watched Claire Finnerty's eyes narrow. "Benedict Kavanagh. The car belonged to him."

"Yes, Mairéad told me about Benedict when she arrived just now."

"Did you ever meet Mr. Kavanagh?"

"No." Stella wasn't sure if she was taken aback more by the lack of apology or by the tiny note of challenge in Claire Finnerty's voice.

"But you didn't like him."

"I really couldn't offer an opinion. As I said, I never met the man."

"And Ms. Broome never spoke about him?"

"Not really."

"A man goes missing and ends up dead less than a quarter of a mile from here, the place where his wife came to work twice a year for the past six or seven years. You don't find that rather odd?"

"It is strange. But I don't have any idea what Benedict Kavanagh was doing here. If you don't mind, I need to get on with my herbs." Claire gestured toward the kitchen, and Stella followed her back to the table.

"What else can you tell me about last April?"

"You mean, can I remember anything incriminating about anyone here?"

Stella found herself rankling at the antagonistic edge in Claire Finnerty's voice. "I just need to know what you recall," she said. "Anything unusual. We're trying to figure out, for instance, how Mr. Kavanagh's car came to be buried in the bog, whether anyone would have had access to a mechanical digger during the last two weeks of April."

Claire Finnerty offered a grudging glance. "I suppose I ought to just tell you now, because you'll find out sooner or later. There was a digger here, for installing the geothermal system. The workmen had to excavate a portion of the hillside behind the house to bury the coils." She gestured toward the courtyard, and Stella noted how the ground sloped away beyond the garden wall. "We had a company down from Boyle to do the work," Claire continued. "GeoSys, they're called. They brought in a JCB and a bulldozer."

"And this gang from GeoSys, they'd just leave their equipment unattended when they'd knock off? Weren't they afraid someone might pinch it?"

"They never said as much."

"Did the workers stay here?"

"No, they preferred staying nearer the pubs in town."

"Do you remember hearing anyone using the equipment after hours?"

"No, I don't."

"Do you know if anyone here has experience in heavy construction?"

"I don't interrogate the people who come to work here, Detective. You'll have to ask them yourself."

"I will," Stella said. "I assume everyone returns here to the main house at some point during the day?"

"They'll be here for lunch in about an hour, when they've finished their chores, and then everyone's free in the afternoon."

"I'll come back then."

Claire Finnerty didn't look up from her work but raised no objection.

Stella headed for the door but turned back just before crossing the threshold. "There was one more thing I wanted to ask. How much do you know about Vincent Claffey and his . . . activities?"

"As little as possible," came the terse reply. "We're not on great terms, if you want the truth."

"But he is your closest neighbor. Which means you'd have more opportunity than anyone else to observe what goes on at his place. Any idea why he would be digging in a protected bog?"

"None whatsoever."

Stella thought for a moment. "How deeply would you say his daughter is involved in any of his schemes?"

A flicker of anger seemed to travel through Claire Finnerty. "Deirdre Claffey is a child, Detective. She doesn't know anything."

Outside, Stella took the long way back to her car, skirting the perimeter of the haggard between the outbuildings to see what she could see. She darted between the goat barn and the cheese storehouse, keeping an eye out for that nasty gander. The whitewashed wall of the storehouse had scorch marks from the ground and hastily sprayed graffiti—a couple of rudely drawn human figures with exaggerated private parts. Rain had made streak marks in the soot. The fire must have been fairly recent. Why hadn't Claire Finnerty bothered to report this, or tell her about it just now? Stella reached out to touch the scorch marks. This fire had been put out before any great damage was done, so perhaps they figured it wasn't worth reporting. Or was there some other explanation?

7

Nora pulled on a new pair of nitrile gloves for the second forensic exam of the day, on Killowen Man. Catherine Friel was the primary point person, given her experience with bog remains and suspicious deaths. After Nora had removed as much peat as she could, Dr. Friel began the external exam, first noting the appearance of the body into her mini-recorder.

"The deceased appears to be male, approximately sixty to sixty-five years of age. The body has been dismembered, more likely the result of disinterment by machines than by homicidal violence or postmortem mutilation." Dr. Friel's voice was calm; she was focused on her subject, as if she had long ago learned to concentrate not on the horror but on the physical form before her and what that physical form had to contribute to the story that was about to unfold. "The deceased appears to be wearing a woolen cloak, which will have to be removed eventually, but I want to make a note first of cuts in the outer garment that seem to align quite precisely with sharp-force wounds on the body." She pointed to the gashes in the woolen fabric where it was wrapped around the truncated torso and then lifted the cloak to show the corresponding cuts in the dead man's flesh. "If we measure the length of these wounds"—she nodded to Nora, who reached for the measuring tools—"it looks as if these cuts were made right through the cloak." She pressed the dead man's skin with a fingertip to flatten the surface. "See how the wound narrows at both ends? That shows the shape of the weapon. It looks as if he was stabbed with a double-edged blade, something like a dagger. And not just once but at least a half dozen times."

Dr. Friel stepped back again and began to scan the rest of the body, and Nora observed the differences in the way they each approached the corpse: she immediately took in details that told of the man's life; Catherine Friel seemed to zero in on what the body revealed about his death. A slight but fascinating divergence in perspective.

"Look here," Dr. Friel said. She was examining the other side of the torso and pointed to a similar set of cuts in the cloth on the victim's left side, underlaid once more with sharp-force wounds. "What do you think—two assailants, or one person with two knives?" She stepped back and mimed an attack with a short blade in each hand, thrusting up toward Nora's rib cage. "Could have happened either way, but I'm betting on two assailants—see how there are many more cuts here, on the left side? Points to one attacker being a bit more . . . enthusiastic than the other. A symmetrical pattern is more likely if it's only one person."

Dr. Friel stepped back again, taking in the whole body once more. "Really quite amazing," she said. "He's so well preserved that we've got enough evidence for a real case. Suspicious death is suspicious death, even centuries later. Pity whoever did it is long gone."

She pointed to several locations on the body with a gloved finger. "There are two distinct areas where the wounds appear to be clustered: there's one grouping in the infraumbilical region, just below the navel; another in the epigastric region, which probably punctured the stomach. The different characteristics of the wounds in each area suggest that there was more than one assailant. That, plus the upward thrust of the blade, which is more usual for attacks than self-inflicted wounds, plus the holes through his garments that correspond with the wounds, all of that together suggests cause of death was exsanguination brought on by homicidal violence. That's what I'd put in my autopsy report."

"So he was stabbed, possibly by two assailants, and bled to death?"

"That's certainly what it looks like. And from the lack of any decomposition, particularly around the wounds, I would also say that he must have gone straight into the bog after he was killed. What else can we tell about him, given the physical evidence?" Dr. Friel pointed to one of the bog man's hands. "There's a pronounced callus on the middle finger of his right hand. Also, the thumb and first two fingers of the right hand are stained darker than the rest of the body. Mishap with a leaky quill, perhaps?" Dr. Friel held up her own right hand, showing off her own discolored fingers. "Unfortunate incident over the crossword last night."

"If it is ink, we should be able to tell from trace analysis." Nora studied the bog man's face, the open eyes and lightly stubbled cheeks, the gaping mouth. She wondered what, if anything, you could tell about a person from his expression at the moment of death. What were the words on his lips at the instant the knives plunged into his gut? And what did he believe would happen to his spirit when his life was so rudely extinguished? The expression was perhaps a function of death itself, the muscles relaxing into primary flaccidity. She thought of the words of the requiem: *Earth to earth, ashes to ashes, dust to dust.*

8

The sun had gone behind a bank of dark clouds when Stella pulled into the driveway at Vincent Claffey's house. Just as she remembered: three junked cars and a rusty washing machine, a trio of unlicensed dogs with the run of the place, a broken baby swing and a pushchair, rolls of fencing. No clamp of turf, so he wasn't likely burning the stuff here at the house. There was plenty of greenery, and every bit of it weeds—not a potato drill or a cabbage in sight. The chipper was parked alongside a shed in the haggard and gave off a greasy reek. What a place to rear a child, Stella thought, realizing that she was thinking of Deirdre Claffey and not the baby she'd seen balanced on the girl's hip yesterday.

She ought to go straight to the door and knock, but the shed door had been left open, and investigative instinct overcame her. She might be able to find out what Claffey was up to with the peat if she could just happen to walk past an open door. She glanced at the house, and seeing no one, made her way to the shed just beyond the chipper.

Just as she reached the door, Deirdre Claffey's voice rang out across the haggard. "What'dye want?"

Stella turned around. "Is your daddy here, Deirdre? I was hoping to speak to him."

"He'll be back soon."

"Maybe I could wait for him? I just have a few follow-up questions."

The girl said nothing but moved away from the door, which Stella took as an invitation. She stepped across the threshold into a dim room with blinds drawn, television blaring, and a dozen spuds peeled and ready for boiling on the stove. Stella's suit, rumpled as it was, made her feel out of place amid the squalor, but with the father's checkered history, she was probably not the first Guards officer or social worker Deirdre Claffey had ever met.

The baby lay on his back on a blanket in the middle of the tiny sitting room, staring up at her from the floor with those giant blue eyes. He shrieked when she made eye contact, delighted to have a playmate.

Stella couldn't help it—she picked up a set of plastic keys from the floor and rattled them in front of the child's face. In contrast with nearly everything around him, the baby's face and clothing, Stella noticed, were immaculately clean. Hard to know which stories to credit amid the local gossip. The child was loved—was that any sort of a clue?

"What's his name?" Stella asked.

Deirdre's voice, floating from the kitchen, sounded tired. "Cal."

"Well, Cal, you're a great little fella, aren't you? What age are you, hmm?" She poked the baby playfully in the stomach, and he shrieked again. Was there any sound more irresistible?

"Don't be getting him excited, now—he's about to have his dinner," Deirdre sounded exactly like someone's nattering old granny. "He'll be nine months next week."

Stella felt her antennae picking up signals from all around the room: large stash of nappies in the corner, the brand-new clothing on the baby, and a new battery-powered swing to replace the knackered one out in the yard.

"Deirdre, do you remember the man I asked you about yesterday, Benedict Kavanagh?"

"I told you I didn't know him."

"But you also said you met all sorts, working the chipper van. I'm sorry to have to tell you this—Benedict Kavanagh is dead, Deirdre. That was his car in the bog. His body was in the boot."

The baby began to cry, and Deirdre quickly plucked him up off the floor. "Shhh," she whispered. "Whisht now, whisht." She began to rock slowly and hummed a little tune until the child began to settle. Unclear, Stella thought, who was comforting whom.

"How well did you know Mr. Kavanagh?" Stella asked as gently as she could. No response. "When was the last time you saw him?"

The girl's voice had dropped to a whisper. "I told you I didn't know him." She lifted the baby's hand and stroked his dimpled fingers. The child began to suck his thumb and laid his head on her shoulder.

"Did your father know you were acquainted—"

"No!" Deirdre shot back, almost as if she was defending her father against some as-yet-unmade accusation.

Before Stella could form her next question, she heard a noise of tires skidding in gravel, and Vincent Claffey was through the door and only a few inches from her face.

"What the fuck do you think you're doin' here? You'd better not be talking to my girl—she's underage, and you know it. Say nothin', Deirdre, I'm warning you. She's no right to be here asking questions."

"Mr. Claffey—" Stella began, but her voice was drowned out.

"Did you get what you came for, then? Did you?" Claffey's voice had risen in pitch, as if he was frightened of something. He turned to his daughter. "You, get to your room, and don't come out 'til I say." He moved to shove Deirdre, who was still holding the child, and Stella stepped forward to block him. Had she put the girl and her baby in danger by coming here?

"Mr. Claffey, I think there's been a misunderstanding. I came to speak to you. Deirdre and I were just chatting." Claffey was not a big man; he was short and wiry but prone to explosive outbursts, as Stella knew from reading his form. He'd never been arrested for striking his daughter, but that didn't mean it never happened. Surely he knew better than to lay a hand on a Guards detective.

Deirdre spoke up: "She was only waitin' for you."

Claffey eyed his daughter over Stella's shoulder, jabbed his finger at her. "I said shut up, you! Not another word."

Stella held her ground. She was taller than Vincent Claffey and confident that she could take him down, if it came to that. "I'm here as part of an official murder inquiry, Mr. Claffey. Of course, if you'd rather not talk here, we can go to the station in Birr. It's up to you."

After a tense moment, in which he seemed to consider his options, Claffey's stance began to soften. But his eyes continued drilling into her, and Stella wondered again whether she'd totally bollixed up this case by coming here today.

"I expect by now you've heard that there was another body in the car," she began. "I asked you about him yesterday, Benedict Kavanagh. And all the evidence at this stage points to murder. I just wanted to double-check and make sure you'd never seen him around." Stella proffered the photo on her phone once more, but Claffey ignored it. "We've discovered that his wife was a regular visitor at Killowen—"

"Wasters," Claffey muttered. "All their crunchy-granola load of fuckin' bollocks. Can't stand seeing anybody making a few bob." Stella filed away this tidbit of information. She could just imagine the difference of opinion between the owner of a chipper van and his totally organic neighbors.

"So you never had any dealings with Kavanagh?"

"What do you mean, 'dealings'? I hope you're not accusing me—"

"I'm not accusing anyone of anything, Mr. Claffey, just trying to get a picture of the victim's movements before he disappeared—where he went, who he might have spoken to. I'm just doing my job, trying to figure out what happened. And I wondered if you could help me."

The tongue darted between his lips. "I've told you, I didn't know the man."

"What about his wife? Her name isn't Kavanagh—it's Mairéad Broome."

Claffey's eyes had gone cold. "Never heard of her."

For a petty criminal, he was a pretty piss-poor liar. But the bruises on Deirdre's wrists came back to her, and Stella knew she couldn't push any further without the risk of putting the girl and her child in danger. She'd have to leave it for now. "Well, if you're certain . . ."

The slight smirk that lit up Claffey's face said he was pleased for having won—this round, anyway. He turned away and started rooting through a cardboard box that sat beside the door, pawing through its contents until he came up with a sturdy padlock.

He followed her out to the yard, and as Stella executed a slow three-point turn in the haggard, he made a show of slipping the lock through the hasp on the shed door and fastening it securely.

9

Low clouds had settled over Killowen by the time Nora returned to the farm. Her first task was locating Joseph, to try to find out what had been troubling him this morning—she'd promised Cormac. The front door of the main house was wide open, but no one answered when she called. The house felt peaceful, a diffuse light from the cloudy sky leaking in through the windows out onto the courtyard garden. The sitting room and kitchen were empty, so Nora stepped into the herb garden, refreshed by the pungent whiff of oregano. As she crossed to the other wing of the house, a small movement caught her eye. Stepping through the doorway, she called out, "Hello, anyone here?"

The stillness in the air refuted another living presence. Probably just her imagination. The interior walls of this corridor were plain whitewash, perfect for displaying the work no doubt donated by resident artists: there were woodcuts, flat metal sculptures, a few abstract seascapes, and a series of elaborate calligraphy pieces.

The first room she encountered seemed to be some sort of scriptorium: beside the windows stood a couple of tall desks, angled surfaces covered in large sheets of vellum. Shelves hanging on the back wall held rolled-up parchments and jars of brightly colored pigment; a long table between the writing desks held a mortar and pestle and several clamshells with brilliant colors crusted in their cupped surfaces. A basket of eggs stood on the center table as well, along with metal rulers, white cotton gloves with the index fingers cut off, a jar of long feathers and others holding tiny brushes and sharp knives. She ran a hand over the vellum on the nearest table, struck by the anatomical quality of the medium. You could still see blemishes, fly bites, spidery veins. She remembered reading stories, at the start of her training, about ancient medical books bound in human skin.

A few samples of the writer's art hung framed upon the walls here in the studio as well. Unlike the precise, perfect character of most calligraphy she had seen, there was a certain extra degree of expression in these pieces, a primitive spirit that came out in the arrangement of shapes and colors. The staring animal forms that inhabited the pages seemed ready to blink. She turned to read the labels on the pigments: auripigmentum, verdigris, lapis, azurite, cinnabar, yellow ochre, purpura, malachite, red lake. Some of the names hinted at far-flung origins.

Nora began to feel self-conscious, wandering through someone's private workroom, and was about to retreat when she was stopped by the sight of a large bowl of black marble-sized spheres. She picked one up to examine it more closely. Turning the thing over in her palm, she found a tiny hole drilled in one side.

"Can I help you?" The man's voice came from the doorway, startling her and causing the pod to fly from her palm and roll under one of the writing desks. The speaker was a tall, lean man, perhaps in his early sixties, dressed in jeans and a plain black sweater. His hair was arranged in a thick fringe above his ears, ginger going to white, and behind the smile in his blue eyes was an inquisitive expression. Nora felt flustered, caught snooping where she probably ought not to have been. When the man spoke again, his voice held no accusation. "Would I be right in guessing you must be one of our guests from the National Museum?" The rolled *r* and rising inflection pegged the accent as Welsh.

"Yes, sorry, Nora Gavin."

He took her hand. "I'm Martin, Martin Gwynne."

"Is this your studio? I didn't mean to blunder in here. Sorry if I'm intruding."

"Ah, no, you're all right." Gwynne bent down to pick up the object she had dropped. He began to play with it as he spoke. "You're interested in illumination, are you?"

"I teach anatomy, so I'm naturally interested in calfskin, but I'm also intrigued by all the exotic pigments." She gestured toward the shelves.

"Ah, you're thinking of lapis lazuli—the truest blue, brought all the way from Afghanistan in the Middle Ages. But there are local sources as well. Woad grows here, as an example. Irish monks also used ground-up shellfish, charcoal, red earth." He reached for a jar containing a yellow powder. "This one, auripigmentum, is made from the gallbladders of eels." He enjoyed Nora's reaction.

"Do you still use all the old pigments?"

"Well, I've given up on a few of the more poisonous compounds. Orpiment, for example, a beautiful golden color, is actually arsenic trisulfide, not something into which I wish to be dipping my quill. And cinnabar—Chinese red—is mercuric sulfide. I've managed to find suitable substitutes for some. But somehow the modern pigments are never quite as vivid."

"I've always wondered, how did the monks discover all those bizarre compounds?"

"That's a good question. It must have been a process of experimentation, I suppose. Some knowledge carried through from even more ancient cultures. And every scriptorium had its Book of Secrets, where the monks would record their recipes. Knowledge was passed down, refined along the way, as with any branch of science or alchemy."

Nora glanced toward the illuminations in progress she'd spied earlier. "Is this your own work? It's beautiful."

"You're very kind. Yes, most of it is mine, but I've been working with an apprentice recently, so a few are hers." He pointed to a couple of smaller works hanging beside the door and an unfinished piece on the nearest writing desk. "Anca's still a bit hesitant about her design, but there is a certain boldness at the back of it. The power is in her, no doubt. She just has to learn to let it out." Martin Gwynne frowned. "At a certain point, you can't teach people anything further. They have to make their own mark."

As they talked, Martin Gwynne was still playing with the pod he'd picked up from the floor and was now rolling through his fingers with the deft skill of a magician.

"What do you call that?" Nora asked. "I know I've seen them before, but I can't—"

"This?" Gwynne said, stopping the little orb on the flat of his palm. "It's an oak gall, sometimes called a gallnut."

"Of course!" Nora felt the knowledge returning.

"We get all we need in the oak wood just beyond."

"And what do you use them for, if you don't mind my asking?"

"For ink, of course. Grind up a few of these, add iron shavings, wine, and gum arabic, cook it all down, and voilà!" He handed her the gall and picked up a stoppered bottle of dark liquid. "You get a very serviceable black-brown ink. It was the basic everyday stuff used all through the Middle Ages, right up to the nineteenth century. Not much in favor these days. Too caustic, you see, eats right through paper. A surface like parchment is able to withstand the bite of acid."

And all perfectly harmless, Nora thought. Unless you'd just seen a handful of these gallnuts in the mouth of a corpse.

A voice came from the doorway. "Martin, love, do you happen to—" The woman who entered stopped short when she saw Nora. She was slender to the point of gauntness, probably in her midsixties, dressed in a hand-knit linen sweater and jeans. Her hooded eyes were dark pools that called to mind a wild creature constantly on the lookout. "So sorry, my dear, I didn't realize you were occupied." The accent was English, a cultivated drawl that suggested private school and money.

"My wife, Tessa, this is Dr. Gavin, one of our visitors from the National Museum," Martin Gwynne explained and then turned to Nora. "I believe you came to help with our bog man, isn't that right, Dr. Gavin?"

"Yes," Nora said, and then hesitated. Was it possible that they hadn't yet heard about the second corpse? Perhaps it was better not to divulge too much. She began to get the impression that she was holding up a private conversation and hastened to make her exit. "I stumbled in here looking for someone, so I'll just keep hunting, if you'll excuse me. Very nice to meet you both."

She withdrew to the cloister walk outside the studio and stopped a short distance down the corridor to examine the gallnut still in her left hand. It looked exactly like the objects they'd found in Benedict Kavanagh's throat, she was sure of it. She ought to share this new bit of information with Cusack, but she'd also promised to find Joseph. She tucked the gall into her pocket for the time being and set out for the kitchen.

As she crossed the courtyard, she could see Joseph and Eliana coming up from the bottom of the garden. They were accompanied by a tall, awkward-looking figure dressed all in brown, from the worn corduroys to his tweed jacket and cap—even his wellingtons were brown. He carried a couple of fishing rods and a basket.

"Nodding!" Joseph cried. "Noddy in the busker—in the biscuit." He pointed to the creel, and the brown man opened it to show off their catch: a tangle of gray eels, still alive and wriggling in the bottom.

Eliana said, "We helped to catch them." She gave a mock shudder. "So horrible, but very . . . em . . . tasty?"

"You actually eat them?" Nora asked, unable to take her eyes from the writhing mass in the basket. She glanced up to see the brown man's chin jutting forward.

He shrugged and blinked rapidly a few times, then let out a series of small barks, looking mortified and blushing furiously all the while, until Eliana intervened, speaking under her breath: "Oh, yes, we eat *anguilas* many ways at home." The fact that she was standing between two grown men who couldn't manage to put two coherent words together didn't seem to faze her in the least. "This is Anthony Beglan," Eliana said, stumbling a bit over the foreign surname. "And this is Nora, Anthony. I think you will like her."

Nora endeavored not to stare at Beglan but found herself fascinated by the tics that seemed to take him over whenever he tried to speak. All the signs—the rapid gestures, the facial tics, and vocalizations—pointed to Tourette's. She had read a bit about it in the medical literature, of course, but never before had such an up close and personal encounter with the disorder.

Anthony tipped his head back, his jaws snapping together fiercely as his eyes searched her face for the familiar look of alarm he must have encountered daily.

"Pleased to meet you, Mr. Beglan," Nora said. "Are you one of the . . . I don't quite know what to call them . . . the residents here?"

The jaws snapped shut a few more times before he could manage a response. "No, I live just bug-bug-bug-beyond, but"—again the tics interrupted—"we share the work. I keep cuh-cuh-cac-cattle."

"And what about these eels? Are they really going to be our dinner?" Nora smiled, and Anthony Beglan's glower split into a reluctantly wolfish grin, a complete transformation. "Because if they are, I hope Eliana's telling the truth."

She glanced at Joseph, who was gazing intently at Eliana again. Whatever disturbance Cormac had seen this morning seemed to have dissipated. When the girl moved past him, he reached out and grasped her hand, in a gesture that neither surprised nor annoyed her, so it clearly was not the first time. Nora felt a small twinge of trepidation, remembering Joseph's attraction to Cormac's friend Roz Byrne last year before his stroke, and worried about where this new attachment to Eliana might lead. He'd still not managed to recognize Roz, and although she stopped by the house every few weeks to see how he was getting on, there had not yet been any flicker of recognition in his eyes. Each time Roz came for a visit, she went away bereaved yet again.

Eliana's hand looked so small and pale tucked inside Joseph's large fist. Was the attachment significant enough to mention to Cormac? The girl hadn't been with them even two full days. Nora decided to let things be, at least for the moment.

"Anthony, are you coming?" The woman they'd awkwardly encountered in the bath last night emerged from the French doors. "I've got the pot ready for your catch."

Anthony's jaws snapped together a few more times before he could answer. "Be there stuh-stuh-straightaway. Just have to take cuh-cuh-care of these." He lifted the creel slightly.

The woman waved and then retreated.

Nora lowered her voice. "Shawn, isn't it? She said she was an archaeologist."

Beglan nodded. "That's right."

"And what does she do now?"

"You ask a luh-luh-lot of questions," Anthony Beglan said. He turned and strode away.

10

Nora stood in her room, looking over the available change of clothing. She always required a shower and change after a postmortem. Through the open window she could hear a smattering of electronic music, someone's mobile phone. A man's voice floated upward from the drive. "Christ," he muttered, "what the fuck is it now?"

Glancing out the window, she could see it was the same rather scruffy young man who had been with Kavanagh's wife at the hospital earlier. He was in the middle of retrieving two cases from the boot but had set them down after receiving a text message. He stared at his phone and spoke aloud to whoever had sent the text. "Not here, you bollocks. Are you mad?" He texted furiously, then sent off the message and picked up the cases again, heading toward the other end of the car park. His phone jingled again, a real ring this time, before he'd traveled to the other side of the car.

"What the hell are you doing?" Nora heard. "I told you I'd be in touch. No, no, that's not going to happen. I explained to you how we were going to handle it—"

Just then a small motorbike carrying Vincent Claffey came puttering up the drive from the road. He stopped at the outer edge of the farmyard and trundled the bike off the drive and up against the nearest shed. Claffey had a mobile pressed to his ear all the while, and soon it became clear that he was the person on the other end of the call with the young man. They both hung up, and the younger man headed over to meet Vincent Claffey, glancing around in case they'd be seen. Nora watched from her invisible perch, fascinated. The young man pressed a brown envelope into Claffey's hands. "You've got what you want now—and you know what we want."

Claffey's expression seemed to hold both amusement and triumph. He held up the envelope. "Oh, yes, I know what you want. But it's a lot to ask of any man." He slipped the envelope inside his jacket and patted it. "I'm afraid ye'll have to give me a little more time to think it through. Don't worry, I'll be in touch." When he reached the bike, he threw his leg over it, and sped away down the drive.

Alone again, the young man leaned forward and banged his head slowly against the wall of the shed. Then he returned to the car to pick up the cases and trudged down the path that led into the oak grove, disappearing from view.

Nora realized she'd been holding her breath. It was some sort of payoff, had to be. Blackmail? The thickness of the envelope suggested it was no small consideration. She finished changing and made her way outside once more. Mairéad Broome's young man seemed awfully familiar with Vincent Claffey. They must have been here before. What did Claffey have on him? Maybe a bit more knowledge than anyone realized about Benedict Kavanagh's disappearance?

She followed in his footsteps, passing the sign that pointed to the cottages. The broad macadam path cut through a gentle slope that was covered with green mounds, hundreds of moss-covered stones like an army of turtles marching through the oak grove. She spied three or four small dwellings farther down the path, glimpses of thatch and stone and whitewash through the leaves. Towering above the sparse undergrowth of saplings stood a few stout old trees and one giant in particular whose girth must have been twenty feet or more. Nora slowed her pace and circled the massive tree, resting her palm on ancient bark that had grown into folds upon itself, looking up into gnarled branches that stretched outward like enormous crooked arms that drooped gracefully toward the earth, practically begging to be climbed. Garish green moss grew straight up the trunk and clung to a snake-like root that slithered into leaf mold underfoot. How long had this ancient life been rooted here? What ravages of wind and weather, what natural and man-made firestorms had it withstood through all those centuries?

Nora leaned forward and peered up into the branches. She could, if she wished, step from one limb to another and vanish up into its leaves. Testing her balance, she set one foot gingerly on the lowest limb, then stepped quickly up the ladder of branches. Soon she was fifteen feet above the ground, lost amid the rustling foliage. Their thick leaves gave oak trees a particular sound, a deeper timbre than the music of sycamores or beech trees or firs. Nora glanced down and felt a little dizzy. What was she doing, acting like a child? And how on earth was she going to get down?

A growing murmur of voices came from back along the path. The slouchy young man walked beside Mairéad Broome. Her cottage must be along this path, but they seemed headed back to the main house, passing under the oak where Nora was hidden.

"I had to give him the money," the young man was saying. "Coming here like that, in broad daylight? It's not like I had a choice, Mairéad."

Mairéad Broome stopped just under the tree, and Nora held her breath. How could they not hear her or at least sense her presence above them? She hung on tight, pressed against the oak's mighty trunk.

"No, you did the right thing, Graham."

"The trouble is, he'll just keep asking for more, unless we do something."

"What can we do? We'd all be in jeopardy if he says anything, and I won't risk that."

"But he's using you, Mairéad."

"I know he is. Just leave it be, please, Graham—"

He stopped her saying any more with a fervent kiss, pressing her back against the oak.

Nora nearly had to stifle a cry as a fat acorn dropped from a branch directly in front of her eyes, glancing like a stone off Graham's unprotected head.

"Ow!" he yelped, jumping back. "Jesus!" One hand reached up to rub the spot where the acorn had made contact, but to Nora's relief, he glanced up only briefly and didn't see her. The acorn had provided sufficient disruption, however, and the pair moved on and were soon out of earshot.

Nora slowly let out her breath and started to climb down the same branches that had been her ladder on the way up. Reaching out to find a grip, she noticed a small branch bearing a spray of leaves and a marble-sized brown sphere. There was no hole in it, like those she'd seen in Martin Gwynne's studio, but the thing was definitely not an acorn. Nora felt the lump in her pocket and looked around, spying other brown galls on the branches all around her. She hadn't even noticed them on the way up. She plucked the false fruit from the tree, slipped it into her pocket, and climbed carefully to the ground.

It was difficult to imagine that anyone she'd met so far at Killowen could have been responsible for Benedict Kavanagh's death, but the oak galls must be a significant clue. From what she'd seen in the morgue, Kavanagh's death had been planned in some detail. And the anger felt personal. What could Kavanagh possibly have done to warrant such a dreadful vengeance? A little research might be in order.

She found Joseph and Eliana in the kitchen. "I'm back," she said. "Thought it might be time to give Eliana a well-deserved break."

The girl shrugged. "I don't mind."

"Wouldn't you like to take a walk or read a book, anything?"

Eliana finally nodded, eyes downcast. She headed for the door and turned as she crossed the threshold. "One hour?" It sounded as if she was being forced to stay away for an hour, rather than being granted her liberty.

"I'm sure you'll find plenty to do," Nora said. She turned back to Joseph. "You and I are going to do a bit of research. Stay right here—I'll be back."

Nora fetched her laptop from upstairs. She reached into her pocket for the oak galls she'd collected from the studio and the wood and showed them to Joseph. "Here's what we're looking for," she said, setting them down on the table in front of him.

His eyes seemed to light up. "*Bugallas,*" he said. "*Tinta, la tinta!* Uncle!"

Nora wondered if he made as little sense in Spanish as he did in English.

"Uncle!" Joseph said again. He moved his right hand, miming the act of writing.

Nora looked at him. "Do you know what this is?" He nodded slowly, reaching out for the gall she held in front of him.

"*Bugalla,*" he said. He held up the second gall as well. "*Dos bugallas-uh-uh-duh—roble.*"

"You've seen something like this before?"

"*Sí, sí, la medicina.*"

Nora couldn't quite believe her ears. "*La medicina*—for medicine, you mean?"

Eliana's voice came from the doorway. She was back already. "And '*la tinta*' is ink—or perhaps, em, what do you call this . . . for changing colors." She gestured to her clothing.

"You mean dye?" Nora asked.

"Yes, dye, that's it."

"What about '*bugalla*'? Is that a real word?"

"I don't know," said Eliana. "I never heard it before."

Nora swung her laptop around and found an online translation engine. She typed *bugalla*, set the boxes for Spanish to English, and pressed Translate.

The answer came in a flash: oak gall. Was it possible Joseph had come across these odd little things in Chile?

"*Amargura*," Joseph murmured. He was looking now at Eliana. "*Mi dolor. La cara de mi dolor.*"

Nora observed them both. "I can see that you understand. He is speaking Spanish, right? Is it something about a friend?"

The girl shook her head. "No, no—he says *amargura*, em . . . 'bitterness,' and . . ." She hesitated.

"What is it, Eliana?" Nora asked. "What else did he say?"

"He said, 'My sorrow. The face of my sorrow.'"

"What does that mean? Is it some sort of expression?"

"I don't know." The girl seemed bewildered and suddenly close to tears.

"Will you excuse us for just one second?" Nora asked Joseph. She took Eliana aside. "I'm so sorry about all this. We ought to have warned you. The stroke seems to have made Joseph's emotions a bit more volatile. I know he's not saying or doing things on purpose to upset you. I'm not sure where all these cryptic phrases are coming from, and I'm not sure he knows either. If you're finding it too much, we can try to contact the agency and see if they can send someone else."

"No! I'm not upset. Please, don't send me away."

"No one wants to send you away, Eliana. I know you're trying your best. But if he upsets you, if you're not comfortable, we can ask for someone with more experience—"

"Please don't get someone else. I will try harder. Please!"

Nora looked into the girl's dark eyes, and something clicked. There was one advantage Eliana had over someone with more rehab experience, and it had just been demonstrated before her eyes. "You know, I'm not sure whether Cormac mentioned that his father lived in Chile for many years. He's only recently come back to Ireland. It's possible that English feels strange to him, especially after the stroke. It's hard to know. But if you can understand him, I don't know, maybe you could try doing the flash cards in Spanish."

Eliana's face brightened immediately. "I could do that, yes, let me try!" She went off in search of the cards, and Nora returned to Joseph and her laptop in the kitchen. She typed "oak gall" into the search box. The first entry that appeared was from a very old medical text:

Galls or gallnuts are a kind of preternatural and accidental tumour, produced by the Punctures of Insects on the Oaks of several Species; but those of the oak only are used in medicine. We have two kinds, the Oriental and the European galls: the Oriental are brought from Aleppo, of the bigness of a large nutmeg, with tubercles on their surface, of a very firm and solid texture, and a disagreeable, acerb, and astringent taste. The European galls are of the same size, with perfectly smooth surfaces: they are light, often spongy, and cavernous within, and always of a lax texture. They have a less austere taste, and are of much less value than the first sort, both in manufactures and medicine. The general history of galls is this: an insect of the fly kind, for the safety of her young, wounds the branches of the trees, and in the hole deposits her egg: the lacerated vessels of the tree discharging their contents form a tumour or woody case about the hole, where the egg is thus defended from all injuries. This tumor also serves for the food of the tender maggot, produced from the egg of the fly, which, as soon as it is perfect, and in its winged state, gnaws its way out, as appears from the hole found in the gall; and where no hole is seen on its surface, the maggot, or its remains, are sure to be found within, on breaking it. [See also: *Serpent's Egg*.]

Nora stared at the last two words, her memory flashing back to Benedict Kavanagh's distorted face and bulging eyes. The name—serpent's egg—offered yet another meaning, altogether unforeseen. Filled with bitterness, the gallnuts were the imagined spawn of serpents. How many of these were forced into Benedict Kavanagh's mouth—a half dozen? All at once she could taste the bitterness, the rancor, and the resentment contained in each one.

She thought of Kavanagh destroying a youthful Niall Dawson in that debate so many years ago, saw again in slow motion the scene from this morning: Kavanagh's wife pulling the sheet from her husband's body, such a primal, visceral reaction. Nora shook her head, trying to erase the memory of the expression on Kavanagh's face, the bulging eyes and distended cheeks. She looked down at the gall in her hand once more, a chilling message from a vengeful killer.

11

There were a few more signs of life when Stella returned to Killowen in the late afternoon. With their morning chores out of the way, the farm's residents were now pursuing their own work. Stella heard the *tap-tap-tap* of a chisel on stone as she rounded the corner of a small shed across the yard from the main house. Inside, wearing a leather apron and holding a hammer and chisel, was a fortyish man, his jaw elongated by a dark beard, his large blue eyes framed by shaggy brows and a floppy fringe of hair. His hands moved deftly as he chased a groove along a round stone into which he was carving a spiral design. One knuckle bled a bit where he had scraped it.

Stella waited until he'd finished before she spoke. "Excuse me, I wonder if I could have a word?"

He turned, unstartled by her presence, and began to lay down his tools as soon as she produced her Guards ID. "I expected you'd turn up sooner or later," he said. "Saw the cars out on the bog yesterday."

"Just routine questions," Stella admitted. "I'm talking to everyone at Killowen, Mr.—"

"Lynch," he said. "Diarmuid Lynch. What can I tell you?"

"Well, we've received confirmation that the second body in the boot was this man, Benedict Kavanagh." Stella held up the photo of Kavanagh. "He and the car went missing about four months ago. So, for a start, did you know him?"

"No," came the terse reply. Lynch barely glanced at the picture and instead picked up a rag from the bench beside him and began to wipe the stone dust from his tools, moving slowly and deliberately, replacing each in turn.

"How long have you been here, at Killowen?"

"Eighteen months."

"And before that?"

"Knocked about. I was living in Spain for a while."

"Working?"

"At a vineyard for a time, then another farm. 'General labor,' I think they call it."

"How did you come to this place?"

"When I came back after being in Spain, I didn't really have a home to go to. My parents were dead, the farm sold. I'd no other family. So I did whatever work I could find. Spent a good bit of time sleeping rough. Just my good fortune to fall ill so near to this place. I have Martin Gwynne to thank, for finding me out on the bog. I was in pretty bad shape—pneumonia, they said. Martin brought me here, and they managed to nurse me back to health. I decided to stay on after that."

"We're trying to find out what Mairéad Broome's husband, Benedict Kavanagh, might have been doing in this area at the time he was killed. Any thoughts?"

"I really couldn't say. I never met the fella."

"Can you tell me what sort of work you do here at the farm?"

"The same as everyone else: tilling, planting, cultivating, harvesting, the odd bit of construction—and my own work here, of course." He gestured to the stone before him.

"You don't happen to have experience operating heavy machinery?"

"We have a small loader that we use for moving stones like these and for building projects. I drive it sometimes, as do Martin and Claire and Anthony and Shawn. Never operated an excavator, if that's what you wanted to know." He calmly continued wiping his tools with a rag, checking their edges, replacing them on the bench.

"Do you remember anything unusual happening last April, anything at all out of the ordinary?"

"Well, we got the new heat in last April—had lashings of hot water for the first time. That was unusual. And that's when Shawn Kearney—the archaeologist—came to stay with us, attending the excavation on the heating coils. She turned up a few interesting bits, as I recall. I really don't remember much beyond that. Everything else was pretty normal."

He finished with the tools and turned his gaze upon Stella once more. For some reason, she had a sudden urge to put his name through the system.

12

Martin Gwynne looked up at Stella Cusack as he worked the flaws in a sheet of parchment with a short, sharp knife, scraping away rough patches. "Ask away," he said. "I hope you don't mind if I keep working; this commission is due in a few days, and I've still a lot of work to do." He set aside the knife and reached for a sheet of fine sandpaper, scouring in a circular motion.

Stella studied his hands at work, the fingers long and sensitive, the fingertips floating over the vellum's pale surface. Gwynne saw her glance at the text he was working from, a formal commemoration of a wedding, no doubt suitable for framing. As if he'd been reading her thoughts, he said, "Yes, decidedly less elevated than transcribing the word of God, but the written word has lost some of its mystique in the modern world, I'm afraid. This is what pays the bills nowadays."

"I'm here about a second body found in the boot of that car out on the bog."

Gwynne didn't look up, but the sheet of sandpaper in his hand stopped dead at the center of the vellum. After the briefest pause, it continued, making circles within circles.

Stella continued, "I'm trying to reconstruct the victim's last known whereabouts, to find out what could have brought him to this part of the country."

"And you think I might know what he was doing here?"

"You shared an interest in manuscripts, from what I understand. His name was Benedict Kavanagh. That name ring a bell?"

Martin Gwynne put down the sandpaper and ran his fingers across the calfskin again, like a blind man, feeling rather than looking, paying close attention to the sensations that passed through his fingertips. "I knew Kavanagh. We met once, long ago, at some conference or other. As you said, he studied old manuscripts, and he was sometimes known to consult with persons such as myself about some of the finer nuances of ink making or handwriting."

A very carefully couched reply, Stella noted. "And did he happen to consult with a person such as yourself last April?"

"No, he didn't. Now, as to whether he was on his way to see me, I couldn't say. But we had no arrangement or appointment. He never came here to consult with me."

Again, the way it was phrased, Kavanagh could have come to Killowen for some other reason than to consult Martin Gwynne. Was he being deliberately evasive?

"Had anyone mentioned him being in the area?"

"Not that I recall." He began riffling through a jam jar full of white goose feathers, examining each shaft minutely before selecting the stoutest and cutting through it with his small, sharp knife, so that it was about ten inches in length, with a V-shape at the top. He got a firm grasp on one end of the V, and in a single swift motion stripped the lower barbs from the shaft. He repeated the motion on the other side, again leaving a few inches at the top of the quill.

"What do you recall about last April?"

Gwynne stopped to consider. "That's the time for sowing leeks and onions. And Anthony—our neighbor, Anthony Beglan—was working on a new batch of calfskins for me. It might help if I just consult my diary." He set down the half-made quill and crossed to the desk beside her. "I keep a note of deadlines and other important dates in here." Quickly flipping back a few months, he found April and began looking down the entries. The small book was filled with a calligrapher's careful hand, a rainbow of different-colored inks. He saw her taking in his handiwork. "If something is important enough to write down, it's important enough to write properly. It's a mark of respect for the person who will read what you've written." Gwynne replied absently, repeating words he must have said a thousand times. "What sort of time frame are we talking about?"

"We only have a few details. Mr. Kavanagh taped his last television program on April twenty-first. We believe he might have come here shortly after."

Martin Gwynne perused the entries in his book. "Well, we had the workmen in for the new heat, from April twentieth through the end of the month. No visiting artists during that time, with all the upheaval from the construction." He paused to consult the diary once more. "What else? Ah, yes. I always prefer to work in daylight, but I had a commission due at the end of the month, quite a large piece, so I was working late. Burning a lot of midnight oil, as they say."

"Are you the only person with a prior connection to Kavanagh?"

"I met him once, years ago, as I said. I'd hardly call that a connection."

"To your knowledge, had any of the others here ever met Mr. Kavanagh?"

"Well, my wife would have met him at the same time I did, but I doubt she would remember. It's twenty years ago."

"And where was this?"

"At an academic conference in Toronto—a meeting of the Eriugena Society. A little-known group, medievalists and philosophers and paleographers. I believe Kavanagh was presenting a paper—I'm afraid I don't remember the subject."

"What was the name of the group?"

"The Eriugena Society."

"Could you spell that for me?" She handed him her notebook.

"Medievalists, philosophers, and—sorry—what was the last group you mentioned?"

"Paleographers. Specialists in the study of ancient handwriting."

"And what were you doing at the conference?"

"A colleague and I had just finished work on a late-ninth-century text, and the conference organizers thought it might be useful to have me give a talk about the process. I warned them that I wasn't much at public speaking. How is all this relevant? I've really no idea what Kavanagh was doing here."

"It's possible that his visit to the area had something to do with his wife. I believe she's stayed here a few times."

Gwynne looked confused.

"Her name isn't Kavanagh—it's Broome. Mairéad Broome."

A light dawned in his eyes. "Yes, of course, Mairéad. She's often stayed with us."

"And you'd no idea she was married to Benedict Kavanagh?"

"She never mentioned it. I suppose I thought—" He broke off suddenly, as if aware that he ought to be a bit more circumspect.

"What?" Stella asked. "That she was attached to her assistant, perhaps? Maybe I ought to mention that she's here at Killowen now. She came down to identify her husband's body. I believe she and Graham Healy will be staying on here for a few days."

Gwynne looked slightly distracted. "Yes, better to be away from Dublin. The newspapers and the television can be merciless."

Spoken like someone with firsthand experience, Stella thought. He looked up, and she understood that he would say no more today. "Thank you for your time, Mr. Gwynne. I wonder if you could point me to"— she consulted the handwritten list Claire Finnerty had made for her— "Lucien Picard."

He stepped to the door and directed her across the far corner of the yard to a single-story whitewashed shed. "Ah, the French contingent. He'll be in the cheese storehouse, and Sylvie with him. Never apart, those two."

The rank scent of mold greeted Stella's nostrils when she stepped through the door of the storehouse. "Lucien Picard?" A wiry, energetic-looking man in his midthirties looked up from his work as she entered. He was slicing through a thick wheel of cheese with an implement that looked like a knife with handles on both ends.

"*C'est moi,*" he said. "Sorry—that's me. Try some of this? Six months aged." He cut a thin wedge and popped it into her mouth before she could protest. "Very good, eh? To me, it is the best ever!"

Stella tasted the cheese on her tongue; it was perfectly tart and crumbly. She struggled to swallow. "Yes, very good, but I'm not here to . . . I have to ask you about Benedict Kavanagh." She held up her identification. "The dead man found in the bog?"

His look of triumph vanished, replaced by seriousness. "Ah, yes, we heard about this. Do you need Sylvie as well? Sylvie!" A slightly younger woman emerged from the next room. Her short platinum hair was swathed in a turban-like pink headband, and beneath it strong features—large hazel eyes, a long, refined-looking nose, and generous lips—made a striking impression. Sylvie wore a blue peasant blouse and jeans, topped with a starched white chef's apron. Resting on her shoulder was a four-foot plank that held two dozen or more petite creamy white cheeses.

"We have the police here, Sylvie, about the man in the bog—"

"Benedict Kavanagh," Stella added.

"Yes, what about him? Is it true what they're saying, that he was murdered?" Sylvie set her plank down on the counter and began loading her cheeses into a box. She avoided eye contact, concentrating instead on her task, her hands moving quickly, efficiently. Sylvie was careful to grasp each round of the soft cheese very gently so as not to damage it.

"Did either of you happen to know Kavanagh?" Stella asked. "Here's a photograph, in case you might recognize him."

Her cargo safely stowed at last, Sylvie looked up at the picture. "No. I've never seen this man. I'm sorry."

"We think he disappeared sometime in late April, so I'm asking everyone at Killowen what they recall from that time. Anything out of the ordinary."

Lucien and Sylvie regarded each other briefly, and Stella got the impression that they had already conferred about what they were going to say. Difficult to tell if she was reading the signals right; it was always slightly disconcerting when interview subjects spoke a language with its own nonverbal nuances.

"Out of the ordinary?" Picard made a wry face. "Difficult to say, because you see, there is no 'ordinary' here. Every day is different. That last part of April, we were making the chèvre, Sylvie, do you remember? The soft goat cheese, also *crottin* and *pyramide*." He held up his hands to describe the shapes.

"We also had many, eh . . . *Lucien, qu'est-ce que 'chevrette' en Anglais?*"

"'She-goat,' *je crois.*"

"Many of our she-goats, they were having kids at the time. So much to do."

"We didn't sleep a lot," Lucien added.

"Did you have any guests or artists in residence at that time?"

Lucien squinted, trying to recall. "A few, I suppose. I can't remember. Claire would have their names, if you need them."

"Do you happen to know the name Mairéad Broome?"

"Yes, the painter. She has been here a few times."

"And was she one of the artists who were staying here at the end of April?"

"You know, she might have been. As I said, Claire would know for certain."

"And you know that she was married to Benedict Kavanagh?"

"I didn't know. Sylvie, did you know this?"

She shook her head. "No."

Once again, Stella got the distinct impression that a certain amount of forethought had gone into the answers these two were providing. Why should anyone lie about knowing the identity of Mairéad Broome's husband? The reactions of the people here to Benedict Kavanagh's death were strange. Each knew less than the one before, as if they were in some sort of competition for who could display the blankest expression, who could know the least about the dead man. She still had three more people to interview: Tessa Gwynne, Shawn Kearney, and Anthony Beglan.

"Thank you. If you do think of anything else, please give me a ring?" She handed each of them a card, wishing she could double back and listen to the conversation that would be in progress a few minutes after she'd left. Of course it would help if she had a bloody word of French.

As she crossed the haggard, there was a clatter of stones that sounded like a wrecking ball had gone through the side of the house. Stella rounded the corner of the barn to find Diarmuid Lynch's heavy loader driven by a lanky middle-aged man in a brown peaked cap. Beside the pile of stones the driver had just deposited on a patch of meadow stood a woman with short dark hair and vivid blue eyes. Stella glanced at her list. "Shawn Kearney?" she asked.

The woman raised her hand in reply, then removed her dusty leather gloves as her colleague parked the loader and shut off the engine. "Yes, I'm Shawn."

The accent was American, Stella noted, as she held up her ID. "Detective Cusack. I'm here about the body found in the bog yesterday. You're the nearest neighbors, so I'm talking to everyone at Killowen. Does the name Benedict Kavanagh mean anything to either of you?"

Shawn Kearney shrugged. "No, I don't remember hearing that name. Do you, Anthony?"

"Cuh-cuh-can't suh-say that I do," he said. His right arm shot out forcefully, as if he was going to land a punch, but he struck at the air. Stella drew back involuntarily.

"It's all right, Detective," Kearney said. "It's just a reflex." As if to demonstrate, Beglan's hand shot out twice more, uselessly punching the air before him, and he let out a series of high-pitched squeaks. Shawn Kearney stood by as if this conversation were the most normal thing in the world. Stella had to concentrate on her questions and tried to keep eye contact with both of them. "We're looking at the last two weeks of

April, asking everyone if they remember anything unusual from that time."

"I was the on-site archaeologist as the new geothermal system was going in," Kearney said.

"So you'd only just arrived?"

"That's right. Never set foot on the place before the middle of last April. And now I can't leave." She raised her arms, as if astonished to find herself standing in a meadow next to a heap of stones. "Life is full of surprises."

"You had no previous connection to Killowen before coming to work on the project?"

"No. I was at one of the big contract archaeology firms in Dublin."

"You're American," Stella noted.

"Yes, I got my Irish citizenship after grad school—my gran was from Sligo. Ireland was a great place to find archaeology work—until the economy went to hell. I was lucky to be working when the job here came up, and when it finished, they let me go. With so much development on hold, there aren't as many jobs. But I made out all right. I love it here."

"What sorts of artifacts turn up in an excavation at a place like this?" Stella asked.

"There's not much left aboveground in these early Christian settlements. We did find a stylus, a medieval writing tool. That's how we met Niall Dawson—he came down to collect it."

"When was Mr. Dawson here?"

"I put in the call to the National Museum right away, as soon as the stylus turned up. He was here the next day, the twenty-second of April. I showed him around a bit, but nothing else turned up, so he went back to Dublin."

"What about you, Mr. Beglan?" Stella asked. "What do you recall from April?"

He opened his mouth to speak but instead began to yip like a small dog—once, twice, three times—and then said, "Nothing . . . strange." His chin jutted forward and his jaws snapped shut, as if he were trying to recapture the words he'd just spoken into the air.

"Is the name Mairéad Broome familiar to either of you?"

"No, not really," Kearney said. "But I'm fairly new here."

"Picka-picka-painter," Anthony Beglan sputtered. "Often cuh-cuh-comes here."

"That's right," Stella said. "Benedict Kavanagh was her husband."

Shawn Kearney's eyes widened. "You think there's some connection? That's horrible."

Stella eyed the loader Beglan had been driving. "Do you use a lot of heavy equipment around here?"

"Just that loader for stones, and the tractor," Shawn Kearney replied. "Nothing heavier than that."

"Never have need of a JCB?"

"No. Claire would usually hire out those sorts of jobs. Like when they brought in the digger for the new heating system."

"Let me ask you, did anyone at Killowen have access to those diggers after hours, when the workmen had knocked off for the night?"

"Not that I recall," Kearney said. "Besides, you'd have to know how to drive one—"

"I've operated a juh-juh-JCB," Anthony Beglan said. "Not them ones, though. Huh-had their own, that crowd."

"Where exactly were the new heating coils installed?"

"Just down this hill, Detective. Do you see that post in the ground, with the red flag attached? That's where the coils went in."

Stella turned back to the main house, trying to imagine the decibel level of a JCB and the distance from the house. "Did you ever see or hear anyone else using the machinery?"

"No," said Shawn Kearney. Beglan shook his head.

"Well, thanks for your time." She turned to leave, then pivoted on her heel. "I meant to ask, what are you doing with that load of stones?"

"Building a labyrinth," Shawn Kearney replied. "A meditation path."

The last person on Stella's list, Tessa Gwynne, wasn't difficult to track down. She was in the cottage that she shared with her husband, at the end of a path that wound through Killowen's oak wood. The cottage was either authentically old or built to look that way, with small windows, rough whitewashed walls, and a rosebush, a vigorous climber that arched over the doorway.

All at once, a most exquisite ringing swelled from inside the house. Stella peered in through the open window and saw Tessa Gwynne on a low stool behind the door, playing a harp that looked as if it were strung with gold. Was that even possible, or was it just a trick of the light? Tessa Gwynne's eyes were closed, and her whole body moved to the music, the harp in her intimate embrace. Stella stood, rooted, feeling her chest tighten as the melody grew in urgency. As the music grew from a thrum of low notes to a thrilling race up the scale, she leaned into the wall, overtaken by a wild grief that welled up from nowhere and kept spilling until there was no more, until the miraculous notes finally settled into plaintive dignity, the feeling receding and fading with the notes like lapping waves.

Stella felt exhausted. She tried to collect herself, remembering what she'd come for. She rapped on the door and found herself looking into a pair of dark, heavy-lidded eyes that regarded her over a pair of half-moon reading glasses. The woman's collarbone stood out like a yoke beneath her flesh. "Mrs. Gwynne? Detective Stella Cusack. I'm investigating the murder of the man whose body was found in the bog yesterday."

Tessa Gwynne seemed to shrink slightly. "Ah, yes, a terrible business." She didn't step away, and Stella had to drag her gaze from the hand that gripped the door—thick nails, uncannily powerful fingers. Strange how playing heaven's instrument could give one a hellish harpy's claws. "You've found out who he is, then? We hadn't heard."

"Benedict Kavanagh." Mrs. Gwynne's long white hair was done up in a coil at the back of her head, and the claw fluttered at the wisps of hair at the base of her neck. "So the name is familiar to you?"

"Yes, my husband and I met him once. It's many years ago now. Although there is a more recent connection. His wife is a painter—she sometimes stays with us."

"So you knew that Mairéad Broome was married to Benedict Kavanagh? How is it your husband wasn't aware of that fact?"

Tessa Gwynne gave a tiny, exasperated smile. "Because my husband is—like most men—off in his own world, never quite paying attention to all that's going on around him." Her voice was mild, the accent English and decidedly upper-crust, but she looked slightly frazzled, and a touch too thin. The word "careworn" popped into Stella's head—probably the word her mother would have used.

"So only you and Claire Finnerty knew that Mr. Kavanagh was related to one of your guests?"

"I can't think how anyone else would have known, except from talking to Mairéad. Benedict Kavanagh was something of a celebrity because of his television program, but it's unlikely that anyone else would have known who he was."

"Why's that?"

"Because we haven't got a television at Killowen. Never have. This is a meant to be a place for contemplation, a retreat."

"Then how did you happen to know about Mr. Kavanagh's program, if you don't mind me asking?"

"Mairéad is my friend. She shared a few things with me about Benedict and his work."

"Did you ever discuss the state of her marriage?"

Tessa Gwynne turned an even gaze upon her. "Are you married yourself, Detective?" Stella felt her face flush. "And do you speak to many people about the state of your marriage? I wonder. I'm sorry, I don't mean to be rude. Only I wonder how much we can ever really know about other people's lives."

"But perhaps you were able to form some impression?"

"My impression was that Mairéad loved her husband."

Stella paused for a moment. "She told me that she and Graham Healy were lovers and have been ever since he came to work for her."

Tessa Gwynne's spine straightened, and her voice betrayed a glint of ice. "Well, since Mairéad has been so forthcoming, I'm afraid my impressions can be of no use to you."

"Thank you for your time, Mrs. Gwynne," Stella said. "I won't trouble you any further today." She took her leave and returned to the path up to the main house, thinking about Tessa Gwynne's spellbinding music—and about what sort of friend tries to protect someone who doesn't want her protection.

13

It was a few minutes past five when Nora spotted Stella Cusack coming up the path from the oak wood at Killowen. She hurried out to the drive, glancing around and feeling just a tiny bit paranoid about being seen talking to the police.

Cusack stood beside her car. "Dr. Gavin."

"Detective, do you remember those marble-like things we found in Benedict Kavanagh's throat?" Nora handed over the two galls she'd collected this afternoon. "I did a bit of research, thought you might like to know what I found. They're oak galls, gallnuts. And they have another name as well. In folk medicine and magic they're called serpent's eggs."

Stella Cusack's brow furrowed. "Where did you get these?"

"Martin Gwynne's studio. He uses them to make iron gall ink," Nora said. "That's where this one came from." She pointed to the slightly more dried-up of the pair. "But I also found some in the wood just beyond the cottages. That's where Mr. Gwynne gets his supply. Apparently Anthony Beglan collects them."

"I see. May I keep these?" Cusack glanced up at her. "Is something else bothering you, Dr. Gavin?"

"It's just . . . I happened to overhear a bit of conversation this afternoon. I'm sure there's a perfectly innocent explanation—"

"If you wouldn't mind, Dr. Gavin, just tell me what it was that you heard and let me worry about explanations."

"It was about two o'clock. I was upstairs changing, when I saw Mairéad Broome's young man—"

"Graham Healy," Cusack said.

"Yes, the fella at the mortuary with her this morning. I heard him take a call from Vincent Claffey."

"How did you know it was Claffey?"

"Because the man himself pulled up on a motorbike a few seconds later, and they were still talking on their mobiles. They must not have realized that I was at the window. Graham Healy didn't want Claffey here, that much was clear, didn't want anyone seeing them together. They had evidently made some prior arrangement about how and when they were going to meet, and Claffey was upsetting the plan. They were arguing about it."

"What else did you hear?"

"Well, it looked to be some sort of payoff. Healy handed over a fairly thick envelope, and he said to Claffey, 'You've got what you want now—and you know what we want.'"

"And what was Claffey's response?"

"He said he knew, but it was a lot to ask of any man, that he needed more time to think about it. He said he'd be in touch."

"And then what happened?"

"Claffey got back on his motorbike and rode off."

"Was there any indication that Mairéad Broome knew about this meeting?"

"Well, actually, I happened to hear her discussing it with Healy a few minutes later." No need to mention the fact that she'd been up in a tree when that conversation took place. "Graham Healy said he had no choice but to hand over the money, since your man had the nerve to come to the farm in broad daylight. He seemed afraid of what Claffey might say unless they did something. Mairéad Broome seemed a bit more resigned—she said she knew Claffey was using them. But she didn't want Graham to do anything; she told him just to let things be. Then they were out of earshot, and I couldn't hear any more."

Cusack thanked Nora, told her she had done the right thing in reporting what she had heard. Still, Nora felt a bit grubby. What if it was nothing? And what if the people she'd just blithely implicated were innocent of any crime?

As she entered the kitchen, a low murmur of conversation came from the corner where Claire Finnerty stood with the Gwynnes and another couple she hadn't met.

"—but do we know how long she's staying?" Martin Gwynne asked.

"I'm not sure," Claire said. "She's evidently helping the police with their inquiries—"

Spotting Nora, the group quickly broke apart. Claire returned to sawing through a crusty loaf and Tessa Gwynne began tossing a bowl of fresh greens. The new couple tended to something in the oven as Martin Gwynne began pouring the wine. Just another Friday evening at Killowen, evidently. One could hardly blame this crowd for their slightly somber mood, considering that a pair of murders had just turned up a quarter mile from their doorstep.

Claire Finnerty looked up. "Glad you could join us this evening, Dr. Gavin. Where are your compatriots?"

"Just back from the bog," Nora said. "Getting cleaned up. They said not to wait." In fact, Niall and Cormac were just returned from the hospital, after depositing the ancient leather satchel they'd discovered at the crime scene this afternoon—a detail they'd asked her not to share in company just yet. She turned to find the archaeologist, Shawn Kearney, coming through to the kitchen behind her, accompanied by a bushy-bearded man in his forties.

Claire Finnerty said, "I don't think you know everyone." She presented Nora to the new people, Lucien and Sylvie Picard, Diarmuid Lynch, and Shawn Kearney, who laughed and said, "That's all right, Claire. Dr. Gavin and I have already met."

"As have we," Martin Gwynne said, with a gesture to include his wife as well. "In the studio this afternoon."

Claire waved at the far end of the table. "And this is our neighbor, Deirdre Claffey." Nora recognized the girl from the chipper van yesterday, now clapping the pudgy hands of the child she held on her lap.

The long table was laid out with hand-thrown stoneware, woven linen place mats and napkins, and candles, along with a heavenly smelling pan of something under bubbling red sauce. There was an impressive-looking cheese plate and three unlabeled bottles of red wine. Through the glimpses she'd gained these last couple of days, Nora was beginning to form an impression of life here at Killowen. It seemed both profoundly simple and elegantly sufficient—growing the bulk of your own food, using the rest of your time for creative pursuits. Here it seemed possible to imagine a proper sort of balance. Compared to this, the rat race of life in the city suddenly seemed seriously out of whack.

Anthony Beglan slipped in the garden door and removed his cap, the whiteness of his high forehead contrasting with the weathered cheeks. Difficult to tell his age—he looked to Nora like some of her grandfather's mates, men who had worked farms in Clare for fifty years or more, never married, and had no one to whom they could bequeath the fruit of their labors. Was Anthony Beglan also the end of a line? He sidled into the room and stood next to Deirdre Claffey and her baby.

Claire looked around the room, gathering everyone in with her eyes. "Just so you're all aware, we have another couple of visitors as of today. Mairéad Broome is in her usual cottage. It's a dreadful time for her. I know you'll all respect her privacy."

"So it was her husband in the boot of that car?" Shawn Kearney sat at the table and popped a mushroom from the salad into her mouth. "That detective was asking everyone—"

"I think that's a subject we'd better leave right there for the moment, Shawn," Claire said, casting her eyes discreetly in the direction of Deirdre Claffey, who stopped playing and sat with her arms wrapped around the baby, much to his displeasure. He tried to squirm away, but Anthony Beglan began to mug and dance, lifting the cap in front of his face in a game of peekaboo. Nora wondered whether Deirdre Claffey was a regular guest here—or perhaps tonight was unusual?

Claire took a seat at one end of the long table and motioned Nora to take the opposite place. Martin Gwynne took the seat beside Nora. "I hope you like aubergines," he said. "I must admit I never did, until Lucien and Sylvie applied a few secret herbs and tomato sauce. Try this." He held a steaming forkful to Nora's lips. She took the offering and tasted an explosion of flavor. Gwynne looked on expectantly. "What do you think?"

His wife said softly, "For heaven's sake, love, let the poor girl enjoy her meal in peace."

Nora had to admit that she had never been convinced about eggplant—until that moment. "Mmm," she managed, groping for the appropriate word.

"Fantastic," said Gwynne. "Isn't it?"

"Ah, non, non," said Lucien, waving off the compliment. "Pas du tout."

Joseph and Eliana came through from the sitting room, and Joseph took the other chair beside Nora. "What's a dingo?" He pointed at her plate. "Your eeking."

"Eggplant," Nora said. "It's eggplant parmigiana."

"Upland," Joseph repeated. "Ugglamp—good."

The food made its rounds of the table, and when Cormac and Niall Dawson finally arrived and took their places, the only sounds in the room were the clinks of serving spoons and the low murmur of voices.

"Shawn, you mentioned last night that you're an archaeologist," Nora said. "Are you doing excavation work here?"

"Not at the moment. But that's the reason I came here last April. With the new heating system going in, my company got the contract for the archaeological survey, to see if anything might turn up in the excavation."

"And what did you find?" Nora looked up to see a worried look on Niall Dawson's face.

"Well, plenty of pits and postholes that fit with what we already knew about the site," Shawn said. "From the name, Cill Eóghain, Owen's Church, you know it's a monastic settlement, and there's even a brief mention in the *Annals of the Four Masters*. The postholes we found showed pretty typical early Christian wooden structures—although there is a beautiful tenth-century stone chapel over beside the orchard—"

Niall Dawson jumped in. "You know how surveys go, Nora—a lot of digging and not much to show for it."

Shawn Kearney looked curiously at Dawson and continued. "We did find one really spectacular piece—a metal stylus, the sort used on wax tablets. And that's how we met Niall—when he came down to take the stylus back to the museum."

Nora felt the pull of several threads at once. "You'll have to pardon my ignorance. What's a wax tablet?"

"Notepad of the ancient world," Shawn Kearney said. "Until the advent of cheap paper, they were the best—well, really, the *only*—temporary writing surface. Suppose you wanted to scribble something down—a poem, a shopping list, whatever. You'd take a flat wooden board and carve out a shallow reservoir, and into that you'd pour melted wax. Once it cooled, you could scratch down your thoughts in the wax. And when you didn't need whatever you'd written any longer, you could just rub it out and start again. People used them right up to the nineteenth century in some places."

Cormac added, "The fragments of writing that have turned up on tablets are amazing—Greek, Latin, Old Irish—sometimes they've even found the writer's fingerprints in the wax."

"And the stylus was the writing instrument?" Nora asked.

"That's right," Shawn said. "Most would have been made from wood, but there were metal versions, too, some quite elaborately wrought."

Cormac asked, "Where did you find it, exactly?"

Shawn pointed out through the French doors. "Just down below the garden outside. We left a stake at the findspot."

"This part of the country would have been fairly rotten with monasteries at that time," Cormac said. "You've got Birr only a short distance from here, and Clonmacnoise and Sier Kieran. How did Killowen compare, do you think?"

Shawn Kearney shrugged. "Well, it wasn't quite as important as any of those places, obviously, but there was an interesting mention in O'Donovan's notes for this area." She turned to Nora. "You know about John O'Donovan, the famous nineteenth-century antiquarian?"

Nora nodded, and Shawn continued. "Well, he made a note about a curious figure carved into the doorway of Killowen Chapel—"

Glancing at Niall Dawson, Nora thought she detected a shadow passing over his face.

"Yes," he said. "That was a fascinating twist."

Shawn Kearney continued, gesturing with a chunk of eggplant on the end of her fork. "—And he was able to tie it to the mention of a monastic settlement called Cill Eóghain in the *Annals of the Four Masters*. Usually with those sorts of carvings, you might see the monastery's founding saint, or a bishop with his miter and crozier, but this one was different. I'll take you over to see it tomorrow, if you like."

"Yes, I would like," Cormac replied. "Especially as Niall has neglected to tell me a single word about any of this. Did O'Donovan happen to mention any manuscripts associated with this place?"

Shawn Kearney turned to Gwynne. "Martin can probably answer that better than I can. He's our resident manuscript expert."

Gwynne cleared his throat before speaking. "Well, any early medieval scriptorium worth its salt would have been turning out Gospels and Psalters and sermons—"

Shawn Kearney interrupted, "But I believe the monks at Killowen may have been copying and translating works by Greek and Roman writers."

"And what makes you think that?" Cormac asked.

Shawn Kearney offered a mysterious smile. "That's what I'm going to show you tomorrow. I'd hate to ruin the surprise."

The baby began to squawk at the end of the table, until Tessa Gwynne said, "Give him to me, Deirdre. I'll mind him while you finish your dinner." The girl handed over the child, who seemed glad to have a new playmate. Tessa began making faces and poking the baby's belly to make him laugh. Nora glanced at Martin Gwynne and caught him observing his wife with what she could only describe as a mixture of compassion and consternation. What was their story?

"I enjoyed seeing your work today," Nora said to Martin Gwynne. "Plenty to pass on to your apprentice. Tell me her name again—was it Áine? No, Anca."

Gwynne suddenly looked acutely uncomfortable, and Claire Finnerty said, "Oh, yes, she was from Romania. We've had loads of international volunteers—WWOOFers, they're called—after the group that matches us up, World Wide Opportunities in Organic Farming. Most stay only a few weeks, but Anca was with us a long time—nearly nine months, I think. We were sorry to see her go. She left over a month ago now, wasn't it, Diarmuid?"

"That's right," came the reply. Lynch's shaggy head lifted as he turned his gaze toward Dawson. "Six weeks ago."

Without warning, the kitchen door slammed open with a loud bang, frightening everyone, but especially the baby, who began to wail. Vincent Claffey stood in the doorway, fists at the ready and practically breathing fire. "What have I told you?" he shouted at Deirdre. "I told you to stay away from this place. Have nothing to do with those fuckin' hippies, I said. So what are you doing over here again?"

He moved to Deirdre and seized her by the arm, but Claire Finnerty jumped up to intervene. "Leave her alone."

Claffey looked daggers at Claire. "Shut your trap. You're the cause of all this. She's my daughter, and I'll do with her what I fuckin' like." He pushed Claire out of the way. She fell against Diarmuid, who'd risen from the table as well. The baby's cry turned into a terrified shriek, but Tessa Gwynne held on tight.

"Come on," Claffey said. "We're going. You, missus, give her the child," he said to Tessa, shoving his daughter sideways.

Deirdre nearly stumbled as she went to collect the baby. "I'm all right," she murmured to Tessa as she reached for the child and settled him on her hip.

"Will yeh shut up!" Claffey shouted, making the girl flinch. "This crowd don't give a flying fuck about you, my girl."

"And you do?" Claire Finnerty's eyes blazed.

Claffey turned to her and smiled. "Don't you go gettin' any ideas, because I know your secrets, the lot of yez. Think you're safe out here, far from prying eyes? But I know, I *know*." He tapped his temple and leveled a warning gaze at each one of them, as each, in turn, looked away. In the eerie silence, he took hold of Deirdre's free elbow and walked her straight out the door, not pausing to shut it after them.

Claire Finnerty was the first to speak. "Bastard!" She straightened up and separated herself from Diarmuid, trying to regain a little dignity, but her hands were shaking. "We've got to get Deirdre away from him."

"Yes, but how?" Martin Gwynne's voice betrayed a helpless frustration. Clearly this was not their first confrontation with Claffey. "If no one's actually witnessed an instance of abusive behavior, and Deirdre refuses to talk about it . . ."

"I'm sorry, but wouldn't you call what just happened here 'abusive behavior'?"

A loud sob escaped from Tessa Gwynne. Her husband pushed his chair back and circled around to her. "Don't fret now, love, we'll find some way to help the child." But Tessa would not be consoled. Martin Gwynne helped his wife to her feet and led her out the open door.

"Poor Tessa," Shawn Kearney whispered. "She and Martin had a daughter who died, so it tears her apart to see Deirdre treated like that. She just can't take it."

Nora looked across the table, directing Cormac's attention to his father. Joseph had Eliana by the hand and was squeezing hard. His grip was strong, as Nora knew from experience, and the poor girl looked stricken. Cormac reached out and placed his hand over his father's. "Will you let go, please? You're hurting her." Joseph looked down at his own hand as if it belonged to someone else and slowly loosened his grip, his eyes imploring Eliana's forgiveness.

Up and down the table, everyone stared glumly at their plates, poking at the formerly delicious-looking parmigiana with their forks.

"I'm sorry you had to see that," Claire Finnerty said to Nora. "As you've probably gathered, we've been trying to figure out how to deal with the situation."

Claffey's dark threats cast a new meaning on the scene Nora had witnessed earlier in the day, the handover of the brown envelope by Mairéad Broome's assistant. In addition to being a cruel father, Vincent Claffey might be a brazen blackmailer who'd just terrorized everyone in this room. Nora observed the faces around the table. What dangerous secrets could any of these people have to hide?

14

The dinner party was breaking up, the mood shattered by Vincent Claffey's intrusion. Guests were politely banished to the sitting room at the front of the house while the Killowen residents cleared the table and started the washing up. Cormac had been hoping to have a few tunes with Niall Dawson after supper, but proposing a session after the strange scene they'd just witnessed didn't seem right.

The sitting room at Killowen was more library than formal drawing room. Bookcases stretched from floor to ceiling—art books, Irish history, science and natural history, architecture, fiction by some of the country's most respected writers, a small but choice selection of crime novels. Had some of these authors stayed here? Cormac tilted his head to read the spines as he circumambulated the room, feeling restless and unsettled, thinking about the abrupt way the meal had ended, Vincent Claffey's eyes drilling everyone.

His father had stuck close to Eliana ever since Claffey had barged in. She'd found a box of dominoes and had enlisted Joseph's help in setting up a game. There was such a . . . what would you call it? An ease between her and the old man, a camaraderie he himself had never shared with his father. Seeing it stirred up a few unexpected and unwelcome feelings. Added to that was a tiny but undeniable concern. The old man was acting as though he knew this girl, when they'd only just met. What if the attachment strayed over the line of what was appropriate? The thought had never before occurred to him, and now he couldn't shake it. He kept checking on the little scene playing out in the corner, Eliana and his father, heads conspiratorially close as they overturned the ivory-colored tiles. She was so natural with the old man, no doubt blissfully unaware of the undercurrent of familial tension into which she'd stepped. Probably for the best. He turned away and caught the last bit of what Nora was saying to Niall Dawson. "—and the middle finger is quite discolored."

"What's this?" Cormac asked. "What am I missing?"

Nora turned around. "I was just telling Niall that Dr. Friel and I wondered whether Killowen Man might have been a scribe."

"And what made you think that?" Dawson frowned.

"Proper-looking calluses, for a start, and what seemed to be ink stains, just here." She held up her right hand, indicating the thumb and first two fingers. She lowered her voice to a whisper. "And now with the satchel, from the same spot where the body turned up . . ."

"You're wondering if Killowen Man might have been a resident of the monastery at Cill Eóghain?"

"Well, it's possible, isn't it? I haven't even told you the most interesting detail we found in the postmortem," Nora said. "I had a suspicion, but Dr. Friel was able to confirm. He was definitely murdered."

Dawson sat forward in his chair. "How do you know?"

"Cuts through his garments, matching multiple stab wounds to the upper torso. Dr. Friel said both sets of wounds looked as if they were made by some sort of double-edged blade, like a dagger."

Dawson's eyes narrowed. "*Both sets* of wounds?"

"There were two groupings. Probably too early to say for certain, but it looks as if he might have been waylaid by two assailants. Viking raiders, maybe?"

Dawson seemed stunned, trying to take it all in. "We'll have to see what else the evidence says. Oh, I meant to tell you, I got through to the textile expert. She'll meet us in the mortuary at eight, if that's not too early."

"Not at all." The mention of a phone call reminded Cormac that he'd left his mobile in the car. "Will you excuse me for a second? Be right back."

Outside, the clouds had dissipated, and the sky was almost unnaturally clear. No need for a torch this evening. Cormac went to the jeep and found the phone on the front-seat floor where he'd dropped it. He was rounding the corner of the house, checking for missed calls, when he ran full on into Anthony Beglan. Beglan cursed as he dropped the plate of food and a full carton of cigarettes he was carrying.

"Sorry," Cormac said, rubbing his jaw where it had made contact with Beglan's fist. "I didn't hear you coming. It's Anthony, right? Don't know where my mind was—"

Beglan's jaws snapped together three times before he could answer. " 'Twas an accident," he said, the words rushing out in a torrent. "You're all right." He was trying to gather up the spilled food, but it was no use; everything was dirt and gravel. When he had the plate partially reassembled, he climbed to his feet and took off at a quick trot up over the field without another word.

Why was Beglan carrying that plate of food? He'd sat down to table and eaten along with the rest of them, so where was he carrying leftovers? Cormac thought he remembered Claire Finnerty saying that meals at Killowen were communal. He glanced down and saw something glinting in the gravel. A key. Beglan must have dropped it when he'd fumbled the plate. Cormac turned it over in his hand. He could feel its sharp edge—newly cut, not worn down from use. Perhaps Anthony hadn't noticed that he'd dropped it.

Cormac set off, following the shortcut Beglan had taken, over the fields and then down a small lane. He followed the curving lane for about a hundred yards, the last fifty of which was bounded by high hedges. Tucked away and a bit overgrown, Beglan's farm was definitely rough-and-ready. A foul odor permeated the air—no wonder Anthony seemed to spend most of his time at Killowen.

The first building Cormac came upon was an old house—a water-damaged two-story ruin, its gaping door and broken windows crisscrossed with lengths of baling twine, on which hung glinting bits of aluminum and discarded CDs. Evidently an attempt to keep swallows from roosting inside. The adjacent barn looked as if it had been converted into a dwelling; a power cable stretched between the two buildings, there were patterned curtains in the windows, and an old cast-iron pot sat beside the door. The window beside the kitchen door was open, and a pair of voices came from inside—one male, one female.

"Don't worry, Anthony," the woman said. The voice was heavily accented, Eastern European. "I'll find something else to eat."

"I haven't anything to give you. Muh-muh-bollocks barged right into me," Beglan explained. "Sorry, eeh-eeh-Anca. Got your cigarettes, though."

The girl gave a mirthless laugh. "That's good. Cigarettes are more important than food."

Anca. The name Nora had mentioned at dinner. Martin Gwynne's apprentice, the one Claire claimed had left Killowen more than a month ago. She was obviously still here, so why would Claire lie? If the girl was a foreign national, maybe her papers weren't in order. That could get a bit dicey, with the police everywhere, digging into everything at the farm. Whatever the immigration rules were for Eastern Europe these days, they weren't likely very strict. Dublin was still full to bursting with Romanians and Bulgarians and Poles, although some had legged it off home when the Irish economy soured.

He looked down at the key in his hand. Perhaps it would be better if he didn't make himself known. Not his business, any of this. He edged up to the door and set the key gently on the threshold, moving away silently the same way he'd come. One of them was bound to find it there, and he'd have discharged his duty. He felt guilty for ruining the girl's dinner. She'd go hungry, and all because he'd been fixed on the bloody phone and hadn't looked where he was going.

He found Niall and Nora still in the sitting room. They had cracked open the bottle of twelve-year-old whiskey from the side table. Nora looked up, and Cormac tipped his head at the corner where Eliana and his father had been. "Gone to bed already?"

"Yes. Your father was tired, so I helped Eliana get him settled. You were gone a long time."

"Oh, yes, found my phone right where I dropped it. But then I ran into Anthony Beglan—literally, ran smack into him in the car park. Completely destroyed the plate of parmigiana he was carrying home."

"So that's how you got tomato sauce on your face?" Nora's eyes glinted as she directed him to his left eyebrow. "Just there."

"What? Oh." Cormac touched his own forehead and brought away a small splodge of red sauce. "I guess it must have—" He looked around for something to wipe his fingers and finally took the handkerchief Niall Dawson offered. "But that's not the most curious thing."

He told Nora and Niall what he'd overheard at Beglan's place.

"So Anca's not gone away at all," Nora said. "I thought it was strange that she'd left half-finished work on the writing table in the studio. Martin Gwynne seemed to regret my mentioning her tonight at dinner, didn't you think?"

Cormac agreed. "I thought Claire seemed miffed as well, to tell you the truth. So they don't want us to know she's here, but why not?"

"The girl's probably illegal," Dawson said. He shifted in his chair, looking almost as uncomfortable as Gwynne had been at the dinner table.

"I thought of that," Cormac admitted. "But even if that is the case, they're going to an awful lot of trouble to hide her, from us or from the police."

Nora asked, "Did you ever meet the girl, Niall? She must have been here when you came last April."

Cormac studied Dawson, watching his friend's expression subtly change in response to Nora's gentle probing.

"I don't really remember," Niall said. "I was only here briefly."

Cormac thought back to the intimacy of the dinner table tonight. How could you forget the people you'd broken bread with at that table, even if it was a few months past? Nora seemed to register a touch of disbelief as well. "Come on, Niall, how could you not remember?"

"Well I don't."

Nora shot him a questioning glance, but Cormac signaled her with a tiny frown to drop it. Something was not right. He'd have to take up this subject with Niall when they were alone.

15

At nine o'clock on Friday night, Stella Cusack was at home watching the first of several digital videos she had requested from the RTÉ archives—Benedict Kavanagh's chat show. The format featured an intellectual duel, each guest challenging the host over philosophical points that had about as much to do with any ordinary person's life as how many angels could dance on the head of a pin. After twenty minutes or so, all the blather about "being" and "nonbeing" made her head ache. No surprise at all that the debaters were men, who evidently had time to sit around and think deep thoughts while their wives were at home managing the house and the children and the cooking and every-feckin'-thing else.

Still, it wasn't difficult to understand people's attraction to Kavanagh. He had a kind of effortless grace, a full head of hair just unkempt enough so that you knew he wasn't vain—at least not in that way. Kavanagh seemed to focus on his guests, to take in and process what they were saying. Each guest would fall under his spell, relaxing into easygoing, spirited conversation. Which made it all the more surprising when the smiling host suddenly went on the attack at the end of the program.

Stella began running the video again, fast-forwarding through the arguments, instead focusing on what interested her, which was Kavanagh's body language and that of his guests. If gamblers had their tells, so did philosophers, apparently. At some point in each of the debates, Kavanagh would purse his lips and wait a few moments, then interrupt whoever was speaking and cut him off at the knees. She watched another three videos, fast-forwarding through the chat just to watch the body language, and it happened at the same time in each one. It was as though Kavanagh knew exactly when to stop the discussion and make his fatal thrust before the credits rolled. She studied the faces of the guests as their host cheerily signed off: fuming at their own impotence, trying to make nice for the sake of the audience, but ready to strangle the man as soon as they got off camera. Had anybody ever thrown a punch at the studio? Easy enough to find out. Stella thought back to her conversation with Mairéad Broome. Did Kavanagh resort to the same tactics in the inevitable marital disagreements? Barry Cusack, for all his faults, had never made her feel like murdering him because he could lap her in an argument. But if Benedict Kavanagh was capable of outmaneuvering his brainy professional colleagues, what might he have done in a spat with the wife? Not forgetting the live-in assistant who might have rushed to her aid.

Stella dialed Fergal Molloy. She could hear music in the background as he picked up and remembered that it was Friday night. He probably had some girl at his flat.

"Sorry to bother you, Fergal—"

"No, it's fine." The volume of the music dropped.

"I was going through the archives of Kavanagh's television program and wondered if you'd found out any more about the land records."

"Have you had dinner?"

"No, actually, I started in on these—"

"Because I could pop round, pick up a curry, and we could go over a few things. What's your usual?"

Stella surprised herself with a quick response: "Saag chicken and garlic naan."

When she hung up, Stella was taken aback at what had just transpired. They'd sometimes stayed late at the office, going over case notes, but Molloy had never volunteered to bring dinner before. Was she missing something? And was the house presentable enough to receive a guest? She jumped up to clear away the few pieces of dirty crockery that tended to pile up in the sink when she was home alone, and then turned to the files that were spread across the kitchen table. Finally, she checked the fridge and found some bottles of ale still there from a few months back. That was fine—Smithwick's was rather good with Indian.

Just then the bell went, and she opened the door to find her partner laden with a file tucked under one arm and two carrier bags full of take-away containers. "Didn't realize your flat was so near," she said.

"All right, I confess, I was in the car when you rang. Going for curry on my own."

She showed him to the kitchen and they began unloading the food. "And here's me, thinking you'd have someplace to go on a Friday night, somewhere a bit more exciting than going over case notes."

"And if I was looking forward to it?"

"Then you are officially a pathetic human being." The spicy curry smelled wonderful. Stella licked a bit of sauce from her thumb and realized that she was ravenous.

Molloy pulled the last package from the bag. "And garlic naan, as requested."

"Thanks, Fergal. You didn't have to do this."

He waved away her thanks. "Best option I had for the evening, by a long shot."

She leveled him with a look. "You can leave off the slagging right now."

His gaze was steady as her own. "I happen to be deadly serious."

A small voice at the back of her head told Stella something had just happened, that she ought to be paying attention. But whatever it was, the moment was so small, and so subtle, that she couldn't say what it was. She went to the fridge and brought out two bottles of ale.

Molloy sat down to his curry and began flipping through the pages of his notebook.

"Killowen, including the turbary rights to turf cutting in the adjacent bog, belonged to a Thomas Beglan, bachelor uncle of Anthony, until his death at age eighty in 1992. Thomas had no heirs but his nephew, so the whole parcel went to him. Anthony Beglan still owns the land, both his own family farm and Killowen."

Stella's interest piqued. But first things first. "Kavanagh's wife and her assistant are top priority in this case. I found it curious that even though they'd stayed at the farm multiple times, everyone I spoke to this afternoon denied that Mairéad Broome and Graham Healy were at Killowen during the last two weeks of April. And no one seemed to know what Kavanagh might have been doing in the vicinity. But Dawson, the archaeologist from the National Museum, he was at Killowen for a couple of days in April, right around the time of Kavanagh's disappearance. Odd that he never mentioned it."

"Want me to check him out?"

"Not yet. Dr. Gavin was telling me about an interesting encounter she witnessed this afternoon: Graham Healy passing a fat brown envelope to Vincent Claffey in the car park at Killowen."

"Did you get anything from Claffey?" Molloy asked.

"More from his daughter than the man himself, not surprisingly.

When I spoke to Deirdre Claffey, she didn't admit knowing Kavanagh, but she seemed quite upset that he was dead. It's going to be difficult getting anything more out of her—the father doesn't want her talking to us. But we'll have to find a way to get to her again. And it looks as if Claffey's hiding something in his shed. He made a show of locking it up as I was leaving, almost like a deliberate two fingers to the world. I wish I knew what the hell he's playing at."

"What do you want me to do?"

Stella clicked through the list of interviews in her head. "I keep going back to that car buried in the bog. It's partially drained, so the surface is pretty solid—you can't just push the car in. Someone used a digger. And that's the thing: you can't just pick up and drive a JCB— it's not that easy. Whoever buried that car must have had some experience with an excavator. But everyone at Killowen seems to have things they're not telling us. I found out that the calligrapher and his wife, Martin and Tessa Gwynne, both knew Kavanagh, or were at least acquainted. Met at a conference in Toronto twenty years ago, some group called the Eriugena Society. Let's see if we can find out more about that. And maybe you could also get some background on Claire Finnerty and Diarmuid Lynch. He gave me a story about being a farm-hand in Spain—I don't know, it sounded dodgy. Obviously, it would be great if we could take a closer look at everyone, but we've got to pri-oritize. Unless we can make progress—and soon—Special Crimes will pull this one from us."

"Let's make some progress, then," Molloy said. "I've been through the missing person file on Kavanagh, and there are a couple of things that don't add up."

"Such as?"

"Well, if he was out here in April for more than just a day trip, where's his luggage? Presumably he'd bring a toothbrush, a change of underpants. But there was no case in the boot of the car, right? So if he did have an overnight bag, where is it?"

"Come to think of it, there wasn't any laptop in his Dublin office either. But no one ever came forward with those things when his disap-pearance was in the news. Speaking of, did you put out that photo to the television people?"

"Just like you asked."

"So maybe we'll get something. Good work so far, Fergal." She glanced at her watch and sprang to her feet. "God, will you look at the time? It's nearly midnight."

"We're only getting started."

"No, it's time you were off home. I want your little gray cells firing on all cylinders in the morning."

"Yes, ma'am." He offered a small, crooked smile, and Stella felt once more that she'd just missed something. She pushed him toward the door. "I won't be responsible for dark circles under your eyes. What would your mammy say?"

He stopped short and gave her a curious look. "It's all right, Stella, I don't live with my mammy anymore."

16

Cormac stood at the kitchen window, gazing out at the herb garden in the moonlight. It was after three o'clock, and everyone else at Killowen seemed to be asleep. He'd come downstairs, unable to stop the thoughts circling in his head, mostly worries about Niall Dawson's connection to a murder victim and his strange reaction to the mention of that Romanian girl.

And it wasn't just thinking about Dawson that kept him from sleep. Every time he had closed his eyes tonight, he'd sunk immediately into shadowy dreams: standing at the edge of a bog, surrounded by faceless assassins and dagger blades glinting in the darkness. He'd jerked awake the last time with a strong taste of bitterness on his tongue and headed downstairs for a drink—something that might take away the lingering sharpness. He'd found a lone bottle of cider in the fridge and had gone outside into the courtyard to drink it, sitting in the shadows of the cloister-like walkway.

It would certainly have been his preference to let the police get on with their job and solve Benedict Kavanagh's murder. He didn't want to be mixed up in all this, now with Claffey threatening people, and worrying about whether Nora, or his father, or Eliana might be in danger. And yet there were bits of information to which he alone was privy that raised questions perhaps not best answered by the police. He'd have to find some opportunity to speak to Niall. Why was it so difficult to know what to do?

He finished the cider and set the bottle gently in the recycling bin in the kitchen corner. Climbing the stairs, he decided that perhaps he ought to poke his head in, make sure the old man was safe and comfortable.

Cormac paused as he grasped the handle on his father's bedroom door, conscious of making noise in the still night. But the sturdy hinges seemed to be well oiled, and the heavy door opened silently. He let his eyes get used to the darkness, focusing on the old man flat on his back, the barrel of his chest rising and falling steadily, one arm flung out to the side. A pile of extra bedclothes on a chair next to the bed shifted, apparently on its own, and Cormac stared, trying to make sense of it. Again, the pile moved, and he squinted into the darkness. Was he seeing things? At last his eyes became more accustomed to the darkness, and he could see a pale arm snaking out of the blankets, a small hand clasped in his father's large one. The old man wasn't alone.

Cormac crept into the darkened room and knelt by the chair. "Eliana," he whispered, trying to rouse the girl without waking his father. "Eliana."

She started, groggy with sleep. "What is it?"

Cormac said, "Listen to me, you shouldn't be here. You ought to be in your own room."

"He couldn't sleep, so I came to sit with him," Eliana explained. "No trouble, really—"

"But you can't let him talk you into these things."

By this time, the old man was awake. He sat up and reached for the girl's hand again. "Have a projection!" the old man mumbled. His hair was a fright, standing on end all over his head. "He can projector. Projecture." He tried to push Eliana back into her chair.

Nora's groggy voice came from the doorway. "Cormac, do you need some help?"

"Eliana was sleeping here, in the chair." Cormac could feel his blood pressure rising, not sure how to explain what he'd seen, what he feared. None of this was good. "My father won't let her go back to her room."

"Let me speak to him—you can see Eliana to her room."

Cormac hesitated. "He's my responsibility, Nora. I can't let you—"

"Will you stop? Just go with Eliana. I'll be fine here."

Eliana pulled her blanket from the floor and led Cormac to her own room next door. She piled the fluffy duvet onto her bed and sat beside it.

Cormac pulled up a chair beside the bed. "First of all, I'm not angry with you. I want to make sure you understand that." The girl nodded. "Can you tell me what happened tonight?"

Tears welled in Eliana's eyes. "I try to make sure he is all right before I sleep," she said. "And tonight, he didn't want me to go, I don't know why, so I brought this." Her fingers played with the edge of the duvet. "I didn't mind."

How was he going to explain to her? "Now, listen, Eliana, I want you to tell me, honestly. My father hasn't said or done anything that's made you feel . . . well, uncomfortable?"

"No, he's very kind." Then she pulled back, her eyes widening, suddenly aware of what Cormac was asking. "No, no, nothing has happened, I swear! I would never . . . please, you must believe me."

"I do believe you, Eliana. Calm yourself."

Back in their own room, Cormac's conversation with Nora turned on what had just transpired and how they ought to handle it. He said, "I don't think we should send her back to Dublin."

"No, I agree."

"So if we can just stick things out here for the next day or two, that would be best."

"Do you want to call the agency, request someone else?"

"No, let's wait until we get home and take things from there. It's not as if Eliana has done anything wrong—perhaps she's not exercised the best judgment—it's my father who's been making unreasonable demands."

Nora smoothed the worry lines from his forehead. "We'll figure all this out. And remember that it's only temporary. Mrs. Hanafin will be back in ten days."

Ten days. And then everything would go back to normal—at least to the ordinary strangeness of their quotidian life.

A whisper came from the darkness. "I meant to ask, Cormac, what were you doing up in the middle of the night?"

"The usual. Couldn't sleep," he said. No need to mention his fears about Niall, the shadowy dreams. He pushed all that away. Let Stella Cusack worry about solving Kavanagh's murder. Not his business, any of it.

Nora's silence told him that she had slipped back into slumber. He lay still and concentrated on breathing until he heard the faint sound of a footfall out in the corridor. If his father was going to start wandering the halls at four o'clock in the morning . . . He threw off the duvet and went to the door, cracking it open. No sign of his father, or Eliana. The only movement was Niall Dawson's door across the way, closing silently.

BOOK THREE

Oráit annso dona macaib fogluma
is catad in scel bec he
na tarbra aithbhir na litir orum—
is olc in dub
in memram gann
is dorcha an la.

A prayer here for the students;
and it is a hard little story:
do not reproach me concerning the letters—
the ink is bad,
the parchment scanty,
the day dark.

—A scribe's note in Old Irish, inserted into a medieval
Latin manuscript about Saint Finnian

1

Regina Mullens, the National Museum's textile consultant, was already waiting outside the hospital morgue when Nora, Cormac, and Niall arrived a few minutes before eight. "I drove down last night," she said in response to Dawson's surprise. "Stopped with a friend who lives near Birr. I wanted a crack at your bog man as soon as possible."

"Sorry to drag you all the way out here," Dawson said. "Not exactly museum conditions, I'm afraid, but we're not able to transport him back to Dublin just yet."

"Extenuating circumstances," Cormac explained.

"Really?" Mullens was intrigued. "Do tell."

Dawson frowned and turned away slightly, so Cormac said, "It turns out that our bog man was found at a crime scene."

"You're joking." Cormac shook his head, and suddenly Regina Mullens's eyes opened wider. "Not that car buried in the bog? I saw the news reports last night. That was somewhere round here, was it?"

Dawson seemed annoyed. "Sorry, Regina, that's all we can say, except that we can't transport our man here to the Barracks until the crime scene has been thoroughly investigated and cleared. You understand, I'd have to ask you to keep this all under wraps anyway, extenuating circumstances or no."

"Naturally." Mullens pulled a zipper across her lips. "I shall be as silent as the grave."

Niall Dawson opened the door to the morgue's refrigeration unit where Killowen Man and the satchel were being stored. "I wanted to show you this first—we found it yesterday." He and Cormac transferred the board supporting the satchel to the exam table and lifted away its form-fitting cast. The wet leather glistened under the mortuary lights. Mullens began to remove some of the surrounding peat, revealing a messenger-style bag with a full front flap.

"A beautiful piece of work," Mullens said. "Look at those double-bound seams. I'm not sure we'll be able to date it from construction alone; leather fabrication methods haven't changed all that much over the years. I might guess somewhere between seventh and tenth century, but don't hold me to it. Where did you say this was found, in relation to the body?"

Dawson's eyes narrowed. "Nice try. What else can you tell us?"

"Well, the material looks like vegetable-tanned cowhide. DNA is iffy with bog specimens, but you can usually get a read on the species from the hair follicles." She peered at the leather surface with a magnifier. "In sheep and pigskin, the hairs are grouped in threes, but on cow and calf hide they're more evenly spaced. The seams appear to be sinew, which is good; vegetable-based thread would have been more fragile. I hope you had a look inside."

Dawson shook his head. "No joy. I suppose it was daft, even thinking about it. No one's ever found a book in a bog. Let's wrap it up, have a look at our bog man."

All four of them gloved up this time and began uncovering the body, one portion at a time. Each time they removed Killowen Man from his wrapping, they were opening the door to mold spores and bacteria, the destructive elements he'd so far managed to avoid, protected in his anaerobic, antiseptic bed. Mullens's eyes grew large as she glimpsed the knob of the humerus protruding from the peat beside bog man's chin.

"Jesus," she whispered when the full extent of the damage was revealed. "You didn't tell me he'd been pulled apart."

"Whoever buried the car must have accidentally discovered the body," Nora said. She glanced at Niall Dawson, who warned her with a frown not to say more. "Sorry, I shouldn't have—"

Regina Mullens was watching both of them. "Now I'm dying of curiosity. But all right, I won't ask any more questions. We'll stick to his clothing. The good thing about wool is that it's quite tough," she said, "even after this long in a bog. From what I can see of the construction on this outer garment, it looks to be medieval, which could mean any time between the sixth and the sixteenth century."

"Well, that helps narrow it down," Cormac said.

"Dates might be difficult," Mullens admitted. "It's probably easier to figure out what social class he came from—there were all kinds of laws about who could wear what in ancient Ireland. Everything from permissible colors according to your status to the size of your brooch—it was all set down in the *Senchus Mór*."

Nora shot him an inquisitive glance, and Cormac understood exactly what she was asking. "Ancient Brehon law books," he murmured.

With Mullens supervising, they each worked on a small area, lifting the wet wool with long, flat probes, holding it away from the bog man's flesh, spritzing frequently. Trying to undress someone who'd been in a bog for centuries was delicate work. The body and the clothes were all dyed a uniform shade of dark brown, looking as if they'd been soaking for hundreds of years in a vat of Guinness.

"Early medieval construction didn't vary a lot. Looks like a rather plain overgarment," Mullens said, almost like a pathologist scrutinizing a corpse. "From the amount of material here, I'd say it was an ankle-length woolen *brat*—a basic cloak, no embroidery or special trim. You didn't happen to find a brooch of any kind?"

"Not so far," Dawson said. "Although the body had been moved from its original location. We'll know more after we're finished at the site. If that bollocks Claffey took it—"

Nora said, "Niall, isn't it possible that the people who killed him also pinched his brooch?"

Regina Mullens looked up. "What's that?"

"Maybe you noticed these cuts through his cloak," Nora said, gently lifting the fabric to show her. "They correspond with stab wounds to his stomach and back."

"But this fella's murder can't be the reason you've got a crime scene. He's been dead for centuries." Regina Mullens was trying to work out the details of their intrigue. "All right, all right, no more in that vein." She kept working, her nose only inches from the brown corpse. "So no brooch, at least for the moment. But I would expect to see a girdle or belt of some sort. Belting a cloak like this was fairly common—the draped material made handy pouches that medieval travelers used to carry things. Ah, here we are."

Nora said, "We were wondering, given the bald patch and the stains on his hands, if perhaps he was a monk or a scribe."

Mullens nodded and handed her the magnifying glass. "Well, you can take a look for yourself, but I'd say he came by that naked pate quite naturally. If you notice, the hairs on top of his head are very soft and fine, not like they've been shaved. Irish monks wore a distinctive tonsure." She gestured, as if to pull a gloved thumb across her skull. "The whole front of the head shaved from ear to ear, with longer hair in back."

Nora said, "You'd think he'd be wearing something under this wool."

Mullens looked up. "Well, undergarments as we know them didn't really exist until much later. But supposing he had gone into the bog fully dressed in the fashion for his time, he'd likely have been wearing a *leine*, a sort of linen shift, under his *brat*. But linen's rather delicate. Doesn't usually survive, even in a bog." She paused, feeling through the wool. "There seems to be something underneath him here. I don't suppose we could try turning him over?"

After about twenty minutes, they'd managed to flip the body, and Regina Mullens had peeled away enough of the woolen material to find what had been hiding inside Killowen Man's cloak. "I'm dying to know what this is," she said.

The object looked like some sort of diptych: two flat, rectangular pieces of wood, about the size and shape of a small paperback. Cormac could make out two holes drilled along one of the longer edges, looped through with a leather thong.

"Bloody hell, we were just talking about these last night," Dawson said. He reached in very gingerly and lifted one of the pieces of saturated, bog-preserved wood. The thing opened quite easily on its leather hinge, revealing two reservoirs of darkened wax, scratched with words in an ancient script. "Looks like Latin," he murmured. "And a few words in Greek. My God, there's been nothing like this since Springmount."

Nora moved in closer, crowding in with the rest of them. "What's Springmount? Will someone please explain?"

Cormac spoke without turning his head from the object on the table, as if it might disappear if he looked away. "A set of seventh-century wax tablets discovered at Springmount Bog in Antrim in 1914."

"And there was writing on those as well?" Nora asked.

"A couple of verses from the Vulgate text of Psalms." Dawson shook himself, glancing between the body and the wooden object on the table. "I still don't quite believe it. You realize we have not just a tablet— pretty miraculous in and of itself—but we may also have *the person who wrote it*." Dawson's voice trembled with excitement. "See how the passage fills the panel on the left side? And the right side is incomplete—"

"A work in progress?" Cormac wondered aloud.

Dawson rubbed his forehead, still not able to take it all in.

"What happens now?" Mullens asked.

"We carry on here with our cameras and spray bottles," Niall Dawson said. "We take as many notes and pictures as possible, then pack everything back up in peat and keep working out at the site. And I suppose we'll have to go and talk to Vincent Claffey."

Cormac's eyes were drawn to a pair of marble-shaped objects nestled in a fold of wool beside the body. "Did you see these, Niall?" He managed to tease one of them out of the crevice and handed it to Dawson.

"Hmm . . . they look like oak galls."

"For making ink," Nora murmured.

"That's right," Dawson replied. "How did you know that?"

Something wasn't right. Nora looked as if someone had walked on her grave. Cormac moved closer. "What's wrong, Nora?"

"I don't know. Just a weird coincidence, I guess. Dr. Friel and I found a handful of those yesterday—forced down Benedict Kavanagh's throat."

2

Stella and Fergal Molloy were working on an incident wall in their tiny office at the back of the Birr police station. On the wall so far were Benedict Kavanagh's photograph, a map of Ireland, and a fairly sparse time line marking the victim's movements the last few days of his life. They had tracked down dates from credit card records in Kavanagh's missing person file: he'd stopped for petrol at the Topaz on Donnybrook Road near the RTÉ studios, and then vanished.

"So the first question is: Would he come straight out to this place from Donnybrook, not even go home first? Maybe he finds out what the wife and her boy toy are up to and tracks her out here," Molloy said.

"He seemed to have no problem with Graham Healy," Stella said. "Knew all about the two of them, according to his wife. And Mairéad Broome wasn't even here at the time—she and Healy claim they were in Mountrath."

Molloy traced the distance from Killowen across the Slieve Bloom Mountains to Mountrath. "It's only about forty kilometers. Do we believe them?"

"I'm not sure. If they're lying about it, so is everyone else at Killowen."

"Well, so maybe they are. Kavanagh could have been lurking about, spying on the wife. Suppose he confronted her and Healy, and there was an altercation. I think the motive was personal, not professional," Molloy said. "Look at the way the body was left, with split tongue and those seeds or whatever they are in his mouth."

"Dr. Gavin identified them, for what it's worth—oak galls. Said she saw a whole load of them yesterday afternoon in Martin Gwynne's studio. Any joy from Central Records?"

"Still waiting on most of my queries, but they were able to give me a rundown on Martin Gwynne." He flipped open his notebook. "Studied medieval history at Cambridge, worked as a manuscript specialist for the British Library for fifteen years, until—get this—he was let go over a missing book. He claimed he was innocent; they declined to prosecute. It was never really resolved to anyone's satisfaction. After that, he worked as a private assistant to his old tutor from Cambridge, the paleographer T. A. Priest, until Priest died, which was nineteen years ago. Gwynne and his wife arrived at Killowen not long after that."

Stella took in this new information. "What about that academic conference where they met Kavanagh?"

"That group he mentioned, the Eriugena Society, is based in Toronto and meets every four years or so. They're supposed to be sending me a copy of the program for that year."

"Who or what is this Eriugena, anyway? Seems like I read that name in Kavanagh's file."

"Some medieval Irish philosopher," Molloy said. "Used to be a picture of him on the old five-punt notes. That's all I know."

The phone on Stella's desk gave three chirrups in rapid succession, and she reached for the receiver. "Cusack here."

The voice was hesitant. "They said on the television this was the number to ring . . . about the man that went missing." The caller sounded not well educated but respectable, and certainly not used to telephoning the police.

"Yes, this is the number. I'm Detective Cusack. We're trying to find anyone who'd have information on Benedict Kavanagh."

"Well, that's not the name he used when he came here to me. But I recognized him straightaway from that photo they showed on the television. Always suspected he was up to no good, but murdered! I've no wish at all to be mixed up in things like that," she said, though it was clear from her breathless tone that it was exactly what she wished.

"First things first," Stella said. "Where are you ringing from?"

"The Groves B and B in Crinkill."

"And your name?" There was a pause, as if the caller finally realized the situation she was in and might be entertaining second thoughts.

"I only kept his things because he left without paying, you see." The woman spoke in a rush, worried how the situation might begin to reflect badly on her. "I don't take money up front like most of them are doing now. Old-fashioned, I suppose, but he was the first whoever left without paying, and—"

Stella cut her off. "Are you saying that you kept Mr. Kavanagh's things?" She said it for Molloy's benefit and gestured for him to stand by with his notebook and Biro.

"It's not much, only one bag, and a briefcase with some papers and a small little computer yoke. I thought I'd just tuck them away until he came looking for them, and get what was owed us before he'd get them back. No harm in that, is there? We've all got to make a living."

"We're going to pop round and collect Mr. Kavanagh's belongings, Mrs. . . . what was the name? Right, Mrs. Dolan." Molloy was ready with paper and pen, as Stella repeated the address. "The Groves, Roscrea Road, Crinkill. Thanks, yes, I've got it. Imelda Dolan. We'll be out to you straightaway, Mrs. Dolan. If you would do us a favor, and not touch any of the items, just leave them exactly where they are. Thanks very much for ringing."

They rolled up to the house twenty minutes later. It looked a lot like the place Stella had imagined while speaking with Imelda Dolan. Immaculate, with every shrub in the garden pruned into a perfect globe. Sharp edges on the flower beds, a completely weed-free lawn, and gravel so clean it appeared to have been run through a dishwasher. Three stars from Bord Fáilte, no doubt, but nary a whiff of warmth or personality. What was Benedict Kavanagh doing at a place like this? She'd had him pegged as a five-star man all the way.

Imelda Dolan answered the door with excuses at the ready, before they'd even crossed the threshold. "I'd never have kept his things, you see, only he'd gone off without paying his bill. Then I was out of the country, visiting my sister in Tasmania, so I mustn't have heard the news about the poor man going missing. Bernard—that's my husband—he said I shouldn't get fussed about it, but it certainly puts the heart crossways in you, doesn't it, hearing about someone you know being murdered?"

Stella showed her the photo of Kavanagh. "Is this the man who stayed here?"

"That's him, and no mistake."

"How can you be so certain?"

"Oh, I'd know him anywhere. I knew there was something strange about him. A bit unnatural, he was, the way he'd probe at you with those eyes—"

"And did he say anything about the reason for his visit?"

"The first time, he was looking at some historic sites in the area."

"Excuse me, 'the first time'?"

"He'd stayed with us once before, oh, it must have been right around eighteen months ago. I can check our visitors' book, if you like. But the second visit, not a word out of him. And I refuse to pry, not like some—"

"Can you tell us anything more about the day he arrived in April?"

"I remember, 'twas a Thursday night—the twenty-first of April it was—and he booked in through the weekend."

"And when did you discover that he'd gone missing?"

"He was out a lot, not much in his room. But when Sunday came around, and he didn't turn up for his breakfast, I went to the room and found his bags on the bed. All packed and ready to go, if you don't mind. There was no sign of him, not that day, nor the following morning. I suppose it was a bit strange to leave the bags. But I suppose he didn't intend to leave, did he, if he was murdered? Still, you can't blame us for thinking he'd scarpered. Took his room key and all. Very annoying, that. Because it's hard to get keys for the old locks anymore, you see. Bernard's been after me to just replace the old doors, but I—"

Stella interrupted. "Excuse me, Mrs. Dolan, could we see Mr. Kavanagh's belongings, please?"

Imelda Dolan kept talking as she led them through her sterile-looking house to a small room with a wall of built-in cupboards beside the back door. She spoke under her breath, almost like rubbing at a bruise, Stella thought. "Didn't call himself Kavanagh when he was here. Scott, it was, Mr. John Scott. 'Twasn't his real name at all—I should have known." She pulled open one of the doors to reveal a small black leather overnight bag, a laptop, and a zippered briefcase. "I had to move his things, you see, to make way for the next guests."

"And you didn't happen to look inside the bags, or remove anything from them?"

"I resent the suggestion. I run an honest house here—"

"I wasn't suggesting anything, Mrs. Dolan," Stella said. "Only asking." She grasped the handle of the overnight case.

Mrs. Dolan said, "Take it all away, right now, this minute. I want nothing more to do with any of it. Imagine if word were to get round about where the man was staying when he was *murdered*." She crossed herself hastily.

Stella resisted the small urge to point out that any association with a gruesome murder might actually boost business. After a few more questions, including checking the register for the earlier visit, they took their leave, bringing the cases and laptop back to the station for further inspection.

"What are you hoping to find?" Molloy asked as they spread out Kavanagh's belongings on the table in their small back room.

"Maybe some indication of what he was doing here," Stella said, taking inventory of the usual items in the overnight case, all ordinary things a man would take with him on a trip out of town for a few days: clothing, toiletries, prescription bottles for various tablets—blood pressure, allergies, vitamins. "What do you make of these?" she asked, pointing out a small vial of blue tablets.

"Interesting," Molloy said. "Especially if those tablets are what we think they are."

"Oh, they're the 'little blue pills,' all right."

"So the question is, did he carry them on principle, or had he made plans?"

"Exactly." In among the pill bottles, Stella noticed a small gold cross with a broken chain. She picked it up, squinting to see the letters engraved on the back: *From Mum.* Not a man's jewelry, that much was certain. "All right, let's have a look at the briefcase."

Molloy placed the attaché case on the table and flipped it open, perusing the papers inside. "Looks like notes for a book or a paper about marginalia—"

"Why does that sound a bit unsavory?"

Molloy smiled. "It's just the little notes that monks used to write at the edges of their manuscripts. Some wrote poems, or scribbled down random thoughts they had while copying."

Stella was pleased to see that Molloy's secondment to the Antiquities Task Force last year was paying off. But she was thinking about Benedict Kavanagh, not about monks. "So this trip may have had more to do with his work than with his wife?"

"Seems that way, so far at least. There's nothing at all about her and quite a lot about old manuscripts. He seems to have made a translation of a poem in Irish. Here, read this." He offered her a handwritten page, alive with scribbled notes and underlines.

"This Kavanagh's handwriting?" she asked.

"Looks to be."

Stella turned the page sideways, following several lines of text that seemed written with particular force:

A little hut in the wood, none knows it but myself.
A lowly, hidden hut, among the paths of the forest,
Will you return with me to see where it lies?
The stags of Feadán Mór leap from its streams amid sweet meadows.
From my hut great Arderin can be seen to the east.
A clutch of eggs, sweet apples, heath peas, and honey;
haws, yew berries, nuts from the branching green hazels.

After the poem came a cryptic code in Kavanagh's hand: "i¹ !!!!?"

"Any idea what this means—i-one?"

Molloy shrugged. "No, but the poem sounds like something a monk would have scribbled at the edge of his manuscript. We read a few of these, studying Old Irish at school."

Stella remembered that Molloy had been educated at a *gaelscoil*, where everything was taught through Irish language—maths, physics, geography, the lot. And at that moment, the distance between the two of them seemed incrementally wider. They might as well have come up in different centuries, for all they had in common.

"What's this?" Stella pointed to another notation, where Kavanagh had written "An Feadán Mór, 8k sw Birr, off N52." She paused for a moment, thinking back to something Mairéad Broome had said in Dublin, about the breakthrough her husband had just made in his work. *This is going to rattle some bones,* he'd said. Two bodies in the boot of a car was a rattling of actual bones. There was something right under the surface here, she could feel it.

"Fergal, do you think Kavanagh could have been mixed up with treasure hunters?"

"Not out of the question, I suppose. They try to get all sorts of people in those smuggling rings—museum staffers, even coppers." Molloy grinned. "They know we're always skint."

"But Kavanagh wasn't. He'd plenty of money, according to the wife."

"Ah, but some of them aren't in it for the money," Molloy said. "For them it's all about getting your hands on something very old and rare. And book people are especially fanatical—or so I hear."

Stella took a marker and started writing on the time line. "So, from the landlady we know Kavanagh arrived at the B and B in Crinkill on the evening of Thursday, April twenty-first, where he stayed for at least two nights, and went off between Saturday the twenty-third and the morning of Sunday April twenty-fourth and never returned."

"Let's put the wife's time line up next to his," Molloy said, grabbing a blue marker. "She and Graham Healy drive down to Cork for the exhibition installation on April fourteenth; they supposedly arrive at the friend's house in Mountrath on April twenty-first and stay for a week, then head home to Dublin on the twenty-eighth. She waits around three days before reporting the husband missing on the first of May."

Stella added a red line. "Work on the geothermal system at Killowen commences on April twentieth, and wraps up on the thirtieth. Niall Dawson is there for a couple of days around April twenty-second." She paused, thinking of the way Kavanagh's body had been left—tongue cleaved down the middle, gallnuts blocking his airway. There was a message in all that, but what was it? "What does a split tongue say to you, Fergal?"

"Signifies a liar, doesn't it, someone who can't tell the truth?"

"The serpent in the garden," Stella murmured. "Let's fire up that laptop."

Molloy was keen on computers of all kinds and had no trouble navigating his way through the laptop to find out which files Kavanagh had accessed most recently.

"Seems like he's downloaded quite a few images," Molloy said, squinting at the monitor. He looked up at her. "Internet porn—what'll you wager?"

"I'm not betting on anything. Let's have a look."

Molloy pushed a button, and dozens of files opened on the screen.

"Hah! Well, they're skin pictures, right enough," he said, "just not the sort of skin you'd expect." Rather than rosy human flesh, the images were close-ups of parchment pages, Latin words inscribed in translucent brown ink. "Old manuscripts," Molloy said. "Book of Kells old."

"They were Kavanagh's thing," Stella said. "Isn't that what everyone's been telling us?"

"It's the same poem as he's translated." Molloy was staring at the image on the screen. "Amazing."

"What's amazing?"

"Well, think of it: there used to be whole libraries full of books like this, copied out by hand. Jesus, all the time and effort those poor buggers the monks put into each one. We take it for granted now, don't we—the printing press, the copy machine, the Internet. I mean, words lose their value, in a way, don't they, when you're drowning in them?"

"Never thought of it that way, but I suppose you're right."

She returned to the briefcase, finding numerous modern handwritten pages in the same distinctive rounded hand as the notes. They were beautiful to look at, although the words were mostly incomprehensible, the kind of scholarly language that made her eyes glaze over. She turned the page around to read tiny shorthand notes in the margin:

> *Extant mss:*
>
> *1) Reims, B municip, 875, ff. 1ʳ–358ᵛ; s. ix² (apart from ff. 212–7, c. AD 1000); numerous additions and corrections in Irish hands, i¹ and i²; origin perhaps Saint-Médard de Soissons; provenance Reims.*
>
> *2) St Gall, Stiftsb, 274, p. 4; s. ix [fragment of book 1].*
>
> *3) Laon, B municip, 444; s. ix² (AD 870–875); origin Laon.*
>
> *4) Feadán Mór?*

There was a gap below the last entry and then a hastily scribbled note:

> IOH *returns to* IRL, *great work unfinished*—Malmesbury *mentions An Feadán Mór, revised ed* Gesta Pontificum Anglorum *(ff. 153–200v).*

Stella frowned. "I don't know what any of this has got to do with Kavanagh's wife being here at the artists' retreat. But I don't think we're on the wrong track with her. I'm going out there to have another chat. In the meantime, Fergal, why don't you get on the phone and see if you can do some checking into Graham Healy's background."

"Looking for . . . ?"

"Any experience with heavy machinery. Somebody dug that hole in the bog."

"Art school type," Molloy scoffed. "Doubtful if he's ever got his hands dirty."

"You never know," Stella said, remembering the construction materials piled in Mairéad Broome's house. "Sometimes art can be more industrial than people imagine." Stella looked back at Kavanagh's notes. "While you're at it, Fergal, why don't you also put in a call to your pals on the Antiquities Task Force? And what about Interpol—they investigate art forgery and book theft, right? Give them the names of the players in our little drama, see if any of them have form in that area. You said Martin Gwynne was suspected of nicking something from the British Library. Let's see if there's anything else in his record."

Molloy nodded. "They had us read a few case histories on the task force. Did you know the Brits once nailed this fella who'd stolen over a million pounds' worth of old books? They called him 'The Tome Raider.' Good, isn't it?"

"Very clever." Stella was fond of books. She liked holding them, savoring their inky, wood-pulp smell. She especially loved wasting a whole weekend whenever she could manage it, holed up with a glass of wine and a juicy potboiler. But how could a book—any book—be worth killing for?

3

A lowering sky threatened to unleash a midmorning shower as Cormac and Niall Dawson set out for Vincent Claffey's farm. The time had come to speak to Claffey about the recovery of the artifacts associated with Killowen Man. The law was fairly generous when it came to rewarding citizens for turning over any found objects. Still, trying to keep those citizens honest was a constant challenge when it came to priceless ancient treasures, especially considering the current state of the economy.

The shed door was open. A whirr of machinery caught Cormac's ear as he stepped from the car. He glanced over at Niall, trudging toward the door wearing a grim expression, clearly not relishing the prospect of the conversation before them.

There would be no negotiation. Vincent Claffey lay on the conveyor belt of a contraption that filled almost half of the small shed. The machine was whirring and clanking, jerking the man's body from side to side. Cormac took a step closer. Claffey was completely encased in cling film, and his eyes were open and glassy. His mouth gaped open, and several dark round objects protruded from it. Gallnuts. *I know your secrets*, Claffey had said last night at dinner. Someone had clearly taken his words to heart.

From slightly behind him, Dawson managed a strangled whisper. "He's dead, is he?"

"I'm afraid so," Cormac said. He located a red emergency switch, at last putting a stop to the machine and its futile whine. Claffey's head sagged, and Cormac had to resist the urge to support it. They really ought not touch anything. He placed two fingers gingerly on the man's temple. No pulse, and through the plastic, the skin felt cold. He must have been dead for some time.

Cormac found himself counting the hours since four A.M., until a voice inside his head said, *Stop.* He glanced up at Dawson, who was staring at the corpse, unable to move. "We should ring Detective Cusack,"

Cormac said. "Will you check and see if Deirdre Claffey is around? We don't want her wandering in here."

"No, no, of course not." Dawson began backing slowly away from the body.

Cormac had dealt with plenty of corpses in the course of his work, but there was something uniquely unsettling about this one. Now his training kicked in. Something in him turned on automatically in situations like this, reading a site for what it could tell. Vincent Claffey's apparent penchant for clutter continued inside this shed. The only really remarkable item was the machine, fairly new and astonishingly clean, compared to everything else. What was Claffey doing here? A cardboard carton on the ground beside him was half filled with plastic tubes, with labels that read: "Tir na nOg—Authentic Irish Moor Peat, 500 ml."

He looked at the gallnuts again. Nora had told them about the handful she and Dr. Friel had found in Kavanagh's mouth. They were clearly some sort of message, but in a language as yet undecoded. It was as if someone knew that he and Niall would be coming to visit Vincent Claffey today, and his body had been left for them to find.

He thought of Niall Dawson's old connection to Benedict Kavanagh and wondered about all the unknown threads that bound together the people he and Nora had met at Killowen. And how many more connections would Cusack begin to uncover, once she started to dig?

"The girl's not here." Dawson spoke from the shed door. "I've looked everywhere. No sign of the child either."

4

Stella Cusack was on her way to Killowen on the N52 when her phone rang. It was Cormac Maguire. Her stomach sank as she received the news of Vincent Claffey's murder. "There's something else as well, Detective," Maguire said. "We can't find Deirdre Claffey or her baby."

When she hung up, her first impulse was to ring Lia, just to hear the sound of her daughter's voice. It was almost noon on Saturday. Where would Lia be now? She pictured her daughter with a small knot of friends, wandering aimlessly through piped-in music and shiny window displays at the Bridge Centre in Tullamore. When Lia answered, Stella could hear the echoing background noise and knew she'd guessed correctly.

"You don't need to be checking up on me, Mam. Everything's fine. Everything's *wonderful*."

Tears welled up as Stella rang off. Everything wasn't wonderful. She couldn't help thinking of Deirdre Claffey. If something had happened to that girl, or her child . . . Lia had no idea how fragile life was, how everything could be fine one minute and gone in the next second.

Still sitting in her car at the side of the road, she rang Molloy, then Dr. Friel, her third call to the state pathologist in as many days.

"It's getting to be a regrettable habit for both of us, isn't it, driving the N52?" Catherine Friel said. "I do hope this will be my last trip down that road."

Arriving at the Claffey farm, Stella slipped immediately into crime scene mode, wading through the uncut grass that brushed against her legs. The shed she'd wanted to get inside for the past two days was wide open, and Maguire was standing to one side of the door with Niall Dawson.

Stella found Claffey's body cocooned in cling film, his mouth open and stuffed with gallnuts, exactly like Benedict Kavanagh. A grubby plastic tub at one end of the machine held a glistening mass of wet black peat, the wonder substance Vincent Claffey was apparently packaging for sale. She should have known what he was up to in that protected bog. Pulling moor peat out of the ground, slapping on a label, and selling it for a hundred euros a liter—so obvious now. It was almost like free money. Claffey wouldn't have been able to resist.

Stella returned to the door to speak to the two men. "Tell me what happened."

Maguire began. "We found a few more artifacts from the bog site, so Niall and I came here to talk to Mr. Claffey about a possible reward. As the landowner, he'd be due some compensation. He was dead when we got here."

"What exactly did you notice when you arrived?" she asked.

Again, it was Maguire who spoke. "We heard a sort of clanking noise from the shed—"

"That's when we came in and found him," Dawson managed to add. He still looked shell-shocked. "The machine was still going."

"You haven't touched anything?"

"No," Maguire replied. "Well, apart from switching off the machine, seeing whether he was still alive."

Dawson said, "I must have touched the door handle when I went to look for Deirdre."

"I'll need statements from both of you. Have either of you seen Deirdre Claffey in the past twenty-four hours?"

"She was at Killowen last night; she and the baby were with us for dinner," Maguire said. "But her father came and collected her—"

"Dragged her off, you mean," Dawson said. "It was a bit of a scene."

"What time was that?" Stella asked. "And what happened, exactly? Tell me as much as you can remember."

Maguire told her. "Must have been about half-seven, maybe closer to eight. Vincent Claffey called everyone at Killowen 'fuckin' hippies.' Said he knew our secrets. He looked at every one of us, Niall, didn't he? If I'd any secrets, I'd have the wind put up my back by that look, and no mistake."

"What happened after they left?" Stella asked.

"Claire seemed to imply that it wasn't the first time Claffey had come after Deirdre, that they had to figure out some way to get the girl away from her father," Dawson said.

Maguire added, "Someone—Martin Gwynne, I think—mentioned having no evidence of abuse."

"Nothing but the evidence of our own eyes," Dawson murmured.

"He was pretty rough on the girl. And he shoved Claire Finnerty at one point, as well."

"But no one rang the police?"

Dawson shook his head. "Not as far as we know."

"And no one said any more about the incident?"

Maguire glanced at Dawson. "We wouldn't know. It was all guests out of the kitchen after that, so we didn't hear any more discussion."

Stella was processing all that she'd heard so far. Claffey could have been killed by someone wishing to protect his daughter, or someone with a secret so great he or she couldn't afford to risk exposure. "Tell me who, exactly, was at the dinner table."

"Claire Finnerty and the Gwynnes, Diarmuid—I'm sorry, I don't know his second name," Maguire said. "Shawn Kearney, the archaeologist, Anthony Beglan—"

"The French couple," Dawson added. "Lucien and Sylvie."

"My father and his minder, Dr. Gavin, and Niall and myself."

No mention of Mairéad Broome or Graham Healy. Perhaps Vincent Claffey had seen something he wasn't meant to see, perhaps someone, or even more than one person, coming back from the bog where they'd buried Kavanagh. Stella had to admit, she still liked the widow and her young man for Kavanagh's murder, maybe this one as well. She walked closer to Vincent Claffey, his head dangling at an awkward angle. "Can you describe for me how you found the body?"

"The machine was going," Maguire said. "Back and forth, like it was stuck, and he was on the conveyer belt, just like you see. I found the emergency switch and turned it off, then checked for a pulse, but it was no use, he was long gone. I sent Niall to look for Deirdre and phoned you as soon as he returned."

She said, "If you would stick around until my partner gets here, he'll take your statements. You can wait outside if you like."

Alone inside the shed, Stella reached for her torch. The place was filthy, which made the one clear spot on the floor under the hayloft stairs particularly noticeable. The torch beam showed a rectangle on the floor, devoid of dirt or peat, with a footprint about the size of a small chest. At a crime scene, sometimes what was missing ended up being just as important as what remained.

Stella crouched and peered under the stairs, shining her tiny light all around the cramped space. In the farthest corner, tucked in under the

steps, she could see the corner of a yellowed cutting from an old newspaper. She got down on her hands and knees and reached for the paper.
The cutting was torn in half, but she could tell from what was left what
it was about: a bombing in a small border town called Cregganroe. A car
packed with Semtex had peeled shop fronts from buildings in the high
street. The blast that had gone off without warning. She was familiar
with the story.

On her very first day as a lowly *bean garda*, she had been assigned to
evidence collection at the bombing scene. Nobody really covered those
sorts of situations in training courses. And how could they? How on
earth could anyone prepare trainee officers for the horrors they might
encounter? After an hour searching the scene, relieved to find nothing,
she'd been heading for the stairs when her gaze fell upon a small bright
stone on the roof's pebbled surface. Round and shiny, a shade larger
than the others. And then she'd realized it wasn't a stone at all but a
lone detached eyeball, staring up at her.

The bomb makers had been found out and put away—too late, after
their handiwork had killed seven people. During their trial, the bomb-
ers swore that a warning had been phoned in to Special Branch, in
plenty of time to evacuate the area. They charged the authorities with
letting the bomb go off—an act of calculated, cynical murder to harden
the hearts of the people against the cause. The charge wasn't all that
uncommon in the bad old days of the Troubles. Stella knew which of
the two scenarios she believed but had never admitted it aloud. Garda
detectives weren't supposed to have political views.

What was Vincent Claffey doing with this old newspaper cutting?
She thought of the threats he'd uttered just last night. Perhaps Claffey
was making someone at Killowen pay for what he knew, or thought he
knew. She saw the faces of the people she'd interviewed yesterday, imagining each of them in this shed with Claffey. Who among them would
have been physically capable of lifting the dead weight of a body onto
the machine? Hatred was a powerful thing; it could give an attacker
an almost inhuman physical power. Or perhaps the deed had been carried out by more than one person. She searched for signs of a struggle
and found a small pool of blood near the outside wall. Perhaps Vincent
Claffey never suspected that he was being attacked until it was too late.
Blackmail, if that was Claffey's game, was like playing with a serpent: in
order to profit, you had to get close enough to risk a deadly bite.

5

Nora had just arrived back from the hospital and was standing in the kitchen at Killowen with Joseph and Eliana when Shawn Kearney came through the door. Her usually animated expression was gone. She pulled Nora aside and spoke under her breath.

"Vincent Claffey's been found murdered," she said.

"But that's not possible. Niall and Cormac just went to see him."

Shawn's grim expression told her everything she needed to know.

"My God, they found him, didn't they?"

"It seems so. And Deirdre and the baby are missing. A few of us are going to help with the search."

"I'll come, too," Nora said.

The Claffey place was still being processed as a crime scene, so the search for Deirdre commenced from the nearest three-way crossroads. A group of uniformed Guards officers was milling about with volunteers, and Detective Molloy was handing out assignments to small groups. "Each team will have a detailed map of the area," Molloy said. "We'll be doing a grid search of the areas marked. The girl we're looking for is Deirdre Claffey. She is sixteen years of age, approximately 1.65 meters tall. She has short brown hair and brown eyes. We're working on the assumption that she has a child with her—her son, Cal, nine months. If they were on foot, it's quite likely they haven't traveled far. If you find Deirdre, try and persuade her to stay put; make it clear that we just need to talk to her. And ring that number on your flyer straightaway."

Cormac and Niall Dawson arrived while Molloy was talking, and they joined Nora and Shawn to make a full search party. At last their turn came with the organizers. They were assigned a small area of meadow and woodland rising up from the edge of the bog just below Anthony Beglan's farm. Nora studied the map as they began making their way to the assigned area. They had to circumvent a hedgerow of furze, a wall of thorns, obviously untrimmed for several years. Once they'd reached the area marked on their map, they walked along in close flanking formation, scanning the ground and the undergrowth for any sign of human activity. About a hundred yards up the hillside from the bog, they were nearing a small stone ruin.

"I didn't imagine bringing you here under these circumstances," Shawn Kearney said. "This is Killowen Chapel, the place we were talking about last night."

They passed by a flat corbelled doorway, completely filled with rubble, and the stump of a round tower, sheared off about ten meters above the ground.

"The carving I mentioned is just inside," Shawn Kearney said, leading them through a fine Romanesque arch on the far side.

"Here he is, the scribe of Killowen," Kearney said. The carving beside the doorway showed a figure holding what appeared to be a stylus and a wax tablet. He wore a flowing cloak that pooled around his feet, and his head seemed to be naturally balding rather than tonsured in the Irish style. Nora felt the tug of intrigue.

"See the Greek letters on his tablet," Cormac said, stepping closer. "Alpha and omega. That's unusual. Most tenth-century inscriptions were in Latin. There's a kind of monogram as well—interlacing letters, it looks like an *I* and an *O*, maybe an *H*. Hard to see. You were never at this place before, Niall?"

Dawson glanced away. "As I said, I was only here briefly. Had to get back to Dublin."

"Listen, we can come back to that carving later," Nora said. "Remember why we're here."

They spread out and began to search, poking through the tall grass that grew up through the floor of the chapel and all around the exterior. Nora spied the open door to the round tower and stepped inside. The tower had no roof, but a piece of blue tarp material was secured to the wall to make a kind of shelter inside. Somebody had been here, and fairly recently, too. Nora knelt and found a plastic carrier bag under one corner of the tarp. Inside the bag were a few items of clothing for a young child. If Deirdre were running away, why would she not go back to Killowen Farm, where she obviously felt safe? Or perhaps Deirdre and the baby weren't running at all but had been taken away by force—an especially frightening possibility if Deirdre had seen the person who killed her father.

"It looks like they might have been here," Nora said, rejoining the others. "I found a bag in the tower, with some baby clothes and some extra nappies."

"Look at this." Cormac pointed to several cigarette butts on the ground next to a crushed packet. "Silk Cut. That's Anca's brand, isn't it, Shawn?"

Shawn Kearney turned to him. "How do you know that?"

"I'll spare you the long story. We know she's still here somewhere. The real question is, why are you all pretending otherwise?"

Shawn stared at the ground. "Anca's been hiding out. I'm sure you've read stories in the papers about the Romanian gangs and what they do to young women, promising them good jobs here and then forcing them into prostitution. The people who brought Anca to Ireland were into all sorts of things—not just prostitution, but cigarette smuggling, identity theft. It's a huge operation. Anca was so afraid of what would happen if they ever found out where she was, and she was our friend, so of course we hid her. You'd have done the same."

Nora turned to Niall Dawson. His face betrayed a greater degree of concern than one might expect from someone who didn't even remember the girl. A quick glance at Cormac told her that he'd seen it, too.

"Let's leave everything here just as we found it," Nora said. "I don't think there's any way around it, Shawn. You'll have to tell the Guards what you know. They'll protect Anca."

"Can they protect her? You have no idea how much money is involved. That makes it impossible to trust anyone, even the police."

"There's also Deirdre and her child to think about," Nora reminded her. "I'm afraid we have no choice, Shawn. We have to call this in."

Shawn Kearney turned away with a frustrated sigh. "Do what you have to do."

As they waited for Cusack and her team to arrive at the chapel, Niall Dawson was standing a few yards apart, speaking to Shawn Kearney. Cormac moved closer to Nora and lowered his voice. "I haven't told Cusack about what I heard last night at Beglan's place, about Anca. I don't know why—"

"Because of Niall? He has been acting strangely, I'll admit."

"There's something he's not told us about that girl, Anca. You must have seen his reaction when you mentioned her at the dinner table, and just now. I didn't have a chance to tell you before, but I saw him going back into his room after that episode with my father last night. It was close to four in the morning, Nora. I'm not sure what to do."

"Can you talk to him?"

"There's something else, too. When we found Vincent Claffey this morning, he had a handful of those gallnuts in his mouth."

"You're not serious."

Cormac glanced over at Niall and Shawn Kearney, still deep in conversation. "I am. And I can't help asking myself who could have known that detail about Kavanagh's body, apart from the people with access to the excavation site."

Nora considered what he was saying. "So, the Garda contingent and the coroner's crew, Dr. Friel, the two of us—and Niall."

"That's it. You see, maybe Claffey's murder was a warning to anyone else who might consider making threats. I want to get you and Eliana and my father away from here."

"But surely we're in no danger, Cormac. You and I know nothing." She considered for a moment. "Well, next to nothing . . . very little, anyway."

"Do you see what I mean? Every minute we stay, we learn more and more. We may be gaining knowledge completely by accident, but that doesn't make it any less dangerous."

"And what about our work here? All the things we're finding out about our bog man, the satchel, and the wax tablet."

"Yes, of course that's all very important, but, Nora—"

She took his hand. "We'll be fine, Cormac, really. Rest easy. Nothing will happen."

Dr. Friel was just stitching up the Y incision on Vincent Claffey's chest when Stella joined her in the mortuary.

"Another tongue cleaved down the middle, I'm afraid—postmortem again. And those were in his mouth." Catherine Friel glanced down at the metal tray resting at her elbow, which held five dark brown objects that Stella now recognized as oak galls. "One fewer than Mr. Kavanagh had; I don't know if that's significant. Have you found out what they are?"

"Dr. Gavin said they're gallnuts—they grow on oak trees, apparently. Still not clear what they mean. Any fix on the cause of death?"

"Blunt force trauma. He either fell or was on the receiving end of a pretty vicious blow to the back of the head. Fractured the occipital bone. He was at least incapacitated—most likely dead already—before he was wrapped in the cling film and placed on that conveyer belt." Dr. Friel kept stitching. "It's all in my report."

"What about time of death?"

"From the core temperature and onset of rigor, I'd say he was killed in the wee hours, somewhere between one and five A.M."

Stella's phone rang as she stood at the table. It was Molloy.

"One of the search parties found a bag with some baby togs and a few nappies at a ruined chapel not far from Killowen. We haven't found the girl yet, but here's a new twist: she may be traveling with a Romanian national, Anca Popescu. This girl, Anca, was working at Killowen for the past nine months, but when you turned up asking questions about Kavanagh, Claire Finnerty and the others told everyone she'd left weeks ago."

"How do you know she's still around?"

"Maguire overheard her at Anthony Beglan's place last night. And we found some recently smoked butts and an empty packet of her brand of cigarettes here at the chapel."

Why had Cormac Maguire neglected to mention any details about the Romanian girl when they spoke this morning at the Claffey place? Too many people connected to this case were keeping secrets.

The baby's anguished cry cut through the quiet forest. All other noise seemed muffled by the soft green moss at their feet. Deirdre stumbled, struggling to keep up with Anca, who was forging ahead through whipping branches of undergrowth. A thin branch brushed the child's face, and he howled louder. Deirdre said, "He's hungry, Anca. I've got to stop and feed him. He'll only cry harder if I don't."

"All right," Anca said, pulling up short. "But not too long. We have to keep moving."

Deirdre settled into the mossy crook of a massive oak tree, hitched up her T-shirt, and put the baby to her breast. The split in her lip throbbed. "Where are we going, Anca? Why do we have to keep on? I'm so tired."

"Because . . . because we have to, that's all." Anca looked desperate for a fag, but she'd run out back at the chapel.

"Can't we just go back to Killowen? They'd feed us and look after us—"

"No, we can't go back!" Anca's voice was rising. "The police are everywhere." She clasped her arms around her, as if they were crawling all over her.

"But we've no place to go." Deirdre's voice quavered.

"Be quiet! I don't want to hear about it." Anca covered her ears with both hands and continued pacing back and forth in front of the tree. "Don't talk to me. You had to get away from your father, and I—" She dropped her hands and pulled the sleeves of her jumper over her balled fists. There was something strange going on, Deirdre thought. Something Anca wasn't telling her.

She'd been fast asleep last night when Anca came into her room. *Get up*, she said, *we have to go. Be quick about it and don't make any noise.* So Deirdre had gathered up some clothes and a few nappies in a couple of carrier bags, and they'd set out across the fields in darkness. It was no use asking what happened; the few times she'd tried, Anca had got very angry. Deirdre didn't want to make trouble. Anca was the only friend she'd ever had, so she had kept quiet and followed along. But now she was beginning to feel frightened. She'd never seen Anca so upset. They'd gone as far as the chapel and waited there for first light. Deirdre looked at her friend now. The mascara had gone all splodgy around Anca's eyes, and she looked like she'd kill for a cigarette. Cal seemed to catch their restlessness, pulling at Deirdre's hair as he nursed. Why hadn't she thought to bring him anything to eat? She reached for the handle of her carrier bags and realized that she'd only one. Where was the other? She had no nappies at all if she'd lost that other bag, and Cal would be needing a change very soon.

They'd have to turn around and go back to Killowen. Why didn't Anca want to go there? Deirdre knew her father might get angry and drag her home again like he had last night, but Claire and Diarmuid did say she could come to them whenever she needed a place to stay. Her da wasn't that bad, really. Mad as a snake, right enough, but he'd never hit her. Well, never before last night, anyway. And she had gone against him, after he warned her more than once about going to the farm. He said again last night that Claire and her crowd were not to be trusted, that he was just looking out for her, and maybe he was. Hard to tell sometimes who exactly he was looking out for. She looked over at her friend, stripping the bark off a thin branch. There was something wrong. Why wouldn't Anca look at her?

"Did you see my da last night?" Deirdre asked. "Did you speak to him?" Anca just glared straight ahead and continued breaking bits of dry bark from the stick and pegging them at the ground. "Does he know where I am?"

Anca threw down her half-stripped branch. "Stop talking about him! Why do you care about him, anyway? Look at your face! He gave you that, didn't he?"

"He never did it before."

"So that makes it all right?" Anca made a face as if she'd swallowed something that was shredding her insides. She gripped her stomach as the words burst from her lips: "You don't know what he was doing, how he was using you, and Cal." She buried her head in her arms.

Deirdre felt cold all over. The baby stopped nursing and pulled away. She looked down at him and watched his mouth make a perfect O before his loud wail pierced her eardrums. She tried to soothe him, patting his back and murmuring little comforts. He always got an air bubble, that's all it was. An air bubble. If she only walked him and rubbed his back, it would go away, stop bothering him. She climbed to her feet, trying to keep the child balanced on her hip.

They were deep in the oak wood now, the far side, no place she recognized. She had played in this wood as a little girl and had never been afraid, but now there seemed to be strange noises around them, shadows stealing up from all sides. What did Anca mean, that her father was using them?

All at once Deirdre found herself running through the woods, Cal bouncing heavily on her hip. She didn't know which way to turn, so she just kept running. The baby had stopped crying, his arms tightening about her neck as she ran. She could hear someone behind her, crackling noises of branches breaking, feet pounding the earth, and heavy breathing, but she dared not stop or even look back.

8

Mairéad Broome answered the door to Stella this time. Her face looked pallid, as if all emotion had been wrung out of her over the past several days. Seeing who it was, she left the door open but turned and walked away. Stella stepped into the sitting room. The cottage was slowly taking on the look of a squat, with cups and plates, clothing strewn about, along with a few empty wine bottles. It was as if the two people living here had given up on appearances and surrendered to whatever was troubling them.

Mairéad Broome said nothing, sinking onto the sofa and pulling her loose jumper close about her. A cigarette burned in the ashtray beside her on the table, next to a nearly empty wineglass.

Graham Healy came in from the other room. "Why are you here, Detective? We've told you everything we know."

"Forgive me, but that's not quite true, is it now? It's actually you I've come to see, Mr. Healy," Stella said. "I had a question about your conversation with Vincent Claffey yesterday afternoon."

The young man's face betrayed his alarm, but Mairéad Broome's voice broke in before he could answer. "Graham did have a brief conversation with Vincent Claffey after we arrived here. What about it?"

No immediate denial, then. Stella kept her focus on Healy, who was clearly unnerved. "You were seen passing Mr. Claffey a brown envelope. I have to ask you what was inside."

Healy hesitated, thinking.

"Our witness said it was quite obviously a transaction. Mr. Claffey took a thick envelope from you, said he needed more time to think about what you were asking—I think those were the words he used—and then he rode off on his motorbike." Cusack considered her bargaining position. She really had nothing beyond Dr. Gavin's statement that would compel this suspect to say any more. Not yet, anyway. "So what were you asking of him? Shall I tell you what I think?"

Mairéad Broome leaned forward in her chair, her mouth set in a grim line. "You don't have to say anything, Graham."

"I've been imagining all the possibilities, why you'd be paying off Vincent Claffey. For instance, what he might have known about the two of you that would be worth a significant amount of cash."

"I've told you, Detective, neither Graham nor I had anything to do with my husband's death. I can't help it if you don't believe me, but that's the truth."

Healy's eyes grew defiant. "If you need to know what was in the envelope, why don't you ask Claffey?"

"I certainly would, except for one small detail—he's dead."

Mairéad Broome looked up. "What? How?"

"His body was discovered this morning. He was murdered."

Graham Healy's mouth dropped open, but no words came out.

Stella continued, "So I have to ask where each of you were between the hours of one and five o'clock this morning."

"We were here." Mairéad Broome's voice was adamant. "We stayed in all night. And as far as the contents of that envelope are concerned, Graham was acting on my behalf, Detective. Vincent Claffey had done some work for me, and—"

"What sort of work?"

"Pardon me?"

Stella repeated: "I asked what sort of work he did for you."

"Odds and ends, mostly, framing and stretching canvases, that sort of thing."

Stella turned to Healy. "I thought those sorts of jobs were handled by your assistant."

"They are, usually, but Graham's got a lot on his plate at the moment, dealing with galleries and all the exhibition planning. Things have been busy lately, so we needed some help with . . . some of the more basic tasks. And Vincent Claffey always needed money."

"So you're quite certain it wasn't blackmail? I understand that Claffey was here last night, making threats. He claimed to know the secrets of everyone here at Killowen. I presumed that might include yourselves."

"If that's true, we've heard nothing about it. I told you, we've been here at the cottage since we arrived."

"I probably ought to inform you as well that Claffey's daughter and grandson have gone missing. You wouldn't happen to know anything about that?"

"Deirdre and the baby are missing? Since when?"

Stella thought she detected a note of increased tension in Mairéad Broome's voice. "All we know is that she was gone when her father's body was discovered. We're searching for her and the child now."

"You have to find them, Detective! It's bad enough that she should have that odious man for a father—"

"Mairéad." Healy shot an imploring look.

"I can't help it, Graham. He was. I'm not sorry he's dead."

Stella's phone pipped. "Cusack here."

Molloy sounded breathless. "We've got them, Stella. The two girls and the child. They're all right. Uniform are bringing them in."

Stella felt a surge of relief. "Where were they?"

"Just the other side of the oak wood at Killowen. Like you said, they hadn't got very far. Had to keep stopping to feed the child, to keep him quiet."

Stella turned around to find Mairéad Broome's gaze fixed on her.

"Was that news about Deirdre? Is she all right?"

Stella decided to probe further. "She's physically fine. But I am concerned. I mean, if the girl happened to witness what happened to her father, or if she were somehow involved—"

"*Involved?* For God's sake, Detective, she's a child."

"Old enough to have a child of her own," Stella said. Mairéad Broome turned away abruptly, as if she'd been slapped. There was some deep, unspoken link here, but what was it? Stella filed this information away, next to Deirdre Claffey's reaction to news of Benedict Kavanagh's death. "We discovered that Deirdre was traveling in the company of a Romanian girl, Anca Popescu. What do you know about her?"

"Not a lot. She's been living here for the past year or so, working as Martin Gwynne's apprentice. He'd know more about the girl, you can ask him."

"I have a few more questions, about your husband's visit to this area," Stella said. "We've found the B and B where he was staying when he disappeared; some of his personal effects were still there. You've no idea what he was doing in this part of the country?"

"Not the foggiest."

"Did he know that you were a regular visitor at Killowen?"

"I sincerely doubt it. He didn't really pay me that much notice."

"Doesn't it seem odd that he'd come to this remote, rural area—to a place that you happened to frequent—and that his visit had nothing whatever to do with you?"

"Lots of things seem odd, Detective, when examined under a microscope. The only thing my husband was interested in was his research."

"But he never happened to mention a connection to Killowen? What about Faddan More?"

"As I told you back in Dublin, he mentioned a breakthrough, but he offered no details. All I can think is that he was interested in medieval manuscripts, and this place was once a monastery . . ." Her voice trailed off, as if she'd just realized something significant, but the recovery was swift. "Then again, this whole bloody country is peppered with monastic ruins. I have no idea what brought my husband here. I wish I did."

"All right, let me ask you this: in your husband's belongings, we found a few interesting items. There was a gold cross with an inscription, *From Mum*. Not familiar to either of you?"

"No."

"There were also some handwritten notes. In one of them your husband mentioned a person—at least I'm assuming it's a person—with the initials *IOH*. Do those letters mean anything to you?"

Mairéad Broome gave a short, bitter laugh in reply. "Only the object of my husband's affections, my nemesis—my only true rival."

Not quite the answer she was expecting, Stella had to admit. "You're saying that your husband and this IOH were involved?"

A tiny, cryptic smile played across Mairéad Broome's features. "That's a good word for it—involved. Most definitely."

"In that case, I'll need to speak to—"

Mairéad Broome cut her off. "That won't be possible, I'm afraid, since he's been dead for a thousand years. I am sorry, Detective, I've been toying with you. The initials belong to the ninth-century philosopher my husband studied. It was more than just study, if you want the truth. Benedict was completely besotted with the man—his intellectual hero, the great mind he tried to emulate. I know that level of devotion is hard to understand; in my experience, it seems to be a disease peculiar to academics."

"So the manuscripts he consulted—"

"—were all to do with Eriugena, yes. He was obsessed."

Stella paused for a moment. *Eriugena.* That name from Kavanagh's papers again. Someone else had mentioned it as well—Martin Gwynne and the conference in Toronto. "How do you get Eriugena from the initials *IOH?*"

"That was evidently how the man signed his work. Don't ask me why. I don't know."

Stella's mind returned to the handwritten note mentioning IOH and his great unfinished work. "Do you think your husband's remarks about turning the world of philosophy on its ear had something to do with this . . . Eriugena?" Stella nearly stumbled over the strange name.

"John Scottus Eriugena, John the Scot—call him what you like. Everything Benedict did had something to do with that bloody man. I'm sick to death of hearing his name."

9

At a quarter past three in the afternoon, Cormac and Niall Dawson returned to the excavation site. With the discovery of the wax tablet in Killowen Man's garments, it became vitally important to search for other any other associated artifacts.

Cormac stood at the edge of the cutaway with his clipboard and pencil, ready to climb down into the pit. Niall had been silent and withdrawn since they'd discovered Vincent Claffey's body.

Cormac knew this moment was his best chance to excavate the past, as it were, to begin turning up whatever his friend was hiding. He took a deep breath.

"Niall, I've no wish to pry, but you've not been yourself these past few days. You flinch at the mention of this Romanian girl, Anca; you're wandering about at all hours of the night. I saw you coming back to your room, Niall, it was nearly four in the morning. I haven't said anything to Detective Cusack because I wanted to get your side of the story first."

From the length of the pause before Dawson spoke, Cormac surmised that his friend was wrestling with a heavy conscience. "If I tell you what's happening, can I count on your discretion?" Dawson asked.

"Of course."

"My visit here in April was in connection with a treasure-hunting investigation for the Antiquities Task Force. No one at Killowen knew the real reason I was here. I received an anonymous tip about someone poking about, a ring of treasure hunters operating in this area. Sometimes it's a group of amateurs with metal detectors, sometimes it's professionals who've identified a particular artifact or group of artifacts from the records about a site. It happened that this group, according to the caller, was looking for an old manuscript. Then, only a day later, and apparently out of the blue, I got Shawn Kearney's call about the stylus. That gave me an easy excuse to come down and have a look around."

"Your tipster didn't happen to say who it was, poking about?"

"No names were mentioned."

"You're saying a disembodied voice on the phone told you that someone was digging up this little corner of Tipperary searching for an ancient book?"

"Sounds completely daft, I know, but that's about the size of it."

"But surely the phone records—"

"The call came in on the museum's main line, and you know yourself, our system is so antiquated there's no way to tell where it was coming from. And I didn't think to record anything."

"What about Benedict Kavanagh? Did you know he was in the locality when you arrived?"

"I hadn't a clue, but of course I can't prove that. I've spent the last two days trying to work out whether he might have been involved with the treasure hunters. Kavanagh had a very particular field of study, you see, the Neoplatonist philosophers of the late ninth century, and one man in particular, John Scottus Eriugena. It did make sense that if Kavanagh was here, it had something to do with his work on Eriugena."

Frankly, this wasn't at all what Cormac had been expecting to hear. "So you think these treasure hunters have got something to do with his murder?"

"That's what I've been trying to work out. Without access to any of Kavanagh's papers, I haven't been able to crack what his connection might have been to Killowen. So I started reading up on his man, Eriugena. It's a bit insane—we're talking about someone who was born around 815 A.D., apparently educated in Ireland. He went to France to run the palace school for Charles the Bald, the Holy Roman Emperor, around 845. But the most interesting detail I found about Eriugena was his reputation as a Greek scholar."

The import of what Dawson was saying took a moment to sink in. Cormac flashed back to the Greek words on the wax tablet, the figure in the chapel doorway holding a tablet with the letters alpha and omega. "You think there might be some sort of connection between this Eriugena and our bog man?"

"I don't know. What I'm saying is that we need to find out more about him. It's tempting to jump to conclusions, but we have to do our work and see where it leads."

"I still don't see what any of this has to do with Kavanagh being murdered."

"Eriugena's work was his singular obsession," Dawson said. "Bene-

dict Kavanagh would have paid any price to get his hands on information about the man, something no one else knew. Suppose the treasure
hunters came across new evidence, something they realized Kavanagh
would pay for, and something went awry in the transaction. Suppose he
wouldn't pay, or threatened to expose their operation. That's sufficient
motive for murder, don't you think?"

"Wait a minute, how would they know to contact Kavanagh?"

"If you're stealing ancient manuscripts, you've got to be something
of an expert at what you're doing. To know what they're worth, who'd
pay for them. Treasure hunters are not your garden variety thieves. They
have to understand enough about the potential market to know which
pieces will fetch a good price."

"What sort of 'new evidence' about Eriugena were you imagining?"

"Well, look, we've already got a stylus, a wax tablet, a satchel, but
what haven't we found? Something you'd expect to find with all those
other artifacts that we still haven't got our hands on?" Dawson's voice
had taken on a kind of fevered urgency.

"Well, a manuscript."

"Exactly! We've found the body of a murdered scribe, his wax tablet,
and very likely his stylus and satchel, but there's no sign of any book so
far. Maybe his book survived, or was stolen for some reason."

"You're not making sense, Niall. Whoever killed Kavanagh wouldn't
have known there was an ancient body in the bog until he dug the cutout for the car. The satchel and tablet were found with the ancient body.
The stylus was the only artifact that turned up here before we arrived.
It's just not tracking."

"I know. I know it's not making perfect sense, but I'm convinced that
we're on to something here. Can you not feel it?"

"Maybe. But you're avoiding my real question. None of this explains
where you were last night, Niall. Where were you until four in the morning? It's something to do with that girl, isn't it? With Anca."

Niall Dawson's face fell. His hands moved nervously. "I know it
doesn't look good, with what happened to Claffey. That's the reason I
haven't said anything, to you or to Cusack."

"It also doesn't look good to be covering things up. Surely you see
that."

Dawson rubbed his forehead, frustrated. He began to pace. "All right.

I went to try and find Anca. I just needed to talk to her. She wasn't at Beglan's place, so I went to Claffey's."

"Why did you need to speak to her? And why look for her there?"

"Just let me tell you what happened, all right? It'll all become clear soon enough. When I got to Claffey's place, he was already dead. I didn't see anyone else. But here's the thing, Cormac—he wasn't up on that machine when I found him. He was on the floor, and there was blood." Dawson pointed to the back of his neck. "It looked as if he'd fallen and hit his head on an old engine block up against the wall. I didn't know what to do. I suppose I panicked. I just wanted to get the hell away from there as quick as I could. I headed straight back to my room at Killowen. Couldn't close my eyes after that. I kept seeing his face, those eyes staring at me."

"So there was no cling film, no gallnuts in his mouth?"

"No, no, none of that. He was definitely dead, though. If there had been any chance to save him, I would have rung for the ambulance straightaway. You do believe me, don't you?"

"Why are you so jumpy when anybody mentions the girl?"

Dawson ran a hand through his hair, even more agitated now. "There are a few more bits I haven't told you, unfortunately. About Anca. How she and I—"

"You had an affair with the girl?"

"No, no, not an affair. God, how I hate that word. It was just sex, and only the one time. I can't even explain why it happened. I love Gráinne, Cormac. She's the mother of my children. You know I'd never purposely do anything to hurt her. I've never been unfaithful, until that one fleeting moment of . . . I was at the chapel, and Anca was there, too, and we got talking. She seemed so . . . so alone, so fragile. I suppose it sounds stupid to say that I felt sorry for her. I can't even tell you what happened. It was just this brief moment of delusion or connection or both, and then it was over and done with and forgotten." Dawson ran both hands through his hair again. "Until the photographs started showing up in the post."

Cormac's thoughts raced back to Claffey's threats at the supper table. *I know your secrets*, he'd said, the small, dark eyes drilling into every one of them. He winced. "Jesus, Niall, you were set up."

"I know that now. The photos were taken from that tower at the chapel. I realized it as soon as I saw them. But don't you understand, even if it was a setup, that doesn't absolve me. And it didn't mean that Vincent Claffey couldn't ruin my marriage, destroy my family. I didn't know what to do except pay him off. I couldn't risk him saying anything to Gráinne. But I never killed him, Cormac. I wished him dead, so many times over, but I never . . . I swear to you on the lives of my children—I am not a killer."

"But, Niall, if they've found the girl, Anca, all this is bound to come out. There's no way to stop it."

"Help me." Dawson's eyes pleaded. "I can't think what to do. Everything's falling asunder."

Cormac took a moment, considering. He thought of Niall's wife, Gráinne, his three lovely children, all the hours he and Niall had spent playing music together at sessions, all the meals and countless bottles of wine he'd shared in the Dawsons' back garden, and the sight that always affected him, his friend's arm slung around Gráinne or one of the children. Niall stared at the ground, his shoulders sagging.

"If Vincent Claffey was blackmailing you, how likely was it that he was holding things over other people as well?"

Dawson's head lifted suddenly. "Yes, if we could just work out who *did* kill Claffey and Kavanagh, none of this ever need come out."

"I'm not sure about that," Cormac said. "But perhaps we can stop you being the focus of the investigation. Back up and tell me again about this tip you got about the treasure hunters."

Dawson took a deep breath and pulled himself together. "The caller was a man. He seemed to *know* things."

"What did he say, exactly?"

"That there was some illegal activity going on around Killowen that might bear looking into."

"You're sure the caller mentioned Killowen by name?"

"Yes. Made sure I knew it was Tipperary he was talking about and not some other Killowen."

"And Shawn Kearney's news about the stylus came the very next day—that didn't strike you as odd?"

"Of course it did. But when I arrived, she seemed forthcoming about what they were finding. Her license was up to date, and she had her whole excavation very well documented."

"And Shawn didn't seem worried about security?"

"Apparently not. She never mentioned it to me."

"I don't like to cast aspersions, but how can you be so sure of Shawn Kearney's honesty? There's no way, for instance, she could be in league with the treasure hunters, perhaps accidentally left something out of her report?"

"She'd have had to enlist the cooperation of everyone at Killowen— they were all helping with the excavation. Everyone living there would be complicit in the lie."

"And that's not possible?"

"I honestly don't know. A lot of our business depends upon trust. You know we can't possibly keep an eye on all the sites that need monitoring, so we have to hope that national pride can overcome baser instincts."

"If we could just figure out what Kavanagh was doing here," Cormac said. "You know more about his work than I do, and you think he wouldn't have come here except for some new discovery about this philosopher, Eriugena. He couldn't have had any other motivation—his wife being here, for instance?"

"But that's just it—she wasn't here at that time. There were no visiting artists during the excavation and construction those last two weeks of April. They only let me stay because I convinced them that I was used to rough conditions."

"What could have made Kavanagh drop everything and rush out here? And doesn't it seem like there are only a few people in the world who would have understood the sort of information he'd be interested in? So the question is, who around here knows a thing or two about old manuscripts? What about Gwynne? Shawn mentioned him as the resident expert, but he's only a calligrapher, isn't he?"

"Try paleographer with a degree in medieval history from Cambridge."

"I can't believe you haven't mentioned it before now. Why the hell is he working out here in the back of beyond and not at some great university?"

"He used to work at the British Library. I gather that he left under some sort of cloud, but I haven't had time to find out what it was. I dread prying into people's personal lives."

"We might have to pry, if we're to save you from becoming a suspect. You've got to come clean to Cusack, tell her that Claffey was blackmailing you, and why, that you and Kavanagh were friends at university. And you have to tell Gráinne what's going on. You have to do it, Niall. Can you really justify keeping this from her when it's bound to come out? That would be even more hurtful. She loves you. You have to trust her."

Dawson swallowed hard. "It could all go pear shaped."

"Tell her the truth. It won't."

Niall Dawson was still trying to convince himself. "Gráinne first, then Cusack."

"You're a decent man, Niall."

"A decent man doesn't end up making a fuckin' bollocks of everything." Dawson held his gaze for a few seconds, then climbed up out of the pit. He looked down at Cormac from the bank. "I can't just ring her. I've got to go home. I don't know when I'll be back—it'll depend on what happens."

"Go, then. Don't worry about me. I'll carry on here, and I can walk back to the farm."

Watching Niall Dawson's disconsolate posture as he trudged across the overgrown bog, Cormac felt a twinge of guilt, having urged his friend to come clean. Some things between people were better not said.

10

The house was empty when Nora returned to Killowen. She headed to the kitchen to work on her report about Killowen Man, curling herself onto a short sofa with camera and laptop. Time to concentrate on work.

But all the events of the past few days had her head in a muddle, especially after seeing Cormac's anxiety about staying here.

Nora had felt enormous relief when word came that Deirdre Claffey and her baby had been found. They all should have stood up to Vincent Claffey last night, kept him from taking his daughter away. He might still be alive if they had just found a way to resist. And what would become of Anca? She was probably not much older than Deirdre. Impossible to know how bad things had been for Anca at home, that she'd had to seek a better life here.

Nora shook herself, trying to clear these thoughts out of her head. There was nothing she could do to help right now. Better to stop worrying and just stick to her work. She pulled the memory card from her camera and slid it into her laptop to begin downloading the new pictures of Killowen Man, the ones they had taken this morning with the textile expert.

The first images were shots of the stab wounds in Killowen Man's chest. She clicked through the pictures, pulling descriptive details: the visible pores in his brown skin, the size and placement of the wounds. From all these elements she could begin to weave at least a fragmented story for an unknown, fragmented murder victim. He did have a name, once.

Looking at close-ups of the gashes that had allowed a man's lifeblood to escape, Nora suddenly felt the spark of vitality that had once been in the form before her. She felt the man's pulse, his breath inside her, along with the fierce burst of mingled fear and joy that must have seized him at the very instant that he merged with the infinite. All at once, the letters on that stone carving on the chapel loomed forward in her consciousness. Alpha and omega. The beginning and the end. Nora found she couldn't breathe. She reached forward and snapped the computer shut.

She pushed the laptop away from her, and as she did so, her elbow brushed against a tweed throw that someone had left tossed casually over the arm of the sofa. She looked down to see the corner of a Moleskine notebook peeping out from under the dark woolen fringe. Her curiosity aroused, Nora opened the cover to discover whose book this might be. It was a journal. The writing was small, compact, and in a female hand, it seemed—and in Spanish, which perhaps answered her question. Was this the sad story that Eliana had been reading on the evening they arrived? Nora tried to recall whether the book she'd seen in the girl's room had a yellow cover like this. She scanned a few phrases at the top of the page: . . . *y la forma en que me mira . . . A veces parece que diga el nombre de mi madre, pero quizás es sólo por accidente.* Something about an accident? She could read the letters, but the words themselves formed a cipher, a code she could not crack.

She heard someone coming. She quickly closed the cover and slipped the journal back into its cushioned crevice.

It was Claire Finnerty.

"Wonderful news, that they found Deirdre and the baby," Nora said.

"Yes, a great relief. We're all very glad to know they're safe."

"And Anca as well," Nora said.

Claire threw her a suspicious look. "Yes."

"I don't blame you for trying to keep her name out of the investigation, telling us that she'd left. Shawn gave us the whole story this afternoon."

Claire Finnerty swung around to face Nora full on. "Did she, now?"

"We found Anca's cigarettes during the search. Shawn had to tell us. She said you were trying to protect the girl. I think that's commendable."

Claire offered no response.

"It's hard to know what to do, sometimes, to protect people." Nora knew she was in danger of overstepping, but she couldn't seem to stop herself. "Maybe last night wasn't the first time you'd seen Deirdre's father treat her that way. But I know what it's like, not having any legal standing to intervene—"

"Please stop, just stop talking!" Claire Finnerty was grasping the edge of the sink. Her voice sounded strangled. After a long moment, she turned and fled the kitchen, leaving the water running over some salad greens.

Nora turned off the tap. She shouldn't have pushed Claire so hard just to satisfy her own curiosity. And yet, recalling the shock and anger in the faces around the dinner table, she was sure that her memory wasn't mistaken. It had been Claire Finnerty insisting that they find a way to get Deirdre Claffey away from her father. Someone had found a way, but perhaps it wasn't what Claire had in mind.

Joseph and Eliana came ambling up to the kitchen through the courtyard garden. Both of them had witnessed the scene at dinner last night, but as far as Nora knew, they were still ignorant of Vincent Claffey's death. Better if they were spared the details. The way Cormac's father had clung to Eliana's hand after Claffey's outburst last night—you could read it as a protective gesture. Was that what was going on later on as well, when the girl was in his room? *He didn't want me to leave,* she'd said. Was he afraid Vincent Claffey would come back to Killowen? Cormac had the same protective streak as his father, which could be maddening at times, but it was also oddly reassuring. And Cormac probably had no idea where he'd picked up that character trait.

"Time to wash up for supper," Eliana was saying to Joseph, letting go of his arm. "Would you like to rest a minute here before we go upstairs?"

Nora saw Eliana check under the throw on the sofa and slip the yellow notebook out between the cushions and into her bag.

"I'll take him to get washed up, Eliana, if you'd like a break before supper," Nora said. She motioned Eliana a short distance away so that Joseph might not overhear their conversation.

"Did you have a good day?" Nora asked.

Eliana glanced at her briefly. "Yes, everything is fine today. We were studying these cards—what do you call them?"

"Flash cards."

"Yes, the flash cards. He likes the pictures, but he gets eh . . . nervous?" She tried to find the proper way to express it.

"Flustered? Or perhaps you mean frustrated?"

"Yes, that's it—*frustrated.* I try to tell him he will learn the words again. That it will take patience."

"That's true," Nora said. She glanced over at Joseph, who seemed to be nodding off in his corner of the sofa. "I wanted to ask if there's anything more that Cormac and I could be doing to help you."

Eliana's eyes flicked away nervously. "I hope I am doing the right things . . ."

"You're doing great work, Eliana. He seems to enjoy the time spent with you." Nora reached up to give the girl's shoulder a squeeze. "I want to make sure you know that we're here, both Cormac and myself, if you have questions about anything, or just want to talk." Eliana nodded without looking up. "Now, a little time off."

"I don't need it."

"I insist," Nora said. "I can stay with Joseph, and you can do whatever you'd like to do."

Eliana looked doubtful. "You're certain?"

"Yes, go and enjoy yourself."

Eliana rose slowly from her chair and headed for the stairs, not visibly cheered by the prospect of time to herself. This reluctance to leave Joseph was becoming a pattern. A worrisome pattern, if she were honest.

Nora turned back to find that Joseph had cracked one eye open. He'd been watching them the whole time, the sly old devil. "Narb a fisking torrit," he said, drawing his hand over his face. "Her fox, it's a looken peas. Peas." He shook his head and with one hand seemed to bat the words away, a gesture that said he knew what was happening and was buggered if he could do anything about it. Here he was, back at the peas again. That was the way this thing seemed to work; he'd make steady forward progress and then would come a sort of verbal hiccup, and he'd drop back to where he'd been a week ago. Back with the vegetables.

"I think Eliana's all right," Nora said. "Probably just a bit homesick."

He looked puzzled.

"Missing her family, you know."

He looked at her with such a fixed stare that she wondered if he understood.

"Neary, shows a brick." He put his palms together, then opened them like a book. Like an endless game of charades, Nora thought, and he can't even tell us when we've guessed right. "A brick," he said, and made the book gesture again.

"A book?" She exaggerated the O shape of her lips, trying to show him. "What is it about a book?"

"Hermakes a voil." Here he scooped one hand, as if to say, *Come here*, and she moved closer. "No! A voil in it, a spog, a spogget." Beads of sweat were beginning to form on his forehead, as if the effort of making oneself understood was hard physical work. She searched his face for hints, clues to the meanings he was going for, to no avail. He definitely had something to tell her, perhaps something important. That was the trouble—no way to know.

"Bollocks," he muttered.

"Now *that* I understand," Nora said. "And you'll forgive me if I concur."

11

Cormac looked up from his work in the cutaway. He was digging directly below the spot where they'd found the satchel, hoping there might be a few more clues buried in the peat. Killowen Man's brooch was still unaccounted for, not to mention the contents of his satchel. The likeliest scenario was that both the books and the brooch were stolen by the assassins who had stuck their blades into Killowen Man's belly.

It was nearly five; Niall had probably made it back to Dublin by now. Cormac tried mightily not to think about Gráinne Dawson's reaction, not to feel in his own gut the punch his friend was about to deliver at home. He had never been married, so how could he possibly know what it was like? Surely a true marriage required a certain acceptance of all the shades of human complexity; to deny imperfection, or to allow a momentary weakness to undo years of connection seemed extraordinarily severe. And yet what would his reaction be if Nora came to him with a similar story to Niall's, not a long-term affair but giving in to a brief flash of desire? He looked down at his feet, stuck into wellingtons that seemed to be melting into the wet peat, and realized that he was still standing on shifting ground. Was there nothing solid at the bottom of it all? After a full year together, he found himself still craving assurances that Nora, no matter how desperately he loved her, might never be able to provide.

He started packing up his tools. They hadn't had any security out here since the crime scene detail left, and now he wondered if they should ask the Guards to post someone on site overnight. That's when treasure hunters usually did their work, going over sites with their outlawed metal detectors.

Niall's anonymous tipster had mentioned a manuscript. The real question was whether there was a manuscript, or whether the tipster only wanted to draw the National Museum's attention to Killowen. The stylus was discovered a few days before Benedict Kavanagh went missing and just before Niall had received the tipster's call. Considering Vincent

Claffey's obsession with rewards, could he have been the anonymous voice on the phone? Not likely that Shawn Kearney and the others at Killowen would have kept Claffey posted on their excavation, given the frosty relations between them. Then again, Claffey seemed to have no problem spying on people. He should have asked Niall a few more questions: what sort of accent the caller had, the exact language he had used.

As Cormac stood in the cutaway, he heard someone moving through the scrubby birch saplings at the bog's edge. A strong, low voice carried over the heather: "How, hi, hi, how!" Anthony Beglan carried a thin hazel rod as he drove his cattle home from the pasture beside the bog. Cormac could see only the top half of Beglan's body and the tip of the hazel. He had to struggle to make out the language—not English, that was certain, nor Irish. Straining to hear, he climbed up out of the cutaway, trying to follow without being detected, safely screened behind the saplings at the edge of the road.

Every language had its own music, Cormac thought, tuning his ears to the sound. If it wasn't English or Irish, what were the possibilities, logically speaking? The sound was almost like Italian, or perhaps Beglan had begun to learn a few words of Romanian from the girl he'd been hiding in his house.

When they reached his farm, Beglan penned the cattle and slipped the leather strap from the basket over his head. Cormac followed at a distance. The rank smell he'd noticed the other night was stronger now and seemed to be coming from the shed across the haggard, a low building with a corrugated fiberglass roof.

Beglan crossed to an open lean-to against the shed, where he took an eel from his basket. Cormac looked away as Beglan held a nail to the creature's head, and he flinched as the first hammer blow drove the nail through its skull. Cormac looked up to see the eel's tail flex once and then lie still. Beglan took a knife and scored around the creature's neck, then used pliers to peel back its skin. Finally he slit the belly and gutted it, paying close attention to the entrails and carefully separating out one small portion, which he slipped into a cup on the nearby bench. The eel went into a bucket at his feet.

As he watched Anthony go about his work, Cormac wondered about the conversation he'd overheard here the other night between Beglan and Anca. Shawn Kearney said the Killowen residents were trying to protect the Romanian girl. So why had she run away with Deirdre

Claffey? Why not flee to Killowen? If Niall had been set up by Vincent Claffey, the girl must have had something to do with arranging the incriminating photos of her and Niall, either as coconspirator or unwilling pawn. Either made her a possible player in Claffey's death.

Cormac had no more time for rumination. Anthony Beglan was such a practiced hand that the half dozen eels in his creel were skinned and gutted in the space of about twelve minutes. He rinsed off his hands under the tap in the shed, reached for the bucket of eels and the small container from the workbench, and set off down the lane toward Killowen.

Anthony never slowed or turned around. As Cormac struggled to keep up, it occurred to him that the old spelling for Beglan would have been Ó Beigléighinn—*beag* for small, and *léighinn* from the word *léigh*—to read or to study—scholarship, in other words. Put it all together and the name meant "descendant of the little scholar." In all the conversations about Cill Eóghain, they'd gone back and forth about what sorts of scholarship might have been carried on at the monastery here more than a thousand years ago. Was it possible that Beglan's family had some connection to this place from that time? Centuries had passed, to be sure, but it was true in Ireland—as it was true everywhere, in fact—that artifacts, roads, structures, and even people sometimes did not stir from where they'd remained for generations. There was clearly some powerful force that connected human beings to their ancestral places.

Cormac watched Anthony Beglan fifty yards ahead of him. Here was a man far removed from the bookish pursuits of his presumed forebears. How ironic it would be if this descendant of the little scholar could himself neither read nor write.

Arriving at Killowen, Beglan went first to the kitchen, where he dropped the bucket of eels, then crossed to the north wing of the house, where Martin Gwynne kept his studio. Still in Beglan's left hand was the small cup from his workbench, with whatever he had taken from the eels' insides. He stuck his head through the door and spoke to Martin Gwynne. Cormac could hear a few words of the conversation:

". . . like you asked," Beglan said.

"Very good, Anthony, I appreciate you going to the trouble," Gwynne replied.

"Nuh-no trouble, really," Beglan said. "All for a guh-good cause. I'll get some more gallnuts as well."

Beglan left by the outside door of the studio, and Cormac tried to get close enough to peer in through the window.

Martin Gwynne fished something out of Beglan's cup, a small bluish organ, and held it steady over a glass jar. He lanced the thing with a sharp scalpel, releasing a bright yellow liquid into the jar. Gwynne carefully repeated the same procedure five more times. What could it be? Best to ask the anatomist—surely Nora would know.

12

Stella Cusack decided to begin by interviewing Deirdre Claffey. The girl was in one of the two tiny, airless rooms they had for talking to suspects and witnesses. The uniforms had taken the baby away for the moment. Deirdre had appeared exhausted when they brought her in. The circles under her eyes were dark as bruises, and she obviously hadn't slept.

Getting information from people wasn't as difficult as everyone imagined. Most of them wanted to speak. Deirdre's head was on the table when Stella entered and took a seat across from her.

"Before we begin, do you need anything, Deirdre, cup of tea, a biscuit, maybe a sandwich?"

The girl didn't raise her head but rocked it side to side. "Where's Cal?" came a small voice from the tabletop.

"He's being looked after by a very nice *bean garda* just outside. He's fine. They're giving him a bit of dinner while you and I have our little talk."

"They won't give him peas, will they? He doesn't like peas."

Stella checked her watch. Where was that bloody child advocate? It was getting late, and whoever Social Services had assigned to the case was taking her own sweet time in getting here. But those were the rules. She'd just have to wait.

Molloy stuck his head in. "She's here, Stella, the advocate."

Five minutes later, Stella sat across the table from Deirdre Claffey, now with the child advocate by her side. "I just need you to tell me what happened last night, Deirdre, in your own words. Take your time. We're not in a rush."

The girl's hands were tucked underneath her. She stared at the table and mumbled her story, about going to Killowen yesterday evening, her father bringing her home, going straight to bed, and being awakened in the middle of the night by her friend Anca. They'd stayed in the chapel until first light and then moved on. Anca seemed anxious about getting away.

"You don't know why Anca wanted to run away?"

"No. I asked if she'd seen my da, and she started shouting at me."

"And what did she say?"

"That we couldn't go back."

"Why did you go along with Anca?"

"I was afraid. She said my da was using us, me and Cal—what was she talking about?"

"Do you know why you're here, Deirdre?" Stella asked as gently as she could.

"Something's happened to my da," the girl whispered. "I know it, something bad. He's dead, isn't he?"

"Yes, Deirdre. I'm afraid he is."

Deirdre put her head on the table and wept. Impossible to know if it was genuine sorrow or relief. The advocate tried to comfort the girl but was pushed away.

As she waited, Stella pulled a gallnut from her pocket, one of the pair Dr. Gavin had given her. When Deirdre looked up again, she set the gall on the table between them. "Do you know what that is, Deirdre?"

"Is it a seed?"

"Not exactly," Stella said. "It's a gallnut, from an oak tree. Some people call them serpent's eggs."

"I used to see them in the wood, where I played when I was little."

Her wrist was exposed as she reached for the gall, and Stella winced at the sight of the fresh bruises—raw, distinct marks of an adult hand.

"Can you tell me how you got those bruises, Deirdre?"

The girl dropped the gallnut, and both hands went immediately back under the table. "Working the chipper," she lied.

Stella tried again. "What about your lip—is that from the chipper as well?"

"Fuck you!"

Stella was unprepared for such vehemence. This girl's father had been killed, possibly for abusing her, had quite likely made her pregnant, and here she was, still trying to defend him. The world really beggared belief.

Through the small window in the door, she saw Molloy out in the corridor. "Will you excuse me?" she said to the advocate. "I'll be back."

There was no sign of Molloy when she got outside. Stella took a deep breath and started to bang her head slowly against the wall. She felt a presence behind her and heard Molloy's voice in her ear. "Hey, everything all right, Stella?"

She turned, surprised to see his look of concern. He leaned closer. "Anything I can do?" How had she never noticed his long lashes, those dark irises flecked with gold?

"Everything's fine," she said. "Just let me know when you've got Anca Popescu set up in the other interview room."

"She's there now," Molloy said.

"What's the word from Interpol? Anything?"

Molloy shrugged. "You know how things are on the Continent— they don't work weekends. Did you want me to finish up with Deirdre?"

"No, let her stay put for a bit. I may want to talk to her again."

Stella pushed through the door of the other small interview room. Anca Popescu sat at the table, smoking, hands toying nervously with a bit of cigarette wrapper. Stella noted some red marks on her wrist, the ankles twined together under the table. The girl's eyes had the look of a cornered animal. Not the most trustworthy source of information, in Stella's experience. Better to try to calm her first. Stella took a seat, moving deliberately. She had no file or notebook in front of her, no recording device. All conscious choices, to say this was just a conversation. She waited perhaps thirty seconds for Anca to glance up and offered a slight but reassuring smile.

"First of all, I want to make it clear that no one's accused you of anything. We need to learn what happened last night. We'd really like to be able to help you, Anca, but you'll have to give us a little information before we can do that. Do you understand?"

Anca didn't respond, just pulled a fresh cigarette from the pack. She lit up with the old butt, then savagely stubbed it out. "I don't have to tell you anything."

"No, you don't. But it may help you in the long run. If you cooperate with us now, we may be able to help if you'd like to stay in Ireland. You would like to stay?" No verbal response, but Stella could see the hunger in the girl's eyes.

"Why don't we start with last Wednesday, when you were still working at Killowen? We understand that your friends there were trying to protect you, to keep your name and picture out of the press." Anca stared at the table, took a drag on her cigarette.

"I know you may be wondering what will happen to you, and to Deir-dre. If you answer our questions, and we have no reason to hold you, you'll be free to go." Still no reaction. "If you're concerned about the people who brought you to Ireland, we can offer accommodation at a safe house when we're finished here. We'll protect you. That's one thing I can promise."

Anca's eyes flicked toward the door. It was the first time she'd lifted her gaze from the table, and Stella's heart leapt just a little. She was in.

13

Claire Finnerty had left a cold supper for Cormac and her three other guests on Saturday evening. Everyone else seemed to have retreated into their private spaces. The atmosphere was quiet but slightly on edge, almost as though the house or the people in it were waiting for something. After dark, a couple of lights glowed from upstairs windows in the opposite wing.

As Cormac passed Dawson's room, he saw that the door was open. Still not back from Dublin. Nora came up behind him. "Where's Niall gone?"

Cormac tipped his head toward the door to their room. When they were safely inside, Cormac stretched out beside Nora on the bed. "Niall's gone home to talk to Gráinne. It seems when he was here last April that he . . . well, he had a very brief thing with that Romanian girl, Anca."

Nora sat up. "Niall Dawson? Jesus, Cormac, what on earth was he thinking?"

"Well, he wasn't thinking, that's the point. He said he felt sorry for her."

"No wonder he was so anxious whenever her name came up."

"From what he said, it also seems clear that he was set up. Vincent Claffey had photos. Niall paid him, but Claffey wanted more. Niall thinks Claffey might have coerced the girl."

"That doesn't excuse him, Cormac."

"No, of course it doesn't, but remember what Shawn told us about Anca running away from that Romanian gang? Claffey may have been threatening to reveal her whereabouts if she didn't do exactly as he said."

"You realize what this does—it makes Niall a prime suspect in Vincent Claffey's murder."

"He swore to me he'd nothing to do with it, but—"

"But what?"

"He did admit that he was there—at Claffey's place—early this morning. Claffey was dead when he arrived. I have to believe him, Nora. Niall's one of my oldest friends, and he's going to tell Cusack everything as soon as he's spoken to his wife."

"And you have to believe that as well?"

"He's not a liar—"

"Except about blackmail, apparently."

"—and he's certainly not a killer."

"Well, if Niall didn't murder Vincent Claffey, then it's likely someone else around here did. And if we're going to help Niall, we have to figure out why. You know, I keep thinking about those gallnuts in Kavanagh's mouth—and Claffey's as well. Martin Gwynne said they were used for making ink. If you look at the other items recovered so far, we've got a wax tablet, a stylus, a satchel. But there's still something missing: a manuscript."

Cormac was pleased that Nora had hit upon the same thing he and Niall had realized this afternoon. He wasn't sure he should share what Niall had told him today, but his friend's whole future was at stake. "Niall said he was here in April following up on a tip about a group of treasure hunters. The caller mentioned that they were after a manuscript. Something very old and very rare, like the books at Trinity."

"With all the monasteries here, there must have been hundreds, even thousands, of books made in Ireland. What happened to them all?"

"Destroyed by the raiders who burned down monasteries, or some would have been hidden and never retrieved, and obviously a great number would have been carried to the Continent. There are still libraries in France and Switzerland full of ancient Irish books. But only a few manuscripts created in Ireland actually stayed here—I'd say less than a dozen."

Nora didn't say anything but reached for her laptop on the nightstand and opened the lid. "I was thinking about what Shawn Kearney was telling us about her research on the site here, and I came across something interesting online earlier. The local historical society just posted the full text of John O'Donovan's Ordnance Survey Letters for this part of Tipperary. Look at this."

1336—Ó Beigléighinn, Coarb of St. Eóghan, dies at Cill Eóghain. [Note: Ó Beigléighinn was the coarb of the church at Cill Eóghain, in the parish of Faddan More, in the northwest of the county of Tipperary, where his lineal descendant and representative still farms the termon lands.—JO'D]

[This appears to be the earliest reference to the Coarb of Cill Eóghain from whom the hereditary custodian of the Book Shrine of Cill Eóghain was descended—the Termon Beglan, as we might call him, from his inherited right to the termon land of that church. J. E. Canon McCarthy cites him in his list of the Abbots of Faddan More as "Ó Beigléighinn, successor of Eóghan." Concerning Killowen, he tells us elsewhere, "The Parish of Faddan More extended along the bog to Carrig, and included the town-land of Killowen in the County Tipperary," and, in connection with the *Cumdach Eóghain* (or the Case of Eóghan's Book, as he translates the Gaelic term) he says, "For many centuries the O'Beglans of Killowen, comharbas of St. Eóghan, were the custodians of this interesting relic, as the MacMoyers were of the Book of Armagh, the Buckleys of the Shrine of St. Manchan, and the parish priest of Drumlane, for the time being, of the Breac Maedóic reliquary. In the course of time, the possession of the shrine was hotly contested between the bishops and priests of these dioceses. Sometime in the twelfth century it fell into the hands of a Faddan More O'Beglan, who, in misguided zeal to end the controversy, was said to have burned the precious manuscript, known as the Book of Killowen. Some centuries later an O'Beglan from Derrylahan was reported to have sold the shrine to a Nenagh watchmaker to have it melted down.]

When Cormac finished reading, Nora looked at him expectantly. "The keepers of this book shrine—they were called O'Beglan."

"It's funny, I was thinking about that name just this afternoon. It means 'descendant of the little scholar.'" Cormac was remembering the dilapidated farm he'd visited earlier in the day. Were it and the place he and Nora sat at this moment part of the termon lands of Cill Eóghain, where the ancient monastery had once stood?

"And is a book shrine what I think it is, like those elaborate metal boxes they have in the National Museum? You said Niall was here checking out a tip about some treasure hunters and an old manuscript.

Do you suppose Kavanagh could have been mixed up with them some-how?"

"From all I know of Kavanagh, he wouldn't have been much inter-ested in an elaborate shrine. He was far more likely to go for the book inside. But didn't O'Donovan say in that passage that the manuscript was burned?"

"No, he says your man O'Beglan was *said to have* burned the manu-script, that the shrine was reported to have been sold and melted down. You'd think Niall would have known about all this. I'm going to see if there's mention of this book shrine anywhere else."

Nora's attention was focused on her laptop again. Cormac's head had begun to ache. He also wanted to check once more to see if Niall had returned from Dublin. "Listen," he said to Nora, "I'm going below for a cup of tea. Do you want anything?"

"No, I'm all right." She frowned at the laptop screen.

Cormac checked Niall's room as he passed—still not back. It was getting late now; maybe he'd decided to stop at home for the night. And maybe that was a good sign. Cormac felt burdened by what he knew. He couldn't abandon his friend now. Downstairs, the moon was shin-ing through the window, so Cormac didn't bother to turn on a light. He ran the tap for a few seconds, then filled the electric kettle. He looked out into the garden, imagining that it must resemble the kitchen garden that had helped to feed a monastery. He remembered the strange sight of Anthony Beglan cutting something from the entrails of those eels this afternoon. He'd have to ask Nora about it.

A harsh whisper came from the courtyard, and Cormac drew back into the shadows. He couldn't make out who was speaking, but he saw two figures creep along the inner wall and leave by the gate outside Mar-tin Gwynne's studio.

Seized with an urge to know who could be skulking around Killowen at this hour, Cormac followed, keeping his distance. His brain registered the silhouettes ahead as male and female, but he could not distinguish their identities. He watched the two figures head for the storehouse, set into the side of a small hill, where the farm's creamery and cheese-making operation was housed. Could it be the French couple, Lucien and Sylvie, or was someone else breaking into their domain? The pair ducked behind a white van, ghostly in the moonlight, parked directly in front of the door. KILLOWEN FARMHOUSE CHEESE was emblazoned on its side, and a pair of cartoonish bearded goat faces glowed eerily.

Cormac hesitated. He couldn't follow any longer without being detected. Perhaps he ought just to wait.

Five minutes passed, then ten, as Cormac kept watch on the store-house door. What the hell was he doing out here? Nora's words reverber-ated through his head: *If Niall didn't murder Vincent Claffey, then it's likely someone else around here did.*

He checked his watch again. No sign of movement in the store-house. He could be out here all night. Bugger that. And bugger the tea as well. It was time to turn in.

Checking Dawson's room again on his way upstairs, he detected a flicker of movement inside. He pushed the door open wider. Niall was sitting on the bed, staring straight ahead.

"Everything all right?" Cormac asked.

"Gráinne threw me out. I've never seen her so angry." He made eye contact. "Thanks for the advice."

"Niall, I'm sorry."

"You know, I don't feel much like talking right now." He reached out to push the door shut, and Cormac had to jump back to avoid being hit.

He'd made a total bollocks of everything. Nora was still staring at her computer screen when he opened the door to their room. She glanced up.

"Niall's back from Dublin. Gráinne threw him out. I urged him to come clean, Nora, and now—"

"The two of them will have to figure out what to do, Cormac. We can't help them." She pointed to the floor beside her. "Come and sit."

Her cool fingers gently massaged his temples, the tension melting away down his neck and shoulders, wherever her hands came in contact with his skin.

"Nora?"

"Hmm? You know, if you keep talking, you'll never relax properly."

"There's something I meant to ask you. I followed Anthony Beglan home from the bog this afternoon and watched him clean and dress about a half dozen eels. He cut something from their entrails—I wasn't close enough to see, but he brought whatever it was to Martin Gwynne."

Nora kept working at the cords in his shoulders. "Go on."

"They were small bluish sacs, about this size." He made a shape with his fingers, held it up to show her. "After Anthony left, Martin cut open each one and drained off a bright yellow liquid into a jar."

Nora stopped kneading. "Ah, yes, he told me about that. I wandered into his studio the day we arrived. We were talking about all the strange sources for pigments, and he said the monks used to make a yellow ink from the gallbladders of eels—"

A knock sounded at the door. And another, urgent.

Eliana was outside, in pajamas.

"He's gone, your father. I don't know where he is."

Cormac froze. They'd never had a problem with him wandering off at home in Dublin, but each day out here seemed to hold a new and distressing surprise.

They headed downstairs, with Cormac and Eliana each taking a wing of the house and Nora checking outside in the car park. As Cormac ventured down the corridor of the south wing, he spied the door of the thermal suite ajar.

The old man was up to his chin in peaty water, eyes closed, clearly enjoying himself. "He's here," Cormac shouted. "Nora! I've got him."

Eliana arrived at the door. "I'm sorry, I should have been watching."

"No harm done, none at all," Cormac insisted. "This isn't your fault. It's just that he's very . . . independent."

"Please don't be angry with him. It's my fault. Perhaps he doesn't understand me, my English—"

"Your English is fine," Cormac said. "Now, please don't be upset. No one is in trouble." When Nora arrived, he said to Eliana, "Maybe you and Nora would make us a cup of tea while I get him dressed again."

Nora slid her arm around the girl's shoulder. "Come on, Eliana, I think there's a bit of porter cake left."

When they'd gone, Cormac sat down on the bench beside the sunken tub and studied his father's face: eyes closed, a film of perspiration on his forehead and upper lip. Suddenly the old man's eyes opened, and he seemed overcome by a gust of feeling. Cormac sat helplessly, not certain what to do. He reached out and placed a hand on his father's shoulder, the aging flesh soft as kidskin, loose against bone. To his surprise, the old man's hand covered his. "You're my sum," Joseph said. "My sum."

Cormac sank down on one knee beside his father, not wishing to withdraw his hand too soon. At last the old man sighed heavily. "I'm wet," he said, as though noticing that fact for the very first time.

"Yes," Cormac said, "that you are." He reached over and pulled one handle to begin draining the tub, another to switch on the shower spray.

"Mmm," Joseph said absently. He took Cormac's hand once more and pressed the palm against his breastbone. "My sum."

BOOK FOUR

Ná luig, ná luig
fót fora taí:
gairit bía fair,
fota bía faí.

Do not swear, do not swear
by the ground on which you stand;
it's a short time you'll be upon it,
and a long time you'll be under it.

—Poem written by an Irish monk in the margin of a medieval manuscript

1

As Cormac came down the stairs into the kitchen at Killowen the next morning, Niall Dawson was staring down into a cup of steaming coffee. He looked like hell—unshaven, dark rings under his eyes. But he glanced up as Cormac poured himself a cup of coffee.

"I'm sorry for taking everything out on you last night," Dawson said. "It's not your fault I'm in this mess—it's all down to me. It's probably good that I'm here, actually. It'll give Gráinne time to think."

"She loves you, Niall. You'll work things out."

Dawson nodded numbly. "Listen, before we head back to the site, I was thinking of nipping over to the hospital, to see if I could use one of the scopes and have a closer look at that wax tablet. Thought you might like to come along."

Twenty minutes later, they were pulling into the parking lot at the hospital in Birr. The tablet had been kept with evidence from the Kavanagh murder, which included Killowen Man, his clothing, and other effects. Dawson brought the tablet to the adjacent pathology lab where they could examine it under a microscope.

"I've been thinking about the stylus Shawn found at Killowen last April," he said, placing the tablet gently on the scope's stage and adjusting the angles of the lamps. "I spent hours looking at that thing under the magnifier at the Barracks. One side of it had a small flattened spot—not clear how it happened exactly, but it gave the thing a particular fingerprint. And with a material as impressionable as wax, it just might be possible to prove an association between the stylus and this tablet. Each stylus has a signature, and if there's any way of identifying its mark—if there's a flattened area on one side that could be identified on a microscopic level, for example—we might be able to say with a high degree of certainty that the stylus Shawn found was used on this tablet." He peered through the lens, moving the tablet carefully across the stage to inspect each line of text.

Dawson's voice took on an excited edge. "You're not going to believe this. Take a look."

Cormac leaned in and looked through the lens.

"Do you see it?" Dawson was almost dancing. "I had hoped, certainly, but never . . . can you see it?"

Cormac could see a distinctive flattened impression, repeated wherever the writer had made a mark upon the wax.

"No other stylus could make exactly the same mark. This is enormous."

Cormac understood how Niall was feeling. That sudden, visceral connection with the person who wrote those words on the tablet, or left his mark on metal, his fingerprint in clay. No one talked much about the emotional fallout of these discoveries, rare glimpses so deep into the past. Staring at shapes graved into the wax, he suddenly saw how letters began, as animal signs and drawings on cave walls. The words before him still carried the horns of the ox, the sinuous curve of the serpent.

Dawson began to pace in the narrow laboratory space. "I'm thinking Killowen Man must have been a rare specimen indeed, if he could read and write Greek. Must have been a scholar of some degree." He was thinking aloud. "If we could get a better angle on the lighting, perhaps we could make out the words more clearly." Cormac stepped back, and Dawson began adjusting the lamp to rake light across the surface of the wax. "Better be careful," he muttered to himself. "Christ, that's all I'd need right now, to melt this! Have you got the camera—"

The door swung open to reveal Stella Cusack, with Detective Molloy behind her.

"Mr. Dawson?" she said. And suddenly the tiny room seemed far too crowded. Niall looked up from the microscope, elation draining from his face.

"Niall Dawson, I'm here to arrest you for the murder of Vincent Claffey. You are not obliged to say anything unless you wish to do so, but anything you say will be taken down in writing and may be given in evidence—"

"What?" Dawson studied Cusack's face as if there was some disconnect between it and the words issuing from her lips, and Molloy came around from behind, reaching for a pair of handcuffs from his belt.

"Wait a minute, this can't be right," Dawson said, pulling his arm from the junior detective's grip.

Cormac turned to Stella Cusack. "What's going on?"

"I don't suppose you can vouch for Mr. Dawson's whereabouts two nights ago, between the hours of one and five A.M.?"

"For Christ's sake, Detective, we were all asleep," Cormac said.

Niall still held his left wrist aloft, as though doing so could stave off the inevitable.

Molloy said, "If you would just come along, Mr. Dawson. It's better for all of us if you don't make a fuss."

"I'll make a fuss. I'll make a fuckin' stink if I like," Dawson said. "Because I haven't murdered anyone. You can't possibly have any evidence."

"What we have is an eyewitness who saw you kill Vincent Claffey," Molloy said. "I'm afraid we've got to bring you in."

"What eyewitness? That's impossible. Somebody's lying."

Cusack replied, "If you'd just come with us, Mr. Dawson."

Niall's shoulders sagged as he turned to Cormac. "Please be careful. That tablet is—"

Cormac tried to reassure him. "I'll make sure it's safe."

"Could you take a few photos first?" Dawson asked. "Document that mark. It's very important. I didn't do this, Cormac, you've got to believe me."

"Do you want me to phone someone? Gráinne, or a lawyer? Anyone?"

"No, don't call my wife," Dawson said. "Not yet. And there's no need for a lawyer. I'm sure this will all blow over—it's a misunderstanding, has to be." At last he brought down his other wrist and submitted to being handcuffed. "It's all a dreadful mistake." He sounded as though he was trying to convince himself, and not succeeding.

Cormac was left standing alone in the little laboratory, the microscope lens still focused on a string of words written a thousand years before.

2

Cormac sat at the lab bench, knowing he had to do something to help Niall, but what? Get past all the qualms he'd been feeling last night and actually do something, start digging. If Niall hadn't killed Vincent Claffey—and Cormac believed he hadn't—then someone else had, someone else who also had just as much in the way of motive. Claffey had threatened every person at that dinner table. He had something on all of them, it seemed.

Cormac switched off the lamp. He should finish up here at the hospital and get back to the farm, talk things over with Nora.

He told her about Niall's arrest and about the shadows he had followed to the storehouse last night.

"Cusack said she had a witness to Vincent Claffey's murder?" Nora asked.

"That's what Detective Molloy said."

"But who would say such a thing, if it wasn't true?"

"Someone who wanted to deflect suspicion from himself, I'd imagine."

"Surely Cusack gets that. Maybe she's just playing with the real suspect, making him think the heat's off. Let's wait a minute now. We haven't stopped to put together all the facts."

"We can't rule out the possibility of a conspiracy. Do you remember the way everyone at the table that night seemed to be in agreement about one thing—the need to protect Deirdre Claffey from her father?"

"There did seem to be a general consensus."

"So maybe there was a similar pact about protecting Mairéad Broome from her husband."

Nora rubbed her arms. "Not a very comforting thought. I suppose it's a good thing we're out here where no one can hear us."

They were sitting on the ground in the middle of the open field above Killowen's geothermal system, far from any possible eavesdropping. Joseph and Eliana were doing flash cards under the tree at the edge of the meadow, well out of earshot.

"Claffey might have discovered who murdered Kavanagh, and the killer might have taken his threats the other night seriously," Cormac said. "The cloven tongues and oak galls found in the victims' mouths—those are the details tying the two murders together. Who would have known enough about Kavanagh's murder except the person who put those galls down his throat?"

"Or persons, if you're sticking with your conspiracy theory. So what do we do next?"

"Keep our eyes open, try to find out more about Kavanagh's connections here at Killowen. And anything to do with Claffey's blackmail schemes, manuscript smuggling. There's definitely something strange going on at that storehouse. Conspiracy or no, I get the distinct feeling that everyone here knows more than they're telling."

"What did you find out about the wax tablet?"

"Niall thinks the impressions in the wax came from the stylus that Shawn Kearney found. The point of the stylus has a unique imperfection that makes a distinctive mark."

"You have photos?"

Cormac pulled a memory card from his pocket. "Did you want a look?"

"What would you think of printing off a few pictures and showing them to Martin Gwynne? He's apparently worked with old manuscripts; maybe he could decipher the writing."

"Isn't he one of our suspects?"

"Of course he is, but at this point, who isn't?"

3

Stella Cusack needed to speak to Anca Popescu once more. The girl claimed she had witnessed Vincent Claffey's murder. Stella pulled into the drive at the safe house where she'd sent Anca and Deirdre Claffey and the baby, expecting to see the Guards officer she'd assigned to the door. No one there. The door was open, and she found the officer, Stephen Murray, tied to a chair in the kitchen. Stella felt no qualms about causing pain as she ripped the tape from his mouth. "Christ, Murray, what happened?"

"That little one, the Romanian, she's a right devil. I turned my back for one second, and the next thing you know, I'm trussed up here like a Christmas turkey, and they're away in me car. Sorry, Stella, I know she was your witness."

"I'll deal with you later. Which way did they go?"

Murray pointed with his head. "East on the Mill Road, I think. They can pick up the N52 from there. They didn't say anything about where they were going, like. Been gone about twenty minutes or so."

"What's the number plate on the car?"

Murray rattled off a Tipperary registration, and Stella got on her radio and put out a bulletin for all available cars to check the numbers on all Garda vehicles within a sixty-kilometer radius. She returned to Murray, still strapped to the chair, and cut the tape from around his arms and torso. "You can do the rest yourself," she said, handing him the knife. "Then get back to the station and write up a report. Don't leave anything out."

Stella trudged back to her car. She'd had some serious doubts about Anca's story all along. Now she had a sinking feeling that it had only been a ploy to buy time. If Anca had been any way involved in Vincent Claffey's death, she'd be deported straight back to Romania. The Immigration Ministry had no qualms about ejecting criminal offenders. The girl was running scared. She'd turn up; you could get only so far driving a Garda officer's vehicle, especially with a baby. And petrol cost money. Stella suddenly realized that they'd never found the brown envelope that Claffey had received from Graham Healy. If Anca had taken it, she'd have enough to keep running for a while—but was it enough to leave the country? The way things were with the economy right now, you might easily find a fishing boat that would drop you on some far-away coastline for the right price. Stella couldn't help thinking of the two girls, one the same age as Liadán, and the baby, and all the harm that had come to them already. She could only hope that they would be found again, and soon.

Her thoughts returned to Kavanagh's references in his note to a mysterious manuscript and the curiously few degrees of separation between the body in the boot and the residents of Killowen. Vincent Claffey's gob full of gallnuts—it seemed a deliberate clue, perhaps a little too deliberate. There must be a logical order to all the disparate pieces of information they'd collected so far. She just had to figure out how they all lined up.

Stella set out for the station. Dawson had started to tell her about the anonymous tip he'd received in April, about a mysterious ancient manuscript. Kavanagh's handwritten notes flickered through her head: IOH *returns to IRL, great work unfinished.* What was the great work? Mairéad Broome said the initials IOH belonged to the object of her husband's obsession, this ancient scholar Eriugena. *This is going to rattle some bones,* Kavanagh had told his wife.

When she arrived at the makeshift incident room, Stella began scribbling notes on the whiteboard:

IOH—great work unfinished
Treasure hunters operating near Killowen—manuscript?
Kavanagh here 18 mos earlier—notes on location of Faddan More
Healy/Broome paying Claffey off
Cregganroe?

She stood back and took in the whole picture. Like the debris field after an explosion, there were fragments and bits of things all scattered and mixed together.

"We need to know more about this Eriugena character," she said to Molloy, who'd just come in. "What can you find out about him?"

Molloy opened his laptop and tapped a few keys. "Let's see, John Scottus Eriugena." He went through the history as Stella scribbled a few notes. "Early details are sketchy. Most people think he died around 877, probably in France. They're not sure whether or not he was a cleric."

"Anything there about his 'great work'?"

Molloy peered at his screen. "His major work was a philosophical treatise, *Periphyseon—On the Division of Nature.* Here's something interesting—the last line mentions 'recent discoveries of manuscripts.'"

"How recent?"

Molloy scrolled down to the bottom of the page. "Ah, this was written in 1909."

"No joy from Interpol?"

"Nothing yet."

Stella spotted a fat interdepartmental courier envelope in the wire basket on a shelf behind Molloy's head. "What's that?"

"Case file on the Cregganroe bombing you requested. Arrived this morning." He reached for the file and handed it over. Stella shoved it in her bag; she'd have a look at it later.

"What about Diarmuid Lynch? What do we know about him before he turned up at Killowen?"

"He's no driving license, which is a bit odd in itself. Says he had a passport but lost it when he got back from Spain. So I checked. Forty-six passports issued to people with the name Diarmuid Lynch over the past twenty-five years. The thing is, Stella, it's just you and me on this case. We don't have the manpower to track all these people down."

4

Martin Gwynne was in his studio bent over a sheet of parchment when Cormac and Nora arrived at his door. Nora waited until the quill lifted from the calfskin before speaking. "Mr. Gwynne?" She pulled Cormac into the room after her. "We wondered if you would mind having a look at some photographs."

"What sort of photographs?" Gwynne said, apparently a little puzzled by the request.

Cormac spoke this time. "We had a textile expert here going through our bog man's garments, and we found this tucked inside his cloak." He laid the printed photographs of the tablet on the table.

Gwynne stared at the pictures, as if touching them might make the images evaporate. "My God, a wax tablet." He proceeded to examine each photo in minute detail before turning to the next. "I'm sorry, where did you say this came from?"

"Killowen Man's cloak," Cormac said. "He must have been carrying it when he went into the bog."

"When he was dumped into the bog," Nora said. "After being stabbed to death."

"Is that right?" Gwynne seemed distracted, focused completely on the tablet images and not on his visitors or what they were saying.

Nora said, "We were wondering if you could help us decipher the writing."

Gwynne looked up, as if suddenly aware that he was not alone. Cormac noted a twinge of melancholy—or was it regret?—that seemed to cloud the man's features.

"Yes, of course, I can try." He cleared his throat and settled down to business, pulling his lighted magnifier closer, setting the pictures out in two short rows. He pored over each photo through the thick glass. "The language is Latin, as you probably recognized, with a few Greek words interspersed. The script is Irish majuscule, very like the Springmount tablets." Gwynne reached for a sheet of paper and a pen. "Let's see if we can work out what it says . . ." The nib of his pen began to move across the page, Latin words appearing in a fancy, ancient-looking hand:

> *Si enim libertas naturae rationabilis ad imaginem Dei conditae a deo data est, necessario omne quod ex ipsa libertate evenit, malum seu malitia recte dici non potest*

Gwynne stopped writing and looked at the paper. " 'For if the freedom of a rational nature has been given by God, then necessarily all that from freedom comes—or has come to pass, evil or malice'—no, that's not right—it's 'cannot rightly be called evil or malice.' "

Cormac's eyes were on Gwynne's handwriting as well. "Definitely not Psalms, then. Any thoughts on what it might be?"

Receiving no answer, he glanced at Gwynne to find his face completely blank, the pen tumbled from his hand, his eyes staring into the middle distance. The change in demeanor was so abrupt, and so extreme, that Cormac had to wonder whether something had gone wrong inside his brain. "Gwynne," he said sharply. "Martin, are you all right?"

All at once the eyes seemed to regain focus. "Yes, yes, quite all right. No, it's not Psalms, you're right about that." He peered through the magnifier once more. "No, it's something else entirely, but I'm not sure what. I'd be happy to hold on to these photos and keep working on them, if you like. It might take some time—I'm afraid my Latin has grown a bit rusty."

"Anything you can tell us would be helpful," Cormac said.

When they were out of earshot of the studio, Nora turned to Cormac. "I don't suppose you would have noticed, since that was your first time in Gwynne's workshop, but he's gotten rid of the oak galls. There was a huge bowl on one of the side tables last time I was in the studio, and now they're gone. Listen, one of us ought to spell Eliana for a while—I'll take the first shift. What are you going to do?"

The shadows he'd seen skulking about the storehouse last night lingered in Cormac's brain. "There's something I need to check out. I'll catch up to you in a bit."

When Nora had gone, he made sure he was alone, then crossed the yard to the storehouse. The van was still parked out front. He glanced about once more and shaded his eyes to see in through one of the storehouse's tiny windows. No one. Might be worth a look inside. He was just about to head for the door when Tessa Gwynne emerged from the forest path. He slipped quickly around the corner, hoping she hadn't seen him. Tessa came straight for the storehouse and ducked in through the small doorway. Under cover of a vine, Cormac peered inside to see her looking through the items on the shelves, about two dozen packages, all neatly wrapped in brown paper. She seemed to be searching for a particular parcel. When she found it, she brought it down and pasted a Killowen Farmhouse Cheese label on top, then placed it in the basket she carried over her arm.

Tessa Gwynne left the storehouse and crossed over to her husband's studio. They both emerged a minute or two later, Martin climbing into the driver's seat of the Killowen van.

Cormac could hear Nora's voice inside his head: *What a perfect way to smuggle stolen goods—inside a wheel of cheese. We should at least see where they're taking it.*

Cormac slipped behind the wheel of his jeep and headed down the driveway, careful to keep his distance.

5

Cormac checked his watch. Martin Gwynne was a careful driver, coming to a full stop at every crossroads, checking both ways before pulling out. Wherever the pair of them were headed, they didn't seem in any hurry. The van cruised along a back road from the farm to the N52, followed that main road north for a bit, then turned onto a secondary road that led into the Slieve Bloom Mountains. At the twenty-six-kilometer mark, just past the village of Coolrain, they turned into the driveway of a big house with beautifully manicured grounds. Cormac hesitated at the gate, not wanting to make his presence known. He'd park outside and see if he could figure out what this place was. The sign at the gate said simply HAWTHORN HOUSE.

Driving on for a bit, he turned around and found a field gate and parked beside it. He tapped "Hawthorn House" into his phone and found that it was part of a network of residential rehabilitation centers for people with brain injuries. If the Gwynnes were smuggling a stolen manuscript hidden in a wheel of cheese, why bring it to a place like this?

Cormac drove onto the grounds. There was a small car park at the side of the main building, a rambling old gray limestone mansion. He left the car there and circled around to the front door. Perhaps he could see about a tour . . .

No one was at reception. Cormac waited, taking note of the surroundings. All the furnishings were new, none of the draperies yet faded by sunlight. Someone was spending a bit of dosh, keeping this place updated. It was private, which meant fees were probably steep. If the Gwynnes did have someone here, how on earth could they afford it? Their own modest living arrangements boasted no such luxury, and calligraphy, unless you were the warranted scribe of some royal family, wasn't exactly a lucrative profession these days.

Cormac walked to a tall window that looked out over the back garden, a spectacular formal arrangement, with miniature boxwood hedges, rosebushes, and other colorful blooms. The edges of the beds were as sharp as if they'd been cut with a razor.

From the window, he could see the Gwynnes strolling through the side garden, coming upon a younger woman sitting at a table on the terrace, under the shade of an oak. They greeted her warmly, but she remained diffident, barely looking at them. Tessa Gwynne reached into the basket and brought out the brown paper package, unwrapping it carefully. She'd brought a knife and cut into it—nothing but a wheel of soft cheese.

He turned his attention to the younger woman. She was short and slight, dressed in a pair of pale green corduroys, a patterned blouse, and what looked like a hand-knitted cardigan; a long dark plait fell down her back. She sat up eagerly to the table now, looking for a taste of the cheese. Tessa Gwynne reached out to touch the younger woman's hair, but she pulled away, shrugging off the attention. Tessa's disappointment at the rebuff was visible, even at a distance. Who was this person? The touch implied some sort of close relationship, but he could have sworn he remembered someone at Killowen saying that the Gwynnes' only child had died. Cormac felt ashamed, following these people like some sort of half-arsed private investigator, prying into their personal business.

Tessa Gwynne seemed to have recovered. She stood close to the younger woman, speaking softly. Cormac was so intrigued by the miniature drama unfolding in the distance that he didn't hear the footsteps approaching behind him.

"Can I help you, sir?"

He turned to find a fresh-faced receptionist standing at his elbow. Her name badge read FIONA.

"Are you here for an appointment with Dr. Carnahan?" she asked brightly. "I can ring and let him know you've arrived."

"Sorry, no," Cormac said. "I just happened upon your website and thought I might have a look around. My father's recovering from a stroke, you see, and we've got him at home just at the minute, but my wife and I, well . . . we're looking for a place where he might receive more intensive therapy." He'd just managed to spit out a plausible lie. "I suppose it's not all stroke patients here."

"Oh, no, we get the lot—car accidents, sport injuries, strokes, and falls."

Cormac threw a glance over his shoulder. "Your garden is certainly stunning."

"Isn't it, though? Designed by the father of one of our residents," the girl explained. She joined Cormac at the window. "There she is now, with the parents—Derryth. They're here every Sunday, but she's in that garden all the time. Hard to get her indoors, even when it's raining. Anyway, the father's some class of artist, I think. He made up the plans for the garden. Fantastic, isn't it?"

"Yes," Cormac said. He didn't say any more, hoping that Fiona would try to fill the silence. He didn't have to wait long.

"Very sad, what happened to her, poor craythur." The girl's voice dropped to a whisper. "They say she tried to hang herself, over some boy. By the time they found her, she'd gone without oxygen for too long. She's been here near on twenty years like that." A shaking of the head suggested the extent of the damage done. "You'd never catch me trying to top myself over some man. Nothin' but a shower of shites, the lot of 'em—well, present company excepted, I'm sure." Fiona suddenly seemed embarrassed. "God, I'm an awful eejit. Shouldn't have gone and opened my yap. I'll just go and ring Dr. Carnahan for you, will I?"

When the girl turned and left the room, Cormac slipped out the front door and made his way to the car. He had what he'd come for, to see where Tessa Gwynne had taken her package. And he had something else: the knowledge that the Gwynnes' daughter was not dead after all.

6

Pulling into the car park at Killowen, Cormac had a notion about how he might be able to find out more about the Gwynnes. He reached for his phone and punched in a number.

Robbie MacSweeney was Cormac's oldest friend. He and Niall and Robbie had a regular session at the Cobblestone, which of a Wednesday night became an island of wild, wind-tossed West Clare music in the heart of Dublin. Perhaps he should tell Robbie about Niall being arrested—but Niall wasn't ready for that information to reach Dublin quite yet.

"Robbie, I'm ringing to ask a favor."

"Fire away."

"Could you find out anything about a fella called Martin Gwynne? He's something to do with handwriting or old manuscripts, I'm not quite sure."

"Say no more. That's *G-W-Y-N-N*?"

"And an *e* at the end," Cormac said. "I think he's Welsh—he worked at the British Library and may have been in academia at one time, if that helps."

"I don't suppose you're going to tell me why I'm on the lookout for this fella?"

Cormac hesitated. "I wish I could, Robbie. Just ask around and see what you can suss out, will you? Ring me back as soon as you have anything."

A wise decision, ringing MacSweeney, the best researcher Cormac knew. If past experience was any guide, he would have something from Robbie within a couple of hours.

The house was quiet. Everyone must be outside. Cormac went straight to the sitting room, curious to see if there was any pattern to the books collected there. He crossed to the Irish history section and paid closer attention this time to the titles, all about the early Christian era into the Middle Ages, and a great preponderance of books about books,

manuscripts, scribal arts. And a large-format book about artifacts, treasures of the National Museum—a treasure hunter's sourcebook hiding
in plain sight. He found an appendix at the back, a gazetteer of priceless
objects, including exact GPS coordinates of each findspot. How exactly
had Shawn Kearney happened upon that stylus?

But she had turned it in. Perhaps that was why Niall seemed to trust
her.

He felt a presence behind him and turned to find Shawn Kearney
herself standing in the doorway. He closed the book and slipped it back
on the shelf.

"Is it true?" she asked.

"Is what true?"

"About Niall Dawson being arrested?"

Word traveled fast here. He didn't have time to weigh the pros and
cons of telling the truth. "I'm afraid so."

"He didn't harm anyone. He couldn't."

"You don't have to tell me that," Cormac said. "Niall's one of my
oldest friends."

"Then you want to help him, too."

"Is there something you know, Shawn? Something that could help
Niall?"

She came closer and lowered her voice. "He told me this morning
why he was here in April, investigating a ring of treasure hunters—"

"Shawn, have you ever heard of the Book of Killowen?"

"How do you know about that?"

"Nora found John O'Donovan's notes online last night, with the
reference to the shrine and to the book being burned. We thought that
might have been a ruse."

She glanced behind her, checking to see that they were alone. "I
need to know exactly what's on that wax tablet you found on the bog
man."

"How did you—"

"Martin told me. He showed me the photographs you left with him.
Do you still have the originals?"

Cormac took the camera's memory card from his pocket. "On here."

"Let me have a look. Please."

He handed over the card, and she plugged it into the laptop on the
corner table. Her reaction was similar to Gwynne's. What did they all

know that he and Niall were missing? "Shawn, do you know what it says?"

She turned to him. "I should let Martin explain, he's much better at translation than I am. How much do you know about the Book of Killowen?"

"Only that it's mentioned in the *Annals of the Four Masters*, and there are stories about people coming to blows over it, and that neither the book nor the shrine has surfaced since the eighteenth century—a hundred years before O'Donovan wrote about it in his Ordnance Survey letters. He was basically reporting on rumors on something that might not even exist anymore. One of the Beglans was supposed to have burned the book because he was fed up with the controversy."

Shawn Kearney threw him a skeptical glance.

Cormac took a step back. "Hang on, is the Book of Killowen still here? What about the shrine?"

"I can't say any more."

"Wait a minute. Does the book have anything to do with the death of Benedict Kavanagh or Vincent Claffey?"

"I don't know. Please don't ask me any more. Look, you've got to be careful. There are certain people here who would—" A sudden noise in the hall pulled her up short. "I'm sorry, that's all I can tell you." She opened the door and looked both ways, then slipped away.

Cormac's memory snaked back to Anthony Beglan following the cattle, the foreign-sounding words flowing from him, and Martin Gwynne's reaction to the Latin script on the tablet, the ancient writer's thoughts about evil and malice.

7

Nora studied Joseph Maguire's sleeping face, searching for traces of the family resemblance. She found hints in the cut of his jaw, the shape of the earlobes, the curve of his lower lip. Joseph had been subdued all day, after the bath incident last night. He shifted in his lounger, opening one eye only briefly to see that she was there. "Nero," he said, one of his many names for her.

She checked her watch: nearly four. Eliana should be back soon. From where she sat, she could see the gap between the car park at the front of the main house and the path that headed off toward the cottages in the wood. Graham Healy pulled a black BMW into the car park's end space and hefted a couple of large carrier bags—one filled with clinking bottles of wine—and what looked like a petrol container from the back of the car. He disappeared down the path. Strange that no one had seemed too concerned about Healy paying off Vincent Claffey. Why was that? Come to think of it, had anyone found a fat packet of cash when they searched Claffey's farm? The Garda Síochána weren't exactly immune to opportunity; there had been ample proof to the contrary. But somehow Stella Cusack didn't strike her as the light-fingered type. So why was Graham Healy still walking around while Niall Dawson was sitting in jail? If stopping blackmail was the motive for Claffey's murder, surely both men had at least an equal stake in that. Everything came back again to Benedict Kavanagh and what he was doing in the boot of that car.

Nora looked to the woodland path again, surprised to see Eliana emerging from the oak grove. The girl walked quickly, and Nora detected a disturbance.

"Is something bothering you?" she asked when Eliana joined them.

"No!" The girl's eyes darted back to the edge of the wood.

"Eliana, please tell me. That man who just went down the path, did he say something?"

"No, he said nothing." She paused. "He only stared at me."

Nora looked through the woods where Healy had gone. "Perhaps it's better to stay away from that path. There are plenty of other places to walk."

Nora glanced back at Joseph. His eyes were open, and he'd apparently been listening in on their conversation. "Who's stack-stack-staring?"

"It's nothing at all," she said. "Nothing for you to be concerned about."

"Is it all right if I leave you two here for a bit?" Nora asked. A notion was taking shape, her curiosity catching on Graham Healy's odd manner just now.

She'd have to double back around the orchard so that Joseph and Eliana wouldn't see her go down the path. Easy enough, just head for the bog and turn right behind the goat barn and the cheese storehouse. Lucien and Sylvie must have rooms dug into the hill for aging their cheese; they sold their produce at the local markets, and there was no way all that could fit into the tiny storehouse. There must be caverns full of cheese in there.

She made sure no one was watching, then followed along the barn and ducked behind it. To her left was the road leading to Anthony Beglan's farm and the bog, and straight ahead a narrow path led back up into the wood above the storehouse.

The light was different on this visit to the oak grove. The cloud cover was heavier, and the sky cast a yellow light that made the moss underfoot glow a most unnatural fluorescent green. A crack sounded ahead, and Nora slowed her pace. She was off the path entirely now, stepping over hummocks and boulders, the snake-like and moss-eaten roots of giant trees. She detected movement about a hundred yards ahead. Healy, it had to be. But what was he doing? She crept closer, moving only when his back was turned, until she was close enough to observe him. He'd heaped a large pile of dead branches in the center of a circle of fallen logs and was breaking branches over his knee and pitching more wood onto the pile. He bent over, and Nora spotted the petrol can at his feet.

Healy left the container at the edge of the woodpile, evidently not ready to start the fire just yet. Maybe they were waiting for cover of darkness, so that smoke from the fire wouldn't be visible. This far from the house, you wouldn't smell it or see the light through the trees. It wasn't Midsummer, or Samhain or Imbolc, or any cusp of a changing season, so what was this fire for—a celebration, some sort of ceremony? Or perhaps the simplest reason of all: to burn something.

8

Stella Cusack had reached an impasse with her prisoner. Niall Dawson sat across the table with his head in his hands.

"I don't know how many more times I can say it. I did not kill Vincent Claffey."

"But you admit that he was blackmailing you. How much had you paid him?"

"I already told you—two thousand euros. It was all I could manage."

"And he wanted more."

"Yes, but I was going to work that out. I would never have killed anyone over something as . . ." Dawson shook his head and sighed.

Cusack kept silent, waiting for the weight of guilt to do its work.

"Look, I went home to Dublin yesterday, told my wife everything—about all the mistakes I'd made, about Anca, about paying off Vincent Claffey to keep him quiet. I should have told her everything ages ago. I wouldn't be here now if I had."

He looked as if that wasn't all he had to say. Cusack waited.

"I was there, in Claffey's shed, two nights ago. He was dead when I arrived, I swear. But he wasn't up on the machine, the way we found him the next morning. He was on the floor, and there was a small pool of blood under his head. I panicked. I didn't know what to do, so I left him there. I ran. I'm not proud of it, but there was nothing to be done."

"You could have rung emergency services."

"And made myself a suspect right away?"

"So what were you doing there, in the middle of the night?"

"I needed to speak to Anca. Cormac said he'd heard her at Beglan's, so I headed there first. But no one was about, so I headed over to Claffey's—she obviously had some connection to the man. They might have been working together, or he might have been forcing her to do things, I don't know." He stopped and looked at Stella. "I never did find her."

"There was no one at home at Beglan's, at three o'clock in the morning?"

"No, but the door was open. I just needed to talk to Anca. But there was no one home."

"Where was Anthony Beglan?"

"I don't know. I told you, I never saw him, or Anca, or anyone except for Vincent Claffey, who was—"

"—already dead when you arrived. Did you bother to check for a pulse?"

"There was no need, Detective. It was obvious that he was dead." Dawson let out a breath, reliving the moment of discovery.

"Anca Popescu says she was hiding in the shed. She says you and Claffey argued, that you pushed him, and that he fell backward, hit his head—"

"That's not true! Anca might have done for Claffey herself, did you not think of that? She had as much in the way of motive as I had. And easy enough to pin the crime on me, stumbling over the body like some feckin' gombeen—"

The phone on her hip began to play Lady Gaga, and Stella rose from the table. The tiny screen said, "Home," and Stella remembered with a stab of regret that it was past five on Sunday. Lia was due back from her father's now. She'd hoped they could have dinner together, maybe watch a film on television. Shit.

Stella took the call in the corridor. "I'm sorry, I'm right in the middle of an interview here, Lia." She couldn't say anything about the case, or the Serious Crimes Unit. All of that meant sweet F-A to a seventeen-year-old anyway. "Why don't you have something to eat, just to tide you over until I get home? I can swing by and pick up a pizza on my way—"

Lia put her hand over the mouthpiece, and the muffled sounds seemed as if she was conferring with someone. "Lia, is someone there with you?"

After a brief pause, a familiar male voice came on the line. "It's me, Stella. I can take her back to the flat if you're tied up."

"I'm not here all night, Barry, I just have to take care of a couple of things, and then I'll be home. It's not a problem."

"Look, it would be easier, wouldn't it, if I just take her out for dinner? You can let us know when you're home."

"Are you not busy with Allison this evening?" Stella cringed at the sound of her voice, the tone that managed to sound both chilly and pathetic.

There was the briefest pause before Barry said, "No, not tonight."

Stella held the phone to her ear, trying to stay calm. "Could you put Lia back on?" When her daughter took the phone again, Stella said, "Your father says he'll take you for a bite to eat. That might be best—I'm rather tied up here at the minute. But I'll see you when I get home—"

"No you won't. I'm going back to stay at Da's."

"I'll only be a couple of hours—"

"That's what you always say." There was a curt beep as Lia rang off.

Stella gave the wall a vicious kick before joining her suspect once more.

"We had a look around your room at Killowen," she said to Niall Dawson, "and we found these in your case." She opened her hand and let a handful of gallnuts spill onto the table. Dawson stared at the incriminating evidence, then up at her.

"They're not mine, I don't know where they came from. Someone else must have put them there."

"You do know what they are?"

"Of course I do. They're oak galls."

Stella set one of the gallnuts on the table directly before him. "Can you think of any reason why these might have been left as a calling card in two murders?"

"Two murders?"

"You've admitted you were at Killowen between the twenty-second and the twenty-fourth of April, when Benedict Kavanagh disappeared into the bog. Tell me something. If I start digging, will I find that you have a prior connection to Kavanagh as well?"

Dawson looked at her, jaded now, mistrustful. He reached out and carefully moved the single gallnut back to her side of the table. "Back to you, Detective. Someone's trying to frame me. I suggest you find out who it is."

9

Cormac stood at the top of the stairs, listening to the conversation around the dinner table below. A different, quieter sort of crowd tonight. Niall was missing, of course, but there were two new voices—Mairéad Broome and Graham Healy had evidently joined them. Why had they suddenly become sociable, after three days in isolation? Cormac started down the stairs, realizing that he was seeing everyone at Killowen in a new light since the visit to Hawthorn House and his conversation with Shawn Kearney this afternoon.

He'd been thinking of the stunning detail on the book shrines in the National Museum, with their elaborate metal covers studded with jewels, the intricate knotwork designs and large-eyed human figures that mirrored the high crosses. The *Cumdach Eóghain*, if it was like the book shrines he'd seen, would be priceless, something that might prompt a private collector to offer a huge sum. The tricky part was finding a person or an institution not so particular about provenance. Such buyers did exist; there was no doubt about that. But would the sale bring a fortune worth killing for? Two men were dead—perhaps therein lay the answer.

When the phone in his pocket vibrated, he stepped into the sitting room at the bottom of the stairs and closed the door behind him.

"You'll owe me two bottles of whiskey when you hear this," Mac-Sweeney said.

"Done. What did you find?"

"I rang up a friend at Cambridge, the one who invariably has all the gossip. Seems your man Gwynne is an expert on ancient manuscripts. He got his start at Cambridge, doing research under the famous paleographer T. A. Priest, the top man in medieval history there. When Gwynne left Cambridge, he went to work for the British Library."

"Thanks, Robbie. I'm not sure how all this will help, but it's good to know."

"I'm not finished. The scuttlebutt is that Gwynne was let go from the

British Library, more than twenty years since, when a rare manuscript in his charge went missing. He claimed innocence, of course, and I gather there wasn't enough proof to prosecute. When are you going to tell me what this is all about?"

Cormac was trying to process all he'd just heard. "I'm sorry, Robbie, I'm not even sure what I'm looking for."

"Hang on, I'm not done. This is all something to do with Benedict Kavanagh, isn't it? We do get the news here, you know, everyone's talking about him turning up in a bog out there."

"I can't really say anything. It's an ongoing investigation."

"The reason I ask is that after he was sacked from the library, your man Gwynne went back to work for his old tutor, Priest, and apparently they put together the definitive work on the handwriting of the ninth-century philosopher John Scottus Eriugena. Everyone knows Eriugena was Benedict Kavanagh's main subject."

"Yes."

"So all this about Gwynne is something to do with Kavanagh after all, isn't it?"

"I am sorry, Robbie, but I still can't tell you anything."

"Don't you at least want to know what the book was?"

"What book?"

"The one Gwynne was supposed to have pinched. It was a revised edition of *Deeds of the English Bishops* by William of Malmesbury."

"Is that significant?"

"Well, William of Malmesbury was one of the preeminent sources of information about Eriugena, although most people took the stories as apocryphal. There's a great one, though, about Eriugena having dinner with the Holy Roman Emperor, Charles the Bald, where the emperor posed him a question: '*Quid distat inter sottum et Scottum?*'—What separates a sot from a Scot? And your man shot back, '*Mensa tantum*'—Only a table. Cheeky wee bastard."

Cormac couldn't help smiling at his friend's enjoyment of the legend. "Listen, Robbie, I can't thank you enough."

Everyone at the dining table was absorbed in passing plates and filling bowls. Paella and salad tonight, fresh greens fragrant with garlic and the tang of fresh blood orange. No one said a word about Niall's absence, and Cormac could only assume that they knew what had happened. And that someone at this table might be willing to let an innocent man go down for a crime he hadn't committed. A strange wave of apprehension surged over him. He ought to get Nora and his father and Eliana away from this place right now, tonight. But he couldn't do it—he couldn't abandon Niall.

It was almost as if Nora was reading his turbulent thoughts as she tried to make conversation. "Cormac and I have just been reading up on the history of Killowen. Easy to be overshadowed by the monasteries at Clonmacnoise and Birr, I suppose. Still, the monks at Killowen had their own thing, didn't they?"

Martin Gwynne looked up from his salad. "What did you find about our monks?"

"Just that they were known for their work as scribes, apparently," Nora said.

Martin Gwynne said, "Oh, indeed. They saw it as their sacred duty to copy every book they could get their hands on."

Nora considered for a moment. "Do you mean they copied absolutely everything, word for word? Never changed or embellished anything?"

Gwynne smiled. "Well, there were mistakes, obviously. They were human. And they certainly added glosses and annotations in various editions. But you have to realize the significance of the 'faithful copy' to these men—and women, too; there's plenty of evidence of female scribes, but that's another discussion. The notion of a 'faithful copy' was absolutely central to the worldview of a scribe. You'll find that even books that were badly damaged were copied out exactly, with blank spaces left where they were illegible."

Nora pressed on. "You know, all those stories you hear about hedge schools, about ordinary Irish people reading old Latin and Greek texts, right up through the eighteenth and nineteenth century, are they really true?"

"Well, there was certainly a great tradition of scholarship in Ireland," Gwynne said. "History and poetry and writing of all kinds have always held a vaunted place in Irish culture—Welsh culture, too, going way back. When Christianity came, and with it the great wave of written language, the Irish weren't particularly interested in censoring content, even if the monks writing down the old stories thought they were a load of pagan rubbish."

Cormac's gaze wandered across the faces around the table. No particular reactions to what Gwynne was saying, but the man was apparently just getting started. Only Tessa Gwynne's expression said she'd heard this all before.

Gwynne held his wineglass in front of him. "Imagine living in a time when the written word was so special—every book was an individual work of art, unlike any other in existence. Not like today, when all we have is mass-produced, so-called content, and—God help us—'physical books.' Imagine stumbling upon a unique collection of words and ideas and images so fantastic that it was worth spending months or even years of your life copying it out so that others would be able to share in and appreciate its splendor."

Cormac decided it was time to show a little of his hand, despite Shawn's earlier warning. "You know, I've always been intrigued by handwriting," he said. "Such an intimate thing, really. It's amazing how much of one's personality comes out in the act of writing."

Gwynne was enjoying himself now. "I couldn't agree more—almost akin to the unique qualities of a human voice, or a fingerprint. For me, the act of writing has always been a kind of out-of-body experience. It starts with the spark here"—he pointed to his temple—"but then the head, the hand, the pen, and the ink all become one in the act of writing. Of course, all forms of creativity are a way of dipping one's toes in the essence of the divine."

Cormac glanced over at Anthony Beglan, whose head was bent over his plate. Sylvie poured herself another glass of wine. "What do you think of that, Lucien? *The divine*, Martin says."

The Frenchman dismissed her question with a glance. "What do I know about the divine? I'm only a *fromager*. Although one thing I do know—a *crottin* is as close to heaven as a man can get." He lofted a small plate of goat cheese for all to see.

Cormac couldn't catch Shawn Kearney's eye. The woman knew something, or at least had her suspicions. He was conscious of Nora watching him as well, no doubt wondering what he was at. He wasn't quite sure of that himself.

Perhaps warmed by wine, Martin Gwynne began to wax on again about the scribal arts: "We tend to think of the monks' copying as rote work, but it wasn't. Each copy was distinct, a permutation, a way for the writer to put his own signature and stamp on the work, adding his own interpretation, his own embellishments and flourishes."

"It's the same in traditional music," Cormac said. "The individual embellishments may be subtle, but they're peculiarly individual."

"Just so. You know, in the days of copying by hand, books were precious, even magical, but they were meant to be read and handled, studied, and above all, argued over! It was only much later that they were turned into artifacts of veneration, objectified like saints' relics, used only on special occasions."

"I suppose you're talking about book shrines?" Cormac asked. He saw Shawn Kearney's head jerk upward, and he could feel the tension around the table shift. "Nora and I were reading about a shrine associated with this place and the family that was supposed to have kept it—"

Claire Finnerty stood abruptly and said, "There's blackberry crumble with cream for dessert. Who'd like some?"

As Martin Gwynne approached the front door an hour later, Cormac asked quietly, "I don't suppose you've had a chance to look over those photos?"

"I'm sorry, it's been a rather busy day, busier than usual, even. I'll have a go at them as soon as I get back to the cottage."

Cormac said, "You might be interested in our other discovery this morning. Niall compared the marks on that wax tablet with the stylus found here last April, and he's convinced that it was the writing instrument used on that tablet. He thinks he'll be able to prove it without much doubt."

"Takes your breath away, doesn't it, what science is able to do these days? I meant to ask about Dawson—we did hear about his trouble. I think we'd all like to help, but no one is sure what to do. I was quite certain that Vincent Claffey had something to do with Benedict Kavanagh's death. Now I suppose we'll never know, will we?"

Tessa came up behind her husband, and for the first time, Cormac could see the way the blade of her jaw stretched her skin, sharp and insistent. Her eyes seemed to look out from a deep well.

"It's time to go, my love," Tessa said to her husband. He took her arm and tucked it in the crook of his own, and led her out across the gravel. Cormac recalled a gesture he'd seen that afternoon—Tessa Gwynne's hand reaching out to touch her daughter's hair.

10

It was after nine on Sunday evening when Stella arrived home. She changed into pajamas but kept her phone close by, just in case there was word on Anca and Deirdre and the child. Where could they have got to? She remembered the delight on the baby's face when she'd dangled the plastic keys in front of him. Cal. Short for Calum? Where had Deirdre had come up with the name? She hadn't thought to ask. Such a wonderful age, nine months. Not quite walking, but you could see all the wheels turning inside a baby's head. She'd never forgotten what Lia was like at that age. It made her heart ache now, remembering how she had watched the words form on her daughter's lips, the first time the spark of knowledge appeared in Lia's eyes as she said *mama.*

She punched in Barry's mobile number but hesitated before pressing the green button. What would she say? She wasn't finished with this case, not by a long shot. She'd likely be working strange hours for days to come, so perhaps it was best if Lia stayed with her dad for the time being. When the school term started, they'd have to work out a more regular schedule, but until then . . .

She felt a punch to the gut, realizing just how many times she had left Barry and Lia to fend for themselves over the past seventeen years. How many times Barry had had to feed their daughter and put her to bed when she was off on some training course, or when she'd served on the Drugs Task Force. Spending more time with criminals than with her own family. She stared at the number on the tiny screen, then let her hand drop. There was nothing she could say right now that would bring her daughter home. Time to crack this case, then she could work on making things right with Lia.

Stella retrieved the Cregganroe bombing file from her bag, poured herself a glass of wine, and slid the file out onto the table. It was thick, gray with fingerprints, and stuffed with all the photographs and intelligence reports that led to the arrest of the bomb makers. CLOSED was stamped across it in large black letters. Another successful resolution.

She flipped through lists of all the physical evidence collected at the bomb makers' worksite. There was a list of suspected and known associates. Not all the associates had names; sometimes physical descriptions or code names were all investigators had to go by. The file was filled with photos of shaggy young men, cigarettes dangling on their lips, on street corners and in pubs. Stella studied the faces in the photographs, taken by a hidden camera inside a pub. She remembered those days, the heady talk from the young intellectuals about freedom from tyranny, the corruptibility of governments looking out for one another against the will of the people, the whiff of socialism that had laced the struggles in the North. So much had changed, and so much had stayed exactly the same.

There were photos of the bomb makers' hideout after it was uncovered, stuffed with detonators, plastic explosives, and Semtex. It was a wonder they hadn't blown themselves up, as so many others had done before them. The investigators had managed to track down all but one of the group—the instigator, the head of the serpent, as it were. They'd given him a fitting code name, the Snake.

A rap at the door broke her concentration. Molloy was holding a striped carrier bag full of fish and chips. The smell made her mouth water and reminded her that she'd skipped dinner once again. She only wished she'd put on a robe before answering the door.

Molloy grinned. "Seeing as you're working late again, I thought you might be hungry."

"How do you know I'm working?"

He glanced at the contents of the file spread all over the table. "If you're not, I'll go straight home and reckon myself a very bad detective indeed. What are you at there?"

She led him to the table. "I don't know." She showed him the bag with the newspaper cutting. "I found this in Vincent Claffey's shed. It's about the Cregganroe bombing. Not sure what it has to do with the rest of the case, if anything, but thought I should check it out, at least. I'm just going through the file." She held up the bottle. "Wine?"

It took them all of about ten minutes to demolish the fish and chips.

Stella had vowed a thousand times to eat healthier but always knew she'd never be able to give up battered cod and salty vinegar-soaked chips. She'd had almost a full glass of wine before Molloy arrived, and he filled her glass again. He said, "The Cregganroe bombing—that's awhile back now, isn't it?"

"Yeah, a bit before your time," Stella said. "My first assignment out of Templemore—"

"Christ, Stella, not your first day on the job?"

"It was." She didn't have to say any more. A silence lapsed between them.

"Found the bastards, though, didn't they?" Molloy finally asked.

"Oh, they did," Stella said. "Four of them went down for it. But not the brains of the operation, or the girl who was supposed to have phoned in the warning, which nobody admitted receiving." Stella held the cutting at arm's length. "It does strike me as just a bit curious that this particular cutting should turn up in Vincent Claffey's shed. He was making threats at Killowen the night he was killed, intimating that he knew all their secrets. What if this is one?"

"You think somebody at Killowen could have been mixed up in that bombing? It's more than twenty years ago, Stella."

"So anyone over the age of forty would be in the running."

Molloy considered. "The Gwynnes, Claire Finnerty, Diarmuid Lynch, Anthony Beglan—everyone else would have been too young."

"Yes, unless it's an indirect connection, through a family member maybe? And just because Shawn Kearney is American doesn't mean she's off the hook. She said her gran was from Sligo." Stella spied a speck of grease at the corner of Molloy's mouth. "You've got something there," she said, reaching over to wipe it off.

He caught her wrist and pulled her close. She felt his other hand against her back, through the thin pajama fabric. Her immediate reaction was to push back, but he leaned into her.

"Don't fight, Stella. You've been pushing me away for days. You don't even see it, do you?"

"What are you talking about?" She struggled harder, but he still had her wrist, and the other arm around her waist, so that she couldn't move. He smelled good, a mixture of soap and chips and healthy sweat. This could not be happening. They worked together, for God's sake.

And not only that, he was far too young. "Fergal," she said, a note of warning in her voice.

Suddenly he let go of her. "Ah, Christ, Stella, you must know—"

Before he could finish, she grabbed his collar with both hands and pulled him to her, this time tasting that errant dab of grease and salt on her tongue.

11

Cormac made sure that Nora was deeply asleep, then dressed and grabbed his torch and headed downstairs. It was time to check out the storehouse. Two a.m. The farm was in complete darkness as he slipped through shadows to the building that housed the cheese-making operation. The wind had picked up, and the leaves rustled in the steady breeze that blew inland from the bog.

Cormac thanked Providence or whomever that the van was still parked in front of the storehouse and could serve as cover for his intrusion. Cracking open the door, he slipped inside. Cormac was conscious of every noise and could hear his own heart as the moldy odor of aged cheese greeted his nostrils. This was madness, he knew, but he couldn't stop. Something strange was going on in this place, and it must have something to do with both a missing ancient manuscript and the artifacts they'd just recovered from the bog. There were too many facts lining up to suggest otherwise.

He made his way through the workspace that was the front room, walls lined with shelving and all kinds of strainers and separators, metal and plastic molds. He picked up each wheel of cheese as he passed and tapped it, listening for the sound of a hollowed-out space, a void that could be used for smuggling. No luck. Every cheese large enough to hide anything sounded solid to the core. Beyond the workroom, a cave had been carved out of the limestone hill, the perfect spot for aging. The ceiling was supported with large oak timbers, and the cave seemed to go back about ten meters. The beam from his torch played over the walls, showing more cheeses waiting on wooden shelves, built in a way that increased air circulation. It was all about the flora, Lucien had explained at dinner the other night. Allowing the spores to work their magic in concert with other varieties of mold was the secret to great cheese. The shelves were stacked floor-to-ceiling with large wheels the size of car tires, and miniature gray-black pyramids, the last rolled in ashes as a contrast to the creamy white goat's milk, undergoing a miraculous transformation inside.

"Cormac?" Nora's whisper came from the workroom door. "What's going on? What are you doing out here?"

"Nora, you shouldn't be here. It's not safe."

"If it's safe enough for you—"

He didn't let her finish but pulled her deeper into the cave. "I saw two people sneaking out here the other night. I couldn't see who they were or what they were up to, but I thought I'd probe around a bit, in case there's something out here that could help Niall."

"It seems unlikely. What are you looking for?"

"I don't know. Treasure, a manuscript, some evidence of what Kavanagh and Claffey were after." He began to feel along the shelves, looking for a crack or a set of hinges, a hidden doorway, perhaps. All at once, his fingers found a break, the cool metal of a hidden hinge with a spring-loaded mechanism. Only the bottom half of the shelf came forward when he pulled on the latch. They'd have to crawl through.

On the other side was a small room, carved deeper into the hill behind the storehouse. The contents of the room took Cormac's breath away. There were several books—old, leather-bound volumes on a worktable, along with a half dozen magnifiers.

The light of his torch fell upon an ancient book open to an illustration of a plant, its leaves and roots drawn on vellum with a delicate hand. Below the plant was some Latin script and a drawing of a man being administered a draught of liquid from a wooden tankard, his limbs writhing, eyes rolling in his head.

"Looks like a medical text," Nora said, coming up behind him. "I've read about these, but I've never seen one. Doctors called them 'leech books.'" She closed the book and turned it over, pointing her light to the title stamped into its leather spine. "*Regimen Sanitatis*," she read. "These other titles are different kinds of books—geography, astronomy, a Bible."

By this time, Cormac had spied a laptop computer on the far side of the table. "Nora, come look at this." He pointed to the screen, which had come back to life listing a number of North American colleges and universities, private libraries, and museums, each with an abbreviation of several letters and numbers. "An inventory," he said to Nora. "Someone is selling these books to the highest bidder."

"But where have they come from?"

"You said you suspected that an ancient manuscript was somehow part of Benedict Kavanagh's murder. If Kavanagh found out about this stash, if he was a potential customer—"

"Someone might have killed him to keep him from exposing this operation."

Cormac nodded. "I think we know whose office this is, but let's see if we can confirm it." He started looking at the files on the computer desktop. Clicking on a folder marked "Photos," he found hundreds of images of the French couple, Lucien and Sylvie—skiing in the Alps, dressed in gauzy tropical gear on a beach, along a wharf on some Mediterranean island. "Here they are."

A sudden *whoosh* came from the opening into the storeroom, and a dozen tiny balls of fire rolled in at their feet as the hidden door slammed shut. There was no handle on the inside, no way to get out. Cormac knelt and pressed his shoulder against the false wall. It wouldn't budge—they were trapped. He turned around to Nora, the question in her eyes answered by the sound of liquid being splashed about on the other side, then a match being struck. Through the cracks in the wallboards, they could see light and hear the roar of the fire before they smelled smoke.

Together they shouted, in unison, as loud as they could, "FIRE!"

The goats in the barn next door began to bleat, helping to sound the alarm. Smoke was beginning to seep into the small room, searing their eyes. Cormac thought he heard someone outside, but it was only the van. Whoever had started this fire was getting away. "HELP!" he shouted again. "FIRE!"

Nora crawled on the floor, chasing fireballs, trying to extinguish them. "Stay low!" she shouted.

He could hear noises outside, indistinct voices raised in alarm.

The wall was beginning to feel warm to the touch, the flames crackling louder and louder, fed by oxygen from the outside. Finally, they heard footsteps running into the storehouse. "Back here," he shouted. "Behind the shelves. Hurry!"

A series of heavy blows sounded, smashing down the shelving and breaking through the false wall. Cormac grabbed Nora's hand and dragged her. As they passed the table, she made a lunge for the stack of books, but he pulled harder. They hadn't time to stop. They made it through the opening just as flames snaked up the table legs and began to consume the ancient volumes.

Diarmuid Lynch stood outside, surrounded by smoke, a sledgehammer in his hands. "Get out, quickly!" he shouted, and they clambered past him and out the storehouse door. "The fire's spreading to the barn. We've got to save the animals. Open the pens and let them out—quickly!"

Although he could barely see, Cormac followed Diarmuid's command, lifting the pins at each gate as he passed and chasing the goats through the opening. Nora worked the other side, driving frightened animals before her. The goats scrambled madly, tripping and falling over one another, spreading out as they reached the huge door and running madly in all directions. The humans outside stood openmouthed in their nightclothes: a wild-haired Claire Finnerty with a mobile in her hand, Martin and Tessa Gwynne, Shawn Kearney, his father and Eliana. Mairéad Broome and Graham Healy were on the path from their cottage, and Anthony Beglan came running up from the back meadow. The only two missing were Lucien and Sylvie. The white van was gone.

Claire Finnerty rushed up to them. "Are you all right?" she asked, as Diarmuid came up behind. "Was anyone else in there?"

Cormac shook his head. "Someone . . . locked Nora and me in the storehouse . . . and started the fire," he said between gasps. He watched the expressions on the faces around him, the glances of disbelief and denial as they all realized who wasn't among them.

12

The phone on Stella Cusack's bedside table intruded into a dream about herself and Barry, the one she had nearly every night, where he'd brought her to the circus, and just as the lights came up on the ring, he said, "I'll be right back," and then disappeared into the crowd. Whatever it meant, Stella was sure she didn't know, but it kept spinning in her subconscious, like bathwater circling a drain.

The clock read 2:38 A.M., and the voice on the phone was the duty officer, Hartigan. An emergency call had come in, a fire at Killowen Farm.

"Anyone hurt?" she asked, fearing the worst. If only she'd been paying more attention.

"A couple of minor cases of smoke inhalation, but somebody got to them fairly sharpish, so they'll be all right, thank God. I already rang Molloy. He's on his way over there now."

Stella rang off and looked over at the other side of the bed. When had he left? She reached out and ran her hand over the sheets. Slightly cool to the touch.

It was a quarter past three when Stella pulled into Killowen's car park. She found a crowd of emergency personnel milling about with Killowen residents and guests, and about sixty goats in a makeshift pen between the house and the damaged barn. The ambulance crews were still tending to Nora Gavin, Cormac Maguire, and Diarmuid Lynch. Molloy was herding the other residents into the farmhouse kitchen, preparing to take statements. He glanced at her with no glimmer of acknowledgment. Probably for the best. She should never have let him into the house last night.

Suiting up, Stella entered the fire scene, noting a stench of burned milk. She addressed herself to the local fire brigade's chief arson investigator, Thomond Breen: "What have you got, Tom?"

"Come through," he said. "One thing I can tell you is that it would have been one hell of a lot worse if someone hadn't turned a hose on. From what I can tell so far, it looks as if an accelerant was splashed about here." They were in some sort of storage room. Strands of melted cheese dripped from charred wooden shelving, and Stella noted the scorched petrol tin tossed to one side. Broken shelves at the back of the room showed the entrance to another space, also steaming and blackened. "Look here," Breen said, stooping to pick up a small black object from the floor. "Looks like these were used as fire starters. Can you smell the petrol?"

He set the charred walnut-shaped thing in her outstretched hand. "Some are burned more than others. That one's not too bad. Just what the hell are they, do you suppose?"

"Gallnuts," Stella murmured.

She headed for the house and found most of the farm's residents and current guests crowded into the kitchen with emergency service personnel. "We'll need statements from everyone," she said to Molloy. "I'd like to talk to them, if you don't mind. I'll take the sitting room, start with Dr. Gavin and Maguire, if you'd send them in. Give me about two minutes. Have we a call out for the two gone missing?"

"Just went out on the wire."

"Bloody Interpol," Stella said. "I'm guessing this all could have been avoided if they'd been on the ball."

Molloy shot her a sheepish look and reached into his jacket. "I meant to show you these last night, Stella," he said, then lowered his voice. "That's why I came over, actually. Sorry I got distracted." He handed over a couple of pages from the station fax machine, mug shots of two Swiss nationals wanted for theft of rare books from a library in St. Gallen. The names were different, of course, but it was definitely the supposedly French couple from Killowen.

She didn't look directly at him. She could still feel the grip of his hands, the heat of him against her. "One more thing, Fergal. What were Maguire and Gavin doing out in that shed in the middle of the night, anyway?"

Molloy gave a shrug and the slight jerk of an eyebrow. "You'll have to ask them."

Often the best witness in an attempted murder was the intended victim. Stella's advantage in this case was that she had two best witnesses, and not just ordinary witnesses, either, but scientists, trained observers of detail. Perhaps this whole case would be wrapped up tonight, if she was lucky. She went to the sitting room and waited for Dr. Gavin and Maguire.

"Have a seat," she said when they joined her. "You were both very fortunate tonight." That came out differently than she'd intended, more like an admonishment. "Can you tell me what you were doing in the storehouse tonight?"

Maguire sat forward in his seat. "I went there. I thought Nora was asleep, but she followed. I went because I'd seen suspicious activity there a couple of nights ago. It was two people, a man and a woman, but I couldn't make out who they were, in the darkness. Tonight I went looking for any evidence that could help Niall Dawson—"

"Evidence?" Stella couldn't help herself. She had almost forgotten about Dawson, still in custody down at the station.

Maguire said, "I had a notion that Benedict Kavanagh's death, and maybe Claffey's as well, had something to do with an ancient manuscript—"

Dr. Gavin jumped in: "And as it turned out, we did find evidence that Lucien and Sylvie were stealing old books. I'm sorry that the fire destroyed the evidence."

"Don't worry, we've got all we need to go after those two," Stella said. "Tell me how you arrived at that conclusion, about Kavanagh's death being connected to a rare manuscript."

Maguire's face was still marked with soot. "This place, Killowen, used to be a monastery. You know about the metal stylus that was found here last April?"

"Niall Dawson told me it was his excuse for being here then. My colleague's just off a stint with the Antiquities Task Force last year—he was very interested in that find."

"Well, a few more things have turned up since then," Dr. Gavin said. "The bog man, for a start. And while we were going through his garments with the textile expert, we found a wax tablet tucked into the folds of his cloak."

Maguire picked up the story. "Niall and I also found a leather satchel out on the bog, the kind the monks used to carry books a thousand years ago. It was empty. We started to think there might be a missing book, but it was all so vague. Then there were the gallnuts turning up everywhere—"

Stella sat forward. "Used to make ink."

Dr. Gavin said, "That's right. Then I happened upon some old accounts of a manuscript called the Book of Killowen—"

"And what sort of manuscript would that have been?"

Maguire was hedging his words. "Perhaps a special illuminated edition of the Gospels, like the Book of Kells or the Book of Durrow, perhaps something else. We don't really know." He looked at Nora. "It's possible that several important books might have come from the monastery here. Tradition has it that the Book of Killowen was guarded by a family called O'Beglan, and that there was a *cumdach*, an elaborate book shrine, made for it sometime in the tenth century. But evidently possession of this particular manuscript was so contentious that one of the O'Beglans got fed up with the fighting between the priests and bishops, and claimed to have burned it in the twelfth century. Seven hundred years later, one of that Beglan's descendants was supposed to have sold the shrine to a clockmaker, presumably to have it melted down."

"But you didn't believe these stories?"

Maguire shrugged. "I think such tales are a good way to throw people off the scent. Saying that you've burned or destroyed something may be the best way to keep it safe."

"Wait, back up for a minute. Who were the keepers of this manuscript?"

"The O'Beglans. The family was connected with the monastery, going back centuries. They farmed the termon lands of the church here. It's not out of the question. Lots of important manuscripts were for centuries in the possession of private families. A few still are."

"So why, in your estimation, would Benedict Kavanagh have been killed over this manuscript?"

"We haven't been able to work that out. Perhaps he was after the same artifacts as the treasure hunters, or maybe he was mixed up with them. A book like that would be worth a lot to the right collector. And even more if there's a shrine with precious metals and stones. If you could just locate Lucien and Sylvie—or whatever their real names are—perhaps we could find out whether Kavanagh and the book were connected. Vincent Claffey could have learned about it as well and wanted his share to keep quiet."

Stella took all this in. "So tell me again what you were doing out in the storehouse tonight?"

Maguire sighed. "Trying to find someone else with a motive for murdering Benedict Kavanagh. It occurred to me that a compartment carved out of a wheel of cheese would be an ideal way to smuggle valuable artifacts away from the farm."

"And what gave you that idea?"

Maguire paused for a moment. "I happened to see Martin and Tessa Gwynne, earlier in the day, carrying a wrapped package to a place called Hawthorn House—it's a private nursing home. Turns out their daughter has been a resident for almost twenty years. Someone told us the daughter had died, but it isn't true. The girl apparently tried to commit suicide after being jilted by some man. I'm not sure if it's anything to do with what has happened here, but you did ask how I got the notion."

Dr. Gavin said, "I saw something earlier as well, Detective. I don't know if it's important, but I was out in back, and I saw Graham Healy park up here beside the house and head down the path to the cottages. Eliana was just coming back that way—"

"My father's minder," Maguire said. "He's recovering from a stroke."

Dr. Gavin continued, "Eliana looked upset as she was coming from the wood, so I asked her what had happened. She said that Healy had been glaring at her. I wanted to see for myself what he was up to, so I went around the back way to the grove, and I saw him preparing a bonfire." She glanced up at Stella. "He'd set out a can of petrol." She shook her head. "That's all I know. But whoever lit the fire in the storehouse tonight used petrol as well, or some sort of accelerant. The thing I don't understand is, if Lucien and Sylvie did this, if they killed Benedict Kavanagh and Vincent Claffey, was it all for money? Then the elaborate staging, with the gallnuts and everything, that was all just for show. You saw the bodies, Detective. What do you think?"

Inside that question was the same vague notion that had been bothering Stella for several days. From the beginning, the two murders seemed very personal. Something about this was not sitting right.

After seeing her witnesses out, Stella called Molloy. "Fergal, can you get Tom Breen to look for a bonfire site in the oak grove, see what he can find there in the way of evidence? And one more thing, did you ever find out whether Graham Healy had experience with heavy machinery?"

Molloy inclined his head slightly. "Sorry, Stella, meant to tell you about that last night as well. I checked with the art school, like you said. Healy was the head of the sculpture installation crew, operated a small JCB they used for digging foundations. You were dead right about that."

The rest of the interviews were unproductive. No one else at Killowen admitted hearing a thing before the fire began. Stella paid particular attention to the accounts of Mairéad Broome and Graham

Healy, but they claimed bonfires were a perfectly ordinary occurrence at Killowen, that they'd half a tin of petrol left after starting the fire.

So many things just weren't adding up. If Kavanagh had been murdered by the Swiss couple, why would they stick around after his death? Wouldn't it make more sense to disappear before the body was discovered and suspicion aroused?

But Maguire and Gavin's theories about an old book being at the center of this case jibed with what they'd found in Kavanagh's things from the B and B. Kavanagh could have been here looking for a valuable old manuscript, one that might raise a few eyebrows, give his academic notoriety a nicely timed kick in the hindquarters. What had he said to his wife? *This is going to rattle some bones.* It would have to be something sensational. But he had to make sure it was real. She could see the notes in his hand: *IOH returns to IRL, great work unfinished.*

Fergal Molloy appeared at the door. "Stella, we've got something you should see. Come out to the grove. Breen and his lads did find the remains of a bonfire."

Out at the bonfire site, Stella got a whiff of woodsmoke with an edge of something acrid, like burned chemicals. She turned to Thomond Breen. "What news here?"

"No petrol container, but we did find a few interesting bits. Photos and papers, mostly, not completely burned. I'll have them bagged up and delivered to you."

Stella felt a twinge of excitement. Vincent Claffey had made a mistake, squeezed the wrong person. And something in this pile of ashes may have led to his death.

She was headed back to the house when she brushed past an old man sitting on a bench outside the door at Killowen. She felt a surge of annoyance, realizing that she hadn't interviewed this man; Molloy hadn't brought him in. "Are you all right there?"

"Nan-nanning a wordoo," the old man said. His diction was perfect, but the words were incomprehensible. "I flang the cubbits snaring." It finally dawned on her. This was Maguire's father, the one who'd suffered a stroke. On the ground at his feet were large white cards with black lettering on one side, pictures on the other. Common household objects, as if he were a child again. In her experience, even children noticed far more than people realized.

The old man seized her hand, a pleading look in his eyes. "I sew the

Free Staters," he said. "You know, the Free Staters." He kept pointing to an upstairs window and making the same gesture over and over, running his pinched-together right thumb and forefinger over his open left palm. Was it some sort of sign?

"Sorry, I don't understand. Do you need pen and paper?"

"No, no." He seemed impatient, urgent.

"Shall I get your son?"

"My sum?" He seemed worried, confused. "No, my author."

"Maguire, the archaeologist, isn't he your son?"

"Yes. Yes." The old man let her go then and sank back onto the bench. No wonder Molloy had left him off the interview list. He had mentioned an author—could it have to do with a mysterious missing manuscript, or was he just talking rubbish? Impossible to tell. And yet behind his eyes, she sensed a kind of light, or intelligence. Or was it only the ghost of the person he had been?

Just then Graham Healy came through the front door of the house, followed by Molloy. Stella felt the old man grip her forearm. "Free Stater," he whispered hoarsely.

She dropped down beside him, so that her face was on a level with his own. He started making the same gesture again, and this time she felt a jolt of recognition. He was lighting a match. She spoke quietly, making sure to keep her back to Healy and Molloy. "You saw that man start the fire last night, didn't you, from the window upstairs?"

He nodded, and Stella continued. "Listen to me, was it the bonfire in the wood, or the fire up here, the one in the storehouse?"

The old man's eyes darted unmistakably toward the storehouse. She had a witness. "You're sure it's the same man you saw? It was dark last night."

He focused on her face with intense concentration and said slowly, "I—sawt—rum-rumaway."

"All right. Thank you for telling me."

As Stella straightened, she glanced up to find Graham Healy staring at them.

BOOK FIVE

Gaib do chuil insin charcair,
ni róis chluim na colcaid.
Truag insin amail bachal;
rot giuil ind shrathar dodcaid.

Take thy corner in the prison:
thou shalt have neither down nor pallet.
it is sad, o prince of crosiers,
the packsaddle of ill-luck has stuck to thee.

—Verse written in the margin by the Irish scribe who copied
Priscian's *Institutiones Grammaticae* (a Latin grammar)
in the mid-ninth century

1

Tired as she was, Stella felt an extra adrenaline jolt as she entered the windowless interview room. Graham Healy sat at the table. She took a seat across from him. "Thank you for coming in, Mr. Healy. I just have a few more questions." She consulted her notes, giving him a little extra time to stew before she began.

"We found evidence of a bonfire at Killowen last night, out in the wood."

"That's not against the law now, is it?"

"No, but destroying evidence in a murder investigation is. Burning down a building with people inside it is a crime."

"I was asleep in my own bed when that fire started at the storehouse last night."

"I have reason to believe otherwise. Let me ask, how far is it from the cottage where you stay to the storehouse? Only a couple of hundred yards, right? Easy enough to start the fire and then double back. You could make certain everyone saw you and Ms. Broome coming up the path when the alarm went up."

"Why would I want to harm those people? I know nothing about them. We'd barely even met. I'd never seen them before dinner last night."

Stella paused for a moment, then tried a different approach.

"All right, let's go back to your relationship with Vincent Claffey."

"There was no relationship."

"But you did work together, isn't that right? Preparing canvases, other sorts of . . . how did Ms. Broome put it? Oh, yes, 'the more basic tasks.' You'd have to instruct him, surely, explain just the way she wanted them, dimensions and so on, and arrange delivery if he worked on the canvases at his own place, all that sort of thing."

Healy offered a grudging glance in her direction. "Yes."

"So you did have an ongoing relationship with Mr. Claffey, if he took care of those sorts of tasks for you on a regular basis?"

"I suppose so."

"What's the going rate?"

"Excuse me?"

"It's a simple question. How much did you pay Mr. Claffey for framing and stretching canvases?"

Healy looked at her for a long moment. "It was a bit more than the going rate; Mairéad was always too generous, especially with Claffey."

"How much more? And do you figure that sort of work on an hourly basis, or is it usually piecework?"

"Hourly." Graham Healy's voice was barely audible. "He was paid forty euros an hour."

"So he must have put in a lot of time on those canvases. Because the witness statement we have says it was a pretty fat brown envelope you handed over to Vincent Claffey on the day you arrived at Killowen."

"He preferred twenty-euro notes, didn't like fifties. He'd particularly asked to be paid in twenties that time. You can check with Mairéad if you don't believe me."

"So where are the canvases?"

"Sorry?"

"Come on, Mr. Healy. If Vincent Claffey spent so much time making bloody canvases, where are they? Is there a special shed at Killowen where you keep a store of materials? We didn't find any materials at Claffey's farm, so I assumed he'd been working at Killowen. But there don't seem to be any supplies there either."

Healy sat stone-faced.

"I have a different theory, Mr. Healy. Would you like to hear it?"

"I don't suppose I can stop you."

"I think Vincent Claffey spied you with Benedict Kavanagh out at Killowen Bog. I think he didn't make anything of it until Kavanagh's body turned up. That was when Claffey saw his big chance to make a bit of money—for keeping his mouth shut."

"No."

"But maybe he threatened to tell anyway. Or maybe he wanted more money, and you couldn't see paying again and again, for years. So you had to get rid of him. Or maybe it was an accident. You went to talk to him, things got ugly, you pushed him, and he hit his head. Nothing to be done about it, so you make his death look like Kavanagh's to distract us."

Stella continued, "You knew the bog was protected, that no one was going to be cutting there for a long time. You have experience driving an excavator. The one thing I can't figure with that whole scenario is how you got Kavanagh out to Killowen. But I have to hand it to you, whatever way you did it, it worked. Maybe it was you who sent him an anonymous message about an old manuscript, something to do with his old friend, Eriugena, the philosopher fella. Some earth-shattering new discovery that would definitely rattle some bones."

"I really have no idea what you're talking about, Detective. I never should have come here. You're dead wrong—about all of this."

"Am I?"

"I told you, Mairéad and I were staying at a friend's place in the Slieve Bloom Mountains when Benedict disappeared. We were nowhere near Killowen. If you don't believe me, ask Claire, ask Diarmuid Lynch—they'll tell you."

"They're also friends of Mairéad's. Maybe they were glad to see her get shut of that bastard of a husband, almost as glad as you were."

"You've got it all wrong. Mairéad would never harm anyone. She was only trying to help—" Healy stopped abruptly.

Stella knew she'd just witnessed a slip. "Who exactly was she trying to help?"

Healy had reached his limit. "I'm done talking. If you've nothing to keep me here, I'd like to go."

It could have happened just as she described to Healy, but there wasn't a shred of evidence that could prove anything, and Healy knew it. Molloy was lounging against the wall outside the interview room when she opened the door. Healy didn't make eye contact with either of them as he left.

"I hate to say it, Stella, but we're going to have to charge Dawson or spring him. All we've got are those gallnuts from his room, which anyone could have planted, and a witness statement from Anca Popescu, who's conveniently scarpered."

Anca's statement was looking more and more like a fable, Stella thought. She remembered Dawson's words: *Anca might have done for Claffey herself, did you not think of that?* The girl had claimed that Dawson pushed Claffey, that the victim had struck his head. Those details had been borne out in the postmortem. But it could have been Anca herself on the other side of that altercation, and Niall Dawson could be telling the truth. They still didn't know who'd mutilated Claffey's corpse and wrapped him in plastic.

"Have we gone over the clothes Dawson was wearing that night? He admitted finding a corpse, for God's sake. I can't believe there's not even a single speck of blood on his shoes. We've no physical evidence that can place him there?"

Molloy shook his head.

"Fine," she said. "Let him go. Christ, this whole case has me round the bend."

Stella could hear the clock ticking, could feel the hot breath of Serious Crimes on her neck. They were going to lose this case in the next day or two, she could feel it.

2

Cormac shook his head. "It's no use, I don't know what you're saying." He threw up his hands and turned away from his father, who sat on the bed, refusing to get up or dress himself. They'd let him sleep late after the excitement over the fire last night, and now he was adamant about not leaving his room.

"I sew the Free Stater. Tolder pleaseworum." He kept repeating the same phrases, over and over again, about a Free Stater. There was a screw seriously loose today, and no mistake. "Will you just please put your clothes on?"

The old man shook his head. "No."

"If you're not going to get up, I'll have to get someone to sit with you."

"No—" He started to stand. "Does she havunn? The Free Stater?"

Cormac said, "I'm sorry, I don't know what you mean." He knelt down in front of his father once more. "What is it? What are you trying to say?" He searched his father's eyes, looking for clues.

Joseph shook his head and spoke slowly, distinctly. "I sew the Free Stater. I sew." He held his fingers up, pointing to his own eyes. "Bollocks. But she . . . she knows I sew it."

"Who knows?" Cormac asked. "Who the hell are you talking about?"

"Her! The worum." He let his head drop into his hands. "You can't hear me."

"I'm trying. I'll keep trying, if you will."

"I'm an awful bosom."

Cormac struggled to keep a straight face. "Well, an awful something, and no mistake."

Joseph reached out to touch Cormac's face, letting his fingertips brush the eyebrow that had been singed in the fire last night, the edge of the bandage that covered a small burn on his forehead. "My poor lad," the old man said. "My sum."

He helped his father to stand and brought his clothes from the bedside chair. "Time to put these on and face the day. Eliana is downstairs waiting for you." The mention of the girl's name drew an unexpected response.

"Can't look. Spuh-puh-puncture of pass. *Pass*. Peas. Ah, I'm a fool of bad words."

Cormac tried to hear what his father was saying. "Has Eliana upset you in some way?"

"No, no. She's a goose to me."

What must it be like, every day facing a barrage of meaningless words that hemmed him in, imprisoned his thoughts? *She's a goose to me.* What could that possibly mean?

The old man was finally dressed. Cormac led the way downstairs, already exhausted before the day had begun. He made tea and buttered some brown bread for their breakfast, though it was nearly two in the afternoon. A strange morning after a strange night.

But both he and Nora had work to do today; he was back on the bog, and Nora had said she'd lend a hand. Bringing the old man out here, even for a few days, had been a mistake. What if he never regained his faculty of speech? Once in a while, some word would come swimming to the surface, stay anchored to its meaning for a few hours, and then recede again. Most days the image he carried was of the two of them, himself and his father, in a coracle, paddling furiously in a vast sea of alphabet soup.

3

By half-two in the afternoon, Stella Cusack felt her energy flagging. Between Molloy's late-night visit and the fire, she'd slept only about two hours, and a heavy fatigue was beginning to settle upon her. But there was no question of taking any rest, not now when the case was in disarray. They had no leads, no suspects in custody. The whole thing was a bloody shambles. She'd been staring at the whiteboard for twenty minutes with no flash of insight.

Molloy set a cup of steaming tea on the table beside her.

"Just got a call back on Claire Finnerty," he said. "Remember, you asked me to look into her background, like I did with Lynch? I checked public records for the birth date listed on her driving license. There was a Claire Finnerty born at the Mater Hospital in Dublin on the fourth of January 1968. I was able to track down the parents, Roger and Sheila Finnerty of Beaumont Road, Dublin. Just got off the phone with them, and get this—their daughter was eight weeks premature; she only lived two days."

Stella said, "So who's your one at Killowen calling herself Claire Finnerty? Any chance we've got her prints on file?"

Molloy shook his head. "Never any reason to collect them."

"Except now we know she isn't who she pretends to be."

"Want me to talk to her?"

"No, I'll go. What else have you got?"

"The arson investigators found a few fragments of the papers burned at that bonfire site. Thought you'd like to see them." He lined up on the tabletop about half a dozen clear polythene bags, each holding a bit of partially charred paper. "Not much left, but . . ."

Stella took the magnifying glass from Molloy and peered at each one in turn. "No, but look—does that seem like a date from a newspaper article?"

Molloy peered at it. "Yeah, *Irish Times*, looks like the eighteenth of August 1991. We can check that. What about this?" He held up one of the other fragments. "That colored pattern looks almost like a bit of a passport."

Stella turned the clear packet over. The numbers 463 stood out clearly at one corner. "Let's start there, get a list of Irish passport numbers ending in four, six, three. See if anything leaps out."

Molloy's phone began to buzz. Stella couldn't hear what the caller was saying, but it seemed to be good news. He pressed the phone to his shoulder. "They've found the girls and the baby. Up in a forestry preserve above Mountshannon. The car got stuck, but they're all right. The local sergeant already called social services for Deirdre Claffey and the child."

"Good! This time we're going to keep closer tabs on Anca Popescu. I don't think Murray will get over the trauma."

"Tied up by that slip of a girl? He shouldn't get over it."

"Fergal, why don't you head over to Mountshannon and bring Anca back here? I'll get to work on these."

Stella locked up the evidence, then stashed her notebook where she'd scribbled the newspaper date in her bag. The local library ought to have newspapers from that era, on microfilm or online. She left the station by the front door, traveling out John's Place to the oval, and then turned right at Wilmer Road, the N52. The Birr library was in a nineteenth-century chapel built by the Sisters of Mercy. Stella stepped into the nave of the old church, now the main reading room. In the center stood a display case, lit from above. She felt herself drawn to the large book inside. The sign said it was a facsimile of the MacRegol Gospels, supposed to have been made at Saint Brendan's monastery, Birr. Stella knew the place, now just a small ruined churchyard around the corner from the Guards station in Church Lane. She read:

> The MacRegol Gospel Book is a manuscript copy of the Four Gospels, written and illuminated by an abbot of Birr about 800 AD. It consists of 169 vellum folios (leaves) about 345 mm high and 270 mm wide. The script used is a formal one called insular majuscule or insular half-uncial and it somewhat resembles one of the hands of the Book of Kells. A translation or gloss in Old English cursive script was inserted between the lines about a thousand years ago. Eight pages are illuminated in the style of the

eighth or ninth century AD with pigments including red lead, verdigris, and orpiment probably bound with the white of an egg. About 1681 John Rushworth presented it to the Bodleian Library, where it was known as the Rushworth Gospels and presumed to be of Anglo-Saxon origin. But Charles O'Conor STD of the O'Conor Don family demonstrated by internal evidence in 1814 that the manuscript must have originated in Ireland. He pointed to the colophon on the final page of the manuscript, which read: *"Macregol dipinxit hoc evangelium. Quicumque legerit et intellegerit istam narrationem orat pro Macreguil scriptori."* (Macregol coloured this gospel. Whoever reads and understands its narrative, let him pray for Macregol the scribe.)

Stella propped her elbows on the glass and gazed at the book. This was only a photographic copy, and yet she felt herself pulled in by the tiny spirals and twisted birds, the serpent that formed the border, the odd rectangular shapes of letters hidden in plain sight. And the colors—red the color of half-dried blood, gold, green, and black—and eyes, everywhere, creatures staring unblinking from every corner of the page.

"Very fine, isn't it?" The librarian's voice startled her. "The original is in Oxford, but it was made at the monastery right here in Birr."

"Yes, I was just reading about it," Stella said. "I suppose there were lots of books like this made in the monasteries around here."

"Yes, but only a few survive. Which makes them all the more valuable."

"I wonder, you wouldn't happen to have heard of the Book of Killowen?"

"Ah, the lost book of Killowen and its shrine."

"If the book was lost, how do you happen to know about it?"

"There are several accounts of it. Monks wrote down the stories of important books, who made them, who kept them, any controversy. They say the first copyright case in the world was over a manuscript illegally copied by Colmcille himself. We librarians are like a secret society, Detective. Even in the digital age, we make it our business to know about books."

Stella was puzzled. "I'm sorry, have we met?"

"Not formally, but I've seen you about. Mary Anglim—I should explain. I know your daughter, Lia. She often comes to our writers' workshops for young people. You must be pleased—she's turning into an excellent writer."

"Yes . . . yes, she is," Stella said, although this was the first she'd heard of any literary aspirations. She'd never even seen her daughter with pen in hand. What on earth did Lia write about? And why had she kept this part of herself so well hidden?

"Must be frustrating," Stella said. "Reading accounts of something like the Book of Killowen and never being able to see it. Especially if it was as spectacular as this. Where do you suppose MacRegol's book was between the time it was made and the time it was presented to the library at Oxford?"

"Most likely in private hands, but there's no way to know for certain. Were you just here to see the Gospels, or was there something else?"

Stella said, "No, I came to see if you have the *Irish Times* on microfilm. I'm looking for a specific date."

"Anything before 1996 is searchable on the *Irish Times* website. Let's have a look. What's the date?"

"Let's start with the eighteenth of August, 1991," Stella said. Mary Anglim brought up a search screen on a library computer beside them and typed in the first date. Smudgy black-and-white images of newspaper pages came up on the screen.

"Thanks." Stella got down to it, letting her eyes wander over the headlines, anything that might pop out as connected to Vincent Claffey and his black market in secrets. Follow-up reports on the freeing of the Birmingham Six and the IRA firing mortar bombs at 10 Downing Street a few months earlier. There were items about the brouhaha over the minister of defense being spotted at an IRA funeral, and preparations for the opening of the Dublin Writers Museum at Parnell Square. A small headline on page six stood out: "Gardaí still seek leads on missing woman."

Stella made the article larger and began to read. "Gardaí investigating the disappearance last month of Co Dublin woman, Ms Tricia Woulfe (23), have not ruled out the possibility that the case could become a murder investigation. But Supt Gerald Murray from Harcourt Street, who is in charge of the investigation, said yesterday there was no evidence to suggest that the young woman has been murdered. Tricia Woulfe, from Greystones, Dublin, was last seen in the Cuffe Street area of the City at around 1 am on 13 August."

That was the day before the Cregganroe bombing. Twenty-two years ago this month. A photograph accompanied the article, a blurry black-and-white image showing a young woman with short dark hair and a broad smile, her friends obviously cropped out of the frame.

Where was Tricia Woulfe now? Stella thought she had an idea.

4

Cormac looked up from his work at the excavation site to see a figure approaching through the small trees and clumps of sedge that dotted the surface of the bog.

"Nora," he said. She stopped digging. Niall Dawson was about forty yards away. Cormac climbed up out of the cutaway and waited for his friend. "They cut you loose," he said.

"Didn't have enough to hold me. Never did. What a mess."

Nora shaded her eyes as she looked up from the pit. "I'm so glad. Welcome back, Niall."

"Tell me what you're up to here," Dawson said. "I'm in desperate need of distraction."

Cormac jumped off the bank into the hole once more, while Niall peeled off his jacket and began to roll up his shirt cuffs. The three of them stood in the middle of the large rectangular void.

"We've finished going over the area where we found the satchel," Cormac said. "So I thought we'd get going on a couple of test pits. I was just going to start breaking the surface in that area." He indicated a plot that he'd finished marking off with stakes and twine. "Maybe you'd care to let off a little steam?"

Cormac handed his friend the pick, and Niall attacked the dense, spongy peat. Once the top layer was broken, they would use spades and trowels and eventually graduate to bare hands to sort through the increasingly sodden material below.

"I stopped by the farm—Claire told me about the fire," Dawson said, breathing heavily as he slung the pick. "She said there were old books in that storehouse."

Cormac said, "Yes. That nice French couple turned out to be Swiss art thieves on the run from Interpol."

Dawson stopped his work. "Lucien and Sylvie? Claire didn't mention that."

"They were the only people missing after the fire," Cormac said. "They must have seen us go into the storehouse and saw their chance to escape."

"Yes, but why start a fire?" Dawson asked. "Why not just lock you in while they made their getaway? That level of violence, it doesn't fit the profile of book thieves I've seen. They like money, or they like books, but very few resort to murder."

"Unless they were involved in Kavanagh's death."

"Why stick around after he was killed? That doesn't make sense either."

"Unless they didn't have what they'd come here to find. Niall, did you ever hear of a manuscript called the Book of Killowen? Shawn Kearney seemed to know about it," Cormac said. "She seemed rather frightened, to tell you the truth."

"I found a brief mention of it in John O'Donovan's Ordnance Survey notes," Nora added. "It was evidently a special book, but it was said to have been burned back in the twelfth century. O'Donovan also mentioned a fancy book shrine, but it may have been melted down after the book was destroyed. And the family that was reported to have done all this were called Beglan."

Dawson stopped swinging the pick and leaned on the handle. "What else do you know?"

"The Beglans were successors to the founder of the monastery at Killowen. But it's all so convoluted," Cormac said. "I meant to tell you, Niall, we showed the photos of the wax tablet to Martin Gwynne. I thought it was rather curious that a medieval manuscript expert should be living here at Killowen, so I rang up Robbie and asked him to check into Gwynne's background. Turns out he was sacked from the British Library over a stolen manuscript, twenty years ago. The thing is, the stolen book was a revised edition of *Deeds of the English Bishops* by William of Malmesbury—"

"I know the one," Dawson said. "*Gesta Pontificum Anglorum.*"

"Then you know it has a connection to Kavanagh's subject, Eriugena."

"Yes, well, William of Malmesbury was probably just repeating all the juicy stories he'd heard. If I'm remembering right, he even had one about Eriugena being murdered, how his pupils were supposed to have stabbed him to death with their styli because he insisted that they think for themselves—a cautionary tale for all academics. Robbie must have explained that William of Malmesbury had a reputation for embellishment."

"Well, he did mention the stories were considered apocryphal."

Nora said, "Hey, guys, I've found something."

She dropped her trowel and began to work with bare fingers while Cormac and Niall Dawson crowded around. A smooth brown ridge began to protrude. Cormac and Niall joined in the digging, working quickly, until they had uncovered a single leather corner and a ragged hash of soft brown material.

"Sweet holy Jaysus," Dawson said. "I don't believe this. It's a book. It's Killowen Man's missing book." He gingerly picked away more peat, and a few words of Latin script appeared under his fingertips, the vellum page shiny with wetness and miraculously still readable. Dawson sat back on his heels. "I really don't believe this."

Cormac tried to get his head around the shape, the book splayed open, the upper left corner folded over and the pages dog-eared, the center almost rotted away, a mass of letters floating free in wet peat, independent of their vellum matrix. "I think you're right. It is a book, though it looks a bit more like—"

"Lasagna," Nora said. "What the hell do we do now?"

"First, we get the camera." As Dawson turned to dig into his bag, Cormac's eyes began to pick out details: a yellow bar appeared, and then an almost circular letter *D*, with an S-curve clearly visible inside. "Look here, Niall, I think this is a capital, and a gold border."

Nora leaned in to try to read the script as Niall peered through the camera lens, snapping away as quickly as he could. He said, "See that line of text, dead center? Can you read it? Looks to me like '*in ualle lacrimarum.*'"

Cormac dredged up his decades-old knowledge of Latin. "Something about a vale of tears. Psalms, maybe?"

"There's one way to find out," Nora said, quickly typing the letters into her phone. "You're right. Psalm 83, verse 7: '*in ualle lacrimarum in loco quem posuit.*' 'In the vale of tears, in the place which he has set.' So our bog man was walking here, maybe reading his book of Psalms, and he's attacked by a couple of assailants, they throw his body into the bog, and then his book, and his satchel after him."

"So maybe he was robbed," Niall said. "Remember what the textile consultant told us, that he ought to have been wearing a brooch, and we didn't find any. Maybe it was as simple as that."

But the words on Killowen Man's wax tablet weren't verses from Psalms, Cormac thought. They were something about freedom of rational thought, and malice and evil. He had often experienced this same sensation out on excavations, a feeling of hurtling down a tunnel through time. Now he felt himself spat out, centuries ago, on this same squelching bog, where the ancient man in the hospital cooler had once walked and perhaps written his last thoughts, and where he'd been brutally murdered. Cormac suddenly understood in a flash how everything they'd found was connected, down through the centuries, all the way from the Dark Ages directly to Benedict Kavanagh. He heard voices from a distance, then felt his thoughts zooming back into the present.

Niall had his face pressed to the wet peat and was using a flat probe to try and get a look between some of the other pages. "I can see another illuminated border."

"We'll have to get it out of there as quickly as we can," Cormac said. "I've got some plywood in the back of the jeep. Would that do as a stabilizer for now?"

Niall nodded. "It'll have to do."

On the way to the hospital, Cormac's thoughts came back to the present as he glanced over at Nora in the passenger seat. She was nodding off. Dawson's eyes, too, were closed in the backseat. Cormac felt tremendous relief, looking at the white gauze wrapped around Nora's forearm, that neither of them had been badly injured last night. They were lucky that Diarmuid Lynch had heard them. Surely the police would track down the book thieves, and the case would be wrapped up shortly. Still, it was chilling to know that someone at Killowen had wanted them dead.

5

Stella was on her way to Killowen when her mobile began to buzz. "Cusack here."

"She's dead, Stella. Anca Popescu is dead."

"Fergal, what are you talking about? What's happened?"

"I met the uniforms at Cappaghbaun, the place above Mountshannon where the girls got stuck on the forestry road. Social Services had charge of Deirdre Claffey and the baby, and I was carrying Anca back to Birr, like you said . . ." His voice broke. "You told me to keep close tabs on her this time, and I should have been watching—"

"Just tell me what happened, Fergal."

"I brought her in the car with me. But I never locked the fuckin' passenger door, Stella. I never thought—"

"What happened?"

"We were coming over the top of the mountain, and the next thing I know she's got the door open and she's trying to jump. I reached out for her, but I couldn't hold on."

Stella was imagining the scene as Molloy described it: a rough forestry road, fir trees, and a vicious drop. She felt a punch to the gut. Did the girl dread being sent back to Romania so much that she would risk losing her life rather than face that? "Are you with her now?"

"Yes. I had to climb down to her. I checked her pulse, but there's nothing. She's dead." He sounded on the verge of tears.

Stella heard her own voice take on a steely edge. "Fergal, listen to me. Stay where you are and ring Emergency Services. Do it now."

She heard a sharp exhalation. Finally he said, "Right. It'll be all right. I'll just tell them what happened."

"Phone Emergency Services right now, Fergal. Don't move her, don't touch anything else. I'm on my way."

Stella rang off, feeling numb. Anca Popescu was only nineteen, but she had probably experienced more horrors than any human being could be expected to endure. And all Stella could see now was that haunted expression in the girl's eyes, the nervous, darting hands, the way she'd sucked that smoke from her cigarette, as if it were pure oxygen. That, and how Anca had turned her gaze into a silent plea as Stella had left the safe house the other day, as if she had somehow known it would be their last meeting. Why the hell had she sent Molloy? She ought to have gone with him, or picked the girl up herself, and none of this would have happened. She sat in the car, hands on the wheel but going nowhere, not sure what to do next.

Her phone buzzed again.

"Mam, it's Lia."

Stella didn't say anything, afraid that if she opened her mouth to speak, she would begin to sob.

"I'm sorry about hanging up on you yesterday," Lia said, her voice sounding less like the stroppy seventeen-year-old she'd been lately and more like the child she used to be. "It was rude. I only wanted . . . it just makes me crazy when you and Daddy are so unhappy. I don't mean to mess things up."

Stella forced herself to speak. "Oh, Lia, you haven't messed anything up. What happened between your father and me, it's not your fault, sweetheart. It's nothing to do with you. Are you all right, staying with Daddy for another little while? It'll only be a day or two more, I promise. I'll ring you."

"But you should talk to Daddy. He's not—"

"I'll speak to him, Lia, don't worry."

"Right, see you, Mam."

"I love you, Lia. I'll ring you back just as soon as I can."

Stella started her ignition and felt the tears begin to flow.

Forty minutes later, she bumped along the road that crossed the top of the mountain at Cappaghbaun and found an ambulance, a Mountain Rescue van, and several Guards vehicles all parked in the middle of the road.

"Stella!" A voice came from beside the ambulance as she stepped from the car. It was her superintendent, Eamonn Brown, looking smart in his expensive suit. Not a bad copper, but too ambitious, always looking for the next opportunity to impress those above him, which tended not to impress the people below him.

"Eamonn, why are you here?"

"One of my officers involved in a fatal accident? It's my job to be here."

And to see how your investigation is coming along, was the unspoken subtext.

"Where's Molloy?" Stella asked.

"The ambulance lads are checking him over."

"Have they recovered the girl's body yet?"

"A bit dodgy, that." He waved her to the edge of the road to look down. "The Mountain Rescue team is rigging up some lines to make sure no one else takes a tumble. Then they'll send a couple of people down and bring the body up on a gondola. Dreadful business. Molloy said he phoned and told you what happened?"

"Yes, that the girl jumped from the moving car."

"I gather she was one of your witnesses on the Killowen case?"

"Yes, although I was beginning to have serious doubts about her story."

"You're saying you've no leads at all?"

"No, we've got substantial evidence for book theft but still not much to go on for either of the murders, unfortunately. I was hoping this girl might finally come clean when we got her back to the station."

"Well, this is pretty damned inconvenient, then, isn't it?"

She got the message: Brown wanted this case cleared up, and fast, before Serious Crimes ran roughshod over all of them, himself included.

The paramedics were just coming up the hill, pulled up by their mates along a couple of nylon cords. Anca Popescu's body was already zipped into a black body bag. A light rain had begun to fall while they were down the slope, and now the valley below was beginning to disappear in the mist.

"Can I just see her face?" Stella asked the nearest paramedic.

He turned to look at her. "It's not pleasant."

Stella unzipped the bag. Anca's face bore cuts and contusions; her lip was split, and there was a dreadful gash at the temple, lots of blood. She looked so young, even more like a little girl now that her wary eyes were closed. Where were this child's parents? Stella wondered. And who would have to go and tell her people that she was dead?

6

The sun was just coming up behind the brow of the hill as Joseph Maguire climbed the rise that led to Anthony Beglan's farm. He felt a little short of breath and paused to rest for a moment against one of the crumbling gateposts along the hedge-lined lane. In his mind was a picture of the eels he'd have for lunch today. He could see their shiny, slippery skins, the intricate and beautiful architecture of their tails.

He closed his eyes and breathed, letting the scent of cattle and grass fill his head, bringing back the animal smells of childhood, the strange gaze of beasts standing out in the rain along the road he walked to school. Everything took such an effort now, and time itself felt slippery as an eel. He was young, and then he was old again, in the blink of an eye.

He pushed off from the gatepost and passed by a field where a dozen pairs of large brown eyes looked up to greet him, ears with yellow tags flapped and twitched as he kept walking. He looked down and saw the bulge of a belly, two stout legs beneath him. Whose were they? Not those of a boy. Hard to keep things straight when his brain was so uncooperative.

A house stood at the end of the road, old and weather-beaten, paint peeling from the window and door frames. No one home. He could see no sign of life, no sounds, but he walked toward it, waiting for something. Glinting shards of light came from the building beside him, and he turned to see the sun broken into hundreds of pieces, bright circles, blinding him as he looked through a missing wall. All a dream, it had to be.

He felt the sharp jolt of the blow before the pain registered. It seemed like he waited for eternity after that, with that hollow roar in his ears as his knees buckled under him and he pitched forward into darkness.

. . .

Joseph felt himself drifting, floating in space. When he tried to move, he could not. Pain in his head. Cracking his eyes open, he saw and then felt the band, something around his chest. His hands were behind him, shoulders pulled back, a shooting pain up the shoulder. Where was this place? Was someone here? His head still lolled forward on his chest, but he could see a table before him, cracked oilcloth, a basin of water—and a shape made of green rushes. He was alone.

He began to move, trying to break free, but he was fixed, immobile. He twisted from side to side, and at last the chair moved, but only to topple over. He landed on his right cheekbone with such force that the pain knocked the breath from him, and he experienced a sudden flashback—the cold floor, the musty smell, the shooting pains through his limbs. Another interrogation? They could beat him all they liked—he knew nothing. The whole right side of his face felt numb. He was ready to pass out when the door opened and a pair of muddy black shoes walked slowly toward him. From his awkward angle on the floor, he could not see the wearer. The silent figure stood and looked at him, as if deciding what to do. He'd let his jaw go slack, feigning unconsciousness, knowing instinctively that it was the wisest course. When the boots turned and proceeded out the door once more, he tried to open his eyes wider but felt himself slipping into an unconsciousness that this time was not feigned.

7

"Sorry about the hour," Catherine Friel said. "I've got to be up in Cavan by noon. You must know I wouldn't have dragged you out of bed for no reason."

Stella was gazing at the mortal body of Anca Popescu, looking in her nakedness on the table here this morning even more like a waif than she had appeared yesterday evening. Again Stella's throat constricted, thinking of how alone this girl was, in death as in life. "What is it? What have you found?"

"Since I wasn't at the scene, I don't know a lot about the circumstances surrounding this girl's death, but I can tell you with a fair degree of certainty that it was no accident. At first I thought perhaps it was the position of the body after the fall, a function of livor mortis. Then I found this." She lifted Anca's arm away from her body and revealed a mark on the skin, a pattern of discoloration.

"What is it?" Stella asked. "What am I looking at?"

"Do you see the outline just here?" Catherine Friel's gloved finger traced the air above the shape. She pointed to a jagged line on one side, a rounded curve on the other.

Stella's brain began to distinguish the significance of the outlines before her, just as Dr. Friel's voice sounded in her ear: "It's a footprint, Stella. This girl didn't jump to her death. She was pushed."

Stella stared at the mark, remembering Molloy's distraught voice on the phone.

"Are you all right?" Catherine Friel's voice had become a low, echoing noise, like a sound traveling down a long tunnel. Time slowed, and all Stella could feel was the touch of his hands upon her skin, his eyes locked on to her own. It wasn't real, any of it—it had only been a distraction, to keep her from seeing what he was. She had to force herself to focus.

"You're sure this happened at the time of her death? It couldn't have happened earlier?"

"The marks would be much darker if the contusions had happened a day or two earlier and the blood had had a chance to settle in the surrounding tissue."

An image came back—those fresh red marks on the girl's arm in the interview room. Stella had let herself imagine that they were self-inflicted, but Molloy had just been with her. Was he threatening the girl? Had he forced her to point the finger at Niall Dawson for the murder of Vincent Claffey?

Of course Molloy knew Anca. Because she was mixed up with Vincent Claffey, and so was he. How could she have been so thick? Molloy and Claffey and the Swiss book thieves, and perhaps Anca as well—they were all in on it. That secondment to the Antiquities Task Force, and all those cracks Molloy kept making about treasure hunters trying to corrupt Guards—she'd heard only what was on the surface and not the truth that lurked below. *They know we're always skint.* He needed money, and for that he'd let himself be pulled into a hole so deep . . . Stella looked down at Anca Popescu's fragile, battered face. Was it money that had driven Molloy to treat another human being like this? She felt the floor shift beneath her, and held on to the table for support.

"Detective?" Catherine Friel's voice was louder now. "Stella, are you all right?"

8

Cormac emerged from his room at Killowen at about half-seven in the morning to find Eliana in the hallway, still in her dressing gown. She raced to his side, eyes wide and slightly frantic. "You're awake, thanks God!" she cried. "He is gone again. I looked in his room, and the bath. Your father is not here."

Cormac put his two hands on her shoulders. "Calm yourself. He can't have been gone long. Have you any idea where he might have headed? Had you made plans for today?"

"Anthony was going to bring us eel fishing again, but not until later."

"He may be mixed up about the time. Let's see if we can find him at Anthony's. You get dressed, and I'll wake Nora and tell her where we're going."

He was trying to maintain a calm demeanor for Eliana's sake, but Cormac could feel fear rising in his throat. It was tempting to believe that two murders had been solved with the discovery of stolen books in the storehouse, but what if Lucien and Sylvie were only book thieves and not killers?

It took nearly ten minutes to cover the fields between Killowen and Beglan's place. They went up over the field and along the perimeter of the orchard, then down the narrow lane that separated the two farms.

Cormac turned to Eliana. "Don't worry, I'm sure he's fine. Probably having a very interesting conversation with Anthony Beglan right now." Eliana allowed the ghost of a smile to pull at the corners of her mouth.

They turned down the lane that led to Beglan's drive. Anthony had been here. The gate was open, the cattle grid littered with fresh dung from the morning's milking.

"Hullo!" Cormac shouted as they approached the sheds. "Anyone here?"

No answer from the ruined cottage or the house. The shed gave off an acrid, rotten smell, as before, and Cormac held his nose as he approached the door. Something was not right here—he could feel it. With Eliana behind him, he pushed open the first door. In the center of the room was a strangely shaped chopping block alongside a crude table holding several rounded blades, plus a dozen or more stretching frames, some with half-dried skins upon them. The light from the grimy window glowed through the rough but translucent skins, casting the room in an eerie yellowish light. *Jesus.*

"Stay here," he whispered to Eliana. "Don't come any farther."

Cormac crossed to the next doorway and pulled it open to reveal two large bubbling vats of opaque liquid the color of heavy cream. A sopping, pale skin lay draped across an old oar that had been adapted for use as a stirring paddle. Cormac felt his blood freeze. He ran forward and seized the paddle, and began feeling around in the cauldron, unaware of the agitator stirring up the bottom. It clamped on to his oar and practically lifted him from the ground, the oar bending and nearly snapping with the weight of him, until he was able to let go. The machinery stopped, and he dislodged the oar and finished stirring each of the vats. Nothing.

Anthony had to be here, Cormac thought. He wouldn't leave this machinery running if he weren't, surely. Cormac heaved himself away from the vat and surveyed the room. There was no place to hide. At the center of the third room hung a chain studded with large hooks, where Beglan evidently hung the bodies of recently slaughtered animals. One calf hung suspended by its hind legs, blood staining the metal trough below. Still dripping. So where was Beglan? Cormac inched around the corner, expecting the worst, but found only a skinned calf's head, pink and white musculature exposed like an anatomical drawing. His eyes scoured the walls, the floors, looking for clues. All he could see were a couple of stalls in the far corner. A closer look revealed a handprint in blood on the dirt floor and a few stray bits of straw that must have been carried in by the calves. Above the print dangled a long pair of tongs on a coil of electric cable. The line ran to a control panel on the far wall. A stunning device of some kind, no doubt used on the animals. A spark leapt from the tongs and landed harmlessly on the dirt floor, prompting Cormac to cross and shut off the power.

A low moan came from the corner stall. Cormac dug through the straw, uncovering a semiconscious Anthony Beglan.

He lifted Beglan's head and began checking for broken bones, obvious wounds. All he found was an angry circular burn at one temple but no blood anywhere. An accident, or a foiled attack? He gripped Beglan's face. "Anthony, can you hear me? Is my father here? Joseph Maguire, is he here?"

Beglan opened his lips and emitted another low moan. He couldn't speak but seemed to be trying to cast his eyes in the direction of the house. "It's all right now," Cormac said. "You're going to be all right."

He shouted for Eliana, and when she came around the corner, he thrust his mobile into her hand. "Stay here with Anthony and make sure he's warm. He may be in shock. Ring emergency services, nine-nine-nine, and do exactly what they tell you. Do you understand? I've got to find my father."

Cormac burst out the door of the shed, heading toward the house. He entered by the back door, trying to remember what his father had said on the morning after the fire. Some nonsense about Free Staters. It wasn't exactly what he was trying to say, but he just kept banging on about it, so it must have been important. Trying to wring the meaning from his mixed-up words was like trying to crack an ever-changing code. Sometimes the words came in spurts, sounds or meanings like the one he intended but not quite the thing he meant. Letters transposed, or dropped altogether. *Free Staters*. Perhaps someone else had understood.

The kitchen was in disarray, although whether from a struggle or just general neglect, it was difficult to discern. Crockery in the sink, peeling wallpaper, the table and chairs pushed from the center of the room. Cormac bent down on one knee to examine the kitchen floor. There was a small amount of blood, about an arm's length from the table.

But for the dripping faucet, the house was eerily still until a strangled cry came from the far corner. Cormac flung himself forward and found his father bound to a toppled chair, eyes wild, his mouth stuffed with gallnuts. He was choking. Cormac scrabbled for the blackened marbles that blocked the old man's airway, spilling a shower of galls onto the floor. But there were more—he had to keep going until he reached the very deepest one, lodged in the windpipe. He couldn't reach it. Too far down. He ran to the sink and seized a carving knife, slicing through the tape and watching the old man go into a spasm. He was dying. Cormac lifted him from behind, and cinching his arms around his father's middle, gave a mighty squeeze. It worked—the last gall shot out of Joseph's mouth and pinged off a windowpane four feet away.

Cormac released his grip, letting his father slide to the floor. They were both still gasping. Stretched there, the two of them resembled a pair of knotwork figures, arms and legs at all angles. The old man's eyes were open, and Cormac searched for any tiny glimmer of recognition, wondering if his father might have had another stroke. At the very least, the lack of oxygen couldn't have done his overtaxed brain any favors. "Stay with me, Da. We're not finished. Stay."

Joseph's hand reached out blindly, as though he couldn't see who or what was before him. Cormac felt the old man's palm, warm against his face.

"Sum," Joseph said, his voice hoarse as a crow's. "My sum."

"I'm sorry I didn't try harder to understand." He smoothed the old man's hair. "Who did this? Can you tell me who tried to harm you?"

The old man shook his head and croaked, "Free Stater."

Cormac's brain began searching for possibilities. It couldn't have been Anthony Beglan—he was injured—and whoever had done this to his father must have just left. Probably still close enough to catch if he . . . no, he couldn't leave the old man here.

Joseph's breathing finally began to slow. He grasped Cormac's shirt-front and pulled him down closer. "My author?" He started to reach for his breast pocket but couldn't find whatever he was looking for. The old man began to plead: "She-she's-my-author. My *author*." More labored breathing. "You see?" Why was it always like this, two steps forward, one step back? Cormac felt lost once more, and frustration was rising in him again. "We'll figure this out," he said at last. "I'll find some way to decipher it, I promise."

The wail of an ambulance sounded, far away but fast approaching, and Cormac struggled to his knees. "Eliana's managed to get through. She's out in the shed with Anthony, I'm afraid he's hurt."

Joseph reached for him once more. "Stay. Stay."

"Don't worry," Cormac said. "I'm going nowhere."

9

Stella Cusack was flying down the N52 when she heard the keening of an ambulance and saw flashing lights overtake her on the narrow road. They turned off, headed for Killowen or Beglan's place—there were no other options this way. She arrived in the yard at the Beglan farm a few seconds after the ambulance.

Eliana Guzmán was at the shed door. "Over here! A man is hurt!"

Cormac Maguire was coming out of the house with his father, the two of them staggering along like punters after a long night at the pub. "Help!" he shouted. "Someone help us."

The ambulance crew split up, two in each direction. Stella headed for the Maguires.

"What's happening here? Who's hurt?"

"My father, and Anthony Beglan over in the shed. Someone tried to kill them. I don't know who it was." He held out his hand, revealing a half dozen gallnuts. "But someone tied my father up and stuffed these down his throat. If I hadn't found him when I did . . ." He shook his head, trying not to imagine.

Stella said, "Did he keep repeating the same word to you?"

Maguire looked at her curiously. "How did you know that? Yes, he kept saying 'Free Stater.' Do you know what he meant?"

"I thought I had it figured out," Stella said. "When I talked to him yesterday morning, he kept repeating that same word over and over, and I thought he was saying 'fire starter.' I believe he saw the person who lit the fire in the storehouse."

"Jesus."

"And that person saw him speaking to me—that's why he was targeted. I'm so sorry. You didn't happen to hear a car just now, before the ambulance arrived?"

"No, there was no car. Whoever did this must have left on foot."

Molloy wouldn't have tried to escape down the lane, Stella reasoned, since that was the way the police and ambulance would have to approach the farm. No, he'd head for the bog. Maybe he'd left his car there, out of sight of the farm.

As she set out toward the bog, Stella felt her soul begin to harden from the inside out. What on earth had possessed her? She felt ill, remembering how sorry she had felt for him, having to witness Anca Popescu's terrible death, and realizing that he would have gotten away with it, too, if Catherine Friel hadn't spotted his footprint on the girl's body.

More sirens sounded in the lane; squad cars were on their way. What would she do if she found Molloy, if he tried to resist? She'd show him the same mercy he'd shown Anca Popescu.

The field in front of her started to slope downward, and a long row of furze bushes about a hundred yards away separated them now from the bog. Stella kept her eyes on the ground, letting her gaze sweep left and right, checking for bent grass, footprints, anything Molloy might have dropped along the way as he made his escape. About fifty yards from the hedgerow, she heard a low moan and glanced up, shocked to see a figure spread-eagled across the huge bank of furze. It was Molloy, hanging upside down, caught on the spiky thorns. He must have been running down the slope and somehow tripped and tumbled into the furze. When she reached the hedge, she saw that Molloy couldn't move without two-inch barbs tearing into his flesh. "Help me, Stella," he pleaded. "You've got to help me, please."

She couldn't move.

"For fuck's sake, Stella!" he began to protest and then winced— every tiny movement caused a dozen fresh wounds. Blood was beginning to trickle from his face and hands. One barb had quite pierced his ear. It must have been extremely painful. Still, she didn't move. She had to know.

"I know about the 'accident' on the mountain," Stella said. She couldn't bring herself to say his name. "You were in this all along, weren't you? Right from the start. Even the assignment to the Antiquities Task Force, it was all just preparation. You deliberately kept those pictures from Interpol until you could warn your accomplices, and then you made it look as if they started the fire. But Maguire, the old man, saw you running away. You put those gallnuts in Dawson's room, too, to cast suspicion on him." She felt sick as the whole story came crashing in on her. Turning away from Molloy, she spied a group of uniformed officers at the top of the hill. They hadn't seen her yet.

Molloy groaned as his weight pulled him into the thorns, and for the first time Stella noticed a cloth-wrapped bundle at the base of the furze bush. She inched closer, realizing that the canvas cloth was marked with bright drops of blood.

Reaching in, she brought the heavy bundle out and began to unwrap it, feeling a chill as she caught the first glimpse of intricate golden metalwork, the checkerboard patterns and knotwork designs, beautifully rounded letters cut into the border, and the glowing bloodred stone embedded in the cross at the center. She said, "This is it, the thing you were after? Tell me, was it worth all the people you had to destroy to get this? Kavanagh and Vincent Claffey, and Anca, that poor child—"

"Poor child?" Molloy tried to sneer through his grimace. "Who do you think helped Claffey blackmail everyone? Who do you think killed him?"

"And if she did, that's supposed to justify what you've done, how you nearly killed two innocent human beings back there as well?" Stella pointed to Beglan's farm. "At least you didn't succeed this time. Jesus Christ, Fergal, why? You were a good cop."

"I was a fuckin' poor cop." His voice was labored. "Look at your life, Stella. Can you blame me for wanting more? You can't prove anything."

Stella couldn't bear any more. "Say you did it," she demanded. "Say you killed Anca."

"No. Just get me down."

"Say you pushed Anca Popescu down the side of that mountain, or I swear to God I'll call off the uniforms and leave you there to rot!" He would recant as soon as he was free, she had no doubt, but she needed to hear him admit his guilt. "Say it!"

"All right, all right! But you can't put any of the rest of it on me, Stella. Claffey was dead when I got to him. I may have . . . rearranged the body, but I didn't kill him. And I never laid a hand on Kavanagh, I swear. I knew nothing about him. You have to believe me."

"That's where you're wrong," she said. "I don't have to believe anything you say ever again."

She hailed the uniforms, and in a few seconds the officers were down the hill and stood gaping at the strange sight of a man hanging upside down in a thorn bush. Stella kept a hand raised to hold them off. Molloy's eyes were focused not on her but on the crimson pool gathering on the ground below his head. "Christ, Stella, I'm bleeding to death here.

You've got to help me, please!" The last word faded away into a whimper.

Stella moved deliberately, wrapping the golden shrine again in its canvas shroud. She looked into Molloy's face, upside down, twisted in agony, and felt nothing but a cold, dead spot in the center of her chest as she recited the words of the caution and arrested her partner for the murder of Anca Popescu. When she had finished, Stella turned to the nearest uniform. "All right, call the paramedics and get him out of there. Don't feel you have to rush."

10

It was after three in the afternoon when Stella Cusack finished writing up her report on Molloy and all she knew about his involvement in the treasure-hunting ring and Anca Popescu's death. He wasn't badly hurt from the thorn bush but remained under arrest and under guard in hospital. How could she have been so blind and stupid? She desperately wanted to go home and have a shower, to wash off any particle of him that might remain upon her skin.

For some reason, she believed Molloy when he said he'd had nothing to do with Kavanagh's death. No, for that piece of the puzzle, she'd reluctantly returned to her original theory, that Mairéad Broome and Graham Healy were somehow involved. There was the liar's forked tongue for a start, not to mention the gallnuts and the burial in a protected bog, both elements they would know about from staying at Killowen. But Vincent Claffey couldn't provide a witness statement about what he knew, and Anca Popescu's lips were also closed forever. That left as her possible witness pool only the people at Killowen, all friends of Mairéad Broome, and one other person—Deirdre Claffey.

Stella thought back to the shock on Deirdre's face when she'd seen Kavanagh's photo. Flipping open her notebook, Stella found the number for Child Protection Services.

Fifteen minutes later, she was on her way to meet Noreen Kilpatrick, the specialist victim interviewer. The timing of the call was fortunate. The SVI was also on her way to interview Deirdre Claffey at one of their designated interview locations, a nondescript building in Limerick. Stella hadn't undergone training to become an SVI, so she'd remain in the other room, but she would be able to watch Deirdre via camera and monitor system, and communicate with Kilpatrick through an earpiece.

The interview unfolded according to the prescribed protocols. Stella found herself only half listening, watching Deirdre Claffey's body language as she answered questions about her family, the daily routines at home. Part of the process of the stripping away of ordinary, habitual behavior that trained interviewers used to get at the truth. The first speed bump was the girl's mother. She'd left when Deirdre was only six.

"That must have been difficult," Noreen Kilpatrick said. "Not having your mum around."

"She didn't love me," Deirdre said. "If she loved me, she wouldn't have gone away, would she?"

"What were things like for you, after your mum left?"

"All right," Deirdre said. "My da and me, we managed. He never bothered me—that's what you want to know, isn't it? Well, he didn't. I could see the way people looked at us, but it's not true, any of it." She began to cry. "My da loved me, he was looking out for me. Maybe he was rubbish at it, but at least he never ran away."

The interviewer tried several different gambits, but Deirdre Claffey was steadfast and resolute in her denials. Stella had to admit she wasn't surprised. A nasty rumor is a nasty rumor, as Deirdre herself had pointed out. But the girl was playing with a gold cross that hung on a slender chain around her neck. Stella hadn't noticed it when she'd spoken to Deirdre before. She spoke into her tiny mike: "Can you ask her where she got that cross?"

"Did someone give you that necklace?" Kilpatrick asked.

Deirdre nodded. "Da gave me it. I had another one, a First Communion one from mum, but I lost it."

Stella's memory traveled back to the items in Kavanagh's overnight case. The small gold cross with the engraved message, *From Mum.*

"Can you ask her about the child's father?" Stella said quietly into her headpiece, and received a minute glance in response from inside the interview room.

"You were close to someone once, Deirdre," Kilpatrick continued. "I'm talking about your child's father. Where did you meet him? Does he know he has a son?"

The girl looked miserable. "I met him at our chapel. It's not really ours, doesn't belong to anyone. It's out in a field beside the bog."

"Was this chapel someplace you went often?"

Deirdre nodded.

Stella remembered with a pang her own desperate need for solitude at that age, and the field where she used to go, to lie down in the grass and feel the vast vault of heaven above her.

Deirdre continued, "One time I went there, and I met this man . . . ."

"Can you tell me what happened, Deirdre? Just as much as you can remember."

"He asked if I knew about the funny little picture of a man beside the doorway. And he showed me some letters. They weren't ordinary letters—alpha and omega, he said they were called. The first and the last. I didn't know what he meant."

The girl's voice had turned a bit dreamy as she remembered. "He was standing behind me, pointing to the letters, and then"—she closed her eyes, and her breathing changed as she remembered—"he said I had beautiful skin, and he put his fingers here." She touched the side of her neck. "I remember he was shaking. And he asked if he could kiss me and I said yes. And then he asked if I would lie down in the grass with him, and I said yes to that, too. I wasn't scared. I let him do everything. I wanted him to do it."

"And that was the first time you met, at the chapel?"

Deirdre's eyes were downcast. "The only time," she whispered.

"And after that, Deirdre, how long was it before you realized that you'd fallen pregnant?" Kilpatrick asked gently.

"I just started feeling ill. I don't really remember when it was."

"Did you understand what was happening?"

"No. I didn't know about any of that. Not until my da found out."

"And what did your father say when he discovered you were going to have a child?"

Deirdre hesitated and looked up at the interviewer. Stella wanted to shake the girl and tell her: *Your father is dead. There's no need to protect him now.*

"He was angry at first, but he never laid a hand on me, I swear. He just kept going on and on about this bein' his ticket. His ticket. I don't know what he was on about."

"You didn't understand what was happening?"

Deirdre brushed away a single tear. "Then I heard him on the phone." Her voice was a whisper. "He said, 'You'll pay for your bastard, you tosser.' He said he'd have money, and plenty of it, for me and the child—or he'd tell the whole world, anyone who'd listen."

Kilpatrick cast a quick glance up at the camera, at Stella. "Deirdre, can you tell us his name, this man you met at the chapel?"

Deirdre's fingers traced the edge of the table in front of her. "I don't know his name. I never saw him again, until that lady from the Guards showed me his picture."

"Kavanagh," Stella breathed into her headset. "That's the photo I showed her. Benedict Kavanagh." But how would Claffey have known where to find Kavanagh? Unless he'd discovered who his daughter had met at the chapel from the camera he'd rigged up there, the same one he'd used to trap Niall Dawson. She'd just about written off Vincent Claffey as a suspect in Kavanagh's murder, but this was further confirmation that he wasn't involved. He'd have had no reason to bury that car in the bog if Kavanagh was about to become his cash cow for life. He must have been sore when the prospect of an easier life evaporated, and just when he was so close.

What would someone in Kavanagh's position pay to keep an underage pregnant girl and her money-grubbing father well out of sight? Another possibility trickled into her brain: What if Kavanagh wasn't at all put out by the news that he was going to be a father? What if he had embraced the possibility, welcomed it? He'd married Mairéad Broome when she was only eighteen, and she'd not given him any children. Perhaps this was his only chance to carry on the family line, and he was making plans to throw his wife over for this girl. Mairéad Broome claimed not to care about the Kavanagh family money, which might just mean that she did. Not to mention being shown up by some brainless poppet who'd only to open her legs once to get knocked up. A thing like that could push a person off the deep end.

11

The kitchen at Killowen filled slowly at dinnertime. There was no conversation, only people going about their mealtime preparations singly or in pairs. They'd all heard about Anca, and about Molloy. It would have been easier to stay apart, to take the blows of the latest discoveries in solitude, but there seemed to be a purpose in gathering around the table this evening above all others.

Cormac sat at one corner of the table, grating a lump of hard yellow cheese. At the opposite end, Nora cross-sectioned shallots into paper-thin slices for the salad. Martin and Tessa Gwynne were helping Shawn Kearney lay the table, while Claire and Diarmuid wrestled a trio of crisp herb-roasted chickens from the oven onto a serving platter. Mairéad Broome and Graham Healy joined the company, each bearing two bottles of wine.

Cormac pressed the block of parmigiano into the grater, watching short curls fall onto the plate below. His father and Eliana were still resting, worn out by the mayhem earlier in the day, and Anthony Beglan was spending the night in hospital. He'd received a nasty shock but was expected to make a full recovery. Niall Dawson slipped in from the sitting room and sat down across the table. He leaned forward and spoke under his breath. "Is it true, what I just heard—about Anca, and that detective, Molloy?"

"I'm afraid so," Cormac said.

Dawson looked bereft. "I was going to try to talk to her, to apologize, something." He stared at the table. Cormac didn't know what to say.

After a moment, Dawson spoke again. "I'm going to see Cusack in the morning, to tell her I'm taking Killowen Man back to Dublin. She's got what she needs from the site."

Cormac glanced up to see Stella Cusack standing behind Niall. "Looks like you can tell her right now."

"Apologies for the interruption," Cusack said. "But I have a few more questions, particularly for you," she continued, turning to Mairéad Broome. "When did you find out that your husband was the father of Deirdre Claffey's child?"

Claire Finnerty reached out to her friend. "It's all right, Mairéad."

Mairéad Broome's voice was quiet but strong. "Vincent Claffey informed me of that fact just after my husband went missing. It seems they'd had a . . . financial arrangement, but Mr. Claffey never had a chance to collect."

"And that's why Mr. Healy was paying him off when you arrived here?"

Mairéad Broome nodded. "I agreed to honor the arrangement he'd made with my husband, but I wanted to add one condition. I don't know why I'm telling you this, I don't expect you to believe me, Detective."

Graham Healy spoke. "What Mairéad wanted was to raise the child and to look after Deirdre as well, give her a better start in life. But Claffey was holding out for more money. He knew Mairéad would give anything to help the girl and her child."

"It was the only way I could think to protect her, to get her away from that man. Deirdre will have to make her own decisions now, but Cal will eventually inherit the bulk of my husband's estate, according to the terms of the family trust."

"You all knew this," Cusack said, issuing a challenge to the assembled Killowen residents.

"Mairéad has suffered enough," Claire Finnerty said. "But you can't accuse her of murder. For God's sake, she loved Benedict. She's still protecting him. Can you not see that?"

Mairéad Broome spoke quietly. "Please, Claire, that's enough. We've been through it all, Detective. Graham and I were on the other side of the Slieve Bloom Mountains when my husband disappeared. I know we can't prove that to your satisfaction, but it's the truth."

"And if I choose to believe you, then that means my investigation will have to focus elsewhere," Cusack said. She looked in turn at each of the people around her. "Do you know what I'm beginning to think? That one of you deliberately brought Benedict Kavanagh here, knowing that it was the perfect opportunity to get rid of him, not only for your friend's sake, but for your own. Or perhaps for all your sakes."

The detective took a few more steps, walking behind Shawn Kearney, as she thought aloud. "I have my former colleague, Detective Molloy, to thank for some of what I'm about to tell you," Cusack said. "Before the worm turned, he'd actually done some police work. You must have wondered where Vincent Claffey got all the material he used for blackmail. Molloy was supplying it. He used his position to dig into your backgrounds, your histories, and discovered that you were all running from something. He'd found out, for instance, that at least one of you is using an alias." She stopped behind Claire Finnerty, who shifted uncomfortably in her seat. Cusack moved to the next person at the table, Diarmuid Lynch. "I even considered that Benedict Kavanagh's death might have been carried out by more than one person. You all had reason to hate him—"

Lynch turned to face her. "Say whatever you've come to say, Detective."

"All right." Cusack continued on her circuit around the table. "We've had plenty of distractions, if you want to call them that. Book shrines and treasure hunters, ancient manuscripts, Vincent Claffey and his blackmail schemes. But it struck me just today that this whole case goes back to what sort of a man Benedict Kavanagh was. Intelligent, yes, but also arrogant, aggressive, blind to his faults, and more than willing to use other people in pursuit of his own aims." Cusack stopped, fixing Martin Gwynne with a steady gaze. "But perhaps most telling was the evidence we found suggesting that Benedict Kavanagh was a serial seducer of young girls. Why did you insist on telling everyone that your daughter was dead, Mr. Gwynne? I can understand if the shame of attempted suicide was too much to bear—"

"No!" A jagged cry erupted from Tessa Gwynne. All eyes were on her as she leapt up from the table and tried to put herself between Stella Cusack and her husband. "No, it was never shame. I won't have you saying that. And don't look at him, don't—Martin . . ."

Gwynne's look pleaded with his wife. "Ah, Tess, you don't know what you're doing—"

"I know, my love. I do know." She turned back to Cusack. "I think you have a daughter, Detective. You cannot know what you would do if someone . . . if someone brought such grievous harm to your child."

Cusack said nothing.

Tessa Gwynne continued: "Our Derryth was such an open spirit, so gentle, so full of joy—"

"Until she met Benedict Kavanagh."

"Until he destroyed her. She met him at that conference in Toronto where Martin spoke all those years ago. I've thought about it so much since then, all those philosophers wasting their breath arguing against the existence of evil when he was right there in their midst, that serpent, that *villain*—" She stumbled, but Cusack reached out to keep her upright. "Martin and I, we didn't know what had happened. When we returned to England, she tried to stay in touch with him, this man to whom she'd given everything—*everything*—and he—" Her legs buckled and she fell against Cusack for support. "He tossed her aside, like so much rubbish. My beautiful, beautiful child. Only fifteen years old. And so she tried to kill herself, by swallowing these, a half dozen or more." Tessa Gwynne brought a fistful of gallnuts from her pocket, her hand shaking. "She believed they were poisonous, you see, just kept shoving them down her throat until she couldn't breathe anymore. It was too late when we found her, too late to reverse the damage. You see, don't you, why I did what I had to do? I brought Benedict Kavanagh here. I didn't know anything about Deirdre, or the baby. Mairéad, I swear, I meant to stop him sooner."

"How did you manage to get Kavanagh down here to Killowen?" Cusack asked.

"It wasn't difficult. I knew he wanted the book, you see, the fabled Book of Killowen. I knew he'd have done anything to get it. I heard Martin and Anthony talking about it and knew that Kavanagh wouldn't be able to resist. So I rang and told him that what he was after was here, that it could be his for the right price. I told him to come and see the carving at the chapel, if he didn't believe me."

"The figure with the wax tablet," Niall Dawson said. "The Greek letters. And the initials below, *IOH*—for Iohannes Scottus Eriugena."

"And that was the first time Kavanagh came here, eighteen months ago?" Cusack asked.

"Yes. I'd whetted his appetite for the spoils but missed my chance to get him alone. He came, and saw the chapel, and then he escaped. I had to wait more than a year for another opportunity. I couldn't fail this time. I rang again, asked him to meet me out on the bog, at night. I was to bring the book this time. He didn't know me—who I was, what

I was doing here. I showed him Martin's copy of the old manuscript, and when he leaned into the boot for his case of money"—her muscles began to spasm, limbs jerking awkwardly—"I hit him," she said, reliving the horror of it. "As hard as I could, and he crumpled, just like a marionette. I tied his hands and feet, and stopped his breath—one bitter serpent's egg for every one my child had swallowed. After he was dead, I gave him a proper serpent's tongue as well." She fell to her knees, arms and shoulders writhing, her face a grimace.

Martin Gwynne dropped to his knees beside her. "Tessa, no!"

"What's wrong with her?" Shawn Kearney asked. "Why is she shaking like that?"

Nora darted forward and seized Tessa's wrist. "Mrs. Gwynne, have you taken something? You must tell us."

Tessa Gwynne pushed her away. "Leave me alone. Let me talk." She turned to Cusack again. "You wanted to know about the car, how I managed to bury it. My father was in construction. He taught me himself how to handle a JCB. Always said I was the neatest excavator he'd ever had."

"And you came across the bog man when you were digging the cutout for Kavanagh's car," Cusack said.

Tessa Gwynne nodded, her lips curling back once more in a ghastly grin. "I had no choice, had to put him in the boot. No one would have found them, but for Vincent Claffey grubbing after money in moor peat." Her breaths were coming shallower. "I'm not sorry he's dead. As bad as the other, the way he used Anca, his own daughter." Tessa Gwynne cried out as her body convulsed, her back arching uncontrollably.

Nora took her wrist again, this time checking for a pulse. "Mr. Gwynne, has your wife taken something?"

"I don't know," Gwynne replied helplessly.

Nora looked around at the circle of anxious faces. "Did she swallow anything in the last few minutes? Did anyone see?"

Martin Gwynne wept as he tried to still his wife's body, now wracked with spasms. "I didn't think . . . she takes so many tablets. My wife hasn't been herself these last few months, she's been ill. Oh, Tessa, my lovely Tess."

His wife looked up at him, between spasms now, and raised a hand to his face. "I had hoped . . . all this would pass, and you would never know . . . but how could I let you or anyone else take the blame? You see that, don't you, my love? Don't forget—" Tessa Gwynne's back arched once more, until it seemed as if her spine would snap. Her husband clasped her to his chest, but her eyes were staring, vacant now. Stella Cusack turned away, her head bowed.

BOOK SIX

Uch a lám,
ar scribis de memrum bán!
Béra in memrum fá buaidh,
is bethair-si id benn lom cuail cnám.

Alas, O hand,
so much white parchment you have written!
You will make the parchment famous,
and you will be the bare peak of a heap of bones.

—Epigram left by an Irish scribe in the margin of a medieval manuscript

1

Nora pushed through the wide door at the morgue just as Catherine Friel pulled the sheet over Tessa Gwynne's body on the mortuary table, shaking her head in resignation.

"The poison was mercifully quick. I think we'll find it's strychnine, when the toxicology reports come through. She hadn't much time, in any case. There were some fairly advanced histopathologic changes in her brain and muscle tissue, consistent with multiple myeloma. I'm sure the disease was beginning to affect her quite significantly by this stage. I'm amazed that she had the strength . . ."

A moment of silence hung between them. Nora thought of the desperate act of a grieving mother, unable to countenance the continued existence of the man she held responsible for her child's living death.

"I would never condone what she did," Dr. Friel said. "But that doesn't mean I can't imagine what she felt. If it had been my child—"

The door opened, and one of the local mortuary staff stuck his head in. "There's someone here to collect one of your patients, Dr. Friel— Anca Popescu." Nora could see Claire Finnerty and Diarmuid Lynch standing just outside the mortuary.

"You can tell them to come through," Dr. Friel said.

"So you're taking Anca back to Killowen?" Nora asked Claire. "Does she not have family in Romania?"

"None that wanted her," Claire replied. "So we're going to keep her here, with us." She looked away, trying to keep her composure.

Diarmuid Lynch asked, "May we see her?"

"Of course." Anca Popescu's body was draped, but her face—pale bluish in hue, bruised and scraped—silenced them all for a moment.

Claire reached out and touched Anca's hair. "She was so often sad. And who could blame her, with the life she had? But if you could see the work she'd done for Martin. There was a quality to it, almost like there was something so immense within her that it couldn't be contained. I don't know how else to describe it."

Nora asked, "Are you planning any sort of observance?"

"Yes," Claire said. "We'll wash the body and wake her tonight."

"If you need help," Nora said, "I have some experience. I know what to do. Why don't I come back with you now?"

Following Diarmuid and Claire in the van, with the simple wooden box visible through the back window, Nora felt herself part of an odd funeral cortège, a small procession that wound its way through the hills that had been crossed in turn by chieftains and cattle herders, monks and raiders, croppies and yeomen, all characters in the great book of human events.

2

Cormac was in the Killowen car park, loading his site kit into Niall Dawson's vehicle, when he heard a voice behind him: "I need to show you something."

Cormac turned to see a figure on the bench outside the door. Martin Gwynne seemed to have aged forty years in the space of a day. He stared out toward the oak wood as Niall Dawson joined them. Gwynne said, "Anthony's back from hospital. And he has something that he'd like you both to see." He turned to Cormac. "Perhaps you'd bring your father along, too."

When they arrived at Beglan's farm, Anthony stepped outside. "You're all right with this, are you?" Martin Gwynne asked. "I want to make sure, Anthony, because it's bound to change things. I just need to know that you're prepared."

"I uh-uh-AM prepared!" Beglan said, his chin thrusting forward.

The kitchen looked exactly as it had been left by the crime scene investigators yesterday, with remnants of Beglan's everyday life everywhere: bread crumbs and tea mugs and a buttery knife beside the sink. A basin of water stood on the table, along with a bowl of oak galls and a small Bridget's cross that Cormac had not noticed before.

Dawson zeroed in on the objects on the table as well and turned to Anthony. "Were you making ink here?"

"No, it's the cuh-cure," Beglan said.

"A cure for what?" Dawson asked.

Beglan grimaced and pointed to Cormac's father, seated at the kitchen table. "Eeh-he can't talk right. I have a cuh-cuh-cure for it." He smiled. "I know, cuh-cure myself first, right? But it hum-huh-doesn't work that way. Un-fuh-fortunately."

"What way does it work?" Cormac was genuinely curious.

"Be patient. You'll see the connection very soon," Gwynne said.

Beglan fetched a bundle from the next room and set it down on the kitchen table. He began peeling back the canvas until he had revealed what was inside. On the table lay an ancient manuscript, its worn leather wrapper closed with three buttons. Cormac could see a knotwork design faintly scratched in the surface of the cover. He glanced at Niall Dawson, who appeared dumbstruck.

"My God," Dawson finally managed. "Is this . . . ?"

"A legacy," Gwynne replied. "An unimaginable treasure, a responsibility laid upon the Ó Beigléighinns, descendants of the little scholar, more than a thousand years ago."

"And was the book shrine connected to this manuscript?"

"Yes, but the police have that. The *Cumdach Eóghain* and its contents had been separated for centuries—Anthony's grandfather only succeeded in reuniting them in 1947. It's strange. There's been so much squabbling over the shrine, with its gold and precious stones, when the real treasure was what lay inside it all those years. Gentlemen, I give you the Book of Killowen."

Cormac felt a surge of adrenaline. He couldn't imagine what Niall must be feeling.

"I thought we'd found our missing manuscript when we came across that Psalter in the bog," Dawson said. "So where does this book fit in?"

"I believe the artifacts you found in the bog—along with this book—tell a story." Martin Gwynne motioned them to sit. "It's a story of philosophical rivalry and heresy and hatred. Let me begin with my own story. I came to this place nearly twenty years ago in search of a dazzling creative thinker, an Irishman with a Greek name, Eriugena—it means 'Irish-born.' I followed him here, based on a brief passage in a medieval history, a mention of his return, at the end of his life, to the place where he had been born in Ireland. That birthplace was named for the first time. And it was this place, an area known as An Feadán Mór—Faddan More."

"This medieval history you mention, it wouldn't happen to be a revised edition of *Gesta Pontificum Anglorum* by William of Malmesbury?" Cormac asked.

"Ah, so you know of my disgrace," Gwynne said. "Yes. But I didn't take the *Gesta Pontificum*. It disappeared a few days after I'd made my discovery, and I don't believe that was pure accident. Someone else must have intended to make it look as if I'd helped myself. After all, I was the last to consult that manuscript, at least according to the library records."

"Who would do such a thing?" Cormac asked.

"I have a few theories, all unprovable. Perhaps archaeology as a field of study is less contentious than medieval history," Gwynne said. "I hope so for your sake. History and philosophy are full of treacheries, rivalries I knew nothing of. And there are certain factions within institutions like the Church who make it their business to carry philosophical feuds from a thousand years ago into the present. People who feel threatened by the ideas presented in books like this."

"I can't believe you actually came here looking for Eriugena," Dawson said.

"And I was not the only one—others followed the same trail. I should explain that Tessa and I lived here for some time before I resumed my work again," Gwynne said. "After my dismissal from the library, and our daughter's . . . injury—" He paused. "It was really all I could manage, looking after Derryth, and Tessa, as best I could. But after a while I began to see signs, undeniable evidence that the man I sought had been here and had left his mark. The first clue was at the chapel."

"That doorway," Cormac said. "The carving of the scribe—the initials IOH. And the letters. Eriugena was one of the few Greek scholars of his time."

"Yes, and so I began to suspect that there was some little truth to the story of his return. But there was no grave, no name carved in stone, no other physical evidence to say that the figure was Eriugena. So I started digging through the old texts, the *Dinnsenchus* and the *Annals of the Four Masters*, and the work of antiquarians like O'Donovan. Through their research, they were able to discover accounts of a mysterious manuscript called the Book of Killowen and trace it right back to the ninth century. O'Donovan reported that the book had been burned, the shrine sold and melted down, because that's what the Beglans wanted everyone to believe. It was their family's sacred charge, you see, to protect the book from harm. I only convinced Anthony to show me his book about two years ago."

Dawson's gaze was still riveted on the manuscript. He glanced up briefly to address Anthony Beglan. "May I have a look?"

Anthony nodded, and Martin Gwynne placed the codex carefully into Niall Dawson's outstretched hands. The cover was rather ordinary, plain leather, more like an envelope than a bound cover. Apart from the one scratched design, there was no gaudy gold or stamped embellishment of any kind. Dawson gingerly undid the buttons and opened the wrapper. His eyes glinted with the curator's heightened passion, a feverish curiosity bordering on greed.

Gwynne said, "I think you may be surprised at what you find inside."

Cormac felt his breath halt as Dawson lifted the front cover to find a page inscribed in Latin. It began with a fantastically decorated capital and contained several margin notes in a tiny hand. "Looks like insular minuscule," Dawson said, his voice filled with awe. "The text is definitely not Psalms. And am I mistaken in thinking there are two hands here?" he asked Gwynne.

"No indeed. The first part of the book has been set down by two different scribes, but the primary hand disappears about two-thirds of the way through. The last portion is completed by the second scribe. Some people know him by the name Nisifortinus—"

Dawson's head turned sharply. "You realize what you're saying?"

"I do," said Gwynne. "And as I've had ample time to study the manuscript, I feel no qualms about making that claim."

"I wish I knew what the hell you were talking about," Cormac said.

Dawson turned to the title page and read aloud: "*Periphyseon. Liber sextus . . .*" Dawson's voice wavered when he spoke again. "My God, you know what this means?"

"That last bit is 'Book Six,'" Cormac said. "If I'm remembering right."

"But there were only five books in *Periphyseon*," Dawson said. "There was never any mention of a sixth book, only a note from Eriugena himself at the end of Book Five that he hadn't covered all the topics that he'd promised to write about." He began to turn the pages, ever so gently, studying the handwriting on the vellum surface. "If this is truly authentic, it's earth-shattering. In all sorts of fields—philosophy, history, paleography. I can't even get my head around it properly." He turned to Martin Gwynne. "If this truly is Eriugena's last work, are you thinking he finished it here, in Ireland?"

"Not quite. I'm afraid he might have died before he could complete it," Gwynne explained. "I've gone over the handwriting again and again." He turned to Cormac. "There are often two Irish hands in Eriugena's major works, two individuals that paleographers have dubbed i[1] and i[2]. Some scholars think one of them might be Eriugena himself, and the second his pupil and protégé, the man some call by the name Nisifortinus, for the way he introduced his additions, '*Nisi forte quis dixerit*'—

Unless, perhaps, anyone shall say that . . . I've often wondered if this mysterious second hand wasn't perhaps founder of the monastery at Cill Eóghain. As I said, the first hand disappears partway through this book, and it's completed by the second hand. I think you may find, when you have a closer look at your bog Psalter, that it may be the work of Nisifortinus as well." Gwynne paused. "I have a theory—entirely unprovable, but plausible all the same, I think—about what transpired here back in the latter ninth century. You'll forgive my wild speculation. I am only a scholar, after all, and not a scientist."

"Enlighten us, please," Dawson said.

"I see two men, scholars and scribes, camped at the edge of this bog. They had come here to withdraw from the world of men, returning to the place from which they'd sprung. But they were not alone. One day while his young companion is absent, the older man is approached by the men who've followed him here, paid ruffians who fall upon him and stab him to death and fling his body in the bog. Since your recent discoveries, I have imagined the book and satchel flung after him, perhaps in frustration, because a Psalter, wonderful though it might have been, was not the book the assassins sought. They were after a book full of dangerous, heretical ideas, mistaken in the notion that they could destroy those ideas by destroying the written word."

"And where was this dangerous book, sought by assassins?" Dawson asked.

"Perhaps the younger man had it," Gwynne said. "One book, one satchel looks much like another. It's true even today. But as I said, I have no proof. I merely speculate."

Cormac said, "So, if our bog man is indeed this philosopher, Eriugena, what reason would anyone have had for killing him? Was there such great harm in what he wrote?"

"His ideas questioned the very foundations of the church in Rome," Gwynne said. "To church theologians, Eriugena's writings skirted too close to pantheism. They were condemned by two separate councils in his lifetime. His argument against predestination, his thoughts about the presence of God in nature, about the nonexistence of evil—these things were considered subversive, heretical, dangerous. They remain so to this day."

"So how did you come to know that Anthony was in possession of this book?" Dawson asked.

"I had noticed that Anthony shared a name with the heirs of the termon lands, the Ó Beigléighinns of Killowen. And I thought it a little strange that Anthony hadn't learned his letters, being the descendant of scholars. Perhaps it should have been no surprise that schoolteachers always underestimated Anthony, because of his tics and stammers. But as it turned out, here was a man possessed of knowledge that none of his ignorant schoolteachers dared dream of. I heard him speak it, when he didn't know I was listening." He cast a weary glance at his friend. "Would you grace us with a bit of that knowledge now, Anthony?"

Beglan had been standing to one side, an arm's length from them, watching the commotion over the ancient book, listening to the story. Now he looked self-conscious, as if he'd rather have been anyplace but the spot where he was standing. "Where shall I stuh-start?" he asked Gwynne, his jaw flexing as he spoke.

"What about '*Si enim libertas naturae*,'" Gwynne said gently. "Don't mind us, Anthony. Just imagine you're out with the beasts."

Cormac felt a twinge of memory, harking back to the strange sounds coming from Beglan as he drove the cattle down the lane. Anthony closed his eyes and began to sway slightly as he recited the words from memory: "*Si enim libertas naturae rationabilis ad imaginem Dei conditae a Deo data est . . .*"

Gwynne turned to what seemed to be a familiar page in the book, marking the words with his finger. Cormac and Dawson could only stand by as Beglan continued: "*necessario omne quod ex ipsa libertate evenit, malum seu malitia recte dici non potest—*"

It was the same passage that was on the wax tablet, the one they'd brought to Gwynne for translation. And it was only after Anthony finished his recitation that Cormac also realized that the tics and stammers had ceased as the Latin words fell from his lips. Perhaps repeating the text of this book over and over like an incantation somehow stopped the errant brain waves that caused his muscles to contract, his tongue to shudder, his voice to come unbidden.

"Is that your cure?" Cormac asked. "That recitation?"

"N-n-n-not exactly," Beglan said. "You take the book and duh-duh-dip it in the basin, and then get two cuh-cupfuls of that down yeh—"

Dawson couldn't hold his tongue. "Wait, you put this book into water?" He looked down at the manuscript in his hands.

"Aye, to buh-bless the water," Beglan replied. "Does no harm."

Gwynne said, "He's right about that. Iron gall ink doesn't just float upon the surface, you see—it bites into the page. Gallotannic acid bonds with vellum. That's why this ink cannot run. Not anymore."

"And that's why the writing in our bog Psalter is intact," Niall Dawson added. "Despite being wet for centuries."

"Indeed," Gwynne said. "It's the gall that makes the words indelible."

"You said you weren't the only one following Eriugena's trail," Cormac said. "We know about Kavanagh, and the corrupt detective Molloy and his accomplices who were after the shrine, but were there others as well?"

Martin Gwynne smiled wearily. "Remember what I said a few moments ago, about Eriugena's ideas being too dangerous still? We have had in our midst these last eighteen months a Catholic priest, an investigator sent here by the Vatican to find and destroy the Book of Killowen."

Cormac shook his head. "How do you know—"

"I have it from the man himself. I always knew that Diarmuid Lynch wasn't what he claimed to be," Gwynne continued. "Tried to pass himself off as an itinerant when he came here, but anyone could see that his hands were far too soft for any farm laborer. Diarmuid finally confessed his true purpose to us just the other night, how the Church had been seeking the Book of Killowen for years and had given him the mission to discover its location. But in doing all that digging, he had a chance to study Eriugena's work in detail, and he'd been won over by the man's ideas. So he began lying to his superiors at the Vatican about new information he'd found, about the book's location. He realized, long before he ever came here, that he could never go through with destroying such an important manuscript." Gwynne looked at Dawson. "And that was why he phoned you with a story about treasure hunters, hoping the National Museum would take an interest and send someone down to investigate. He reckoned that the Church would be in an awkward position if the book's existence were made public in that way."

"Why didn't he just hand it over when I was here?" asked Niall.

"Cuh-cuz he never knew where I kept it," Anthony said.

Cormac was still puzzled. "Kavanagh, he'd been after the manuscript as well for years, hadn't he?"

"Indeed," Gwynne said. "And I was going to show it to him. That was my grand plan, God help me. I wanted to invite him here, to see the blackguard's face as I snatched away the one thing that was most precious to him."

Gwynne sank into one of the chairs, looking spent. "At first, I simply closed my eyes to Kavanagh's crimes, because I knew we could do nothing. We'd no evidence against him, only our daughter's word about what he had done, and since she'd gone from us—" He paused briefly, overcome. "I'd told Tessa about all my discoveries here, the carving at the chapel and the notes in O'Donovan, about the Beglans and their legacy. I never mentioned Kavanagh by name, but I didn't have to—she knew very well that he would stop at nothing to get this book. And she had the courage to act, while I . . ." His head dropped forward, and he let out a long breath. "My beautiful Tess, she suffered a long and painful death, these past twenty years. Punishing herself, wrestling with demons. And I stood by all that time and did nothing. I ought to have protected her, I ought to have helped her."

Cormac's father had been silent, taking in the strange conversation all around him. Now the old man reached over and placed a hand on Martin Gwynne's arm.

"Peas," he said. "Now your author shall have peas."

3

Stella Cusack sat at her desk, just having returned from the required visit to the district commander's office. Since she'd managed to bring embarrassment on the force by arresting her own partner for murder, inquiries had to be made. Just as she anticipated, Molloy had stopped talking the moment he was extracted from the furze. His solicitor was probably going to argue coercion on the confession, but they still had the mark of his shoe on Anca Popescu's skin. And Stella was hopeful in that regard, because Catherine Friel was known as an outstanding expert witness.

Tessa Gwynne's husband had given his full cooperation. He swore that he had begun to suspect his own wife's involvement only after Benedict Kavanagh's murder was discovered. According to the Director of Public Prosecutions, simply suspecting one's wife was not enough to warrant criminal charges as an accessory after the fact. Vincent Claffey's death had finally been ruled an accident, from the blow to the head when Anca Popescu apparently pushed him. It looked like premeditated murder only after Molloy mutilated the body and shoved the gallnuts in Claffey's mouth to throw Stella off the scent. She blushed to the roots of her hair, remembering how had she let that bastard play her. Best not to think about that now.

She turned the key in her largest drawer and brought out a metal strongbox that looked as if it had been through the wars. It had turned up in a search of Molloy's flat, this nest of secrets that he'd removed from Claffey's shed. She hadn't had a chance to go through the whole jumble of newspaper cuttings, official documents, scribbled notes, and photos, but it was clear from the contents that Molloy himself had been feeding Vincent Claffey blackmail fodder for months, a way to keep him mum about the treasure-hunting ring. It turned out that Claffey had been writing cryptic threatening notes to the people at Killowen, hoping to extract money from everyone. And he'd evidently succeeded. Stella found Mairéad Broome's fat packet of cash, along with a few rolls of twenty-euro notes. Hard to fathom how Molloy had managed to scrape up some of this dirt. Everyone at the farm was represented. There was information on Shawn Kearney being slighted by the academic committee that had turned down her bid for a doctorate, newspaper cuttings about Tessa Gwynne's father attempting suicide in police custody after he was charged with fraud in the 1980s.

There was also a series of photographs, taken at Killowen Chapel, of Diarmuid Lynch, lying facedown on the ground at the altar. She found a piece of paper stuck to the back of the last photo. It was an image clipped from a magazine, showing three smiling men looking over an architectural drawing. Stella adjusted her desk light and reached for her magnifier, peering through the glass at the picture. Nothing but a concentration of dots, so close up. Still, the man in the center looked familiar. All three were wearing clerical collars. The caption read: "Monsignor Guido Mariani, the papal nuncio, and members of the Vatican party, Monsignor Andrew Fothergill, and Canon Michael Feery, looking over plans for the new building at the Apostolic Nunciature on Navan Road, Dublin."

She spotted one of her uniformed colleagues approaching and moved to cover the image. Guarda Pollard tipped his head toward the front of the building. "Stella, someone to see you. Duty sergeant asked me to pass it along."

Stella headed to the front reception area, a tiny cramped foyer with a window for the duty sergeant. She pushed open the security door to find Claire Finnerty waiting outside.

"Detective Cusack, I wanted to let you know that we're holding a wake for Anca, tonight, at the farm, in case you'd like to—"

"Thanks for letting me know. I'm not sure if I can make it."

"There was something else I wanted to ask." Claire Finnerty looked away. "We could have done so much more for Anca. She probably arrived at Killowen thinking it would be a safe place, and it turned out to be anything but safe. I don't know how we could have been so blind. None of us had any idea what Vincent Claffey was doing—"

"What was it you wanted to ask?"

"Maybe it's a foolish notion, but I thought you might know of people who find places for young women like Anca, where they can recover from everything they've been through. I've talked it over with the others, and we're all agreed. We'd like Killowen to become a sort of sanctuary. We've got the space, and, well, digging in the dirt and growing things sometimes has a healing effect."

"Interesting proposition," Stella said. "I'm not sure how I can help—"

Claire Finnerty's voice was low but urgent. "You must know people. It's too late for Anca, but we want to do something—we have to do something—to make amends."

Stella looked into the eyes of the woman before her and saw the whole picture: the resolute expression, the sweat-stained clothing and worn hands, dirt under the nails, unruly hair only partially constrained by a head scarf. Here was a simple portrait of human need, a need that, for once, was within her power to answer.

"All right," Stella said. "Let me make some inquiries. I'll see what I can do."

"Thank you." Claire Finnerty's expression was still intense, but something in her eyes seemed to brighten. As she bent to collect her packages, Stella glimpsed a small strip of ink inscribed on her lower back—a delicate scalloped pattern in blues and greens. The shirt rode up slightly as she slung one of the bags over her shoulder, briefly exposing the whole tattoo. Stella could see that it was a snake swallowing its own tail. At the door, Claire Finnerty turned back to her. "Anytime after eight tonight. Just a simple home wake."

Stella returned to her office, feeling that she hadn't probed deeply enough. Why had the person who called herself Claire Finnerty taken the identity of a dead child? What was she running from? It might be wise to find out more about the circumstances of Tricia Woulfe's disappearance before trying to throw the light on someone with an assumed identity. A person could have all sorts of reasons for not wanting to be found. Interesting that Claire Finnerty was so eager to make amends for Anca Popescu's death. Perhaps the clue was embedded in that need.

Her desk was covered with open files and half-finished reports, not to mention all the piles she'd begun to try and organize Molloy's stuff. Time to force a bit of order and logic on the clutter of thoughts and images that filled her mind, as well as the mess of papers on the desk.

Her gaze caught on a photo of the Cregganroe conspirators, and this time her eye was drawn not to the shaggy young men but to a pair of peripheral figures, a young woman locked in an embrace with a tall man at the edge of the frame. Neither of their faces was visible, obscured by moppish haircuts of the time. They seemed disconnected from the others, Stella thought, with the fella's hand right up under the back of his girl's jumper. And then she saw it: the scalloped pattern on the girl's right hip. Stella flipped the photo over, looking for the note about the identities of the subjects, but the label mentioned only the five young men at the table, nothing about the other two. She reached for the magnifying glass, trying to get a read on the tattoo. If she could enhance the image, there'd be a much better chance . . . and all at once, the marks took shape: the head of a knotwork snake, twisted around itself and swallowing its own tail. Claire Finnerty.

The alleged warning call about the bomb was supposedly made by a young woman, but they'd never found any young female associated with the bomb makers. If the call had come in to the police, there would have been phone records, recordings—but there was nothing. Call or not, it made no difference now to the seven people who had died. But allegations in a scandal like that could have shaken both the Irish and the British governments to their foundations.

She set down the photo, her mind reeling. Molloy must have discovered that Claire Finnerty was a party to the Cregganroe bombing, and that was how he kept her silence about anything else she knew.

They'd never been able to nail the Snake, the head of the serpent, because no one knew who he was—that was the way paramilitary cells operated, then as now. But remaining incognito, even to the people you commanded, meant that the bloody Snake could be in their midst, even listening in on their conversations, and they'd never know.

She glanced down at the picture once more and through the distorted glass saw the man's hand magnified. His thumb and first two fingers were tucked up under the girl's jumper, but the last two digits were visible. Stella sat forward and peered at the black-and-white surface of the photo again, not quite believing what her eyes were relaying to her brain. Around his left pinkie the man wore a distinctive rectangular gold signet ring.

4

Nora stood in the shower, letting the hot water course over her. She'd just finished helping Claire wash and lay out Anca Popescu's body for the wake. These were not things she'd learned in medical school, but it seemed now that they should have been. Taking care of people in life ought to extend at least a little past that final threshold. She and Claire had worked in silence, gently washing, applying scented oils, and delicately daubing the girl's dark bruises with makeup.

When their work was finished, Martin Gwynne had come to watch over Anca—according to tradition, the body was never left alone—and he'd brought along a single goose quill. "From her writing desk," he'd explained. "Her favorite. Any scribe will tell you, the quill becomes a part of you—like your own fingernail moving across the page." He gently lifted Anca's pale hand and slipped the feather between her thumb and forefinger." On her way out, Nora saw that Martin also had framed Anca's unfinished work and set it on a small easel at her head.

Anca's body was at rest now, in a plain wooden box in the yoga room adjacent to Martin Gwynne's studio. Shawn Kearney and Anthony Beglan had gathered late-summer flowers, and the normally bare room had been transformed into a bower, filled with the scent of autumn ripeness and even the occasional bee arriving to collect the last and sweetest nectar before the flowers faded.

As Nora stood in the shower, enjoying the pinpricks of the spray, she pictured the intricate letters and patterns from Anca's page, the rich colors, the sharp teeth and staring eyes of the living creatures that leapt off the vellum. There was a nod to tradition, certainly, but also Anca's own individual, inimitable stamp. As if some part of her were still present. And so it was.

Nora had just laid out her clothes when Cormac came through the door. His face glowed with excitement as he took a seat at the edge of the bed. "You'll never guess what Martin Gwynne's just showed us," he said, and began describing the scene he'd witnessed at Anthony

Beglan's farmhouse. Like a boy who has stumbled upon a long-buried treasure map, Nora thought, watching the light that danced in his eyes, the animated gestures that punctuated his story. He told her about the Book of Killowen, the generations upon generations that had taken up the sacred charge of protecting one of the world's most dangerous books.

"I keep thinking about what Tessa was saying, Cormac, that someone like Kavanagh could debate the existence of evil on a purely intellectual level, all the while behaving in unspeakable ways himself. If evil doesn't really exist, does it mean that things like goodness and decency aren't real either? What does it say about me, that I can't bring myself to condemn Tessa Gwynne for wanting to stop Benedict Kavanagh once and for all?"

Nora pulled the robe tighter around her, feeling her limbs take on the character of an ancient furze, a primeval, hobbled thing, covered in spikes and twisted by wind.

Cormac drew her in, as if he couldn't feel the barbs of her bristling anger. "It says you're human, Nora. It says you desperately want to believe that kindness is real and justice is possible. I want to believe it, too."

He held on, tighter and tighter, until her shoulders sagged, the gnarled wood inside her let go its cramp, and she gradually became flesh again.

5

Stella arrived at Killowen at half past eight. The evening light was still bright, but a sliver of moon had risen over the oak wood, a silver crescent magnified by the late-summer damp. She entered by the front door, following the sound of a flute playing a slow air to the yoga studio, where the wake was under way. Flowers and candlelight, and a low murmur of conversation filled the room.

She paid her respects, standing beside the girl's pale body laid out in the coffin, again feeling a twinge at the realization that this was someone's daughter, not much older than her own child. She noticed Cormac Maguire in the opposite corner, elbows on knees, ebony flute in one hand. He must have been playing the air she'd heard coming through the house. As Stella withdrew, he lifted the instrument to his lips again and launched into another slow air, a lament.

Claire Finnerty entered the studio and crossed immediately to the coffin. She stood for a long while, five minutes or more, looking down into the dead girl's face. She bowed her head and began to whisper, her lips moving silently. Was it a prayer, a message to carry into the afterlife, some sort of incantation? Eventually, Claire straightened and reached for a thorny branch among the flowers. She snapped a sharp thorn from the cane, then drew back her sleeve, and plunged it into the flesh of her forearm. She made no sound but drew the thorn out again and pressed the flesh to stop any bleeding.

Stella knew that she must be invisible, behind a huge spray of leaves and flowers. As Claire left the room, Stella slipped from her place of concealment and followed, making sure not to be seen. She peered into the corridor, where Claire Finnerty stopped in front of each of the seven illuminations in turn, repeating the same ritual with the thorn in front of each. What strange sort of penance was this?

After Claire left, Stella approached the first picture. She was standing quite still, and yet there was a feeling of movement, going down and down, like the steps of a spiral staircase, until the outlines of a letter—

no, several letters—suddenly loomed before her eyes: E, D, M. They were not just letters, but words—and they formed a name.

She stared at the picture again, and there was the name, still, where before she had seen only a jumble of shapes. *Edmund Callan.* She moved to the next picture and this time saw the name immediately: *Margaret Rice.* The third bore another, *Gerard Nolan.* And then she knew: these pictures were hidden memorials to the seven victims of the Cregganroe bombing. Visited daily by the person who felt responsible for their deaths. Perhaps there should have been an eighth, bearing the name of Tricia Woulfe, the girl Claire Finnerty had once been.

Stella stopped and gazed out the window. If Martin Gwynne had made these pictures, surely he had to know of Claire's past—perhaps everyone at Killowen had known all along.

She suddenly felt the weight of the file in her bag and began to hear the never-ending echoes that would bounce from the walls of these farm buildings if she were to produce that file right now and start asking questions.

She reached the end of the corridor. Seven pictures, seven names. Stella could see Claire Finnerty's head in the garden, stooping to gather herbs for the meal that would be a part of the wake. Diarmuid Lynch emerged from the kitchen to join her. They worked side by side for a moment, until Claire's head dropped forward. Lynch put out a hand to lift her up, then he set aside his herbs and gathered Claire to him, smoothing her hair, drying her eyes with kisses.

Stella remembered the words Claire had spoken in the entry at the station this afternoon. *Digging in the dirt and growing things sometimes has a healing effect.* And Stella understood what this place was, what it could become, if she made inquiries as she'd promised. She left the farmhouse and crossed the haggard to the burned-out creamery storehouse, pulling a handful of photographs from her bag and setting them on fire in a metal bin, watching as the flames consumed them.

6

"She has my author," Joseph Maguire said. His eyes pleaded with Cormac to draw sense from his urgent words. "My author, my author!" His hands pressed against his chest, then bounded forward. He was in his pajamas and robe, pacing back and forth across his tiny room, refusing to go to sleep this night until they took his meaning.

"Author," he said again, and this time the pitch of his voice rose. Cormac stopped his father pacing and stood directly in front of him.

"Show me," he said, seizing Joseph's wrists and holding his hands up between them. "Please. Use your hands and show me what you mean."

The old man looked down at his hands, and the agitation seemed to drain out of him. "Peas," he said weakly, his voice reduced to a whisper.

Back to the vegetables, Cormac thought. And it always came back around to peas, never runner beans or beetroot or cabbage.

"*La imagen de mi paz. Mi preciosa paz.*"

Cormac cursed his limited knowledge of Spanish. *Paz* was peace, that was all he knew. His father seemed to be saying, My *precious peace*—but what did that mean?

The old man sat down on the edge of the bed, exhausted and frustrated, and with one sweep of his arm sent everything on the bedside table flying: the drinking glass shattered against the wall, and all the familiar, comfortable things Cormac had brought along to re-create his room at home scattered across the hard floor.

He couldn't blame his father for lashing out, even though the sudden violence was jarring. Cormac took a deep breath and sat beside the old man on the bed, looking down into the tumble of books and pictures. Why had he even brought these things on this journey? The books had been on his father's nightstand when he'd had the stroke. It had never occurred to him that the old man might be frustrated that he could no longer read them.

A white square stood out against a book cover. Cormac bent to pick it up and found a photograph with a date faintly penciled on the back:

Noviembre 1983. The spelling was Spanish, but it was definitely his father's handwriting, still so Irish in character. Turning it over, Cormac found a black-and-white image of his father with a lovely dark-haired young woman. A wedding photo. If he hadn't spied the date, he could have sworn the bride was Eliana—

Suddenly, he knew. The subtle evasions he'd sensed when asking about her home and family; his father's obsession with the girl, which he and Nora had mistakenly read as unseemly intemperance. But it was something more.

He knelt beside the bed and reached for the old man's hand, placing the tiny photo on his outstretched palm. "Who is she?"

"Peas-Pease," he began, and stopped. *"PAZ!"* He'd finally managed to spit it out. Then he added, *"Es-esposa."*

Cormac knew that much Spanish, at least—*wife.* "Where is she now?" he asked.

The old man did not reply in words this time but drew together the fingers of his right hand, which then exploded. *Poof.*

"She disappeared?" The old man shook his head, and Cormac suddenly remembered where on the planet his father had spent all those years. "She *was* 'disappeared'? She's so like Eliana—"

Joseph reached out and placed his two palms on Cormac's chest. "My sum," he said. His left hand stretched to the doorway, pointing to Eliana's room next door. "My author," the old man whispered, and this time Cormac felt the sense of it shining through at last. My *daughter.* For days, his father had been trying to tell them who the girl was, and every day he'd been flailing in that whirlwind of garbled words inside his brain.

Cormac glanced up to see Eliana peering around the doorjamb, fist pressed to her lips as if she were afraid of crying out, silent tears streaming down her face. Nora stood behind her.

"You knew," he said to Eliana. "That's why you came to us. You came looking for my father because you knew that he was—"

The girl nodded.

Nora took Eliana's hand and led her into the small room as Cormac cleared a spot beside his father on the bed. He drew the two chairs closer. The whole scene was so unreal.

Eliana had to take a moment to compose herself before speaking. "I didn't know anything about that agency you rang about a minder. I only happened to come to your house on that day, and you said we were going to Tipperary. That we would be in time for lunch. And so I came along. I wanted to tell you, all the time, but I was afraid."

Cormac shook his head. "That doesn't matter now. What I want to know is, how did you find us?"

"It is a strange, sad story. I think you know I'm not from Spain. I was born in Uruguay, in 1984. I have no memory of another place, but I always felt as if I . . . didn't belong. I never knew why until the man I called my father, he was very ill, dying. It was not so long ago. He asked me to bring him a book. I can never forget this book—*Los Años del Lobo*—it was about all that happened so long ago in Uruguay, in Argentina, and Chile—and this man, my father, he asked me to forgive him."

Eliana took a breath and continued. "After he died, my mother—the woman I called my mother—she finally told the truth, that I was not her child. She knew no more than that. But then a few months later, I received a visit from a priest. He said someone was looking for me, a woman in Chile. That this woman was *mi abuela*, my grandmother."

Joseph's expression changed. "Vee-veelet," he said, becoming agitated.

"Yes, you know her, Violeta Mendes-García. She loved you as her son, and she sent me here, to find you. Because she always believed that my mother was eh—" She gestured, giving herself a round belly. "How do you say *embarazada*?"

"Pregnant?" Nora asked.

"Yes, yes, pregnant when she was taken. No one knew but *mi abuela*." Eliana turned to the old man, who crumpled slightly and let out a low groan, the terrible knowledge like a dull spike to the heart. "How could you know? And *mi abuela*, she said she could not punish you that way. What if my mother had been killed, and there was no child? But she could not stop, she had to know. It's strange to think now, but the people in charge, they kept such good records of their prisoners, of all the people they killed. And so my grandmother found my mother's name in the secret files of the military hospital in Montevideo. She found a man there also who remembered my mother and how he was told to put her child into a basket and to bring that basket to the wife of a policeman, a woman who had no children of her own."

Joseph closed his eyes. "*Cóndor*," he murmured.

"*Sí*," Eliana replied. "*Operación Cóndor*."

Cormac felt a knot under his rib cage. Twenty years after it ended, the whole world knew of Operation Condor. About the torture and the killings, the kidnapped children of the "disappeared," who were robbed of their families, their very identities.

"When did all this happen, Eliana? I mean, when did your grandmother find you?"

"Three years ago. But still we didn't know the truth, not for certain. The man in the hospital, he could have lied or made a mistake. And so I went for a test, ADN, which you call by something else, I think—"

"DNA," Nora said.

"DNA, yes." She turned to the old man, gripped his hand. "That's when I knew, when I could be certain. *Yo soy su hija.*"

The old man's fingertips reached out and barely brushed her face. When he finally spoke, his voice was hoarse: "*He soñado—contigo.*"

"And I have dreamed of you also, *papá*—" Eliana broke off, unable to speak. Her eyes locked on the old man's, and his on hers, and upon that thread hung a look of such infinite joy and desolation that Cormac felt his own heart might crack.

Eliana managed to smile through her tears. "How strange it is, to feel at once so full and yet so empty still."

Cormac could bear to look no longer. He turned away. The earth itself had broken open, the continents shifted, and nothing would ever be the same.

7

Stella Cusack snapped into action when she returned home from the wake, pegging all the dirty delft straight into the dishwasher, picking up the sheets she'd stripped from her bed and bundling them into the washing machine. She knew that it was only a feeble attempt to erase all imprints, all residues of Fergal Molloy, but it was the best she could manage right now. She sat on a chair, watching the water sloshing around inside the machine and sobbing like a child.

When the cycle finished, she sat in the silent kitchen, staring at the mobile phone resting on the table before her. She was trying to screw up her courage—time to ring her daughter, see if they could talk things over before it was too late.

Stella reached for the phone and flinched as it began to buzz and vibrate on the table. The blue window said "Cusack." She punched a button to answer.

"Stella, it's me." He'd always been on to her that way, ever since she'd known him. *It's me.* As if he were the only possible *me.* "It's Barry."

But something was up. She picked up on a subtle difference in the sound of his voice, a note of something—was it regret?—that she had never heard before.

"Barry, where are you?"

He hesitated. "Outside."

She found him standing in the shadows, wearing his olive-green mac, even though the sky was clear. "Thanks. Didn't want people to think you had a stalker." He glanced sideways at the twitch of a curtain at the neighbors' window. "Can I come in?" She turned and walked away, leaving the door open. He stepped into the foyer but didn't remove his coat.

"What is it, Barry? What do you need?"

He seemed insulted. "Do I have to need something to come and talk to you? Why do you—" He closed his eyes and stopped himself from saying any more.

"Whatever it is, Barry, just say it and get it over with. We need to talk about Lia."

He looked so awkward and miserable, standing in the middle of the foyer with his raincoat on, that Stella found herself beginning to take pity on him.

"Take your coat off, then. Do you need a drink? I know I do."

"I wouldn't mind, if you've got something. That's one of the things I miss, just having a drink with you, Stella." He was looking at her strangely as he peeled off the mac and draped it over the back of the sofa.

She'd crossed to the liquor cabinet and was pouring out a couple of short glasses of whiskey when she felt Barry standing behind her. So close that she could smell him, could feel his warm breath against her hair.

"Where's Allison tonight?" she asked, her own breath coming fast and shallow.

Barry didn't respond, just slipped his hands around her shoulders. "Stella—"

She turned, seizing the two glasses and ducking under his arm in one motion, before he could react. She shoved one of the glasses into his hand as she passed.

Barry squinted at her in puzzlement. She could almost hear the gears turning inside his skull. They were both adults. What was the point of denying physical need? And besides which, hadn't he got lucky here just a couple of weeks ago?

Stella took a sip of the whiskey to steady herself. "Well, since you won't tell me what you want, I'll tell you what I need: Lia home with me, now. I want her to stop playing us. She knows exactly how to get what she wants, and we both know she's better off here. We also know that you can't keep this up forever, the whole engaged father act. It's been what—four whole days now? That's got to be getting old."

Barry looked at her with an expression she'd never seen before. He was sizing her up, taking her measure. "I'll drop Lia home on my way to the office in the morning."

Stella still couldn't suss out what was going on. Why was he being so agreeable? "You never said where Allison was tonight."

Barry's head dropped forward. "You know, I'm not sure where she is, and I'm not sure I care. I was wrong about her." He glanced up. "And wrong about you as well."

Stella could feel him checking for a reaction, so she didn't react, but she found herself backing up as he moved closer. "Relax," he said, gently bumping her glass against his own. "Just offering a toast. To you, Stella, for being a great mum." He paused. "And, all told, a pretty fuckin' great wife."

8

"Cormac? Are you awake?" Nora's whisper came whooshing out of the velvety darkness to curl around his ear.

He turned to her. "Can't sleep. You?"

She brushed his cheek with a cool palm. "Too much going on. Would you be up for a soak downstairs? Might help you sleep."

They slipped, hand in hand, past the closed doors of the other slumbering guests, down the main stairs, and into the corridor outside the thermal suite. As they passed the courtyard windows, the garden was awash in pale moonlight. All at once a bolt of lightning seemed to flash through the grass at the edge of the herb beds. Nora jumped. "Did you see that? What the hell was it?"

At first Cormac couldn't imagine, but after a moment, he understood. "Do you know something odd? We're quite far inland, but this place seems overrun with eels. They must come up the rivers and canals into the bogs."

"I suppose they've been here forever, if the monks figured a way to use their gallbladders for ink," Nora said. "Maybe they're like salmon, living their whole lives in the sea, until they return to freshwater to spawn."

Cormac had a sudden feeling that he had been forever tracing a line inside the twisted maze of the past. "Strange . . ."

"What's strange?" Nora asked.

"To think that the gold ink in our bog Psalter, or the Book of Killowen, could have been made from the ancestors of eels who still swim up the rivers here. If you keep going backward, it's entirely possible. That homing instinct—part of the great mystery, I suppose. All we know about the natural world at this stage, and we're only beginning to scratch the surface."

They continued to the thermal suite, and ten minutes later the soaking tub was full of brown peaty water, and candles around the room cast a flickering, golden light. Two piles of clothes sat at the top of the stairs down into the pool.

"Have you heard any news of what's going to happen to Deirdre Claffey and her baby?" Cormac asked.

"Claire told me Mairéad Broome is working with Social Services," Nora said. "She's going to see if she can bring Deirdre and the child to live with her. What's going to happen to the Book of Killowen?"

"Anthony's decided to donate it to the National Museum. The book, and the Psalter, and all the other artifacts discovered here will make an amazing exhibit someday. I think that's what Anthony would like, to see his family's legacy preserved. And I'm sure there are academics who'd like to pick his brain about the Book of Killowen and its whole colorful history. What's happened here in the last few days could change his life completely."

"I don't know. It seems to me that Anthony might be content to carry on tending his cattle, fishing for eels, and making vellum for Martin Gwynne. Although Martin did tell me that he's finally teaching Anthony how to read and write."

"I wish you had seen the Book of Killowen, Nora. I can't begin to describe the illuminations. It's almost like the creatures in it are alive—and from what Martin Gwynne says, the ideas in it are equally electrifying. He believes the book contains the handwriting of this ninth-century scholar Eriugena and his scribe. Gwynne says it may be the final proof that scholars needed to establish their identities, once and for all. I don't suppose there's any way to be certain of our bog man's identity, whether he could be the great man himself? I mean, we've got his wax tablet. Maybe the writing in the tablet could be linked to the text in the Book of Killowen—"

"I just don't see how his identity could be definitively proved, unfortunately. We have no way to run his fingerprints, nothing to compare his DNA. We'll just have to be satisfied with the tantalizing possibility, I'm afraid." Her expression turned serious. "Speaking of identity, can I ask you something? Did you ever suspect that your father had another family in Chile?"

Cormac winced. "Jesus, Nora, you make it sound like he was a bigamist."

"I didn't mean—"

"I know, I'm sorry. For so long, I was certain he had another family. Another son. At one point, I had myself convinced that it was the reason he left. It never occurred to me that he might have felt bound to a cause rather than to any flesh-and-blood person. I suppose I always thought if it was danger he was after, he could have found that just as easily in Ireland."

"Some people—and maybe your father is one of them—I don't know how to describe it, exactly, except to say that they aren't born in their own skins. I've known people like that, who have to go looking for a place, or a purpose, that feels like home to them."

"What are you saying? Do you not feel at home here?"

"I wasn't talking about myself. No, I'm afraid you're stuck with me, like it or not." Cormac felt Nora's hand under the water, her fingers twining through his own.

He said, "Do you know what baffles me? That even though they spent all those years apart, my father and mother were still married, right up to the day she died. My father offered to come back to Ireland then, and I wouldn't have it. I sent him packing. It never occurred to me that he would have been grieving as much as I was. That wedding picture we found, of my father and Paz—it was taken long after my mother died."

"Are there not some things that defy understanding, things we just have to let be?" Nora's chin rested on her drawn-up knee, a pale island in their peat-laden pool. Her eyes glowed, even larger and more luminous in the wavering candlelight.

"When my mother died, it seemed as if I'd lost the only person to whom I felt . . . bound. I had to learn to be on my own, and I got used to it. Then came you, Nora. And now I suddenly find my family doubled, tripled"—he glanced up to the ceiling, beyond which his father and sister slept—"quadrupled. Just like that. Difficult to take it all in."

Without a word, Nora slid over and tucked herself around him, wrapping her legs about him, twining her arms through his, until they were bound together like a pair of interlaced figures from the pages of an ancient book. She leaned forward and laid her head on his shoulder, and he could feel her heart beating, through solid flesh, in quiet double rhythm with his own.

HISTORICAL NOTE

The Book of Killowen began, as did each of the books in this series, with a real-life archaeological discovery. In July 2006, Eddie Fogarty was operating a mechanical digger in the bog at Faddan More, County Tipperary, a few kilometers southwest of Birr. He spotted a leather-bound book as it fell from the bucket of his digger into an adjacent trench and immediately called the landowners, Kevin and Patrick Leonard, who had some experience with artifacts previously found in this particular bog. The Leonards knew they had something unusual when they spotted some illuminated pages, and they phoned the National Museum with the news that they'd discovered something like the Book of Kells. The manuscript in question turned out to be a Psalter, a book of Psalms written in the ninth century. Several lines of text were visible, and Dr. Raghnall Ó Floinn of the National Museum managed to pick out one legible phrase: *"in ualle lacrimarum"*: in the vale of tears. It was a line from Psalm 83, verse 7: *"in ualle lacrimarum in loco quem posuit"*: In the vale of tears, in the place which he has set. The Faddan More Psalter is now on permanent display at the National Museum of Ireland, part of an exhibit titled *The Treasury: Celtic and Early Christian Ireland.*

The leather satchel that Cormac Maguire and Niall Dawson discover at Killowen Bog is based on fact as well. After the discovery of the Psalter, previous artifacts discovered at Faddan More took on a greater significance. I visited the Collins Barracks Conservation Department at the National Museum of Ireland in June 1999 while doing research for *Haunted Ground.* On the very day I toured the conservation lab, a technician was beginning work on a leather satchel that had just been discovered in a Tipperary bog—at a place called Faddan More. Ned Kelly, Keeper of Antiquities at the National Museum, told me that the workers who discovered the satchel described it as looking "for all the world like Tina Turner's miniskirt." The satchel was found only a few yards from where the Faddan More Psalter turned up seven years later. Archaeologists say there's no way that the book and the bag can be definitively connected, but Irish monks commonly used leather bags to carry and store their precious books. Depictions of Irish monastic life show satchels hanging from pegs in early medieval scriptoria. The wax tablet discovered in this story is based on the Springmount bog tablets, which you can also see as part of the Faddan More Psalter exhibit at the National Museum in Dublin.

As to the existence of John Scottus Eriugena, the ninth-century philosopher named in this story, both he and his pseudonymous scribe, Nisifortinus, are real historical figures. We know from his name that Eriugena was Irish-born and that he lived from about 815 to 880. He was known for his knowledge of Greek and for the originality and breadth of his ideas; he is often called the most creative thinker of the Middle Ages. He lived and worked for many years at the court of Charles the Bald (grandson of Charlemagne), and his work *On Divine Predestination* (he argued against), and his magnum opus *Periphyseon (On the Division of Nature)*, still provide fodder for lively debate among scholars. Paleographers have long pored over early manuscripts of his work and tried to distinguish between Eriugena's own handwriting and that of his assistants and scribes. The sixth book of *Periphyseon* imagined here is a complete fiction, although Eriugena did leave a note at the end of *Periphyseon* apologizing for all the topics he'd been obliged to omit from the preceding five volumes, "because of the weight of the material I had to deal with and the number of doctrines I had to expound," and offering his pledge to deliver soon, point by point, on the promises contained in the text.

Since Book Six of *Periphyseon* is a fabrication, so, necessarily, is the *cumdach*, or shrine, in which it was purportedly encased. Such jewel-encrusted book shrines are real, however, and you can see some wonderful examples on display at the National Museum of Ireland, or if you're willing to veer off the beaten path, there was a particularly fine example at the Boher parish church in Offaly, but it was stolen by treasure hunters in the summer of 2012 and may not be returned to its original display. The notes that Nora discovers about a particular family charged with protecting the Book of Killowen are also part fiction and part fact, pieced together from actual accounts in *Annála Ríoghachta Éireann*,

Annals of the Kingdom of Ireland, by The Four Masters, from the Earliest Period to the Year 1616, translated and annotated by the great Celtic scholar John O'Donovan and published in 1851, and *Devenish (Lough Erne): Its History, Antiquities, and Traditions*, by Canon J. E. McKenna, published in 1897.

Acknowledgments

I extend grateful acknowledgment to all who assisted with background material for this novel, including Eamonn P. Kelly, Keeper of Irish Antiquities at the National Museum of Ireland, who generously answered questions about archaeological fieldwork and artifacts, and the scourge of treasure hunting in Ireland; John Gillis, Senior Conservator at Trinity College Library, who was responsible for painstakingly rescuing the pages of the Faddan More Psalter; Julie Dietman and Matthew Heintzelman of the Hill Museum & Manuscript Library at Saint John's University in Collegeville, Minnesota, who arranged access to, and answered many questions about the medieval manuscripts in their collection; Dermot O'Mara of Sunny Meadow Farm, Powers Cross, County Galway, for organic farming information; Dáithí Sproule, for advice and assistance with Irish language usage and translations; Molly Lynch O'Mara and all of her Mountshannon farmers' market cohorts; and Ann and Charlie Heymann, for the loan of books about Irish scribal arts. To Jody and Sean Henry, who looked after me with such kindness after the unfortunate misstep at Dun Aengus; and to Mary and Sean O'Driscoll and Brian and Margaret McGrath, who provided me with sustenance and a place to lay my head on the follow-up research trip, thank you. Thanks to Shawn Kearney, both for her enthusiasm about becoming a character in this story, and for her generous donation to the important work of the American Refugee Committee. I'm grateful to my entire extended family for letting me slip off to a quiet space to finish writing this book in the midst of happy chaos. Thanks to my wonderful aunt and uncle, Betty and John Rogers, for jumping into our Irish travels with both feet and for their support through this and all previous endeavors; to Lisa McDaniel, for providing encouragement and distraction when needed in equal measure; to Karen Mueller, who walks along beside me on the daily path of creativity; and to my pal Bonnie Schueler, to whom I am indebted for her example of unbridled joie de vivre and so much more.

Sincere thanks, once again, to the incomparable Sally Wofford-Girand (along with assistants Melissa Sarver and Kezia Toth) of Brickhouse Literary Agents; to Samantha Martin, Shannon Welch, Greg Mortimer, and Susan Moldow at Scribner; and to Susanne Kirk, the most patient and gracious of editors. I'm grateful to my sweetheart, Paddy, for cooking many a splendid dinner (too many to count, really) while I was out wandering imaginary bogs. So, to all of the above, and to any others I have inadvertently neglected to mention here, a toast: Your blood should be bottled. Go mhéimid beo ag an am seo arís.

ABOUT THE AUTHOR

ERIN HART is a theater critic and former administrator at the Minnesota State Arts Board. A lifelong interest in Irish traditional music led her to cofound Minnesota's Irish Music and Dance Association. She and her husband, button accordion player Paddy O'Brien, live in St. Paul, Minnesota, and frequently visit Ireland. Erin Hart was nominated for the Agatha and Anthony awards for her debut novel, *Haunted Ground*, and won the Friends of American Writers Award in 2004. Visit her website at ErinHart.com.

A Scribner Reading Group Guide

The Book of Killowen

Erin Hart

This reading group guide for *The Book of Killowen* includes an introduction, discussion questions, and ideas for enhancing your book club. The suggested questions are intended to help your reading group find new and interesting angles and topics for your discussion. We hope that these ideas will enrich your conversation and increase your enjoyment of the book.

Introduction

What could possibly explain two dead bodies in the trunk of a buried car—murdered hundreds of years apart? Could the two crimes have anything to do with each other? This is the mystery that brings archaeologist Cormac Maguire and pathologist Nora Gavin back to the bogs of beautiful Tipperary in central Ireland. At Killowen, a local artist retreat where Cormac and Nora are staying, secrets simmer below the surface and it seems everyone is a suspect. As the evidence unfolds, mysteries of the past become present again, and questions begin to swirl around medieval manuscripts and ancient philosophies of good and evil. Cormac and Nora work with the local detectives in a race to figure out how the past informs the present, and whose secret was worth killing to protect.

Topics & Questions for Discussion

1. The prologue reveals to us what happened to the bog man all those centuries ago, providing information to readers that the modern-day characters are still in search of. How do you think the experience of reading the story would have been different without the prologue?

2. Nora and Cormac are recurring characters in Erin Hart's books, but the point of view rotates often and there are other important characters featured as well. Who did you consider the most central figure? Whose story were you most interested in?

3. On p. 20, Claire reflects on the eight people, including herself, who have come to live and work at Killowen, thinking of them as "a whole rootless menagerie of misfits [who'd] arrived on her doorstep like strays, all looking for something." What do you think they were each looking for? Have any of them found it?

4. *The Book of Killowen* is a bit of a whodunit—so many of the characters have an air of suspicion surrounding them. Who did you think was guilty of the present-day murders? Did you suspect there were multiple killers, or question different people at different points in the story?

5. On p. 72, Mairéad says, "It's always been a mystery to me how a few words scribbled down a thousand years ago could be so earth-shattering today." Words are a strong theme in the story. Characters struggle with words, search for words, hold them back, study them, etc. Discuss this theme and how words are significant in the overall plot and to specific characters.

6. Do you think the National Museum is the right place for *The Book of Killowen* to be kept, or should it stay with the Beglan family?

7. Do you agree with Stella's decision to burn the photos of Claire? Why or why not?

8. Reread the quotes that open each of the six books within the story. What is their significance? Did they give you any clues to the story, or do they now in retrospect?

9. The peat in the bog has miraculous powers of preservation. While the whole world outside of the bog was changing, the bog man and his possessions were preserved for centuries. Discuss the ways in which preservation is a theme throughout the novel.

10. Killowen is a veritable cauldron of secrets. Nearly all of its occupants have something to hide. Discuss the secrets these people kept and how their lives were affected for better or worse once their secrets finally came out.

11. What do you think of Barry's change of heart? Should Stella take him back? Why or why not?

12. How do you think Cormac's relationship with his father will change now that he knows about his sister? Why do you think Eliana decided not to tell Cormac on her own?

13. Part of the controversy surrounding *The Book of Killowen* is the position its writer takes on the existence of evil. Nora then wonders, "If evil doesn't really exist, does it mean that things like goodness and decency aren't real either?" (p. 314) What do you think? Does evil exist? Can one exist without the other?

14. There were quite a few twists and turns as the story came to a close—secrets revealed, mysteries solved. What was the most surprising plot point to you? Was there something you never saw coming?

Enhance Your Book Club

1. On p. 238, Gwynne says, "Imagine stumbling upon a unique collection of words and ideas and images so fantastic that it was worth spending months or even years of your life copying it out so that others would be able to share in and appreciate its splendor." Try to find a poem or passage that means something to you. Spend some time carefully copying it down into a journal, or perhaps in a letter if there is someone else you'd like to share it with. Consider passing your copied words around at your book club meeting to share their splendor!

2. Lucien and Sylvie were quite the cheese makers. Have a tasting during your discussion, perhaps from a local farm or small cheese shop where you can learn a little bit about the types of cheese you decide to buy.

3. This book is full of authentic Irish sayings. Have you ever heard someone say "half-eight" instead of "eight-thirty"? Exclaim "Jaysus" instead of "Jesus"? Were there any other Irish-isms you noticed in the book? Do a quick look online to see what other sayings you can find.